CLOSE ENCOUNTERS
WITH THE
DEITY

stories by

MICHAEL BISHOP

Foreword by Isaac Asimov

PEACHTREE PUBLISHERS, LTD.

Published by
PEACHTREE PUBLISHERS, LTD.
494 Armour Circle, N.E.
Atlanta, Georgia 30324

Manufactured in the United States of America

1st printing

Library of Congress Catalog Number 86-61070

ISBN 0-931948-96-7 - Hardcover
ISBN 0-934601-07-0 - Trade paper

For my friends Jerry Page,
Steven Utley, and David Zindell

ALSO BY MICHAEL BISHOP

A Funeral for the Eyes of Fire
And Strange at Ecbatan the Trees
Stolen Faces
A Little Knowledge
Catacomb Years
Transfigurations
Under Heaven's Bridge (with Ian Watson)
Blooded on Arachne
No Enemy But Time
One Winter in Eden
Who Made Stevie Crye?
Ancient of Days

Contents

Foreword:

Religion And Science Fiction

By Isaac Asimov

In the November, 1983, issue of the monthly science-fiction magazine that bears my name, the cover story was "The Gospel According to Gamaliel Crucis" by that excellent writer, Michael Bishop. This story deals with a sensitive subject — the coming of a savior, or, in effect, the second coming of Christ.

What makes Bishop's novella even more effective as a science fiction story is that the savior is an extraterrestrial, and not a particularly attractive one to our human eyes, for she — that's right, *she* — is a giant mantis. This speculation is entirely legitimate, it seems to me, for if there is other life in the Universe, especially intelligent life, one would expect that a truly Universal God would be as concerned for these other beings as for us, and would totally disregard physical shape, for only the "soul," that inner intellectual and moral identity, must finally count. What is more, Bishop decided to make his novella more powerful by casting it into a Biblical shape, dividing it into chapters and verses and employing a touch of suitable Biblical wording.

The result is a *tour de force* that the editorial staff at *Isaac Asimov's Science Fiction Magazine* obviously considered successful, or we would not have published it. Still, we were prepared for the fact that some readers might feel uneasy with, or even offended by, the subject matter and/or the style.

One letter to our magazine was quite angry, indeed. The writer was "strongly displeased" and considered the story "a burlesque of the scriptures." Finding no other point to the story, this person decided that it had been written and published only for the sake of the burlesque. Bishop or I could argue with this view, of course, but if a reader sees in "The Gospel According to Gamaliel Crucis" only burlesque, our arguments are scarcely likely to change that reader's mind. Differences of opinion about the value of any work of art are inevitable, and often these differences have their basis in strong emotion rather than reason.

But here a larger question arises, the matter of how science fiction ought to deal with religion, especially *our* religion. (Few people worry very much about how science fiction characterizes other religions, for only our own is the True One.) No one wants to offend people unnecessarily, and religion, as we all know, is a sensitive subject. In that case, might it not be best simply to avoid altogether the religious angle in writing science fiction? As our angry correspondent says, "I suggest . . . that offending any substantial religious group is not the way to win friends or sell magazines."

Yes, we know that, and because we *do* want to win friends and sell magazines, we would not deliberately go out of our way to embarrass or humiliate, just for the fun of it, even *non*substantial groups of our readers.

But we are also editing a serious science fiction magazine that, we earnestly hope, includes stories of literary merit, and it is the very essence of literature that it consider the great ideas and concerns of human history. Surely, that complex of ideas that goes under the head of "religion" is one of the most central and essential of these concerns, and to declare it out of bounds would be rather a shame. In fact, for a magazine to self-censor itself from any fictional treatment of religion would be to bow to those forces that do not really believe in our constitutional guarantees of freedom of speech and press.

Besides, if we were to try to avoid this sensitive subject, where would we stop? In my own stories, I tend to ignore religion altogether, except where I absolutely have to have it. Of course, I absolutely had to have it in some of my early Foundation stories, and in my *Astounding* novelette of 1941, "Nightfall," and so I made use of it. And, whenever I bring in a religious motif, that religion is bound to seem vaguely Christian because Christianity is the only religion about which I know anything, even though it is not mine. An unsympathetic reader might think I am "burlesquing" Christianity, but I am not.

Then, too, it is impossible to write science fiction and *really* ignore religion. What if we find intelligent beings on other worlds? Do *they* have a religion? Is our God universal, and is he/she/it their God as well? What do we do about the faith of these others? What do they do about ours? Writers almost never take up this point, but because it would certainly arise if we actually discovered such beings, science fiction loses touch with reality when it takes the easy way out and pretends that religion does not exist.

Or consider time-travel. I don't know how many SF stories propose someone's going back in time to prevent the assassination of Lincoln, but what about the more spectacular notion of going back in time to prevent the crucifixion of Jesus? Surely, if time-travel were possible, someone would inevitably try to perform that greater feat. Think of the changes that a skillful writer could ring on such a theme. If Jesus were rescued while on his way to Calvary, and if modern technology — a helicopter or something more advanced — effected the rescue while rifle-fire held the Roman soldiers at bay, would not the people of that time suppose that supernatural forces were rescuing Jesus? Would it not seem to them that angels were coming to the aid of the true savior? Would not this event at once establish Jesus' religion, Christianity, as the true religion?

Perhaps not. Clearly, it was God's divine purpose — assuming that the God of the Bible exists — to have the crucifixion take place so that Jesus might serve as a divine atonement for Adam's original sin. In that case, would God allow the subversion of this plan?

It's a nice dilemma and one that legitimately falls within the province of science fiction. Yet with the notable exception of Michael Moorcock's award-winning "Behold the Man," few writers have attempted such a story. Why? Perhaps because that story would be extremely difficult to write. Indeed, I would not feel up to it myself. Still, I think that what primarily keeps us from making the attempt is self-censorship. For that matter, maybe we fear the likely impact of a story in which we go back in time and find that the Biblical Jesus never existed.

The mere existence of time-travel makes all these speculations irresistible. Is it therefore possible that very religious people might object to time-travel themes, deeming them blasphemous, simply because they give rise to such troubling possibilities? The correspondent in his letter says, "Dr. Asimov, I know that you are an atheist," and there may be the implication that because of this I am insensitive to the feelings of religionists, or perhaps even anxious to make them seem ridiculous.

As a matter of fact, I have frequently made it clear in my writings that I have never encountered any convincing evidence for the existence of the Biblical God, and that I am incapable of accepting that existence on faith alone. My stance in this matter makes me an atheist, but, although surprising to some Americans, the Constitution safeguards my right both to be an atheist and to proclaim myself one.

Nevertheless, I am not a proselytizing atheist; I am not a missionary; I do not treat atheism as a kind of true faith that I must force on everyone. After all, I have published more books, articles, and stories than almost anyone else now alive — about twenty million words so far — and I have frequently discussed controversial issues. You are free to go through my published work searching it for any sign that I ridicule religion as such. I *have* opposed those people who attack legitimate scientific findings — evolution, as an example — in the name of religion, and who do so without evidence, or, worse yet, with distorted or false evidence. I do not regard these people as true religionists, however, and I am careful to point out that they disgrace religion. Indeed, they pose a greater danger to honest religion than to science.

And suppose that I weren't an atheist. My parents were Jewish, and I might have been brought up an Orthodox Jew or become one of my own volition. Might one then argue that I would naturally favor any story burlesquing Christianity? Or suppose I were a Methodist. Would I therefore look for stories that parodied Judaism, or Roman Catholicism, or, even more likely, atheism?

If I were in the mood to run *Isaac Asimov's Science Fiction Magazine* in such a way as to offend "any substantial religious group," I would hardly have to be an atheist. I could easily do so if I were of any metaphysical persuasion at all, provided only that I were also a bigot, or an idiot, or both. In fact, I am neither; and, again, I offer my collected writings as proof.

Needless to say, I am sorry that Michael Bishop's "The

Gospel According to Gamaliel Crucis" upset our correspondent. If we lived in an ideal world, we would never publish any story that upset *anyone*. In this case, though, we had to choose. On the one hand, we had a remarkable story that considered, quite fearlessly, an important idea, and we felt that most readers would recognize its legitimacy — if not at once, then upon mature reflection. On the other hand, we had a story that might offend some readers.

We made the choice. We put the story's literary quality and thematic importance ahead of the chance that it might offend. We hope that our angry correspondent will reconsider the matter and see that "The Gospel According to Gamaliel Crucis," like nearly all the other stories with theological themes in this collection, is far more than a burlesque. He might even give Bishop points for skill and courage.

Close Encounter
With The Deity

Everything was set in order ere anything was made.
                                    — Juliana of Norwich

*So maybe the end is in sight for theoretical physicists if
not for theoretical physics.*   — Stephen Hawking

I

They place the deformed Demetrio Urraza in an iridium-
alloy voyager, wish him godspeed, and shoot him
through space toward the bright southern-hemisphere star
Alpha Piscis Austrini, better known as Fomalhaut.

Urraza is a Chilean theoretical physicist and cosmologist.
He is also a devout Catholic of New Reformist upbringing.
In his fragile-looking but sturdy ship (funded by a global
confederation of astronomy and physics institutes), Urraza
will observe part of the multibillion-year process of planetary genesis around the sun whose Arabic name means The
Fish's Mouth.

The honor — not to say the folly — of this expedition has
come to Urraza for his role in formulating a Grand Unified
Theory of the four major forces that structure the physical
universe. To date, his equations have resisted every experimental trial to disprove or modify their import; and his
reputation worldwide puts him in a gallery of indisputably
great physicists including, of course, his immediate prede-

cessors Einstein and Hawking.

Urraza, like Hawking, has had to overcome a physical handicap to do his work. As a result of his mother's daily exposure to radioactive wastes secretly and illegally dumped near Taital, his birthplace, Urraza came from the womb missing part of his small intestine. More important, his body also lacked every extremity but his head, a leg, and one malshaped foot. (His leg and foot the young Demetrio learned to use as most other human beings use their arms and hands.) Had a priest not taken the crippled infant to a doctor in Antofagasta, better than a hundred miles away, and had the doctor not willingly become the child's benefactor, Demetrio Urraza would have died within the week.

Today Urraza enjoys pointing out that his surviving to become a physicist involved a chain of events as unlikely as the fine tuning of a universe in which thinking observers might eventually arise. He is an anomaly, he cheerfully admits, adding that of course life itself is an anomaly.

In a sense, Urraza has won a lottery sponsored by the world's scientific community.

The winning ticket consisted of his publication, less than two decades ago, of the Grand Unified Theory bearing his name, i.e., Urraza's GUT. (In English, this is an ugly — perhaps deplorable — pun that Urraza finds as delightful as humanity's questing sentience in a seemingly disinterested cosmos.) The prize for drawing the winning ticket, now that Demetrio Urraza's GUT has encompassed the centuries-old hunger of theoretical physicists for The Answer, is a one-way trip to Fomalhaut, 22.5 light-years from Earth.

Why Fomalhaut? many have wondered.

Because, eighteen years before the publication of the GUT that most of Urraza's peers agree has put an end to theoretical physics, astronomers detected around Fomalhaut a planetary disk suggesting that the star is sorting out a solar system similar to the one that became our own. Further, although this process — beginning with the creation of the protosun at the system's heart — may take as long as five billion years, Fomalhaut has already advanced beyond the stage at which a blast of flare gas or of scouring ultraviolet has blown the dust in its inner disk out into the transsolar void. In other words, this star is already well on the road to planetary creation and hence — if one has faith — to the oozy birth and chance-directed uncoiling of life.

Conceivably, Earth will have died before Urraza completes his observations of the process, for, waking for week-long periods between dozens of millennia of self-preserving slumber, he will survive several hundred million years. Humanity, during this time, will either perish utterly or escape its inevitable local holocaust by removing to other parts of the galaxy. Maybe Urraza's fellow human beings, arriving later, will find his voyager and resurrect him to life on a utopian Terra Nueva orbiting Fomalhaut. . . .

II

"This is suicide," Talita Bedoya, the man's New Reformist priest, told him an hour before the workers at the lunar launch station put him in his ship's life-support casket. Father Bedoya was trying, as she had all along, to prevent his departure.

"Nonsense," Urraza replied. "I find suicide — in my own case, at least — as sinful as you do."

"But, Demetrio, you'll never be coming back."

"Pardon me, Father," Urraza said, touching the woman's sleeve with his articulate foot, "but maybe I see myself effecting my own salvation by returning to the stuff out of which the Holy Spirit summoned the entire cosmos."

"But if you don't come back —"

"Is it suicide to seek salvation? The reverse, Father, exactly the reverse. No one can sidestep death, but I go to Fomalhaut to see and record, not to surrender and die. For God's sake, then, relent and give me your blessing."

"Demetrio, it's simply not in me to do as you wish."

"Then shrive me. Surely, this is the last time I'll be able to oblige myself of the services of a human confessor."

Father Bedoya prepared herself and then reluctantly heard the physicist's confession. As he had done on several past occasions, he confessed to the sins of detraction, pride, lust, and, now that he was setting forth on a voyage requiring him to take most of his nutrients through his veins or in tablet form, gluttony. The night before, he had gorged on genetically synthesized lobster, lamb, and turkey, to the point of deliberately vomiting and beginning again. Although on launch morning, in Talita Bedoya's presence, he did not feel nauseated, he *was* ashamed of himself. Theory is not the only passion of Demetrio Urraza.

III

Outward into the interstellar ocean, the vessel that this man has christened *La Misericordia de la Noche* glides. Urraza, in his control-casket-cum-pivoting-cryonic-berth, has donned the ship with such happy self-extinguishment that he feels himself to be wearing it like a skin. He wakes and sleeps on the outward leg of his trip almost as he would in his modest home near Santiago. He spends a good deal of time plotting quasar-prediction formulas, sending radio messages Earthwards, and listening to music.

As a whimsical way of connecting to an earlier era of space exploration, Urraza has insisted that *Misericordia* carry duplicates of the recordings hurtled outward aboard the Voyager probes in 1977. Already, then, he has worked on his equations to the sounds of a mariachi band; an erupting volcano; Bach's second "Brandenberg Concerto"; traffic noises; a greeting spoken in Amoy ("Friends of space, how are you all? Have you eaten yet? Come visit us if you have time"); frog-and-cricket cacophonies; Chuck Berry's "Johnny B. Goode"; the sweet whisper and suck of a human kiss; and the soulful Cavatina of Beethoven's late string quartet, Opus 130. He has also played grand opera, the eclecticulture mooings of his own day, and some of the eerie Inca Indian flute tunes taught him by the doctor who saved his life.

Video stimulation — although he could summon almost any image that a connoisseur of either beauty or ugliness could want — the physicist receives only rarely. Such images interfere with his mental picture-making. If ever he chooses to look up from the work at hand, he pivots his control casket to a position giving him an awesome view of the heavens. And feels, despite the tinny voices of his human siblings droning at him over the laser link, like the only human being alive in the cosmos.

"This star-flecked darkness is an unbounded fishbowl, and I'm an insignificant cricket dangling in it for bait."

When listening to music, receiving and sending messages, and plotting equations ceases to amuse him, Urraza reads. For long, self-lost periods, his reading takes him deep into the devotional prose of Saint Augustine, Bernard of Clairvaux, Francis of Assisi, the unnamed English monk who wrote *The Cloud of Unknowing*, Juliana of Norwich, Thomas à Kempis, Francis de Sales, Brother Lawrence, François Fénelon, and others. Speculative theology interests him far less than meditative works that feed the hungering faith that he already possesses. Hence, when he swivels his computer screen to call up reading matter, he nearly always prefers the committed ancient and medieval writers to the besieged, grasping-at-straws, and apologetic moderns.

Bait? He, Demetrio Urraza? To catch what?

God, perhaps. For the line in Juliana of Norwich's *Revelations of Divine Love* that Urraza finds himself inwardly rehearsing again and again is *"I saw God in a point."* The implied physics of the woman's claim, asserted not with braggadocio but with awe-stricken humility, enormously pleases *Misericordia*'s pilot. He is grateful to Father Bedoya for advising him to include Mother Julian's little book in his vessel's computer library.

"I saw God in a point."

"The things that He will keep secret, mightily and wisely, He hideth them for love."

"The beholding of Him — this is an high unperceivable prayer."

And so on, insight after insight, until Urraza realizes that the fourteenth-century recluse who penned these thoughts was on a voyage of discovery as devout as his own aboard *La Misericordia de la Noche*. At the same time, however, he understands that this analogy between a medieval female visionary in her anchorage cell and a twenty-first century physicist flying solo to Fomalhaut would befuddle most of his contemporaries. They respect him for the work he has done, but regard the traditional belief system that has sustained him in this work with, at best, smug or uncomprehending tolerance. "Urraza's quirk," they like to call it.

In his life-support casket, the anchorite from Taital smiles in anticipation of the final Gnostic redemption of his malformed body in a universe-ending return to Pure Spirit.

And gleefully mouths, *"I saw God in a point."*

IV

Eighteen months into his journey, El Sol a glimmering diamond to the rear, Urraza activates the equipment that will ease him into cryonic sleep and then maintain him in this state until his voyager has reached its destination a quarter-light-year above the swarming planetary disk of

Alpha Piscis Austrini. Hibernation, he terms this condition, for the weather between suns is an uncompromising everlasting winter that only rarely clicks on the wheeling furnace of star formation. Now I lay me down to sleep.

And hears a voice say, *"Thou shalt see thyself that all manner of things shall be well."*

His ship accelerates. Its drive is a laser-pulse engine. With this revolutionary motive force, it makes its jaunt to Fomalhaut in eighty-nine Earth-standard years. All but a fraction of this time Urraza spends iced in his casket, dreaming cold dreams and praying to the remotest quasars with the glacier edge of consciousness. His every bad dream is a wintermare, but all shall be well, and all manner of things shall be well. . . .

Misericordia calls Urraza from slumber. Groggily, he awakens, disoriented not only by his trip of 22.5 light-years but also by the icy trash piled up at the front of his brain. Recordings and video displays brief him to his whereabouts and purposes, and he rolls in his casket to look "down" with eye and computer-enhanced imaging equipment at the solar system spread out "beneath" him like an immense gauzy target in the void.

Complicating matters is the fact that Fomalhaut, a young white star, has a small partner of spectral type K a few billion miles beyond it. A dark abyss separates this star from the outer edge of the gauzy disk lumbering about The Fish's Mouth. The *size* of this chasm leads the physicist to suppose — as he supposed even before embarking on his journey — that the emerging planetary system is not likely to be significantly perturbed by the yellow companion. Indeed, the nebulous target spirals around Fomalhaut encourage him to think that in another four hundred million years or so a planet near the star's cooling bull's-eye may acquire an atmosphere, water, lightning-freed carbon and nitrogen compounds, amino acids, enzyme hints, and

— most gracious surprise of all surprises — the molecules responsible for life on Earth. To the creatures arising on this world (should they ever look up), the yellow companion will be nothing more than another good-sized light in the sky.

Mother of God, Urraza murmurs. And after many readings eases himself once more into cryonic sleep.

V

Spiraling down, he recollects reading Juliana of Norwich almost a century ago, an illusory time span that seems but "yesterday." Like the anchoress, Urraza never married. Some, looking upon the crippled body that he refused to "improve" with modern prosthetics, thought him physically unsuited to marriage — but the truth is that the siren song of the flesh has always tormented Urraza. At university, he abused himself, whored, and even played the Casanova with women who would have loved him in a higher way, had only he permitted them to.

Eventually, though, he heard a call more powerful than this carnal siren song and resolved to devote himself to the priesthood of theoretical physics, the fellowship of cosmologists. Ever since, he has redirected the energy of sexual desire into the pursuit of incorporeal satisfactions deriving from either his science or his faith. Like Juliana, like the reformed Augustine, like his confessor Talita Bedoya, he has chosen celibacy as the best means of . . . well, of seeing God in a point.

Had I married, he thinks, going under again, I would not be out here now, for what wife would release her husband to the infidelity of a one-way trip to another star?

And yet he knows that he could never have "oned" his soul — to use Juliana's terminology — with the cosmos (as he feels that he is now doing) had he remained on Earth, his

major accomplishments in physics behind him and nothing
ahead but refinements best left to men and women younger
and more intellectually elastic than he. A superannuated
genius, he knows, is as sad as a faded beauty or an uninhabitable ruin.

But faith may buoy him yet. And when he wakes again,
he finds that *Misericordia*'s displays are showing him a time-
lapse sequence concentrating two thousand years of planet-
forming activity into a week's worth of kaleidoscopic
images. Rocks collide with boulders, orbiting Gibraltars
tailgate whirling Diamondheads and Sugarloafs, the Black
Hills bash into the Rockies, the Urals and the Alps play
demolition derby with a thousand wheeling Himalayas,
and Fomalhaut itself foams and spits, storms and simmers.

Urraza video-records, catalogues, collates, cross-files,
prays, and wonders in passing if his species has died out or
maybe built a postindustrial Garden of Eden on Earth.
Because radio broadcasts from Earth mysteriously ended
during his long recent sleep, he has no way either of knowing or of discovering the fate of his species over the past two
millennia, but he trusts that extinction, if it actually
occurred, was not self-inflicted. It has been a shaky article of
faith with him, ever since graduate school in Boston, that
his own kind would come to its senses before any irreversible catastrophe befell it — *"All manner of things shall be well"*
— but that belief was, has been, and remains harder to
sustain than the conviction that "Everything was set in
order ere anything was made." Hence, not only the loneliness of being light-years from home preys on Urraza, but
also the loneliness of fearing that, even if he and his ship
were physically able to retrace their journey, no real home
would exist to go back to.

Now I lay me. . . .

The chill descends. Urraza winters again in his life-support casket, a corpse laid out for viewing by invisible

mourners. His dreams spiral like the coalescing promonto-
ries and jagged clifflets of Fomalhaut's proto-planetary disk.
Meanwhile, his dreams are indistinguishable from the
actions of the Fomalhaut system or the undergirding
strength of his faith. They assure him that he will live again.

VI

Another two thousand years go by. Because only the
dreaming Urraza is there to count them, they pass in a
midge's span. Not long after the pilot has resurrected again,
he becomes aware of a stunning interstellar phenomenon
five or so light-years beyond the Fomalhaut system.
Streams of distorted light flicker palely on one of the voyager's displays, a sprinkle of lambency pattering against his
vision. Excited, Urraza understands that he has "sighted" a
black hole utterly invisible to astronomers on Earth.

He pivots to figure out how long it will take the laser-
pulse engine to carry *Misericordia* from its anchorage above
the Fomalhaut system to the singularity. Twenty years,
tops. Well, he can do that — making a jest of the matter —
in his sleep. Indeed, for a chance to explore such an anomalous heavenly wonder, he would sleep until Doomsday.
Fomalhaut and the planets taking shape from its accretion
disk be damned; he now intends to visit the black hole — a
tiny anomaly with only five or six solar masses — lurking
like a hidden trapdoor into nowhere.

All his life has pointed toward this exploration, this visit,
and so Urraza programs into the voyager the coordinates
that will take him there. Then he drifts off into yet another
wintermare, to dream away the years whose passage must
finally strand him at the hungry mouth of the singularity.
He also programs *Misericordia* to wake him before disaster
overwhelms the voyager.

Twenty years later, it does. However, as Urraza's ship

rushes toward the maw of this dark sink, every navigational aid in the coal-black skies is bent, blurred, and refracted out of true by the vacuuming forces at the event horizon of the hole.

How could this have occurred? Urraza wonders. He has awakened too close to the singularity, and now he appears doomed to hurtle down to oblivion. He can do nothing to reverse, slow, or abort his fall; and as he approaches the ebony O-gape of the hole, he watches a vast spinning tiara of stars pirouette across the scalp of its event horizon. He sees a mirage of twisted starlight rather than the stars themselves, for the lens of this rotating gravity tunnel has warped and refocused their images into a daunting crown.

Still, some stellar material is actually accompanying him on his fall into the hole. He fully expects *Misericordia* to shudder, shimmy, and, yes, soundlessly collide with spinning chunks of this forced downward migration. Here, several million years too soon, in the prime of his extraterrestrial life, Demetrio Urraza is going to die. Or, perhaps, transcend himself.

VII

The gape of the singularity — the mouth of a fish bigger than the primal carp theorized by ancient cosmologists — lifts higher and higher. The maw looms. Swiveling his screens into place, Urraza begins to do math. This is the ecstasy toward which he has directed his life and work; the formulae marching in jaunty ranks across the display terminals, summarizing, predicting, describing, seem to him not only the abstract hieroglyphics of his science but also the priestly polynomials of his faith in the First Mover behind Creation.

In a period of bodily sickness, Juliana of Norwich saw sixteen visions of the suffering Christ, but Urraza sees the

Holy Spirit — from Whom all else has issued — in *Misericor-dia*'s endless descent into the pit. Down the gravity well, downward to revelation. In fact, the physicist realizes that this specific black hole is not only every other black hole that has ever, or will ever, exist but also the original singularity out of which everything that was made was first made. Neither time nor space has meaning herewhen, but Urraza nevertheless understands that, like a hologram, the interior of this gravity sink reproduces and contains the interior of every other. . . .

And so he plummets toward the Point that exploded, the Mind that made it explode, and the meaning that ever-lastingly abides in the fateful coincidence of the two.

The metal skin of *La Misericordia de la Noche* has long since integrated fully with his own. Urraza, thus perfectly clothed, tumbles into the naked singularity that has seized him. He falls forever through an anomalous medium no longer possessing dimension or duration.

He is being swallowed, but, in an eviternal flash of insight, he knows that he has *always* been "being swal-lowed." What is happening to him "now" was mandated, arranged, and predestined, with his own enthusiastic com-plicity, from the "beginning." The light whirling down this gravity maelstrom with him illuminates him inwardly, and by it he "sees" that he has no body to stymie or bedevil him further, and that "now" it is solely his own discrete mind that hurtles beginningwards.

The heretical Christian gnostics believed that each human being has a divine spark, imprisoned in flesh, whose princi-ple yearning is to reunite with the Godhead from which earthly incarnation has estranged it. Urraza wonders — he has "always" wondered — if his disembodied consciousness is going home in a way that *Misericordia*, even with plenty of fuel and time illimitable, could never have managed. He is Adam, All-Man, and he is Jesus Christ, the Godhead, suffering blissfully, and sempiternally, this new passion of being forever torn apart and sucked downward to union.

"If I might suffer more, I would suffer more," Urraza calmly quotes the words of the Savior as He vouchsafed them to Juliana in one of her bloody visions. And his widening mind — his changing consciousness — quotes this squib not from any leftover biological bent for masochism but rather from all the kinds of love anciently signaled by *agape, caritas,* and, given the ecstasy of his passion, even *eros.*

Light falls in upon Urraza. Although this weird here-when lacks either dimension or duration, the man gets smaller and smaller even as his mind grows larger and more powerful. As his body collapses into a fiery point, his consciousness inflates, acquires spin, and, at one with the Immemorially Cyclical Intention of the Holy Spirit, begins to radiate. . . .

Beyond the event horizon of the black hole that has gobbled Urraza, the universe — by other measures of process than those at work inside this fantastic all-encompassing hole — has long since fallen back on itself. However, some of this fresh radiant energy, a collaboration between God and the representative transhuman mind of Demetrio Urraza, at last escapes the gravity sink compacting all time and matter into the ur-proton of re-Creation.

And Urraza, subsumed by the Increate, hears their huge bodiless voice command, "Let there be light. Again."

— for the students at Clarion '85

Voices

A young man called Hu Shaoqi was possessed of two rare talents. The first he practiced openly, and it delighted nearly everyone who knew him. The second he regarded as a curse and kept altogether hidden from the world. In Hu Shaoqi's opinion, these two talents canceled each other and distinguished him in painful ways from the people whom he loved. That not even his mother and father noticed the signs of his secret unhappiness worked like an evil burrowing worm to undermine his native good cheer.

Hu Shaoqi's first talent was an ability to "throw" his voice. He could make the spotted ponies in the paddock behind the house of the village's chief lord appear to recite poetry. He could project eloquent speeches into the mortar-stopped mouths of stone dogs and lions. He could convince a modest young woman from a fine family that she had just blurted out a curse more appropriate to the lips of a barbarian soldier. He could even make the giant eagles of Xiangcheng and the dwarf dragons of the mountain caves sing like lovely girls.

This talent Hu Shaoqi viewed as a welcome gift. It amused his family, astonished has acquaintances, and so pleased the chief lord (who shamefully exulted in his ponies' recitations of long passages of epic verse) that he often called on Hu Shaoqi to entertain his guests at formal dinners, afterwards rewarding the young man with exotic foods or semiprecious stones. Using this talent, Hu Shaoqi could imagine himself making his way in life without having to marry wealth, or to become a monk, or to devote himself to the respectable drudgery of scholarship. Although not an especially materialistic young man, this idea appealed to him, and already, he felt, he had made a good start on securing his fortune.

Hu Shaoqi's second, and purposely unrevealed, talent was an ability to hear voices that no one else could hear. It did not escape him that this bittersweet talent turned his happier bent for ventriloquism inside-out. Both centered on illusions created by the human voice. (If, of course, the voices that sometimes swept into his mind did not actually belong to dead people or demons.) In the first instance, he, Hu Shaoqi, was the perpetrator of the hoaxing voices, but in the second — frighteningly — he never had a credible notion who or what was trying to empty its fearsome nonsense into his head.

To Hu Shaoqi's shame and confusion, the voices had begun in his thirteenth year, not long after his first nocturnal spurting of man seed. For the next three years, this troubling auditory phenomenon had continued. Although it came to him most frequently at night, occasionally it took place in the midst of conversation with parents or friends. Usually, the voice or voices merely prated at him, telling him that he was not who he thought he was, that no one he knew was in truth the person he believed, and that one day he would be called upon to repay either the gods or his ancestors for his ability to throw his voice. Finally, altogether upsettingly, the phenomenon overtook him during one of his performances in the court of the village lord.

In front of forty people, the sixteen-year-old Hu Shaoqi was making the overweight lady of the lord cackle like a chicken, hiss like a serpent, and bray like an ass. Everyone in attendance was laughing, including the delighted lady herself. Then, completely without warning, a voice insinuated itself into his ears — nay, into some astonished portion of his mind — telling him terrible secrets, cajoling him, *commanding* him.

"Hu Shaoqi," said the voice, sounding at one moment like a great growling bear, at the next like a trio of old women speaking in unison, and at the next like nothing human at all, "you must forsake this village and these silly people and journey at once to the Mountain of Everlasting Winter."

"Silly people?" the boy echoed the voice or voices.

Everyone at court gaped at him. The noblewoman who had been doing such expert animal imitations fell silent. A look of surprised disappointment captured her face, for Hu Shaoqi had just reclaimed his audience's attention and she had foolishly begun to believe that it was hers by right.

"Silly, indeed," the voice or voices reiterated. "You are not who you think you are, doltish boy. Nor are any of these village louts who they so smugly believe themselves to be. So I tell you again that you must leave Xiangcheng and set off this very evening for the Mountain of Everlasting Winter."

Heedless of his onlookers, Hu Shaoqi turned in a circle. "But *why*? You have to tell me why!"

"Why, to discover the underlying meaning of this great and mysterious world. To discover also the real identity of the idiots whom you have been trying to entertain. Therefore, boy, betake yourself to the Mountain of Everlasting Winter."

"But I don't *want* to go to the Mountain of Everlasting Winter!" Hu Shaoqi cried.

"Of course you don't," said the village lord, approaching the ventriloquist, for he had correctly surmised that the young man was at the mercy of some sort of *kuei*, or demon, and wished with all his heart to comfort him. "No one wants to go there."

But, in his distress and confusion, Hu Shaoqi shouted, "Leave me alone, you fool!" Frantically, he shoved the well-meaning lord aside and fled from the court into the streets of the village and from the village streets into the solitude of the evening woods. Alone, he slumped to the ground and put his hands over his ears, horrified by all that had so far happened and terrified that even worse might yet befall him.

"Get up," the *kuei* commanded Hu Shaoqi. "Get up this instant and begin your journey to the Mountain."

"I won't!"

"Would you prefer that I repossess your only distinguishing talent as a human being?"

"Take it!" the boy challenged his tormentor. Then he lay on his side clasping his head and hoping that the demon would accept his ventriloquist's skills as a ransom and from henceforth leave him in peace.

Instead, as if the intelligence behind the voices had been weighing options, the voices said, "Hu Shaoqi, if you do not set out on your journey before sunup, I promise you that tomorrow you will contract a fever and die. You will forevermore cease to *be* Hu Shaoqi, and not even your mother and your father will be able to recall your name."

Threatened in this absolute way, Hu Shaoqi eventually pulled himself to his feet, returned to his own house, and secretly gathered together some few small items that he thought might prove useful on his trek, including a copper bowl, a second set of sandals, and single bag of rice. (He had no wish either to wake his parents or to deprive them of what was theirs.) The Mountain of Everlasting Winter lay several days' journey to the west, over roads that only madmen or monks ever thought to travel alone, for it bore its unusual name — and effectively discouraged visitors to its vicinity — because snow, glacial ice, and clouds like great frozen stones attended the peak year round. Everyone believed that a peculiarly antisocial deity resided there, for almost every "summer" the rock-hard carcasses of one or two adventurers who had thought to climb the mountain would be recovered from a moraine pushing out of a crevice at its base. Indeed, Hu Shaoqi felt a dread certainty that he would meet his own death on the mountain, assuming, of course, that he managed to escape being killed by one of the bandit packs notorious for patrolling the roads that wound into that bleak and forbidding territory.

* * *

And so, in the very dead of night, fear evicted the young ventriloquist from the cradle of his family and the nursery of his native village. Fear — and resentment of the threats that had occasioned that fear — accompanied him through the early stages of his journey. Animals, sensing his fear, avoided him, and he insured their continuing skittishness by tossing taro roots or wild eggplants at those brave enough to stop and look at him. Had he not been under the tyrannical compulsion of the voices (which, since leaving home, he had not heard again), he would have put silly words on the velvet tongue of a deer or filtered one of the teachings of the *Scripture in Forty-two Chapters* through the beak of an unsuspecting owl.

As it was, however, he longed for companionship but had no stomach for the mindless pity of ungulates and birds. Although a solitary exile with no one but himself to talk to,

Hu Shaoqi could easily summon from himself half a hundred different voices. Unfortunately, he knew all these spurious voices too well to take any comfort from their rote exhortations to have courage, practice his survival skills, and meditate on the compensatory beauties of the wilderness. They were little more than children's voices, which echoed in his head like old pottery breaking or dry leaves tiptoeing over cobbles.

As he traveled, the terrain grew more rugged, temperatures dropped, the people whom he encountered wore unfamiliar garments and spoke strange dialects. Their houses looked less like houses than colossal but misplaced beaver lodges. The beasts of burden carrying these folks' firewood and market products resembled animals out of fable. The air smelled of greasy smoke and old snow. The mountains separating the barren villages were like huge, fancifully eroded ant hills. The sky sagging against the peaks contained clouds as splintered and opaque as hammered ice. The channeled and rechanneled wind roared continuously, as if creation itself were in the throes of violent self-disintegration.

Late one afternoon, on a narrow track above a giddy-making abyss, three bandits jumped in front of Hu Shaoqi and threatened him with their staves. From natural towers of rock, another five or six men leapt into the path behind him. Hu Shaoqi had never seen such ugly, brutelike specimens of humanity. They demanded money. He had none. They wanted *any*thing he had. He had nothing but the robe on his back, his copper bowl, one extra sandal (he had already lost its mate), and a walking stick that he had found earlier that same morning. The rice that he had taken from his parents' tiny house was long since gone; he had eaten every bit of it on his very first day away from Xiangcheng.

Not a little frustrated by these discoveries, the bandits resolved to deprive Hu Shaoqi of his life. Their leader, a man with a face so badly scarred that it looked like a platter of broken porcelain ineptly pieced back together, seized the unoffending wayfarer by his robe and told him in grisly detail of all the many methods available to them to free his sniveling spirit, little by little, from his body.

"But why would you wish to do such things to me?" Hu Shaoqi asked. "I've done you no harm."

"You do us harm by intruding," the leader of the bandits retorted. "You do us harm by lacking anything of substance to filch from your nauseating person."

"Then waste no further time on me, sir."

"Only enough to lay you out dead. After which we'll strip you of your lice-ridden garment and leave your body on the path as a warning to any other would-be trespassers. Besides, even the giant raptors who nest aloft must eat, eh, boy?"

"But why not simply let me go?" Hu Shaoqi pleaded. "I'll warn others to stay away."

"Death's the fate of all those stupid enough to intrude upon our strongholds," the bandit said. "And if you should prove too effective in your warnings to others, numbskull, who would we have left to rob? Is it your desire to ruin us completely?"

Realizing at last that there was no arguing with the bandit leader or any of his henchmen, Hu Shaoqi threw his voice. He threw it in several different directions in such rapid succession that the bandits believed themselves surrounded by a far-traveling unit of the Emperor's most able and ferocious troops.

A pillar of granite called out orders.

A roadside shrine whinnied like a hundred horses.

A flock of sparrows divested itself of a dozen dozen murderous battlecries.

A stand of wind-whipped trees clacked its barren branches like so many swords striking steel against steel in cold preparation for attack.

Although the bandits could see no one approaching, this great unexpected clamor so terrified them that most of them fled, without having plucked a single hair from Hu Shaoqi's head. The bandit with the crazed-porcelain face released his captive and turned in a circle looking for the invisible enemy. It seemed for a moment that his ugly shattered face might shatter again, falling to discouraged pieces there on the narrow mountain track. Indeed, when the clamor of unseen opponents persisted (for Hu Shaoqi was putting ungodly strain on his vocal cords and facial muscles to insure that his "allies" grew louder and ever more numerous), the bandit chief lost all heart and went running after the men who had already broken for safety, shouting, "Cowards, come back!" at the top of his heaving lungs. But even when he had caught up with the slowest of this craven lot, the frightened head brigand continued pursuing the others until they had all disappeared.

Exhausted, Hu Shaoqi collapsed to his knees. No longer did whinnying horses or battlecrying birds disturb the loud silences of the windy upland terrain, and the wayfarer, weeping into his hands, principally wept to acknowledge the fact that he was still alive. A moment ago the issue had been in doubt, and yet he had summoned the resources — the god-given skills — to save himself.

And then, for the first time since he had left Xiangcheng, the *kuei* that had sent him on this perilous quest insinuated its voices into Hu Shaoqi's head, laughing in delight, snorting and snuffling like an entire pen of hungry pigs.

"Very good, my little mannikin," the demon said between these snorts and snuffles. "You almost surprise me. Not quite, let me stipulate, but almost."

Hu Shaoqi struggled to his feet and shook his fist defiantly at the leaden sky. "Why are you doing this to me?" he shouted.

But the voices in his head replied only, "To the Mountain, boy. To the Mountain."

Although he begged and expostulated and threatened the *kuei*, it would not say more. The hideous sounds of its hilarity died inside him, fading away until all that he could hear were the groanings of the rocks, the continuous high lament of the wind, and the pounding of his homesick heart.

* * *

Later that evening, to reduce the chances of another bandit attack, Hu Shaoqi left the path and entered a stand of gnarled evergreens. Soon, though, he found himself lost (a paradox not dissimilar to the inherent contradiction of his unasked-for talents) on a carpet of scratchy needles on a higher slope of the mountain. His robe was damp with sweat, the soles of his sandals had begun to shred, and the copper bowl he held in the hammock of cloth between his knees glinted like a miniature moon in the malevolent glow of the wintry sunset. The bowl was empty. Behind the young man's navel, hunger had balled up like a slimy clump of cat's hair. Aggrieved by this uncomfortable knot, he clutched his abdomen and for the second time that day began to cry.

"Stop your shameful display of tears!" he heard a scrawny hare sitting on a nearby rock rebuke him. "Are you truly afraid that you will never eat again, O timid and irresolute *boy*?"

Stunned, Hu Shaoqi stood up. Had the hare actually spoken, or had he thrown his own self-accusing voice into the whiskery mouth of the creature? Or, for novelty's sake, had the ventriloquist demon commandeered the little animal's body in order to chasten him? It *was* humiliating to hear oneself upbraided and disparaged by a mangy forest

animal no larger than an overgrown toad. For which grudging reason Hu Shaoqi had to admire the nasty genius of the
kuei's technique. Nevertheless, he found a stone on the
ground and flung it vigorously at the hare, which leapt
from its rock and disappeared into the underbrush.

"Why, then, boy, I'll just use *your* mouth," he heard his
own hijacked voice say. "Do you like that better?"

This development likewise startled the wayfarer. "Who
speaks?" he croaked, finding it hard to reclaim his voice.
"Who has stolen my tongue?"

Hu Shaoqi's lips and tongue did the bidding of the intelligence that had already scolded him: "Maybe it was the cat
who put that hair ball of hunger in your belly, boy."

His own voice, another's words.

As if retreat would save him, the young man backed up
until his shoulders were against the trunk of a gnarled tree.
No use, he realized, no use at all. The puppet of the master
ventriloquist says *what* it is bid to say, *when* it is bid to say it.

Malicious laughter burst from Hu Shaoqi's lips, terrifying
him even further. The worst part of his fear was the knowledge that he could not escape the demon causing it, for that
cunning immaterial creature had taken alternating control
of his voicebox and the muscles of his lips and tongue.
Flight would avail him nothing, for the demon would
accompany him, all the while mocking his attempts to
escape in the sardonic inflections of his own voice. Hu
Shaoqi wanted to scream, but the *kuei* distilling its caustic
laughter in his throat would not let him.

At last the laughter stopped, and the demon used him to
say, "Not a thought for your mother, lad? Not a thought for
the worry and confusion of your parents?"

Hu Shaoqi wrapped his arms backwards around the tree
trunk and tried to recover his wits.

"Speak, delicate lad! I give you back your voice!"

"About my mother, Peng Chao, I am indeed concerned,"

he said, his own words running so abruptly into the demon's that for a moment the lack of a break between them made him doubt that he had truly suffered possession.

"Doubt it not," the demon countered, again stealing his voice, and during this odd dialigue Hu Shaoqi's head snapped from side to side like that of an actor essaying two parts in a traveling drama. "I am with you always."

"Then you should understand that I deserted my household only because voices told me I must. It was not disrespect for my mother or unhappiness with my father's authority that drove me from Xiangcheng. And if you are one of those nagging voices, demon, then *you* must bear at least some of the burden of her sorrow and disappointment."

"I do, lad. I do. That's why I ask about her. That's why I chide you for seeming to forget her."

"Would you have me return to Xiangcheng to comfort my family?"

"The journey you have begun takes pride of place over all other responsibilities. But not even a hero should forget his mother."

Hu Shaoqi pushed himself away from the tree and pounded hard on his chest, as if to pummel into submission the spirit that was so duplicitously dealing with him. *"Then . . . what . . . would . . . you . . . have . . . me . . . DO . . . monster?"* he shouted, and the echo of each word reverberated like a blast on a war horn of ivory or bone.

Then the young man's head was wrenched about, and when sounds next escaped him, they were oily with the imprint of the demon's personality: "Look into your begging bowl, boy."

"It's empty!" But Hu Shaoqi looked, to confirm the fact, and so confirmed it all too easily.

"Burnish the metal with the sleeve of your robe."

His indignation giving way to cautious curiosity, the

young man obeyed the demon, rubbing the dew-rimmed bowl inside and out with his sleeve. The sun was completely gone now, a skull-like moon had risen in the east, dapples of metallic light fell through the canopy of evergreen needles, and in the bottom of his begging bowl Hu Shaoqi saw reflected a spiderweb of evening stars.

"Blow on them," the *kuei* said.

Peng Chao's son once again obeyed the demon, and, immediately, the concave copper of the bowl showed him his family's house in Xiangcheng and his still youthful-looking mother lying on her side on a pallet in an attitude of grieving weariness. A pug-nosed yellow dog that Hu Shaoqi had named Lung, or dragon, sat at the head of the woman's pallet nuzzling her brow. These images were not static, but, their reduced scale aside, precisely reminiscent of a living human and a living canine figure. Hu Shaoqi could scarcely believe their fidelity to life. His eyes misted, and he glanced up diagonally at the chilly, noncommittal moon.

"See the state she's in. See how you've left her."

"Why do you torment me with the presentation of a scene that I am helpless to alter?" the young man asked, too frustrated by his helplessness to rant.

"You're not helpless, lad. You're a ventriloquist."

"I'm your puppet, rather. And what good is ventriloquism when I am not there in my father's house to amuse the honorable Peng Chao with my talent?"

"Don't amuse her, stupid one! Comfort her!"

"*How?*" The bowl in his hands, Hu Shaoqi was reeling from tree to tree staining the ancient copper with the salt of his tears, but quickly wiping each discoloration away to behold again the poignant picture of his mother's grief.

"Throw your voice, young idiot! Throw your voice!"

The unhappy traveler halted. Still staring into the bowl, he considered the queer advice that had just passed his own lips. Throw his voice? He was better than a week's walk from Xiangcheng. What was the farthest he had ever cast his voice? He had not done badly with the bandits, of course, but that effort had required him to achieve variety and amplitude, not a ridiculously prohibitive distance. Once, however, he had made Madame Duan believe that a stork on a mist-touched hill had called out to her to be its mate, praising her legs as equal in scrawniness to those of any desirable female of its own species. How far had that been? Quite far, really, but he, Hu Shaoqi, had still reposed *within sight* of both the preening bird and the befuddled Madame Duan. He had never tried to project his voice into the mouth of a Mongol horseman half a continent away.

"You're not *that* far from your village, boy. Enter your ugly little dog as I have entered you. To pierce your muddleheadedness, must I explain at even greater length?"

This riposte left an acid taste on Hu Shaoqi's tongue. But, he reflected, it was just. If living pictures could appear in the bottoms of copper bowls, then surely he could exercise his talent for ventriloquism at a distance of as much as even *twelve* days' walk. He concentrated his gaze on Lung, the dog, and tried with all his will to send his thoughts into the creature's head and his voice into its tiny throat.

* * *

Peng Chao, Hu Shaoqi's mother, ignored the little dog's efforts to share her unhappiness. Lung was not her dog, but her son's, and although she was pleased in an absentminded way that her fatigue and melancholy should fret the animal, her fear that bandits had killed her only child, or that he had provoked some stranger's wrath with a misapplication of his eccentric talent, kept her from returning Lung's tender, but sticky, ministrations.

"Mother!" Lung said.

Without looking up, Peng Chao replied, "So great is my unhappiness that I've even begun to hear his sweet voice in this poor animal's mouth."

"Mother," Hu Shaoqi said through Lung, "it's truly I. I'm here beside you."

At these words, Peng Chao sat up on her pallet and stared at the small yellow dog, whose eyes seemed more intelligent than usual and whose head had cocked to one side in a pose of solicitous expectation. Well, those appearances were surely only whimsical accidents. Madame Peng looked away from the dog at various corners of the room, her eyebrows arrowing in over her nose and her mouth assuming a critical involuntary purse.

"No more of your tricks, Hu Shaoqi!" she said. "That you can continue doing such mischief after the cruelty of an unexplained departure will strike everyone who knows us as a failure of upbringing. You shame your father and me. You toy with our goodwill."

"Most Honorable Mother, I'm *not* playing a voice-throwing trick on you," Lung said, wagging his tail.

"Why, of course not. You simply wish for me to believe that your dog has miraculously learned to speak, and that it does so employing *your* voice, and that it calls me Most Honorable Mother only as a doggy courtesy."

"No, Mother, no. I *am* throwing my voice, of course, but not from anywhere in Xiangcheng."

"Come out this instant, you naughty young man," said Peng Chao, still searching the room for a sign of her son. "I will not much longer tolerate the indignity of conversing with your dog."

Hu Shaoqi explained that he was on a mountain

quite remote from the village. "I chose Lung as a vehicle for my words, Most Honorable Mother, not to insult you, but to ease your dear mind about both my whereabouts and the present state of my health." Lung, meanwhile, selected this moment to flop down on his side against Madame Peng's bedding. He exposed his soft belly and began tenderly cleaning his privates with his tongue.

Hu Yong, Hu Shaoqi's father, entered the house, and a long conversation that the dog was unable to interrupt ensued. Peng Chao told Hu Yong that an evil spirit had taken up residence in the animal and was trying to upset her own delicate mental balance by mimicking Hu Shaoqi's beloved voice. The *kuei* inhabiting the dog insisted that their son was throwing his voice in Lung's mouth from a great distance, but this was clearly a lie. Moreover, the whole unpleasant episode was undoubtedly one of the consequences of Hu Yong's impiety last spring, when he had drunk too much at a memorial ceremony for Peng Chao's departed grandfather, once a holy man of great reputation in Kweichow.

"It's truly I," Lung protested on Hu Shaoqi's behalf, looking up from his well-licked crotch. "Please don't argue, honorable parents. I simply wanted you to know that I am well and doing as the relentless voices inside my temples have commanded me."

"Then you aren't well at all," Hu Yong told the dog, angry with his wife for reminding him of his folly this past spring. "You're possessed, just as your mother —"

"I'm *not* Lung's mother," Peng Chao declared.

" — just as Madame Peng has said," Hu Yong corrected himself. "Now all that's left for me is to take you outside and beat you soundly for augmenting our sorrow. In this way, I'll drive the demon from your too compliant dogflesh and put an end to at least a portion of our unwarranted torment."

Lung, detecting the note of menace in Hu Yong's words, rolled to his haunches, lifted his hind quarters, and started backing from the room. "Father," Hu Shaoqi said through the nervous creature's flat, ebony muzzle, "you mustn't do this. Lung's not to blame, Lung's only my innocent mouthpiece."

"If only you had declined that final bowl," Peng Chao chided her husband. "If only you had burned incense."

Although a paunchy man in an ample robe, Hu Yong made a successful leap at Lung, grabbing the dog by the scruff and swinging him up into his arms. He then proceeded straight through the house, out its rear door into the chicken yard, and directly to a rock shrine against which Madame Peng's maid had earlier propped a broom. Bent over like a man planting rice, Hu Yong gripped this broom halfway up its handle and began whisking away at the squirming animal's backside.

"Father!" Hu Shaoqi cried. "Most Honorable Father, you're making a grievously unfortunate mistake!"

"I have Madame Peng to tell me that," Hu Yong managed through clenched teeth, still ineptly flailing at the dog's elusive rump. "I do not require you to second her opinion, Demon-in-the-Dog."

Peng Chao appeared on the threshold of the chicken yard. "That's not the way to beat a dog," she said. "You must grip the broom at the end, you must stand up to your full height, you must . . . ."

Unable to tolerate either further imprisonment in poor Lung's body or the dismaying burlesque of his parents' behavior, Hu Shaoqi withdrew from the dog, reluctantly relocating himself on the high slope of his anonymous mountain redoubt. Cold moonlight still sifted through the trees, and disconcerting images continued to dance in the bottom of his copper bowl. Angrily, then, he flung the bowl off the mountain and into the waiting night.

"Foolish," the demon said through Hu Shaoqi's aching throat.

The young man lifted his hands as if to strangle himself. *"Who are you? What are you? Why do you want me to go to the Mountain of Everlasting Winter? Why have you singled me out?"*

He wrestled himself away from the edge of a gaping chasm, then felt his hands thrust emphatically down to his sides, where they hung from his slender wrists like huge, impotent spiders.

"It's for your talent that I've singled you out, lad. It's so wonderfully akin to my own."

"But why, implacable one? *Why?"*

"Because ever since the world began, and especially since the human race arose from the lice on the corpse of the deity called Pan Ku, I have carried within me a great and amusing secret. It's time to impart it to someone, fortunate boy. It's time to share what only I among all the gods know."

"And the voices that have haunted me ever since I first spilled semen into my nightclothes?"

"All mine, lad, every one."

"Why?"

"To prepare you for manhood and the revelation of my secret."

"I've no wish to learn it. I don't want to know it."

"It's out of your hands," the *kuei* told Hu Shaoqi. "Lie down beneath that tree, and I'll take your hunger from you and give you this one last night of splendid, refreshing sleep — for until I've told my secret, you won't need food or rest again."

Hu Shaoqi could do nothing to combat this suggestion. He lay down beneath a grotesque cedar, surprised to find that the painful tightness in his stomach had disappeared, and fell into a slumber as full of pleasant images of his home and family as the bottom of his dinner bowl had just been with grotesque and farcical ones. In the morning, he awoke rested and stoically resigned to continue his trek to the *kuei's* unimaginable god-home.

* * *

The remainder of this journey took many days, through country even more forbidding than the groaning mountains that Hu Shaoqi had already traversed. Just as the demon had promised, no hunger pangs assailed him and sleep was an unnecessary indulgence that the young man was glad to leave to people who truly required it. Often, he was pinched by anxious thoughts about Peng Chao and Hu Yong, but each time such thoughts arose, the sight of his parents arguing with each other and mistreating Lung was thrown against his inner eye like an estranging shadow. His pity for his mother and father evaporated, his heart hardened, his jaw set. One evening it occurred to him that maybe the demon had allowed him to witness his parents in such an unattractive light for the express purpose of sabotaging his homesickness, but it was too late to go back and it was purposeless self-flagellation to lay upon himself the lash of remorse. He kept going.

Oddly, the *kuei* had relinquished its grip on both his body and his vocal machinery. Hu Shaoqi had no idea where the demon had gone. It had not completely forsaken him, he knew, because whenever he had doubts about which mountain track to follow or which of two icy streams to ford, a voice inside him gave him a prompt that decided the matter. Otherwise, the young man relied entirely on his own wits, and fended for himself, and journeyed ever farther westward like a holy man looking for the one sacred earthly place where he may experience enlightenment. After all, the *kuei* had promised him a powerful revelation in its otherworldly god-home.

It was nearly a week after the episode with the bowl that the troubled young man clambered up a glacial crevasse, high above the layer of clouds covering most of this desolate stretch of the continent, into view of his long-sought destination, the abode of the ventriloquist demon.

Ice clung to the peach fuzz on Hu Shaoqi's cheeks, and to his eyelashes, and to the cold-bruised lobes of his ears. He could scarcely feel his feet. But in the wind at the top of the world, he staggered toward the *kuei*'s miraculous dwelling, marveling at both its beauty and its imperviousness to the onslaughts of everlasting winter. He beheld it by starlight, and through the almond-thin lenses of ice on his eyeballs, and by a secret yearning of the heart that invested every ridge and shingle of the god-home with a saintly fire.

The *kuei*'s dwelling was a rose-colored pavilion beside a pagoda whose upper stories disappeared into the night like the segments of an infinitely tall telescope. A delicate wooden bridge with enameled hand rails crossed another glacial chasm to the pavilion's front door. Despite the roaring wind, beds of lotus flowers with scarlet petals hugged the foundations of the structure, and a pair of mossy willow trees stood sentinel beyond the bridge. Neither the willows nor the lotus blossoms danced themselves to shreds in the recurrent blasts sweeping the peak.

"Come," said the demon, intruding this word into the traveler's mind rather than shaping it on his tongue. "Don't be an idiot. Come out of the cold."

Although astonished by the pavilion and its adjacent

pagoda, Hu Shaoqi hurried to obey. Simultaneously, he understood that *kuei* or demons lacked both the spiritual power and the transhuman prestige to inhabit dwellings like this one. Therefore, no mere evil spirit had possessed him, no mere demon had dictated his strenuous but failure-proof trek to the top of the world. He was dealing not with a sprite or a ghost, but an immortal god. The chief question that remained was, Which one? Hu Shaoqi knew fear again, but nevertheless continued to approach the bridge.

Inside the outer pale of the god-home, a balmy breeze overtook him, and sweet fragrances wafted into his nostrils, and his frozen body began to thaw. Incense mingled with the scent of the flowers. Wind chimes of glass, copper, and polished stone played melodies so much gentler than those of the careering winds on the peaks that the young man kept shaking his head to determine if this action would restore the pitiless roaring. To his considerable relief, it never did.

The throne room of the pavilion humbled Hu Shaoqi. An ivory chair with lion's paws on its legs and a sunlike maned head in the middle of its back support occupied the dais on the room's far west. A pair of embossed gongs — one silver, one gold — flanked the throne. Painted vases, papier-mâché death masks, folding rice-paper screens, and water-colored scrolls complemented these imperial funishings and shone upside-down in the liquid depths of the throne room's marble floor. Hu Shaoqi walked toward the lion chair with an acute sensitivity to the echoes of his own slapping footalls.

"I'm here," he said. "Is that your secret? That no other mortal has ever set foot in this lovely pavilion before?"

To Hu Shaoqi's great surprise, his dog Lung padded into the throne room from one of the pavilion's adjoining wings and hopped up into the lion chair as if perfectly comfortable in so exalted a place. Lung circled about serveral times, slumped down facing his young master, and inclined his head toward his hind quarters so that he could scratch his ear by half-heartedly jiggling one back foot.

"For my own amusement," Lung said, "I've brought plenty of other mortals here, boy. Unlike you, many of them didn't even have to walk to get here."

"Lung," Hu Shaoqi exclaimed. "Little Dragon!" He noted that the dog's voice was not *his* voice, as it had been in the little drama played out in the bottom of his discarded dinner bowl, but an entirely new one appropriate to a creature of Lung's size and disposition. As if the *kuei* — the god, rather — had developed a small growly voice exclusively for the animal. Hu Shaoqi reached to fondle Lung's mite-infested ear, but Lung bared his teeth and snarled, preventing contact.

"You don't really wish to touch me," the dog warned, in a combination growl and articulate snore — so that now it seemed that through Lung's pink lips two or maybe even three voices were speaking in ill-synchronized harmony. "I'm here in the guise of your dog to ease the act of talking with me. The sight of my true form would melt your eyeballs. The sound of my true voice would burst your eardrums." As if to give a credible dignity to these threats, the god's borrowed dog body stopped jiggling its foot against its ear and stared Hu Shaoqi directly in the eye.

Daunted, the young man looked down. "Are you, then, Old Man Heaven? Or Yen Lo Wang, the Judge?"

"I'm far more ancient than even those upstart pretenders," the dog said indignantly, in its eerie double blur of a voice. "Even Shang Ti and the Great Emperor of the Eastern Peak are infants — mere puppies — in comparison to me. I use them as mouthpieces, I sometimes condescend to let them do my barking."

At these words, a strange feeling came over Hu Shaoqi. It consisted of equal parts of terror, reverence, nostalgia, joy,

melancholy, anger, love, outrage, apprehension, content-
ment, perplexity, lust, exhilaration, despair, and mindless
panic — indeed, every human emotion except maybe apa-
thy and boredom.

Hu Shaoqi was lost to himself, frozen in place, and suddenly, without moving from his position before the lion
chair, he found free-floating pieces of himself — his eyes
and his memory — touring the various levels of the infinitely tall pagoda beside the god-home, going from floor to
floor through all the stages of his life that his manipulated
intelligence could divide into discrete and hence under-
standable units. Conception, gestation, birth. Infancy, tod-
dlerhood, childish self-definition. Each level of the pagoda,
as his eyes and memory climbed through the rose-colored
structure, represented a vivid and seemingly self-contained
period of his development as a person; and yet he ascended
through these levels as if his body lacked all substance and
no floors separated these crucial periods. Voices accompanied his ascent, the voices of Peng Chao, Hu Yong, play-
mates, teachers, Lung the dog, other animals, and of course
a host of other half-forgotten or at best half-remembered
children and adults, all of whom had dripped a little of the
lukewarm paraffin of their personalities into his own hot
and ever-flowing one. The cacophony of these voices, their
contending echoes in the well of the infinite pagoda, rang
in Hu Shaoqi's head like the music of either a disintegrating
or a resurgent chaos. He could not tell which, and he hardly
cared.

And then he was in front of Lung again, in the pavilion,
and the strange feeling that had overmastered him grew
even stranger. He was going to speak, but the words that he
intended to say he knew to belong to the god who had
summoned him all the way from Xiangcheng.

"Tell me your secret and let me go."

The dog on the throne cocked its head. "Did you hear

what you've just said, boy? Don't you think it perfectly in character? Why, it even reproduces the underlying anxiety that a callow young man in your position would inevitably experience here. I do it all the time, but it never fails to astonish me. That's why I'm able to revel in my own accomplishment, the surprise of rediscovering the formidable extent of my knowledge and power."

Hu Shaoqi was having trouble following the god's elliptical chain of reasoning. "Please, O Great One, what are you talking about? Have pity on a mortal of lesser understanding."

"There again!" Lung barked. "It's second-nature to me, for I'm the infallible universal dramaturge."

Bewildered, the young man started to frame another plea for compassion.

"Not only that," Lung enthusiastically cut him off, "I play all the parts. I compose, I enact, and I direct. *That's* my secret, boy. Do you understand?"

Hu Shaoqi, every piece of his skin tingling as if it had been sliced from his muscles from the underside, shook his head. "No," he murmured, but the word exploded into the throne room like a canon shot, greatly embarrassing him.

"And I can take you out of character, too," said Lung. "I can go mad inside you to relieve a bit of the pressure of sustaining the world's activity."

"Go mad?"

"As now, puppet. As now. For this *is* a kind of madness, you see, sharing with one of the integers of my dependent creation the secret of its dependency. Haven't you yet begun to understand?"

But he had, Hu Shaoqi, and to show that he had, he spoke words that his interrogator had already scripted for him: "I'm no more obtuse than you want me to be, am I?"

Lung's pink tongue made a circuit of its lips, even flicking up to wet the flat, ugly nose. "Excellent riposte. Excellent."

"Self-praise is no praise at all."

"Better, even better. It's borrowed, of course, but ultimately it's borrowed only from myself."

"I thought of you once as a ventriloquist demon, a mere
kuei with the upsetting ability to hijack — occasionally —
my foolish mortal tongue. But now I know you as the
Ventriloquist God, who has animated us solely for the purpose of throwing your voice, or voices, into every living
husk that has ever been. The meaning of it all is that
although *you* count, *we* don't. Puppets are made for instruction and amusement. We, too. Your amusement, but our
veiled and therefore mocking instruction."

"Hush," the dog said, laughing in its wheezing, doggy
way. "You outrun your allotted dialogue."

Whereupon the creature told Hu Shaoqi to look in turn at
the huge medallions of the gongs, the gold one first and
then the silver. In the surface of the gold gong, as days ago
in the copper at the bottom of his begging bowl, Hu Shaoqi
saw moving pictures. Only gods — Shang Ti, Old Man
Heaven, Yen Lo Wang, Hsi Ho, Pan Ku, Fu Hsi, and a host
of other immortals — disported themselves in the gleaming
gold, whereas in the silver only human beings warred and
partied, wept and sang, argued and reconciled. Both gongs,
however, made it clear to Hu Shaoqi that the Ventriloquist
God who had brought him here exercised total control over
the players, whether divine or human, visible in their surfaces. The sounds conducted through the metals, and
around the rims of the gongs, had their origin in the throat
of the little dog observing Hu Shaoqi, and the dog had its
artificial life through the grace and contrivance of the Pro-
prietor of the god-home.

All life, then, was illusion, just as Buddhist teaching had
long held, but in a peculiarly narrow and degrading way
that the young man had never suspected. It was a shock,
and an annihilating wrench, to find that he and all his loved

ones — indeed, the whole of creation — were mere sub-stanceless effigies through which the Ventriloquist God could pipe the devious excreta of its everlasting vanity.

"You're not amused?" the dog asked.

A kernel of separate being deep inside Hu Shaoqi wanted to say No to the god in its own voice, but the god forced from the young man a No that failed to coincide with that inner one, being playful and sarcastic rather than freighted with true conviction.

"Turn around, Hu Shaoqi. Turn around."

The upright puppet turned, and there in the pavilion stood upright effigies of Peng Chao and Hu Yong, his parents. Their bodies were ashen and airy, like statues made of volcanic pumice, and the hinge buttons at their jaws glittered meaningfully. They began to talk, these two, but in a manner totally out of keeping with what Hu Shaoqi knew of them. Madame Peng was telling her husband a tale of such flagrant bawdiness that the young man's ears began to burn, while Hu Yong was tittering at each repeated obscenity or sexual innuendo like a half-wit girl of thirteen. Immediately, other ashen simulacra of people whom Hu Shaoqi recognized appeared in the pavilion, each with bolts or buttons holding on their lower jaws, and they all began gibbering, ululating, or hacking out hideous noises like persons possessed. The hubbub that Hu Shaoqi had heard in his ethereal flight upward through the pagoda here became a crazy cosmic din that he could no longer tolerate.

"STOP IT!" he shouted. And, for once, the words issuing from his mouth seemed to be wholly his own.

Perhaps for the first time in his life.

Further, at this command, most of the lava-stone statues powdered and blew away. The din diminished. When he shouted the same words again, the remainder of the effigies also disappeared — all but those of his mother and father. Peng Chao was still reciting an indelicate adventure that her son could in no wise credit, and Hu Yong was still giggling girlishly at the outrageous tale. It was a nightmare, their spurious behavior, even worse than what the deity had inflicted upon them in the copper bowl.

"I SAID STOP IT!"

But they would not. The Ventriloquist God was enjoying his discomfiture too much to let the performance end. So Hu Shaoqi whirled on Lung, the dog, whose tongue was lolling from its mouth in the careless, laughing way of all such curs, and with both hands seized the startled animal's throat before it could react. He yanked the creature off the throne and began strangling it, telling himself over and over again, This is not Lung, This is not actually my beloved Lung. The dog's eyes bulged, and its hind feet tried to gain purchase at the midriff of Hu Shaoqi's robe, but the young man kept swinging it from side to side and tightening his grip, with the result that the imprisoned god could not yet wriggle free and manifest.

Over his shoulder, the young man saw that the statues of his mother and father had finally begun to crumble. Their stupid voices continued to sound in the throne room, but more thinly than before, and soon all that was left of either simulacrum was a wind-nudged mound of bleak grit and the whisper of emancipation.

Hu Shaoqi tossed Lung away from him, and the dog broke its back on the rim of the marble dais supporting its throne. Its yelp of pain crescendoed through the pavilion like two great armies colliding, and where a small, twisted dog had been, Hu Shaoqi saw an immense winged serpent with scales like dead leaves and a lion's head unreeling from its toothless mouth a pair of split, snaky tongues. This creature — this being — reared up on the coils of its lower body in much the way that the pagoda next to the pavilion climbed heavenward on its successive stories, and Hu Shaoqi had to tilt back his head to see the ancient leonine face glowering at him like a once glorious sun on the brink of self-extinguishment.

"You're (you're) fortunate (fortunate) I (I) don't (don't) simply (simply) crush (crush) you (you)," the god said in its blurred double voice, and Hu Shaoqi automatically adjusted his hearing to filter out the echo, "but I fear *you're* not solely a walking mouthpiece for my own capricious japeries."

"I'm not," Hu Shaoqi retorted.

"How did you discover your autonomy?" the god asked.

"It was something I always assumed. Until I arrived here, I had no reason to doubt it. It was your purpose to reveal that assumption as an illusion, but it's my gift to you, Ventriloquist God, to turn the tables, to declare from the kernel of being deep within myself that the *real* illusion is your arrogant illusion of total mastery."

"Worship me," the serpentine lion said.

Hu Shaoqi knelt before the monster, casting down his eyes and touching the tips of his fingers to his forehead.

"You submit? You do my will?"

"Voluntarily," Hu Shaoqi replied. "I'm not a god. I'm but a mortal human being."

"Then you comprehend your place?"

"It's a high place, O Great One, for it's no contemptible thing to be a kind of philosophical monkey. To have a voice that splices unintelligible noises into chains of airy import."

The dragon deity spoke no other word, and for the left-over length of that immortal night, Hu Shaoqi remained on his knees before the creature, meditating and praying. When next he looked up, he found himself sitting on the slope of the selfsame mountain on which he had used his copper bowl to witness some dismaying events in his father's household in Xiangcheng. Well, now those events struck Hu Shaoqi as more humorous than otherwise. But although he could laugh at them, a natural anxiety — a concern for the well-being of every member of his family —

prodded him to rise and begin the homeward leg of his journey that would either confirm or cancel his fears.

* * *

So Hu Shaoqi returned to his native village, and his arrival there stupefied many and greatly cheered his mother and father, who had given him up for dead. Lung was there, too, and although the young man tried to show the dog both affection and the rough playfulness that his pet had once insisted on, Lung regarded him with reproachful eyes and tuck-tail suspicion.

But this was the only unhappy aspect of Hu Shaoqi's return, and the hearty meal of chicken and fried vegetables that Madame Peng prepared for him on his first evening home more than made up for the dog's queer lack of enthusiasm. Never had he had a bigger hunger, and never had he so enjoyed a mortal craving.

While he was eating, a choir of children celebrating an autumn festival came down the street and paused just outside to share its song with his family. Hu Shaoqi, even as he ate, listened in wonder, hearing every voice distinct from all the others and then hearing them in unison as if they were complementary pipes on the same joyous wind instrument. And such voices those children had, such beautiful, beautiful voices!

"Throw your voice into theirs," Hu Yong urged his son. "Make Little Dragon there sing with them."

"Forgive me, Most Honorable Father," Hu Shaoqi said, "but it's very hard to do while eating."

Fortunately, Hu Yong accepted this explanation, and it was only later in all their lives that he came to realize that his son had apparently renounced that talent forever.

A Spy In The Domain Of Arnheim

*I am repatriated by a moment of panic. These are
the privileged moments that transcend mediocrity.*

— *René Magritte*

Tourist or Spy? Had I been dispatched to this quaint,
understaffed hotel on a holiday or an errand of
espionage? The spartan Old World elegance of the room in
which I woke — the functional coldness of the furnishing —
told me without my even going to a window that, during a
period of sleep or disembodiment, I had arrived in a region
of rugged mountains and thick snows. Tourist or spy? The
weight of an indistinct obligation made me suspect the
latter, and I was loath to get up, to acknowledge the debt
laid upon me.

Why could not my sponsors have granted me a season of
idleness and recreation? The first elementary condition of
bliss, after all, is free exercise in the open air — for most
human beings prefer the freshness of a montane breeze to
the recycled fetors of a casino or a drawing room. Or
should. But I had no independent choice. Permission for a
carefree stroll along the chanting cataracts, or for a bout of
breakneck skiing down the hotel's hazardous slalom

course, options no less implicit in my arrival at this place than a flurry of unspecified spy work — such permission would have prodded me to rise, complete my morning toilet, and hurry out-of-doors. But I belonged to my sponsors; I was not my own man.

Who were my sponsors? It embarrasses me to confess that I had forgotten. I remembered only that I was an agent — perhaps the only incarnate representative — of their mysterious designs. Although utterly languid in pursuit of their ends, they expected me to subordinate my will to theirs. By no means did I suppose them malign, demented or childish (quite the opposite, in fact), but I was equally certain that they had no right to use me as they did, for at their subliminal bidding I became either a flashlight or a scalpel — an instrument to illuminate the crannies of their ignorance or to lay open the secret tissues of their communal longing. By what authority did they deny me autonomous control of my own consciousness? I had — if only I could find it — an identity altogether apart from their grandiose manipulations.

I have said that my room was both elegant and austere. Let me dilate a little on this point. My bed — upon which I lay clad in a pair of monogrammed drawers, a sleeveless undershirt, and a pair of calf-length black silk hose — was a mere rectangular box with head and footboards. Although I had two lumpy pillows and a bolster, no one had bothered to turn the counterpane back; I reposed supine on this reddish-brown blanket, which had been stretched across, and tucked tautly beneath, my mattress. The only other pieces of furniture in the room were a chair with a lyre-shaped back, a wardrobe with mirrored doors, and a rough wooden table with a cloth the same disquieting color as my counterpane. A phonograph with a large metal speaker sat on this table, beyond which I could see a fire grate and a mantel of salmon-colored marble. The mantel was surmounted by a mirror in a fluted gold frame.

What richness the room revealed — what eclectic elegance — derived from the mirrors, a pair of partially overlapping Persian carpets, the brass cornucopia of the Victrola, the petrified veins in the marble fireplace facing, and the giddily realistic pattern of the wallpaper: puffy, bathtub-sized clouds drifting over a backdrop of robin's-egg blue. A summer sky in a winter room. Although gratified by the whimsical promise of warmth embodied by these clouds, I could not stop shivering. Further, it seemed a sacrilege against the room's intimidating tidiness to pull back the counterpane and climb into the bed.

Resentful of my sponsors, I sat up, swung about, and put my stockinged feet on the floor. Now I could see that beside the mantel was an open archway connecting my bedroom to the suite's parlor, where the floating-cloud pattern on the wallpaper did not extend. Indeed, the walls in there were a deep tomato color, darker than my blanket. Likewise, the hardwood planking of the parlor was perceptibly darker than my bedroom's flooring — as if the more distant chamber enjoyed a late-afternoon rather than a morning slant of sunlight. It seemed to me that by proceeding from here to there I could warm myself without having to don a suit of bleakly styleless clothes. But, standing, I suffered a sudden weakness in my legs and decided that, before venturing forth to greet a later segment of the day, I must submit to the conventional proprieties.

I fingered my chin and jaw. No stubble intercepted these probings; my face was as sleek as an apple skin. It occurred to me that, although an adult, I had never had to use a shaving brush and a straight razor to obtain this immaculate bourgeois smoothness. Nevertheless, I had a vivid recollection of once having used these instruments, not to mention a humming handheld machine that had accomplished the same end. Was my lack of a beard the result of a depilatory substance, or had my sponsors given me the immature hide of a human adolescent? The mirrored doors of the wardrobe — into which I expectantly peered, hoping to overthrow the reign of amnesia — did not give back my image. By implying that I was either an eidolon or some other creature impervious to the laws of optics, this circumstance greatly discomfited me. Frightened, I reached out and touched the glass of the left-hand door. This movement immediately reassured me for the shadow of my hand passed over the icelike surface of the "mirror" and I understood that the images in both doors were imprisoned there by an artifice heretofore unsuspected by me. When I opened the doors, the room's "reflected" wall went one way and its "reflected" Victrola the other, and I was staring into a cupboard of modest dimensions and rather prosaic contents. My panic ebbed.

Have I called the wardrobe's contents commonplace? But for two exceptions (which I will presently mention), perhaps they were.

Arrayed on wooden hangers, a pair of dark trousers, a matching suit jacket, and a long black overcoat greeted my gaze. Warily, I put on these items, which fitted me tolerably well — but my eye kept going back to the *chapeau melon*, or bowler hat, on the recessed shelf above the closet bar. Now I will tell you why.

Someone in a humorous or deranged state of mind had attached a large green apple and its leafy stem to the hat so that the fruit hung down a few inches from the brim. Five shiny leaves clustered above the apple, giving the hat the appearance of an inverted flower bowl. I lifted the hat from the shelf (a block of wood inside the crown had kept the apple's weight from toppling the bowler into the bottom of the wardrobe) and fitted it onto my head. Idiocy! The dependent green apple effectively obscured my vision. Who could have perpetrated such a pointless joke?

Perhaps I was being watched. I hastily removed the *chapeau melon* and struggled to pull the apple and its twig from the hat brim. But whatever fixative the trickster had employed resisted my best efforts, and I was finally obliged to snap the stem. The apple went into my jacket pocket and the bowler with its remaining foliage back onto the shelf. I had no intention of playing the buffoon (at least not again, that is) for the infantile agency that had arranged this absurd trap, and I congratulated myself for so quickly terminating its half-witted concept of fun. Moreover, I had procured my breakfast.

What I now required was footwear, preferably a pair of unassuming black oxfords. Sanguine about finding just what I needed in the wardrobe (which had so far outfitted me like a burgher, without my having made any previous arrangements for it to do so), I knelt and groped about. The oxfords were there, directly under the overcoat, and I gratefully withdrew them. While withdrawing them, however, I caught sight of the backs of a pair of high-topped work shoes, so dirt-caked and worn that I wondered about finding them in this genteel piece of furniture. Curious, I hooked these shoes with my fingers and dragged them into the light.

They hit the carpet but did not fall over. Like the unsuspecting recipient of a torn-out heart, I recoiled from them. Why? Because they embodied a mockery of my expectations, a perverse contradiction of acceptable shoeness, and a threat to civilized mores. How to explain these charges?

Best to say it quickly: they were not really shoes at all; they were lifelike gutta-percha facsimiles of human feet, with horny nails on the toes and the incongruity of laces on the insteps. Bunioned and scarred, they ostensibly represented the feet of a well-built peasant. Had I been so inclined, I could have easily slipped my oxfords into them

— a thought, even in retrospect, altogether repugnant to me. I glanced about the room wondering if the impractical joker who had attached the apple to the hat were secretly remarking my terror and perplexity. This prank, inarguably more vile than the other, had achieved my conspicuous discomfiture. As for the feet-shaped boots themselves, they were poised on the edge of the carpet as if to chase me from the bed chamber.

"How barbarous," I murmured.

Steeling myself, I seized the obscene articles and tossed them back into the bottom of the wardrobe. Then I banged the doors to — those doors with their counterfeit mirrors and artificial reflections — and secured the drop-latch. Drained, I reeled away from the cabinet to the room's only chair. Here I put on my oxfords and caught my breath.

Like a tumor, the apple in my jacket pocket pressed against my hip, attracting my attention. All the while surveying the ceilings, walls, cornices, and baseboards for peepholes or telltale signs of spying equipment, I devoured the tart, juicy flesh of the apple. I saw nothing to confirm or to allay my suspicions, for the glass in the false mirrors bespoke an intelligence of a high, but somewhat deceitful, order. I could not discount the possibility that the very walls were transparent to the unknown eyes beyond them.

Fortified and a little comforted by the apple, I glanced over my shoulder at the Victrola. In a flood of insight, as if eating the apple had restored a portion of my memory, I suddenly knew my *nom de guerre*, my age, and my place of national origin. Starting with the last first, I hailed from one of the southern capitals of the United States of America, I was thirty-five years old, and my sponsors had christened me, for reasons of their own, Elliot Ellison. Indeed, my wallet, containing documentary support of these recollections, lay on the table beside the phonograph.

I went to the table, dropped my apple core into a wine

glass beside the Victrola, and found my wallet. The plastic identity card that I took from one of its compartments gave me a start, for although my name, age, and address were all neatly entered in the proper places, the accompanying photograph would be of absolutely no use to anyone — police, merchants, or custom officials. It would alienate rather than secure their belief in me. Near a lake or an ocean front, I had posed for the camera face-on, but a white pigeon, or perhaps a small albino gull, had swept between me and the camera lens at the precise moment of the shutter's closing. It was this ridiculous portrait — the bird's body and wings obscuring my features — that my sponsors had affixed to my identity card.

What's in a name? I reflected darkly. Elliot Ellison might just as well have been Anson Anonymous or Norbert Nobody.

Angered by this betrayal, I began to crank the phonograph. A moment later I nudged the needle onto the plate of Blue Amberol revolving on the turntable. All this equipment, I decided, must date back to the beginnings of phonographic manufacture. Soon a quintessentially feminine voice began to speak to me through the scratchy static of the record. Although the warp in this disc was substantial, it did not detract from the melodic purity of the woman's recitation.

"One cannot speak about mystery; one must be seized by it," she said, to no accompaniment but the persistent scratching. "Several times this morning, Elliot, mystery has assaulted you, but you have refused to give in to it. You (unintelligible) the banality of explanations. Why? There is really no need, Elliot — no need to embrace the mediocrity of looking for meanings."

It did not alarm me that the voice had used my name. "There is something to look for here," I insisted.

"Of course, but (unintelligible). You must remember that

your identity is negotiable. Familiarity with oneself breeds — death. Find mysteries rather than meanings. Looking for significances abstracts you from (unintelligible) that alone redeem the universe."

"But —" I broke off. Suddenly I was shaken by the uncanny idea that the apple I had eaten was reassembling itself in my gut, expanding inside me like a balloon. Soon, like Athena from the forehead of Zeus, it would burst from my abdomen, annihilating me, its implicit aim being to grow and grow — until it occupied the entire chamber from floor to ceiling and from wall to wall. Humanity banished from its world, the giant green apple would abide forever, listening . . . Imagining the acoustics of metamorphosis, I listened too.

"B e t t e r,   E l l i o t.   Y o u   b e g i n   t o —"

Even though the needle had tracked only the outer third of the record's long spiral groove, the phonograph was running down. Cranking vigorously, I rewound the machine.

" — (unintelligible) the legitimacy of mystery. That's good. You'll soon be a citizen of the living universe again. Don't you see, Elliot? When everything's in transit, it's folly to stand on ceremony. To look for patterns that haven't emerged yet — well, that's even worse."

The needle continued to circle inward, but only the raspy clickety click of static issued from the Victrola's brass horn. I waited, my knuckles pressed against the blood-brown table cloth. Eventually, just as I had begun to doubt, my interlocutor rewarded my patience by addressing me in a lilting, obviously parodic sing-song:

" 'The four elementary conditions of bliss.' " She cleared her throat. " 'First, free exercise in the open air. Second, the love of woman.' No capital 'w' on that one, but it sure sounds to me as if this fellow meant to capitalize. Well. Never mind. 'Third, the contempt of ambition. And fourth, an object of unceasing pursuit. Other things being equal, the extent of attainable happiness is in proportion to the spirituality of this object.'" The stylus scratched inward. "Over and out," the voice added, by way of peremptory afterthought.

"Wait," I implored. "Aren't the third and fourth conditions mutually exclusive? I mean, you've got to have a certain amount of ambition to engage in a pursuit, don't you? Otherwise —"

"Over and out," her enchanting siren voice repeated. "Over and out . . . Over and out . . ."

The needle had hung up on a scratch or an embedded dust particle. Fearful that if my unknown redemptress did not speak again, I would surely go mad, I flicked the tone arm with my finger, then listened in dismay to the hideous, high-pitched screech of its progress across the record. Had I ruined everything? Would the rest be silence or nonsensical distortions? The latter would be infinitely harder to bear for I must then acknowledge my preeminent role in isolating myself from all human intercourse. The Victrola's empty cornucopia would mock me.

"I didn't (unintelligible) these conditions, Elliot. Their lack of consistency means — pardon me — nothing to me. Maybe their formulator defined 'ambition' differently from you. Or 'pursuit', or 'contempt'. I don't feel bound by someone else's conditions, particularly in pursuit of a trivial goal like happiness. Bliss is deadening, Elliot. Too much of it is mindless. That's not Calvinism, either — it's an evolutionary doctrine. You could also consult Plato. Genuine mystery just isn't to be found in mindlessness."

Frustrated by the smugness imbuing these riddles, I shouted at the machine, "WHAT AM I DOING HERE, ANYWAY?"

But the needle had tracked its way to the very center of the plate, where it lapped the last restraining rim like a boat banging its quay in bad weather. Bitterly disconsolate, I set the tone arm aside and plunged my hands into my trouser pockets.

"You're here as both a tourist and a spy," said the woman in a more tender tone. Although the phonograph was no longer operating, her voice issued clearly from the great brass speaker. "Your sponsors have laid the burden of the latter role upon you, but it really wouldn't hurt if you decided to play up the other one a little. Being a tourist's nothing to be ashamed of."

"If you're my enemy, that would suit you just fine, wouldn't it?"

"Listen to me, Elliot. Espionage is a goal-oriented activity; it exists to find meanings in the data it accumulates. And not only meanings, but a basis for future action. Tourism's different. In its purest manifestations, anyway, it's a means of confronting a mystery by generating a context for new experiences. Its goal is perception before understanding. Ideally, I mean."

"A goal is a goal," I countered. "This is all so much talk."

"No human activity is perfectly pointless, Elliot. It's a matter of degree. The way I see it, tourism is less materially goal-directed than espionage. Perception before, or maybe even versus, understanding." To my surprise, she laughed.

"You don't want me to understand, do you?"

"Not yet, Elliot. Not just yet."

"Why not?"

"Everything in time. Be a tourist first, a spy second."

"Who are you?"

But she would not answer, and when next I cranked the phonograph and put the needle on the record, offensive martial music blared into the room. I yanked the disc from the turntable and hurled it against the fire grate. Though the fire grate was empty and cold, the broken shards flickered into flame like so many kerosene-sprinkled coals

— a consequence, I supposed, of the sudden impact. The hooting of a train whistle echoed through the mountain passes beyond the hotel.

"For that matter," I asked myself, "who am I?"

Elliot Ellison was only a name. I approached the mirror over the mantelpiece, half expecting to find another counterfeit reflection frozen in the glass. What I encountered was far stranger. Although I squared my shoulders and looked directly into the mirror, some optical anomaly, which the creator of the looking glass had exploited to sinister effect rendered the back of my head, the back of my collar, the back of my suit jacket. A shudder passed through me. The prankster who had conceived my previous petty torments — the woman whose delightful voice had addressed me through the Victrola — indeed, the entire unforthcoming staff of the Arnheim Hotel — not one of these mysterious persons wished me to behold my own naked face. Their refusal to let me see myself was maddening. To keep my hand from pounding their wicked mirror into hundreds of wicked fragments was a severe test, but by dint of will I passed it.

Atop the salmon-colored marble of the mantel shelf, just to my right, lay a copy of a book bound in fissuring, light-grey paper: Edgar Poe's *Adventures of Arthur Gordon Pym*. It shocked me to see that the mirror reflected the cover of this book exactly as a mirror ought, the letters in the author's name and those in the title — along with the nautical emblem below them — all being properly reversed. Carefully, so as not to crumble the paper jacket or the pages, I picked up the book and curiously inspected it. Now my body (the one in the mirror, I mean) obscured the volume that ought to have been reflected there; and when I held the book to one side or the other, I saw it in my extended hands as if surreptitiously approaching myself from behind. Intolerable! this pointless game-playing.

"La Reproduction interdite," said the woman's voice from the phonograph speaker. "Loosen up, Elliot. Loosen up."

"To hell with you," I told her, and she laughed.

Carrying *Arthur Gordon Pym,* I stormed from the bed chamber into the tomato-red prison of the adjoining parlor. But for a fireplace (it had the same flue as the one in the bedroom), the parlor was bare of furnishings. A pair of empty brass candlesticks and a clock whose hands were stopped at precisely 12:43 rested on the mantel shelf, but I could scarcely contrive to call these items "furniture." This was indeed a miserable sitting room. A person would have to take lessons from a Hindu mystic and collapse into the mind-obliterating toils of the lotus position to find any comfort here. I gazed about me in a fury of despair.

Whereupon I saw, flanked by dark-green curtains, the parlor's only window, which consisted of a large bottom pane surmounted by a fanlight lacking the conventional spokelike sash bars. The view through this window — or, more accurately, its bottom pane — was breathtakingly hard to credit. The wonders (the annoying wonders) of the morning were nothing beside it. In fact, I had never seen a landscape so beautiful, magnificent, and startling. To take in the sight at closer range, I hurried across the empty parlor — only to discover that my eyes had not created, from my nervousness and distress, a wild phantasm.

The high blue mountain enclosing the domain of Arnheim on the east had a prominent central crag resembling, yes, an eagle's head. The rocky peaks to either side of this mighty aquiline profile represented the curves of its outspread wings, and in all the crevices and canyons crosshatching its mountainous body lay immense plumes of downy snow. The mountain had become an eagle, or an eagle had become a mountain, and the exquisite awesomeness of the scene admitted of no improvement. A worshipful impulse lay hold of me, and I made mute obeisance to this avian god of stone — until, that is, a cold suspicion began to undermine my reverence.

"Another trick!" I exclaimed. "Another Arnheim lie!"

The same intelligence that had already sabotaged my peace of mind was at work in this duplicity, too. My wonderful eagle-mountain, or mountain-eagle, owed its existence to the Daedalian trickster who had set its portrait in the very crystals of the windowpane, which had undergone the same subtle alterations as the false mirrors in the bed chamber — with, of course, a different and more miraculous design. Although the sky visible in the unreachable fanlight might be real, the image in the bottom pane was a fantastic sham. It was possible that my hotel suite overlooked an iron foundry, a bog, or a cluttered scrap yard. The only way to determine the truth was to open the window.

I set *Arthur Gordon Pym* out of the way and tried to get a grip on the outer sash. However, this enterprise was doomed by my having to deal with a fixed window; I soon understood that it neither raised nor lowered. If I wanted to see what lay beyond it, I would have to break the window — a vandalism for which I had little experience and even less heart. Struck again by the *outré* beauty of the eagle-mountain design, I stepped back to ogle it and to mull my options.

As I did, the window all at once broke — apparently in response to a sudden geologic tremor or a muted sonic boom — and fragments of glass, some large, some small, dropped from the frame like chips of painted ice. Reacting to this inexplicable concussion, I had gone to one knee, but now, all danger past, I eased myself erect and found my suspicions about the window only partially borne out. Although each window fragment contained a puzzle piece of the eagle-mountain image (the shard bearing the bird's profiled head leaned against the baseboard with several smaller ones), visible through the jagged break was the selfsame scene in very truth. Now I could see that the miniature in the broken glass had corresponded in every detail with the aquiline colossus across the intervening lake from the hotel. Meanwhile, as I stood thunderstruck by this humbling revelation, a blast of icy air rushed through the room, stirring the curtains and flash-freezing my marrow. I myself — Elliot Ellison — had acquired the fragile clairvoyance of a windowpane.

"D-d-dear G-god," I heard myself stammer.

"Are you all right, sir?"

These words issued from behind me in a kind of hoarse whisper, and I whirled to confront the person who had spoken them. One of the members of the hotel staff, a steward, had entered my suite from the corridor. A man of my own height and build, he was clad in a suit exactly like my own, his most unsettling peculiarity being the large linen pouch that he wore over his head. To this astonishing headgear he had attempted to impart an air of commonplaceness by disposing its twisted excess over his shoulder like a scarf. This ruse failed because the sack had neither eyeholes nor breathing apertures, and the man stood before me as if awaiting escort to the gallows or the executioner's block. Was this the man who had arranged all my morning's torments? Perhaps not all. It hardly seemed fair to hold him accountable for the tremors (or sonic boom) that had briefly racked the building.

In that same growly whisper he said, "We don't often have earthquakes, or whatever that was. Anyway, the management have sent me upstairs to check on our guests. If you're all right, sir, I'll call in a chambermaid to sweep up the window fragments and a glazier to perform a temporary repair."

"Why are you dressed like that?" I challenged the man.

As if he could see through the coarse material of his

hood, he glanced down at his person, even shooting his cuffs to facilitate this examination. "We do have similar tastes in clothes, don't we, sir?"

"I meant that — that ridiculous sack! Are you ashamed of your position here? Do you have a deformity?"

"Not to my own eye, sir. Nor, for that matter, to a goodly number of young ladies of my acquaintance."

The man's whisper grated on my sensibilities, all the more so for being nearly, but not quite, recognizable — as if I had met the steward, minus his insinuating manner and exasperating hood, in some other place, at some other time. He stooped, lifted the volume by Poe from the floor, and handed it to me. In transit the book opened of its own accord, and I saw that its pages were all blanks. The hooded man, heedless of this anomaly, stepped to the window and gave every appearance of inspecting the damage.

"Then why *do* you wear the damned thing?"

"Well, sir," the steward returned, "the management wish to treat us all impartially, and these hoods allow 'em to do so."

I tried to protest this explanation.

"They'll be serving dinner in a few minutes, sir. Why don't you go down to the dining room while I'm having this mess cleaned up? Take a stroll along the promenade above the lake. Twilight's a fine time for viewing Mount Aquilonia."

"Twilight? I only just got up."

"That may be, sir," he whispered, "but the moon's rising. Look — a lovely waxing crescent creepin' along the southern wing."

Grudgingly I looked. Seeing that the steward was right, I pivoted on my heel to take myself out of the range of the guttural wheeze of his voice. Downstairs, he had suggested. Very well, I would go downstairs. Free exercise in the open air was what I needed, that and few moments for uninterrupted thought. How else to cure my disorientation and anxiety?

"You'll need your overcoat, sir. It's chilly this evening, and likely to be even chillier later on."

I nodded perfunctorily, then made a detour into my bed chamber. The bogus *Adventures of Arthur Gordon Pym* (obviously this Pym had had no adventures) I tossed onto the mantelpiece. Several signatures of blank pages burst from the binding and drifted out into the room, settling on the Persian carpets. Although my intention was to take my overcoat from the wardrobe and myself rather expeditiously from the suite, one of these pages caught my eye — by virtue of its possessing a single paragraph of printed matter precisely centered between the margins. I picked this page from the carpet (meanwhile cognizant of the entry of a chambermaid, at the bidding of the steward, into the adjacent room) and distractedly began to read:

" . . . In the most rugged of wilderness — in the most savage of the scenes of nature — there is apparent the art of a creator; yet this art is apparent to reflection only; in no respect has it the obvious force of a feeling. Now let us suppose this sense of the Almighty design to be one step depressed — to be brought into something like harmony or consistency with the sense of human art — to form an intermedium between the two: — let us imagine, for instance, a landscape whose combined vastness and definitiveness — whose united beauty, magnificence, and strangeness, shall convey the idea of care, or culture, or superintendence, on the part of beings superior, yet akin to humanity . . ."

There was more, but I lifted my eyes from the page to assimilate this last startling clause. Mount Aquilonia, it strongly implied, was not a natural formation but a prodigious artifact — perhaps I should have guessed as much — and its makers were beings more than human but less than divine. Angels, perhaps; yes, earth-angels whose intelligence had elevated them to a disembodied state that did not prevent their undertaking monumental landscaping projects in the natural world. However much it might annoy me to admit the fact, even the prankster in the hood partook to some small degree of their genius.

I crumpled and cast aside the page, hurried to the wardrobe, and yanked the heavy overcoat from its hanger. The feet-shaped boots in the bottom of the cabinet, I noticed, had oriented themselves so that they could hop into the room — but I slammed the doors upon them, drew on my overcoat, and strode out of the bedroom into the parlor. Here I was embarrassed to find the steward and the chambermaid passionately clutching each other. Because the chambermaid was also wearing a sack over her features, their kiss conveyed a bizarre desperation. Without any thought to either their want of discretion or my own rudeness, I gaped at the spectacle.

At length they separated, and I remembered myself. In doing so, I could feel my face turning as red as the walls. Dangerously flustered, I touched my forehead and sought to leave the suite.

"You've forgot your hat, sir," said the steward in his loudest, most unpleasant whisper.

"Damn my hat."

Coquettish in a short-sleeved red dress the chambermaid rewarded this outburst with a sparkling laugh. "Well, that's a beginning, Elliot."

I halted at the door. The woman's voice — which I would never be able to dislodge from my memory — was the voice that had spoken to me through the Victrola. Although I wished to question her, to ask her to remove her hood, the presence of the steward prevented our having a private interview. I fled from the suite, angrily resolved to depart Arnheim at the earliest convenient moment.

"Enjoy your stroll," the woman called after me.

The corridor, the stairwell, and the lower floors of the hotel were deserted. The salon could have easily been a mausoleum, and the dining room, although set for dinner and delicately candle-lit, seemed a dreamlike fossil from another age. After passing through the vacant lobby, I pelted down a fan of granite steps to the promenade overlooking the lake in the crater below Mount Aquilonia. I followed the wall beside this overlook to a point immediately in front of the mountain's central crag (the eagle's haughty head), where grateful for both the view and a moment of solitude, I paused to gather my thoughts.

But I could not gather them. On the ledge of the parapet rested a tightly woven nest containing three large eggs. Meanwhile, directly above the twilight profile of the mountain hung the white meniscus of the moon. My gaze went back and forth between the earthbound eggs and that celestial fingernail clipping. Did I hope to mediate a meaning out of the gigantic eagle-shaped rock separating them?

I took one of the eggs from the nest and hefted it in my hand; it proved remarkably light, as if its liquid contents had been blown out of the shell through pinholes at either end. Indeed, after finding these pinholes in the egg, I had no scruple about cracking it open to see what the shell might hold, if anything.

A strip of curled paper, like the message in a fortune cookie, came into my hand, and upon unravelling this strip I was able to read the following cryptic phrase: "An object of unceasing pursuit." Because the other two eggs were likewise devoid of meat, I broke and extracted messages from them, too. The second said, "The contempt of ambition," and the third, "The love of woman" (small "w"). I scanned each strip of paper several times, as if the letters might unexpectedly alter at any moment, then tore them into tiny pieces, which I carefully replaced in the eagle's nest. Then I glanced back over my shoulder at the huge, shadowy facade of the Arnheim Hotel. What must I do now?

Someone had picked the remaining glass fragments out of the sash of my parlor window, and bracing herself in this lofty opening was the woman who, only moments ago, had been kissing the insolent steward. Although she was no longer wearing her hood, the distance and the incipient darkness made it impossible to draw any conclusions about her face. She was still an enigma.

"Remember what I told you earlier, Elliot," she called, and her voice echoed in the high canyons of the mountain vale. "You're here to rejuvenate yourself. Act like a tourist first — all the rest will follow."

I gestured helplessly. "I don't understand."

"When next you see me, you will. That's a promise." Whereupon she ducked back into my hotel suite, and I was buffeted by a violent wind sweeping through Arnheim from the north.

Far below, the reflection of Mount Aquilonia rippled in the half-frozen waters of the glacier-excavated lake, and I was ambushed by a provocative thought. So intensely did I concentrate on this notion that neither the wintry air nor the immobility of the moon had any power to distract me. A great deal of time passed without really seeming to.

Eventually, a small, painted bark appeared on the lake, as if it had pushed off from a point slightly north of the hotel, and inscribed a wide arc in the lee of the mountain. Now it was drawing toward the hotel again, its tiny mast pointing straight up at the craggy eagle's head. In the prow of this boat stood a lissom woman dressed in the robes of a Florentine spring and supporting in her arms a garland of luxuriant white flowers. Even before her bark had reached the middle of the lake, I recognized this woman as a figure abstracted from Sandro Botticelli's great painting *La Primavera* — executed in the days when paintings had possessed not only a responsible grounding in both nature and myth, but also the moral force of allegory.

"Come," the woman cried, gracefully beckoning.

Her voice was familiar. It was the summons I had been waiting for. I shed my overcoat, folded it neatly, and placed it on the ledge beside the eagle's nest. I then removed my other clothes, including even my stockings and undergarments, and folded these into the protective womb of my overcoat. The woman hailed me again. In response I scrambled over the restraining wall and picked my way down the precipitous embankment to the lake. Although I had an intellectual awareness of the wind knifing over the waters, and of the consummate folly of my nakedness, my body did not suffer. Whatever Powers and Principalities had sculpted this supernatural landscape could not look with disfavor on my decision to merge with their creation.

"Come, Elliot," cried the tutelary spirit in the bark.

Under the eye of the awesome granite eagle, in the long stasis of twilight, I dove from my promontory to the mirrorlike surface of the lake. Descending, I saw the reflection of my face. It was a respectable face, altogether devoid of mystery — but the mind behind its eyes was furiously conjugating marvels from the gelid air. Then the waters closed over me and I possessed not only the illusory Arnheim landscape but myself.

Love's Heresy

When John Pannell and his seven-year-old son Bubba came into Swainsboro from their farm in the Valley View community, they found the green at the heart of town full of people. The automobiles parked around the square shone like mirrors, and an intense young man in a seersucker coat was haranguing the crowd from the park's bandstand. After glancing toward Osborne's Hardware and the little grocery store beside it, John Pannell led Bubba into the park.

"You are not the only you there is!" the fox-eyed man in seersucker declared, pausing to survey his audience. "Not by any means. In heaven you have a double, another you who is more real than you are. In fact, this double is the *real* you. You here in Swainsboro are nothing but a reflection of your real self in heaven."

Dabney Whitlow, a middle-aged druggist, shook his head, broke away from the crowd, and met the two Pannells halfway across the park. "Hey, Bubba." He tousled the boy's unfashionably long hair. "Hello, John. You're not going to listen to that joker, are you?"

"Who is it?" John Pannell asked.

"He says he's a preacher without a church. Says he's a Baptist, same as you and me and nearly everyone else hereabouts. But . . ."

"But what?"

"He talks some pretty unbiblical craziness, if you ask me. Stay and listen a spell if you want. It's interesting enough, I'll give it that, and he isn't so big a fool that he's tried to take up a collection." Whitlow pulled the neck of his undershirt away from his throat, nodded an amiable goodbye, and crossed the street to his store.

Bubba twisted his father's forefinger. "Let's go shoppin'. C'mon, Papa, let's buy our stuff."

John Pannell gently extracted his finger from his son's hot grip and neared the bandstand wearing a grim, set expression the boy remembered having seen only twice before — once, long ago, when someone gave Pannell's two-hundred-dollar bird dog a near-fatal dose of strychnine, and again in Memphis after Bubba's mother had undergone surgery and the doctors returned a verdict containing the word "malignant." It was a look of dangerous bewilderment, dangerous because bewilderment usually lay outside the range of John Pannell's emotion and experience.

"Papa!"

"Hold your horses, Bubba. I want to give this fella a listen."

"What we do here on earth," the fellow was arguing, nodding at Pannell and son as they wedged their way into the crowd, "influences what happens in heaven. That's how it is. You may as well know it. We may be made of moist and heavy clay, we may be earthbound in our poor, sick lives — but, for better or worse, our actions are reflected in heaven, and they're reflected exactly backwards of things here on earth. In a mirror, you know, your left hand appears to be your right. Well, in heaven the evil you do here is transmuted into good, the good into evil. If your false earthly self drinks and honky-tonks and carries on in a lewd and abominable manner, your double in heaven — the real you — is as chaste as snow. If your false self comforts the sick and gives generously of its time and money, your heavenly double is cruel and tight-fisted in compensation. When you die, your spirit flies to heaven and *becomes* your other self. Your real self."

"How do you know all this?" demanded a woman wearing a straw bonnet with a green plastic window in its brim. "Where do you get these silly notions? Just who do you think you are?"

"My name is Eugene Forbes, ma'am, and I get my silly notions from the Bible."

Several people laughed. "Well, Mr. Forbes," the woman countered, sunlight through her visor painting the upper half of her face a faint green, "it don't sound like we read the same Book."

"I'm sure we do, ma'am. Matthew 11:12 proves that what we do here influences what happens in heaven — 'the kingdom of heaven suffereth violence,' is what it says — and 1 Corinthians 13:12 tells us that everything on earth is seen 'through a glass, darkly' and isn't really real. I know my Book, ma'am. I wouldn't be up here trying to explain it to you if I didn't. My credentials may not be your ordinary ones, but they're sure as hell not a bit phony."

The man's casual "sure as hell" offended the woman in the bonnet, and Bubba hoped that his father, similarly disgusted, would lead him out of the park to Osborne's Hardware or the little grocery store with the cooler full of Nehi soda pop. But John Pannell, who cursed only rarely, raised his right forefinger like a man trying to catch the attention of a busy auctioneer.

Forbes saw this gesture and said, "Sir?"

"If our actions are reflected backwards in heaven, what are we here on earth supposed to do? Should it be good or evil? I can't tell what you're driving at."

"That's because I'm *des*cribing, not *pre*scribing. I'm just pointing out the nature of the situation, that's all. The thing to keep in mind, I guess, is that heaven is what counts, heaven's the reality. Everything here in Swainsboro" — Forbes pointed to the trees, the sweltering automobiles and pickups, the store fronts across the street — "everything here has meaning, but it isn't real. How you personally wish to influence genuine reality, sir, is a measure of the kind of man you are. As for me, I'm going to grab a quick sandwich over at the Mayflower Cafe so my real self in heaven can demonstrate his piety by fasting. Good-day, everybody."

Forbes came down from the bandstand without even attempting to pass his hat, and in a few minutes the crowd on the green had dispersed to park benches, waiting motor cars or trucks, or one or another of Swainsboro's businesses. Bubba Pannell followed his moodily silent father across the street to the hardware store, where Max Osborne apologized over and over again for having to deny them credit.

Almost a year later Bubba's mother died. When they buried her in the small, rock-rimmed cemetery behind the Valley View Baptist Church, a white-washed building on the edge of the rice and cotton fields belonging to John Pannell's neighbors, the mysterious Eugene Forbes was among the mourners.

Forbes wore a dark rayon jacket, a pair of cordovan penny loafers, and a silver buckle as bright as a mirror. The curiously understated funeral rites were presided over by Valley View's young pastor Brian Alverson, who, Bubba heard someone whisper, had once attended the same tiny divinity school as Forbes. That meant that there was nothing really mysterious about Forbes's being at the funeral; he had just happened to drop in on his former classmate when Mrs. Pannell failed for the last time and died. His presence at the graveside service merely signified a kind of simultaneous courtesy to Alverson and the Pannells.

A *double* courtesy, Bubba's father supposed.

"Your wife has joined her real self," Forbes told John Pannell after the burial. "For the first time in her life she's complete and entire in the only reality that counts."

Wiping dirt from his hands, Brian Alverson approached the trio from the flower-heaped grave. His eyes shone fiercely, and his round, usually placid face betrayed an unpastorly resentment. "Don't plague them with your heresies, Gene. This just isn't the time. — Mr. Pannell, Bubba, you know our prayers are with you. If there's the littlest thing anyone here in the Valley can do, just let me know. I'll see it gets done."

His voice as passionless as winter, Bubba's father asked a simple question: "What's Mr. Forbes's heresy, preacher? Is trying to give me a bit of comfort heretical?"

The former classmates exchanged an embarrassed glance. "Of course not," Alverson said. "I just don't see much comfort in Gene's reading of Mrs. Pannell's death. This business of her being complete for the first time in her life, I mean."

"It's what got me kicked out of divinity school," Forbes volunteered, looking at his penny loafers. "Insisting on the falseness of our earthly selves."

"And the existence of doubles in heaven," Alverson added.

Bubba began to cry.

John Pannell knelt beside his son and wiped the half circles under his eyes with an embroidered handkerchief.

"It's all right, Bubba-boy. We may be earthbound, but heaven knows who we are. Never believe it doesn't."

"That's right," Alverson said, touching the boy on the shoulder.

"That's exactly right," Eugene Forbes agreed.

Not understanding this sudden consensus, Bubba put his arms around his father's neck and turned his face to the cloudless blue-grey sky. He was lifted gently from the ground. The three adults bid one another good-bye, and then the boy could feel the intensity of his father's love — warmth communicated through pressure — as John Pannell carried him across the churchyard to their ancient pickup. On the bumpy ride home Bubba saw that his father's eyes were wet, too.

"It's hell, isn't it, Bubba? Earthbound's the same as hellbound, now she's really gone." After a while he added, "I wish this stinkin' truck could fly."

The boy had no idea what to say to this. He put his hand on the window and looked at the crops flash dimly by in the gathering dusk. When the pickup crossed a wooden bridge over an irrigation ditch, its tires played the slats like bones on a makeshift xylophone, and Bubba knew that their old Chevrolet was much too heavy a machine ever to get off the ground. Why did his father wish it could fly . . . ?

That evening after he had put Bubba safely to bed, John Pannell want out to the welding shop next to the shed housing his dry-docked tractor and began picking up all the pieces of scrap iron he could find. Not since the doctors had diagnosed his wife's illness as cancer had he tried to make his living by farming; instead, he had advertised himself throughout the Valley as a mechanic, blacksmith, and machinist so that he could work at home, only twenty or thirty yards from Mary's bedroom window. Business had never been very good, primarily because he was an indifferent mechanic. Now, his wife dead, his son asleep, John Pannell used his acetylene torch in the cramped, musty shop to put together a huge sphere.

The "sphere" was neither solid nor truly round, but irregular in shape, open between its iron struts, and consequently hollow. It resembled a globe conceived and assembled by a student of avant-garde metal sculpture, but to John Pannell it was less a work of art than a means whereby his double in heaven could play Daedalus to his son's unsuspecting Icarus. He worked compulsively for seven straight nights, sleeping only in the final hours before dawn and purposely concealing the project from Bubba — whom he finally sent to the Alversons on the pretext that he needed a little time alone to recover from his loss of Mary. The Alversons said they understood.

The sphere itself was suspended from two iron girders so that its bottommost pole was only three feet from the floor. Once finished, its great size and its crude intricacy its most conspicuous attributes, the sphere dominated the shop, and John Pannell spent the hours after its completion walking about the open-faced globe and trying to come mentally to grips with its weight. No one could possibly lift it, he told himself. A calendar given to Pannell by a man who sold Atlas tires hung over his workbench in the gloom, mocking his assessment of what could be lifted and what not — but he had never believed in any myth but the orthodox ones of Christianity and love, and a single piece of calendar art had no power to alter the plans he had made.

"I'm ready for Bubba to come home," he told Murial Alverson on the telephone that afternoon. "You mind if I come get him?"

"Come ahead, Mr. Pannell. Brian and I have really enjoyed Bubba, though. We wouldn't mind keeping him a little longer, if you like."

"No. I miss him, Mrs. Alverson. I really miss him.

Besides, I've got a surprise for him."

"That's fine. Boys like surprises."

On the trip home from the Valley View rectory Bubba asked his father, "What's the surprise? Mrs. Alverson said you had a surprise."

"I do," John Pannell said. "You just wait."

The pickup swung between the unkempt hedges of the Pannells' gravel driveway and slammed to a neck-snapping stop in front of the tractor shed. Man and boy dismounted and sauntered together toward the welding shop. In its doorway Bubba halted and gaped at the massive metal globe gleaming bluely in the humid dark. Then he scampered inside, closed his hand on one of the grease-blackened iron struts (a bent crowbar, welded into place), and tried to rotate the globe by extending his forearm against the bar. When the globe failed to yield to this pressure, Bubba grinned shyly at his father.

"That's all right," John Pannell said. "It's not supposed to move. If it weren't for those two chains holdin' it in place, it would — but those chains are brakes." He pointed at the girders overhead and the oily chains hanging from them in taut opposition.

"What is it, Papa? What's it for?"

"Come here, Bubba. Duckwalk under the globe and let me help you get into this harness." John Pannell was attaching a pair of leather saddle straps to the underside of the sphere, and in obedience to his father's wishes Bubba crept under the hanging object and donned the harness his father had improvised. Now the globe rode his back like a meteor intercepted a scant three feet above the ground, all its crushing weight miraculously negated. "I know that isn't real comfortable," John Pannell said, "but I don't know how else to rig it up."

"It's OK," Bubba responded. He felt powerful and scared at the same time, grateful and uncertain. But even in the gloom-ridden welding shop his father's face radiated such accomplishment and love that it was impossible for Bubba to think anything terribly wrong.

"Abraham didn't know what I know," John Pannell said. "If he had, he wouldn't've gone up that mountain with so heavy a heart."

These words spoken, the father knelt before his stooping son and kissed him gently on the lips. Then he withdrew. With the aid of a mechanical device he released from the welding shop's girders the chains supporting the globe; these chains fell out of the air like two crumpling iron snakes. Simultaneously, John Pannell's lovingly crafted sphere drove Bubba into the oil-caked dust on the floor of the shop.

Ten or fifteen minutes later John Pannell telephoned the Alversons. "Murial," he said, when the pastor's wife had at last picked up her receiver. "Bubba's dead."

The sheriff in Swainsboro asked John Pannell if he would permit the Reverend Mr. Alverson into his cell for an interview. Pannell refused. "Get me Eugene Forbes," he demanded of the sheriff. "I don't want to talk to Alverson. I want to talk to Forbes."

Forbes was in Memphis, and Alverson had to hunt up and down the city to find his friend, who roamed randomly about preaching his heresies to longshoremen and whores, poor whites and credulous blacks. Even so, the conscientious Alverson found his former classmate and returned with him to Swainsboro and the dilapidated county jail.

"You murdered your son, Brian tells me," Forbes said when he and John Pannell sat opposite each other on Pannell's cot. "You dropped a huge metal sphere on his back, and he was crushed to death."

"So that his double could fly," John Pannell explained. "I wanted Bubba's real self to be able to fly."

"You did exactly right then."

"I know I did. I just wanted to tell you."

"Well, rest assured that Bubba's real self is entire for the first time in his life. Rest assured that he's flying around heaven like a bird."

"I do," John Pannell said. "That's how I rest."

For four days after this interview Eugene Forbes remained in Swainsboro preaching from its bandstand and explaining to the locals why John Pannell had done what he had done. Forbes stayed not in the Valley View rectory with the Alversons, with whom his relations were now severely strained, but in an end unit of a motel on the outskirts of town run by Dabney Whitlow's brother-in-law, Clinton Rule.

On the evening of Forbes's fourth day in Swainsboro, an automobile carrying an unknown number of passengers sped past Rule's motel. One of the passengers hurled a firebomb into the unit where the heretic was thought to be residing. Although the fire department arrived in time to save ten of Rule's fourteen apartments, Forbes's body was eventually found in the sodden ruins of the bombed-out end unit and the county had a second murder case on its hands.

Some time later John Pannell was transferred to a state hospital. For reasons having to do with his initial sanity hearings, the sphere he had crafted was brought into town. The following year Swainsboro's mayor charged a young councilman with disposing of the cumbersome but oddly beautiful sphere, and the councilman, enamored of the object, suggested that it be put on display in the park. This was done.

Today the sphere is an enigmatic monument. Walking across the town's well-trimmed green, one should not be surprised to see children clambering freely upon it, ignorant of its history.

Storming The Bijou, Mon Amour

The world and its central valley were called Pit. In this valley lived the despised groundlings of the omnipotent Count De Mille. The Pittites were ordinary human beings who made their livings in resolute peasant fashion, watching the endless round of motion pictures that Count De Mille showed in the great open windows of the Castle Bijou. This ancient and prodigious establishment rose high into the dark from the valley's northern cliffs; and because the sun never shone on Pit (dusk being the world's closest approximation to daylight), the battlements of the Castle Bijou hovered above the groundlings like the immense, shadowy digits of an obscene gesture.

Night after unending night, shrouded in the acoustic darkness, the Pittites gazed numbly at the castle's windows. Doris Day, Toshiro Mifune, Randolph Scott, Lillian Gish, Max von Sydow, or maybe Mia Farrow — figures as tall as Titans — would stalk from room to room, now and again booming out speeches of incomprehensible urgency or tenderness. It seemed, in fact, that a pantheon of thespian gods lived, died, and underwent resurrection in the huge fenestrae and oriels of Castle Bijou's facade.

It was a hard life, if you were a Pittite. You could break from your mother's womb during *The Birth of a Nation*, experience your first kiss as Sidney Poitier sat down to dinner, and succumb to your own private Bergman metaphor as Robert Taylor defended Bataan. (The groundlings referred to dying, quite earnestly, as "embracing Bengt.") And what was your reward for such a life? The barest necessities. A watching cabana. A sufficient number of canvas-backed chairs to seat your family. Enough tattered costumes to cloak your nakedness. And just enough popcorn and cola to keep the specter of starvation at bay.

After you had gazed obediently at your eighty to a hundred films a week, uniformed hushars on horseback rode out of Pit's rearward concession stands to distribute your earnings, with an occasional grudging bonus for interminable epics like the Russian *War and Peace* and D. W. Griffith's *Intolerance*. Other hushars, probing the dark with their flashlight truncheons, would gallop from watching cabana to watching cabana to insure that the groundlings in their territories were indeed watching. Meanwhile, oceanically, the scores of Mancini, Tiomkin, Steiner, or Legrand swept through Pit like syncopated or raging combers — so that on the aisleways of the inescapable valley theater the hoof beats of the hushars' horses were seldom audible.

No matter. If you were a Pittite, you kept your eyes on Elvis or Marcello and ignored the flashlight beams slicing up the dark. The greatest happiness you could hope to know was to draw your final breath during the ascension scenes in *King of Kings* or *Mary Poppins*. . . .

"I can't stand it anymore," said Gary Cooper Seymour, the patriarch of the Seymour groundlings. He tipped his popcorn box over and let his cola trickle onto their watching cabana's hard-packed dirt floor.

It was night (it was always night), and the movie jumping between the windows of Castle Bijou was *The Return of Doctor X* with Humphrey Bogart. The god himself wore a streak of peroxide in his hair, a laboratory smock buttoned along one shoulder and down the side, and a pair of wire-rimmed glasses. He was not an appealing sight.

"I can't stand it anymore," G.C. Seymour repeated.

"Shhhh," hissed Sissy Spacek Seymour, his only daughter; and G.C. didn't know whether she was shushing him because she was really watching the movie or because a hushar might be riding nigh.

The other folks at the Seymour cabana (left rear center, on the west side of Pit) were G.C.'s wife, Zsa Zsa Gabor Seymour, and his two teen-age sons, Oliver Hardy and Clint Eastwood Seymour. It had long since occurred to G.C. that none of them much resembled their namesakes, but since they spent only a minimal amount of time looking at one another anyway, the discrepancies were of small consequence. The Seymours were all thin and waxen-faced, with bad teeth and sore gums; and everyone's eyeballs glistened so unhealthily that they might have been shellacked.

"This is the second time since Sissy was born that we've seen this turkey," Gary Cooper Seymour groused. He was 301,614 movies old and not getting any younger.

"Groundlings eat their popcorn in the fatigue of their eyeballs," recited Mrs. Seymour philosophically. "So saith the Count."

"Balls to the Count."

"Careful, Dad," cautioned Clint Eastwood Seymour.

In the cabana adjacent to the Seymours, Hermione Gingold Gazehard leaned over her rail and said, "Will you picture-show party-poopers please shut up? Little Tatum's never seen this one before."

"Balls to little Tatum, too." But G.C. was no fool. He whispered this retort and once more slotted his eyes on the smirking histrionics of the Mysterious Doctor Xavier.

"What do you want us to do?" asked Oliver Hardy Seymour in a whisper even more discreet than his father's. "It's watch or die, Dad."

G.C. could not argue with that. In two equally effective ways, it was watch or die. If you could not validate your eighty to a hundred movies a week on the Count's screening examinations (questions were flashed in the windows of Castle Bijou, and you responded on a portable piezoelectric response board), you forfeited your weekly rations. And if you were ever caught either snoring in your chair or fleering at the gods and goddesses illumined hieratically against the night, a hushar would unholster his deadly pistolmatic, shoot your picture, and so deprive you of your soul. To the far south of Pit, indeed, was a graveyard of canvas-backed director's chairs, each with the photograph of a departed groundling displayed conspicuously on its back. During the Count's biannual Intermissions you could make pilgrimages there to visit these rickety folding memorials to your snapped relations. (And, of course, to strike up feeble live relationships with the other pilgrims milling among the chairs. That was how Gary Cooper Seymour had first met Zsa Zsa Gabor Numbrump.) So, yes, Oliver Hardy was right — it was watch or die.

"Don't you think I know that?" G.C. asked his family *sotto voce.* "I saw the hushars take my mother's photograph when she moaned aloud and toppled out of her chair during the last ten minutes of *The Nutty Professor.* It was brutal. The hushars — three of them — rode up to our cabana, and they *all* took pictures, each from a different angle. My mother's soul was extracted from her in pieces, like a pulverized wisdom tooth." Silently, without covering his face, G.C. Seymour began to weep. His mother — Maria Ouspenskaya

Seymour — had been a wonderful woman.

"But what happened to . . . to her . . . to her body?" Sissy Spacek Seymour asked cautiously, her eyes still on the images flickering like a black-and-white conflagration in the windows of the Castle Bijou.

Neither G.C. nor Zsa Zsa had ever told Sissy the facts of death, and the Count's next Intermission was well over 400 films in the future. Perhaps this was as good a time as any.

"The body is an illusion," G.C. whispered fiercely, wiping his tears away and pulling himself up in his chair. "The reality is the soul, which can be externalized only by film. The souls of gods and goddesses —" G.C. gestured at the massive castle on the cliffs. "— are shown forth in images that move eternally. But those of groundlings like the Seymours and the Numbrumps are picked out of us and put on display in *stills*. The gods' souls are vibrant, Sissy, while ours are immobile and monochrome."

No one spoke, except Doctor Xavier. And what Doctor Xavier said was of no importance to the Seymours.

"My mother's body," G.C. went on, gripping the arms of his chair, "underwent a prolonged and somewhat out-of-focus fadeout. And that, my Sissy, is what we all have in store."

Sissy began to cry.

"So what do you want us to do?" urged Oliver Hardy again. "We keep body and soul together by faithful worship. Do you want us to give that up and put ourselves in the way of embracing Bengt? Surely you can't have that in mind."

"The Seven Samurai," said G.C. *"The Dirty Dozen."*

"What's he talking about?" asked Clint Eastwood Seymour.

"Violence," murmured Zsa Zsa speculatively. "Insurrection."

"Guns in the Afternoon," intoned G.C. dazedly. *"The Wild*

Bunch. Straw Dogs. Bring Me the Head of —"

"Shhhhhh," hissed Sissy, frightened. "Shhhhhhhhhhh!"

Two and a half movies later a trio of hushars rode up. *Friendly Persuasion* was lambent in the windows of Castle Bijou, and Gary Cooper Seymour, in partial deference to the performance of his namesake, was holding his tongue and observing the film with rapt dissatisfaction. When the hushars arrived, he heard their snorting horses and looked up to see what sort of change they were going to wreak in his life.

The hushars were uniformed as cowboys (they were always uniformed as cowboys), and the foremost among them dismounted deliberately and approached the Seymour cabana tugging on the belt of his pistolmatic and slapping his chaps with his flashlight truncheon. It was too dark to see his face.

"Seems peaceful enough hereabouts," the man said approvingly. "But we've had a complaint. Seems you folks were disrupting other folks' enjoyment or our programming."

The Seymours maintained a noncommittal silence.

"You got any grass around this here cabana?" the hushar suddenly asked. "I'd sure like to let Trigger graze."

Mrs. Seymour indicated a swatch of ground on the west side of their shelter. Soon Trigger, Silver, and Tony were all nibbling contentedly at the thin grey sprouts of nightgrass there, and the trio of hushars had all come under the dilapidated awning of the Seymours' cabana.

"Everything seems to be in good order here," said the first hushar, shining his flashlight truncheon about and letting his spurs jingle. "Don't see why anybody'd phone in to complain."

"I phoned better than two movies ago," cried Hermione Gingold Gazehard from the cabana next door.

"Well, we was busy then, ma'am."

"I don't see that that's any excuse when you consider that —"

One of the hushar's companions shone his flashlight truncheon into Mrs. Gazehard's contorted face, whereupon the third hushar slapped his pistolmatic from its holster and took the woman's picture

The Seymours, startled, watched their suddenly soulless neighbor fade out of existence like the Cheshire cat in Disney's animated *Alice*. G.C. was glad he'd had an opportunity to talk to Sissy before she witnessed the brutal thing for herself. Thank your lucky stars for small favors.

"What's playing?" the first hushar then inquired amiably.

Oliver Hardy Seymour told him.

"Is that right?" the hushar said. "My name's Gary Cooper Bounzzemout. I haven't seen one of my namesake's movies since I was a little chap. *The Fountainhead*, I think it was."

Of course the Seymours instantly adverted that their patriarch's name was also Gary Cooper, and this revelation made for an uncanny abundance of good feeling. G.C. Bounzzemout introduced his companions, Leo Gorcey Gallup and Sessue Hayakawa Harassman (thereby proving that the cowboyishly attired hushars weren't necessarily named after cowboy gods); and, these introductions out of the way, everyone got along famously. When his print had developed, in fact, S.H. Harassman showed the Seymours Mrs. Gazehard's freshly stolen soul.

"Nice likeness," said Oliver Hardy Seymour.

"That woman was the likeness," the hushar corrected him. "But this — well, this is the genuine article."

"Couldn't we get in trouble talking and carrying on like this?" asked Mrs. Seymour, glancing beyond the grazing horses at the cabana of the Cantinflas Wrinklebrows. "I mean, this isn't Intermission, you know."

"You bet your butt it isn't," said Gary Cooper Bounzzemout. "What I wouldn't give to sit down here and see me a decent movie for the first time in forty thousand flicks. What I wouldn't give."

"Me, too," seconded Leo Gorcey Gallup.

"Me, too," echoed Sessue Hayakawa Harassman.

"What about your horses, your outfits, your pistolmatics, and your flashlight truncheons?" proposed G.C. Seymour hurriedly. "My boys and I could go out for a ride while you fellas took our places alongside the womenfolk. Stand-ins, you could call it. Or sit-ins. Seems a pretty fair trade-off to me."

"I want to go," said Sissy. "Why shouldn't *I* go?"

"And I," echoed Mrs. Seymour. "Why shouldn't *I*?"

"It ain't done," said G.C. grimly. He looked to the surprised but amazingly acquiescent hushars for support.

"No, ma'am," G.C. Bounzzemout agreed. "It just ain't done. A woman just don't know what to do with a flashlight truncheon."

Sessue Hayakawa Harassman and Leo Gorcey Gallup murmured their agreement, quite respectfully; and the ladies reluctantly subsided.

One third of a reel later, G.C. Seymour and his sons Oliver and Clint, outfitted like hushars, were spurring their mounts into the gloomy central aisle of the world-basin known to their people as Pit. The cabanas of the downtrodden groundlings seethed in the dark like popcorn kernels the moment before they bloom. And the cliffs upon which rested the stolid bulk of the Castle Bijou loomed dauntingly.

Maybe, thought G.C. as they rode, maybe, old boy, you've bit off more than you can chew. . . .

For two movies Gary Cooper Seymour and his sons rode northward. Castle Bijou got bigger and bigger, as did the gods and goddesses lounging or cavorting in its gothic oriels. Movie music boomed out across the valley with a volume positively worldquaking — so that G.C. began to

understand why a great many front-row-center groundlings who gathered during Intermission in Pit's chair-clut-
tered cemetery were hopelessly deaf. You could communicate with them only by pantomime. As a consequence, it
did not seem likely that he and the boys were going to be
able to recruit a peasant army to storm the Count's Citadel
of Celluloid Fancies.

Damn, groused G.C in the privacy of his own mind.

All about them, the cabanas of the Pittites and the
angular silhouettes of a thousand watchers in the dark.
Even in the films of Buñuel, Ray, or Fellini, G.C. had never
seen anything quite so lonely or provocative of compassion.
These were his people, these sedentary groundlings. He
loved them. Why were their lives so passive, so monochrome, so devoid of struggle and passion? And why,
except during brief moments of crisis, did they not seem to
notice . . . ?

"Pa," shouted Oliver Hardy Seymour (the boys had
stopped calling him "Dad" the moment they were horseback); "Pa, there's a posse of hushars riding toward us from
the orchestra pit!"

"Get ready to slap leather, then!"

Six fat flashlight beams picked them out and blinded
them. A moment later they were surrounded by just as
many hushars astride just as many horses. G.C. and his
boys blinked and bridled their mounts.

"You Gary Cooper Bounzzemout?" a husky voice
inquired.

"Yep," G.C. lied uprightly.

"You're out of your territory, then; and you shoulda
responded to Mrs. Gazehard's complaint all the way back
during the second reel of that Bogart turkey. I'm afraid
we're going to have to scramble your wavefront reconstruc-
tions, fellas, until the Count sees fit to give you back your
interference fringes."

G.C. had no idea what the man was talking about, but it didn't sound good. It sounded pretty damn scary.

"Now!" he shouted to Oliver and Clint. "Take pictures of their horses!"

Snapping photographs of all six horses with their pistolmatics, the boys were as quick as Kodaks. The hushars didn't know what hit them, but hung in the air above their fast-fading mounts like drop-mouthed marionettes. They were weirdly nonexistent below the chest or waist because it's impossible to separate the lower portion of a rider from his horse when you're taking a picture mostly of the horse. (The horses, by the way, had been nibbling nightgrass when their pictures were taken, noses right down to the ground.) So. The heads and torsos of these unmanned hushars floated helplessly above the valley's central aisle, and G.C. and his boys pretty much had their way with them.

"You sure got the drop on us," growled the hushar who had threatened them with some sort of dastardly disassembly.

Gary Cooper Seymour confessed his and his sons' real identities and asked the hushar about his imcomprehensible but unsettling threat.

"Well," this man responded, "a hushar is a self-motivating hologram, subject to the Count's ultimate control. Punishment for unhusharly behavior is the withdrawal of the laser light that produces our interference fringes. For their goldbricking, Bounzzemout, Gallup, and Harassman were going to be knocked out of existence for fifteen or twenty movies — but you fellas shot our hosses out from under us and disappeared our feet."

"We stole a half of each one of your souls," gloated Clint.

"Souls are indivisible," returned the severed hushar. "And, in any case, being holograms, we don't have any."

"He's right, Pa," said Oliver, shining his flashlight truncheon on one of the developing prints. "Look. Their boots and chaps don't register — there's nothing but horses here."

"Where are your souls?" G.C. demanded.

"The hologramming process stole them, I'm afraid, and the original interference patterns are in Count De Mille's possession. That's why we hushars pretty much hop to the Count's bidding. He's got the *real* us in his fists, you see."

"That's terrible!" Oliver declared.

"Oh, I don't know," replied the hushar. "It ain't as bad as owning your own soul but having to endure half a million movies."

The other hushar heads vigorously nodded their assent, and G.C., even though he and his boys had set out to do something about the life style of the groundlings, almost found himself defending it.

Instead he asked, "In which part of the Castle Bijou does the Count hole up?"

"No one's ever seen the Count," the hushar volunteered. "None of us has ever been up there, anyway." The man's head and torso revolved back toward the south. "We bunk in the concession stands over by the cemetery, you know."

G.C. touched the brim of his hat. "Much obliged. Come on, boys. We'll have to storm the Bijou by ourselves." They spurred their horses past the suspended heads and chests of the dismayed hushars.

"You can't leave us here like this!" shouted the truncated minions of Count De Mille. "You can't!"

"Just see if I don't," murmured Gary Cooper Seymour.

And high on the northern cliffs of Pit one of the films of Michelangelo Antonioni leisurely unraveled.

G.C., Oliver, and Clint dismounted at the foot of the cliffs and manfully proceeded to scale them. To reach a ledge just below the summit took eight full-length feature films, a couple of canisters of Warner Brothers' cartoons, and an early Roman Polanski vignette. The soundtracks of these offerings blared forth at such volume that no verbal communication was possible. Often G.C. would look back over his shoulder to take in the panorama of the valley: row upon row of watching cabanas arrayed in flickering squalor. Could Zsa Zsa and Sissy see the boys and him crawling painfully up the cliff face? Probably not. Straining to find a new handhold, G.C. began to realize why no one had "stormed" the Castle Bijou before.

Near the summit Clint Eastwood Seymour lost his balance and toppled backward into the dark, pulling his brother with him in a last desperate attempt to keep from falling. G.C. could not hear their screams as they plummeted — a deprivation which undoubtedly helped preserve his presence of mind. He unholstered his pistolmatic and took the boys' pictures before they struck bottom, thus sparing them the mortal discomfort of impact. If he ever got back to his cabana, he would have their photographs to show his wife and daughter. Two minute, spread-eagled blurs on an abyss of indefinite depth.

Well, thought G.C. grimly, now it's just you and the Count.

Encouraged by the aesthetic fitness of this imagined confrontation, he found foot- and handholds enough to attain the top of the escarpment. Then he strolled along it in the confusion of eddying lights thrown down from the Castle Bijou's windows. The gods and goddesses above him were too huge to identify. Where was an entrance? Where a way in?

At last G.C. saw the central gateway of the Castle Bijou and headed toward it. As he crept through, reflexively ducking his head in an opening of seemingly immeasurable height, he felt a sudden rippling of wind and glanced up to see the castle's portcullis dropping upon him like the blade of a guillotine. He dove and rolled. Even through the din and dialogue of the movie playing overhead, he heard the portentous clang of the portcullis.

"Jeepers," whispered G.C. "That was close."

He was inside the Castle Bijou, but as he rose to his feet he found that only a short distance beyond him the floor dropped away into a void of absolute nothingness. Here the world ended, and all he could see across the void was the prismatic beam of the Cosmic Projector that animated the windows of the castle.

This beam blazed in the darkness like a sun, a great white hole emptying a multiverse of backwards images into the visions of the Pittites. As he stood transfixed on the edge of his world, this beam seemed to Gary Cooper Seymour the repository and purveyor of all experience. He had come behind the scrim of his and his people's desperately passive lives to the reality sustaining them all. The Castle Bijou, with its battlements and bulwarks, was a cardboard-and-silk false front, a facade whose backside revealed its supports and scaffoldings. G.C. took in the indisputable testimony of his eyes with a weary shudder.

As if aware of his presence, the images being projected across the void suddenly began to stutter madly. They hiccupped, jerked, and danced. Eventually they gave a final unsprocketed shimmy and stopped moving altogether. Frozen in the windows of the Castle Bijou was a single frame of a movie that G.C. was in no position to put a name to. All was still and silent — for the first time since Pit's last official Intermission.

Sternly and resonantly, a voice high above Gary Cooper Seymour inquired, "What are you doing up here?"

G.C. looked up and saw a man seated in a plastic bucket on the end of an articulate metal arm on the vertical shaft of a spidery mobile crane. The man was small and solid, with a bald round head and fierce eyebrows and mustachioes. He wore a beret and riding breeches. He was sharply delineated in the razor-edged light of the Cosmic Projector, and he waved his megaphone with a comfortable awareness of his authority. After he had repeated his initial question two more times and maneuvered his bucket-chair close enough to hear G.C's response, the upstart groundling remarked, "You're Count De Mille?"

"I am," the Count acknowledged. "What of it?"

"*The Wizard of Oz*," intoned Gary Cooper Seymour under his breath, at last grateful for the haphazard catholicity of his education.

"What? Speak up!"

"You're a humbug, Count," drawled G.C. emphatically. "You're a little man with no more brains or spunk than any red-eyed groundling down there in Pit, and I'm going to show you up for what you really are." He drew his pistolmatic and pointed it directly at the Count's bald head.

"Let's not be hasty," blustered the Count. "Let's not—"

"You're not a hologram, are you?"

"No, I'm certainly not a hol—"

Click.

G.C. waited for Count De Mille, whom he had expertly centered in the pistolmatic's view finder, to fade from view. He waited and waited. The Count continued to inhabit his bucket-chair, his legs and boots hanging down like knobby, twisted question marks.

"It seems you're out of film," the Count said sympathetically.

Grimacing, G.C. pivoted and hurled his usless pistolmatic into the void. It was instantly swallowed and lost. Then he returned his gaze to the spiffy little Count, who powered his bucket-chair out over the edge of the world and halted it there. He was cantilevered above the unfathomable abyss and nimbused in the beam of the sunlike projector. G.C., again turning about, had to shield his eyes to look at his adversary.

"What would you have done had you indeed stolen my soul?" asked the Count. "What would you have done if I were no longer here to select and project life's experiences at you in endless, virtually unbroken squence? Tell me that, if you please."

"You select what we see?" G.C. inquired, already knowing the answer.

"I do."

"But there's no sense or sequence to it," he pointed out with what seemed to him killing and irrefutable logic.

"No *unifying* sense nor sequence, you must mean. For of course each individual unit of filmic experience I call up for you is internally structured according to the dictates of the creative intelligence responsible for it. I'm here to keep things going, sir, not to impose an impossible order on the whole. And what would you do if I didn't keep things going, please?"

G.C. blinked and stood gawking into the circular glare at whose heart the Count, dangling his legs, sat confident and inaccessible.

"Supposing, of course," the Count went on, "that all your most basic needs were still provided for?"

"We'd live," said Gary Cooper Seymour. "What else?"

"Here on Pit?" the Count demanded incredulously. *"Here on Pit?* Why, even I don't have that option, sir."

He pushed a button on the arm of his bucket-chair, and the beam from the Cosmic Projector failed, plunging the entire universe into an impenetrable, prechaotic darkness.

The Castle Bijou disappeared into this formless murk along with everything else, whereupon there arose from the groundlings in Pit a gasp of staggering volume, a babble of dismay and terror so unlike anything G.C. had ever heard on a movie soundtrack that it took him a moment or two to recognize it for what it was. Even during Intermissions, he recalled, the Count had not doused *all* the lights in Castle Bijou's windows. Afraid that another step might send him plummeting as his dear lost sons had plummeted, G.C. stood stock-still and waited.

"Now live," said the Count from utter darkness. "Go ahead and live. And should you discover a way, please be sure to let me in on the secret. Your reference to *The Wizard of Oz* was astute in its own limited way, but nevertheless inaccurate as a description of my actual status."

Growing terrified as the babble from Pit became more and more disjointed and ugly, G.C. said nothing.

"I'm not a humbug, sir — I'm the alternately malign and benevolent lackey of an impulse more human and more powerful than any of your poor, put-upon Pittites."

"What impulse?" asked Gary Cooper Seymour tremulously.

But Count De Mille only laughed, and his laughter escaped his megaphone as a thunderous music at once amiable and malefic. G.C. sank to his knees in the scrabble of the narrow cliff and hung on for dear life.

Some time later, after an interval of unconsciousness, G.C. felt himself being scooped up from the cliff and transported giddily across light-years of space and aeons of time by an immense but curiously gentle hand. Like Fay Wray in the clutches of her moonstruck giant ape, thought G.C. desperately. Meanwhile, unbroken emptiness roared by.

"Where we going?" G.C. at last demanded in a small, even drawl that belied his terror.

No response. Only darkness and the whipping slipstream of all-encompassing vacuum as the bodiless hand bore him onward.

When the hand finally swung him to a halt, G.C. rolled up the retaining wall of its curled fingers and then slid back down into the cup of its palm.

"*Lights!*" commanded a voice that wasn't the Count's.

As a feeble wash of illumination from some disembodied source pushed the darkness aside, G.C. raised himself warily to his feet. He saw that an ethereal hand did indeed hold him aloft and that spread out beneath both it and him in the riven void was the unfamiliar nightscape of another world.

"This is Wasteland," said the voice that wasn't the Count's.

Then, so loudly that a hundred constellations trembled like cobwebs in a wind, this voice commanded, "*Camera! Action!*"

Gazing down, G.C. saw that the groundlings of Wasteland were enclosed not in a valley surmounted at one end by a castle with flickering windows but instead in a great sunken living room surrounded on all sides by television screens. Playing simultaneously to the hapless, narcotized inhabitants of this nightmare world were overlapping reruns of "Love of Life," "Hee Haw," "Charlie's Angels," "Gilligan's Island," "Dragnet," "Beat the Clock," "Happy Days" —

"Take me home," G.C. Seymour pleaded pridelessly, again sinking to his knees. "I beg you, take me home."

Five seconds or a dozen centuries later he opened his eyes and found himself seated in his watching cabana beside Zsa Zsa, Sissy, and his miraculously resurrected sons. High in the windows of the Castle Bijou blazed the upright lie of Zinnemann's *High Noon*.

Dogs' Lives

All knowledge, the totality of all questions and all answers, is contained in the dog.

—Franz Kafka, *"Investigations of a Dog"*

I AM TWENTY-SEVEN: Three weeks ago a black Great Dane stalked into my classroom as I was passing out theme topics. My students turned about to look. One of the freshman wits made an inane remark, which I immediately topped: "That may be the biggest dog I've ever seen." Memorable retort. Two of my students sniggered.

I ushered the Great Dane into the hall. As I held its collar and maneuvered it out of English 102 (surely it was looking for the foreign language department), the dog's power and aloofness somehow coursed up my arm. Nevertheless, it permitted me to release it onto the north campus. Sinews, flanks, head. What a magnificent animal. It loped up the winter hillock outside Park Hall without looking back. Thinking on its beauty and self-possession, I returned to my classroom.

And closed the door.

TWENTY-SEVEN, AND HOLDING: All of this is true.

The incident of the Great Dane has not been out of my thoughts since it happened. There is no door in my mind to close on the image of that enigmatic animal. It stalks into and out of my head whenever it wishes.

As a result, I have begun to remember some painful things about dogs and my relationships with them. The memories are accompanied by premonitions. In fact, sometimes *I* — my secret self — go inside the Great Dane's head and look through its eyes at tomorrow, or yesterday. Every bit of what I remember, every bit of what I foresee, throws light on my ties with both humankind and dogdom.

Along with my wife, my fifteen-month-old son, and a ragged miniature poodle, I live in Athens, Georgia, in a rented house that was built before World War I. We have lived here seven months. In the summer we had bats. Twice I knocked the invaders out of the air with a broom and bludgeoned them to death against the dining-room floor. Now that it is winter the bats hibernate in the eaves, warmer than we are in our beds. The furnace runs all day and all night because, I suppose, no one had heard of insulation in 1910 and our fireplaces are all blocked up to keep out the bats.

At night I dream about flying into the center of the sun on the back of a winged Great Dane.

I AM EIGHT: Van Luna, Kansas. It is winter. At four o'clock in the morning a hand leads me down the cold concrete steps in the darkness of our garage. Against the wall, between a stack of automobile tires and a dismantled Ping-Pong table, a pallet of rags on which the new puppies lie. Everything smells of dogflesh and gasoline. Outside the wind whips about frenetically, rattling the garage door.

In robe and slippers I bend down to look at the furred-over lumps that huddle against one another on their rag pile. Frisky, their mother, regards me with suspicion. Adult hands have pulled her aside. Adult hands hold her back.

"Pick one up," a disembodied adult voice commands me. I comply.

The puppy, almost shapeless, shivers in my hands, threatens to slide out of them onto the concrete. I press my cheek against the lump of fur and let its warm, faintly fecal odor slip into my memory. I have smelled this smell before.

"Where are its eyes?"

"Don't worry, punkin," the adult voice says. "It has eyes. They just haven't opened yet."

The voice belongs to my mother. My parents have been divorced for three years.

I AM FIVE: Our ship docks while it is snowing. We live in Tokyo, Japan: Mommy, Daddy, and I.

Daddy comes home in a uniform that scratches my face when I grab his trouser leg. Government housing is where we live. On the lawn in the big yard between the houses I grab Daddy and ride his leg up to our front door. I am wearing a cowboy hat and empty holsters that go *flap flap flap* when I jump down and run inside.

Christmas presents: I am a cowboy.

The inside of the house gathers itself around me. A Japanese maid named Peanuts. (Such a funny name.) Mommy there, too. We have radio. My pistols are in the toy box. Later, not for Christmas, they give me my first puppy. It is never in the stuffy house, only on the porch. When Daddy and I go inside from playing with it the radio is singing "How Much Is That Doggy in the Window?" Everybody in Tokyo likes that song.

The cowboy hat has a string with a bead to pull tight under my chin. I lose my hat anyway. Blackie runs off with the big dogs from the city. The pistols stay shiny in my toy box.

On the radio, always singing, is Patti Page.

DOGS I HAVE KNOWN: Blackie, Frisky, Wiggles, Seagull, Mike, Pat, Marc, Boo Boo, Susie, Mandy, Heathcliff, Pepper, Sam, Trixie, Andy, Taffy, Tristram, Squeak, Christy, Fritz, Blue, Tammi, Napoleon, Nickie, B.J., Viking, Tau, and Canicula, whom I sometimes call Threasie (or 3C, short, you see, for Cybernetic Canine Construct).

"Sorry. There are no more class cards for this section of 102."
How the spurned dogs bark, how they howl.

I AM FOURTEEN: Cheyenne Canyon, Colorado. It is August. My father and I are driving up the narrow canyon road toward Helen Hunt Falls. Dad's Labrador retriever Nick — too conspicuously my namesake — rides with us. The dog balances with his hind legs on the back seat and lolls his massive head out the driver's window, his dark mouth open to catch the wind. Smart, gentle, trained for the keen competition of field trials, Nick is an animal that I can scarcely believe belongs to us — even if he is partially mine only three months out of the year, when I visit my father during the summer.

The radio, turned up loud, tells us that the Russians have brought back to Earth from an historic mission the passengers of Sputnik V, the first two animals to be recovered safely from orbit.

They, of course, are dogs. Their names are Belka and Strelka, the latter of whom will eventually have six puppies as proof of her power to defy time as well as space.

"How 'bout that, Nick?" my father says. "How'd you like to go free-fallin' around the globe with a pretty little bitch?"

Dad is talking to the retriever, not to me. He calls me Nicholas. Nick, however, is not listening. His eyes are half shut against the wind, his ears flowing silkenly in the slipstream behind his aristocratic head.

I laugh in delight. Although puberty has not yet completely caught up with me, my father treats me like an equal. Sometimes on Saturday, when we're watching Dizzy Dean on "The Game of the Week," he gives me my own can of beer.

We park and climb the stone steps that lead to a little bridge above the falls. Nick runs on ahead of us. Very few tourists are about. Helen Hunt Falls is more picturesque than imposing; the bridge hangs only a few feet over the mountain stream roaring and plunging beneath it. Hardly a Niagara. Nick looks down without fear, and Dad says, "Come on, Nicholas. There's a better view on up the mountain."

We cross the bridge and struggle up the hillside above the tourist shop, until the pine trunks, which we pull ourselves up by, have finally obscured the shop and the winding canyon road. Nick still scrambles ahead of us, causing small avalanches of sand and loose soil.

Higher up, a path. We can look across the intervening blueness at a series of falls that drop down five or six tiers of sloping granite and disappear in a mist of trees. In only a moment, it seems, we have walked to the highest tier.

My father sits me down with an admonition to stay put. "I'm going down to the next slope, Nicholas, to see if I can see how many falls there are to the bottom. Look out through the trees there. I'll bet you can see Kansas."

"Be careful," I urge him.

The water sliding over the rocks beside me is probably not even an inch deep, but I can easily tell that below the next sloping of granite the entire world falls away into a canyon of blue-green.

Dad goes down the slope. I notice that Nick, as always, is preceding him. On the margin of granite below, the dog stops and waits. My father joins Nick, puts his hands on his hips, bends at the waist, and looks down into an abyss altogether invisible to me. How far down it drops I cannot tell, but the echo of falling water suggests no inconsequential distance.

Nick wades into the silver flashing from the white rocks.
Before I can shout warning, he lowers his head to drink.
The current is not strong, these falls are not torrents — but
wet stone provides no traction and the Lab's feet go slickly
out from under him. His body twists about, and he begins
to slide inexorably through the slow silver.

"Dad! Dad!" I am standing.

My father belatedly sees what is happening. He reaches
out to grab at his dog. He nearly topples. He loses his red
golf cap.

And then Nick's body drops, his straining head and fore-
paws are pulled after. The red golf cap follows him down,
an ironic afterthought.

I am weeping. My father stands upright and throws his
arms above his head. "Oh my dear God!" he cries. "Oh my
dear God!" The canyon echoes these words, and suddenly
the universe has changed.

Time stops.

Then begins again.

Miraculously, even anticlimactically, Nick comes limping
up to us from the hell to which we had both consigned him.
He comes limping up through the pines. His legs and
flanks tremble violently. His coat is matted and wet, like a
newborn puppy's. When he reaches us he seems not even
to notice that we are there to care for him, to take him back
down the mountain into Colorado Springs.

"He fell at least a hundred yards, Nicholas," my father
says. "At least that — onto solid rock."

On the bridge above Helen Hunt Falls we meet a woman
with a Dalmatian. Nick growls at the Dalmatian, his hackles
in an aggressive fan. But in the car he stretches out on the
back seat and ignores my attempts to console him. My
father and I do not talk. We are certain that there must be
internal injuries. We drive the regal Lab — AKC designa-

tion, "Black Prince Nicholas" — almost twenty miles to the veterinarian's at the Air Force Academy.

Like Belka and Strelka, he survives.

SNAPSHOT: Black Prince Nicholas returning to my father through the slate-grey verge of a Wyoming lake, a wounded mallard clutched tenderly in his jaws. The photograph is grainy, but the huge Labrador resembles a panther coming out of creation's first light: he is the purest distillation of power.

ROLL CALL FOR SPRING QUARTER: I walk into the classroom with my new roll sheets and the same well-thumbed textbook. As usual, my new students regard me with a mixture of curiosity and dispassionate calculation. But there is something funny about them this quarter.

Something *not right*.

Uneasily I begin calling the alphabetized list of their names: "Andy . . . B.J. . . . Blackie . . . Blue . . . Boo Boo . . . Canicula . . . Christy . . . Frisky . . ."

Each student responds with an inarticulate yelp rather than a healthy "Here!" As I proceed down the roll, the remainder of the class dispenses with even this courtesy. I have a surly bunch on my hands. A few have actually begun to snarl.

". . . Pepper . . . Sam . . . Seagull . . . Squeak . . ."

They do not let me finish. From the front row a collie leaps out of his seat and crashes against my lectern. I am borne to the floor by his hurtling body. Desperately I try to protect my throat.

The small classroom shakes with the thunder of my students' barking, and I can tell that all the animals on my roll have fallen upon me with the urgency of their own peculiar bloodlusts.

The fur flies. Me, they viciously devour.

Before the lights go out completely, I tell myself that it is going to be a very difficult quarter. A very difficult quarter indeed.

I AM FORTY-SIX: Old for an athlete, young for a president, maybe optimum for an astronaut. I am learning new tricks.

The year is 1992, and it has been a long time since I have taught freshman English or tried my hand at spinning monstrously improbable tales. (With the exception, of course, of this one.) I have been too busy.

After suffering a ruptured aneurysm while delivering a lecture in the spring of 1973, I underwent surgery and resigned from the English department faculty. My recovery took eight or nine months.

Outfitted with several vascular prostheses and wired for the utmost mobility, I returned to the university campus to pursue simultaneous majors in molecular biology and astrophysics. The G.I. Bill and my wife's and my parents footed the largest part of our expenses — at the beginning, at least. Later, when I volunteered for a government program involving cybernetic experimentation with human beings (reasoning that the tubes in my brain were a good start on becoming a cyborg, anyway), money ceased to be a problem.

This confidential program changed me. In addition to the synthetic blood vessels in my brain, I picked up three artificial internal organs, a transparent skull cap, an incomplete auxiliary skeletal system consisting of resilient inert plastics, and a pair of removable visual adaptors that plug into a plate behind my brow and so permit me to see expertly in the dark. I can even eat wood if I have to. I can learn the most abstruse technical matters without even blinking my adaptors. I can jump off a three-story building without even jarring my kneecaps. These skills, as you may imagine, come in handy.

With a toupee, a pair of dark glasses, and a little cosmetic surgery, I could leave the government hospitals where I had undergone these changes and take up a seat in any classroom in any university in the nation. I was frequently given leave to do so. Entrance requirements were automatically waived, I never saw a fee card, and not once did my name fail to appear on the rolls of any of the classes I sat in on.

I studied everything. I made A pluses in everything. I could read a textbook from cover to cover in thirty minutes and recall even the footnotes verbatim. I awed professors who had worked for thirty-forty years in chemistry, physics, biology, astronomy. It was the ultimate wish-fulfillment fantasy come true, and not all of it can be attributed to the implanted electrodes, the enzyme inoculations, and the brain meddlings of the government cyberneticists. No, I have always had a talent for doing things thoroughly.

My family suffered.

We moved many, many times, and for days on end I was away from whatever home we had newly made.

My son and daughter were not particularly aware of the physical changes that I had undergone — at least not at first — but Katherine, my wife, had to confront them each time we were alone. Stoically, heroically, she accepted the passion that drove me to alter myself toward the machine, even as she admitted that she did not understand it. She never recoiled from me because of my strangeness, and I was grateful for that. I have always believed that human beings discover a major part of the meaning in their lives from, in Pound's phrase, "the quality of the affections," and Katherine could see through the mechanical artifice surrounding and buttressing Nicholas Parsons to the man himself. And I was grateful for that, too, enormously grateful.

Still, we all have doubts. "Why are you doing this?" Katherine asked me one night. "Why are you letting them change you?"

"*Tempus fugit*. Time's winged chariot. I've got to do everything I can before there's none left. And I'm doing it for all of us — for you, for Peter, for Erin. It'll pay off. I know it will."

"But what started all this? Before the aneurysm —"

"Before the aneurysm I'd begun to wake up at night with a strange new sense of power. I could go inside the heads of dogs and read what their lives were like. I could time-travel in their minds."

"You had insomnia, Nick. You couldn't sleep."

"No, no, it wasn't just that. I was learning about time by riding around inside the head of that Great Dane that came into my classroom. We went everywhere, everywhen. The aneurysm had given me the ability to do that — when it ruptured, my telepathic skill went too."

Katherine smiled. "Do you regret that you can't read dogs' minds any more?"

"Yes. A little. But this compensates, what I'm doing now. If you can stand it a few more years, if you can tolerate the physical changes in me, it'll pay off. I know it will."

And we talked for a long time that night, in a tiny bedroom in a tiny apartment in a big Texas city many miles from Van Luna, Kansas, or Cheyenne, Wyoming, or Colorado Springs, or Athens, Georgia.

Tonight, nearly seventeen years after that thoughtful conversation, I am free-falling in orbit with my trace-mate Canicula, whom I sometimes call Threasie (or 3C, you see, short for Cybernetic Canine Construct). We have been up here a month now, in preparation for our flight to the star system Sirius eight months hence.

Katherine has found this latest absence of mine particularly hard to bear. Peter is a troubled young man of twenty, and Erin is a restless teen-ager with many questions about her absent father. Further, Katherine knows that shortly the

Black Retriever will fling me into the interstellar void with eight other trace-teams. Recent advances in laser-fusion technology, along with the implementation of the Livermore-Parsons Drive, will no doubt get us out to Sirius in no time flat (i.e., less than four years for those of you who remain Earthbound, a mere fraction of that for us aboard the *Black Retriever*), but Katherine does not find this news at all cheering.

"*Tempus fugit,*" she told me somewhat mockingly during a recent laser transmission. "And unless I move to Argentina, God forbid, I won't even be able to see the star you're traveling toward."

In Earth orbit, however, both Canicula and I find that time drags. We are ready to be off to the small Spartan world that no doubt circles our starfall destination in Canis Major. My own minute studies of the "wobble" in Sirius's proper motion have proved that such a planet exists; only once before has anyone else in the scientific community detected a dark companion with a mass less than that of Jupiter, but no one doubts that I know what I am doing.

Hence this expedition.

Hence this rigorous though wearying training period in Earth orbit. I do not exempt even myself, but dear God how time drags.

Canicula is my own dark companion. He rescues me from doubt, ennui, and orbital funk. He used to be a Great Dane. Even now you can see that beneath his streamlined cybernetic exterior a magnificent animal breathes. Besides that, Canicula has wit.

"*Tempus fugit,*" he says during an agonizingly slow period. He rolls his eyes and then permits his body to follow his eyes' motion: an impudent, free-fall somersault.

"Stop that nonsense, Threasie," I command him with mock severity. "See to your duties."

"If you'll remember," he says, "one of my most important

ones is, uh, hounding you."

I am forty-six. Canicula-Threasie is seven.

And we're both learning new tricks.

I AM THIRTY-EIGHT: Somewhere, perhaps, Nicholas Parsons is a bona fide astronaut-in-training, but in this tributary of history — the one containing me now — I am nothing but a writer projecting himself into that grandiose wish-fulfillment role. I am an astronaut in the same dubious way that John Glenn or Neil Armstrong is a writer. For nearly eleven years my vision has been on hold. What success I have achieved in this tributary I have fought for with the sometimes despairing tenacity of my talent and a good deal of help from my friends. Still, I cannot keep from wondering how I am to overcome the arrogance of someone for whom I am only a name, not a person, and how dangerous any visionary can be with a gag in the mouth to thwart any intelligible recitation of the dream.

Where in my affliction is encouragement or comfort? Well, I can always talk to my dog. Nickie is dead, of course, and so is Pepper, and not too long ago a big yellow school bus struck down the kindly mongrel who succeeded them in our hearts. Now we have B.J., a furrow-browed beagle. To some extent he has taken up the slack. I talk to him while Katherine works and Peter and Erin attend their respective schools. B.J. understands very little of what I tell him — his expression always seems a mixture of dread and sheepishness — but he is a good listener for as long as I care to impose upon him; and maybe when his hind leg thumps in his sleep, he is dreaming not of rabbit hunts but of canine heroics aboard a vessel bound for Sirius. In my capacity as dreamer I can certainly pretend that he is doing so. . . .

A SUMMER'S READING, 1959: *The Call of the Wild* and *White Fang* by Jack London. *Bob, Son of Battle* by Alfred

Ollivant. Eric Knight's *Lassie Come Home*. *Silver Chief, Dog of the North* by someone whose name I cannot recall. *Beautiful Joe* by Marshall Saunders. *Lad, a Dog* and its various sequels by Albert Payson Terhune. And several others.

All of these books are on the upper shelf of a closet in the home of my mother and stepfather in Wichita, Kansas. The books have been collecting dust there since 1964. Before that they had been in my own little grey bookcase in Tulsa, Oklahoma.

From the perspective of my thirty-eighth or forty-sixth year I suppose that it is too late to try to fetch them home for Peter and Erin. They are already too old for such stories. Or maybe not. I am unable to keep track of their ages because I am unable to keep track of mine.

In any event, if Peter and Erin are less than fourteen, there is one book that I do not want either of them to have just yet. It is a collection of Stephen Crane's short stories. The same summer that I was blithely reading London and Terhune, I read Crane's story "A Small Brown Dog." I simply did not know what I was doing. The title lured me irresistibly onward. The other books had contained ruthless men and incidents of meaningless cruelty, yes, but all had concluded well: either virtue or romanticism had ultimately triumphed, and I was made glad to have followed Buck, Lassie, and Lad through their doggy odysseys.

The Crane story cut me up. I was not ready for it. I wept openly and could not sleep that night.

And if my children are still small, dear God I do not want them even to *see* the title "A Small Brown Dog," much less read the text that accompanies it.

"All in good time," I tell myself. "All in good time."

I AM TWELVE: Tulsa, Oklahoma. Coming home from school, I find my grown-and-married stepsister's collie lying against the curbing in front of a neighbor's house. It is almost four in the afternoon, and hot. The neighbor woman comes down her porch when she sees me.

"You're the first one home, Nicholas. It happened only a little while ago. It was a cement truck. It didn't even stop."

I look down the hill toward the grassless building sites where twenty or thirty new houses are going up. Piles of lumber, Sheetrock, and tar paper clutter the cracked, sun-baked yards. But no cement trucks. I do not see a single cement truck.

"I didn't know what to do, Nicholas. I didn't want to leave him —"

We have been in Tulsa a year. We brought the collie with us from Van Luna, Kansas. Rhonda, whose dog he originally was, lives in Wichita now with her new husband.

I look down at the dead collie, remembering the time when Rhonda and I drove to a farm outside Van Luna to pick him out of a litter of six.

"His name will be Marc," Rhonda said, holding him up. "With a *c* instead of a *k*. That's classier." Maybe it was, maybe it wasn't. At the time, though, we both sincerely believed that Marc deserved the best. Because he was not a registered collie, Rhonda got him for almost nothing.

Now I see him lying dead in the street. The huge tires of a cement truck have crushed his head. The detail that hypnotizes me, however, is the pool of gaudy crimson blood in which Marc lies. And then I understand that I am looking at Marc's life splattered on the concrete.

At supper that evening I break down crying in the middle of the meal, and my mother has to tell my stepfather what has happened. Earlier she had asked me to withhold the news until my father has had a little time to relax. I am sorry that my promise is broken, I am sorry that Marc is dead.

In a week, though, I have nearly forgotten. It is very seldom that I remember the pool of blood in which the collie's body lay on that hot spring afternoon. Only at night do I remember its hypnotizing crimson.

175 YEARS AGO IN RUSSIA: One night before the beginning of spring I go time-traveling — spirit-faring, if you like — in the mind of the Great Dane who once stalked into my classroom.

I alter his body into that of a hunting hound and drop him into the kennels on the estate of a retired Russian officer. Hundreds of my kind surround me. We bay all night, knowing that in the morning we will be turned loose on an eight-year-old serf boy who yesterday struck the general's favorite hound with a rock.

I jump against the fence of our kennel and outbark dogs even larger than I am. The cold is invigorating. My flanks shudder with expectation, and I know that insomnia is a sickness that afflicts only introspective university instructors and failed astronaut candidates.

In the morning they bring the boy forth. The general orders him stripped naked in front of his mother, and the dog-boys who tend us make the child run. An entire hunting party in full regalia is on hand for the festivities. At last the dog-boys turn us out of the kennels, and we surge across the estate after our prey.

Hundreds of us in pursuit, and I in the lead.

I am the first to sink my teeth into his flesh. I tear away half of one of his emaciated buttocks with a single ripping motion of my jaws. Then we bear the child to the ground and overwhelm his cries with our brutal baying. Feeble prey, this; incredibly feeble. We are done with him in fifteen minutes.

When the dog-boys return us slavering to our kennels, I release my grip on the Great Dane's mind and let him go foraging in the trashcans of Athens, Georgia.

Still shuddering, I lie in my bed and wonder how it must

feel to be run down by a pack of predatory animals. I cannot sleep.

APPROACHING SIRIUS: We eight men are physical extensions of the astrogation and life-support components of the *Black Retriever*. We feed on the ship's energy; no one must eat to stay alive, though, of course, we do have delicious food surrogates aboard for the pleasure of our palates. All our five senses have been technologically enhanced so that we see, hear, touch, smell, and taste more vitally than do you, our brethren, back on Earth.

Do not let it be said that a cybernetic organism sacrifices its humanity for a sterile and meaningless immortality. Yes, yes, I know. That's the popular view, but one promulgated by pessimists, cynics, and prophets of doom.

Would that the nay-sayers could wear our synthetic skins for only fifteen minutes. Would that they could look out with new eyes on the fierce cornucopian emptiness of interstellar space. There is beauty here, and we of the *Black Retriever* are a part of it.

Canicula-Threasie and the other Cybernetic Canine Constructs demonstrate daily their devotion to us. It is not a slavish devotion, however. Often they converse for hours among themselves about the likelihood of finding intelligent life on the planet that circles Sirius.

Some of their speculation has proved extremely interesting, and I have begun to work their suggestions into our tentative Advance Strategem for First Contact. As Threasie himself delights in telling us, "It's good to be ready for any contingency. Do you want the tail to wag the dog or the dog to wag the tail?" Not the finest example of his wit, but he invariably chuckles. His own proposal is that a single trace-team confront the aliens without weapons and offer them our lives. A gamble, he says, but the only way of establishing our credibility from the start.

Late at night — as we judge it by the shipboard clocks — the entire crew gathers around the eerily glowing shield of the Livermore-Parsons Drive Unit, and the dogs tell us stories out of their racial subconscious. Canicula usually takes the lead in these sessions, and my favorite account is his narrative of how dog and man first joined forces against the indifferent arrogance of a bestial environment. That story seems to make the drive shield burn almost incandescently, and man and dog alike — woman and dog alike — can feel their skins humming, prickling, with an unknown but immemorial power.

Not much longer now. Sirius beckons, and the long night of this journey will undoubtedly die in the blaze of our planetfall.

I AM FIFTEEN: When I return to Colorado Springs to visit my father the year after Nick's fall from the rocks, I find the great Labrador strangely changed.

There is a hairless saddle on Nick's back, a dark grey area of scar tissue at least a foot wide. Moreover, he has grown fat. When he greets me, he cannot leap upon me as he has done in past years. In nine months he has dwindled from a panther into a kind of heartbreaking and outsized lap dog.

As we drive home from the airport my father tries to explain:

"We had him castrated, Nicholas. We couldn't keep him in the house — not with the doors locked, not with the windows closed, not with rope, not with anything we tried. There's always a female in heat in our neighborhood and he kept getting out. Twice I had to drive to the pound and ransom him. Five bucks a shot.

"Finally some old biddy who had a cocker spaniel or something caught him — you know how gentle he is with people — and tied him to her clothesline. Then she poured a pan of boiling water over his back. That's why he looks like he does now. It's a shame, Nicholas, it really is. A goddamn shame."

The summer lasts an eternity.

TWENTY-SEVEN, AND HOLDING: Behind our house on Virginia Avenue there is a small self-contained apartment that our landlord rents to a young woman who is practice-teaching. This young woman owns a mongrel bitch named Tammi.

For three weeks over the Christmas holidays Tammi was chained to her dog house in temperatures that occasionally plunged into the teens. Katherine and I had not volunteered to take care of her because we knew that we would be away ourselves for at least a week, and because we hoped that Tammi's owner would make more humane arrangements for the dog's care. She did not. She asked a little girl across the street to feed Tammi once a day and to give her water.

This, of course, meant that Katherine and I took care of the animal for the two weeks that we were home. I went out several times a day to untangle Tammi's chain from the bushes and clothesline poles in the vicinity of her doghouse. Sometimes I fed her, sometimes played with her, sometimes tried to make her stay in her house.

Some days it rained, others it sleeted. And for the second time in her life Tammi came into heat.

One night I awoke to hear her yelping as if in pain. I struggled out of bed, put on a pair of blue jeans and my shoes, and let myself quietly out the back door.

A monstrous silver-black dog — *Was it a Great Dane?* — had mounted Tammi. It was raining, but I could see the male's pistoning silhouette in the residual glow of the falling raindrops themselves. Or so it seemed to me. Outraged by the male's brutality, I gathered a handful of stones and approached the two dogs.

Then I threw.

I struck the male in the flank. He lurched away from Tammi and rushed blindly to a fenced-in corner of the yard. I continued to throw, missing every time. The male saw his mistake and came charging out of the cul-de-sac toward me. His feet churned in the gravel as he skidded by me. Then he loped like a jungle cat out our open gate and was gone. I threw eight or nine futile stones into the dark street after him. And stood there barechested in the chill December rain.

For a week this went on. New dogs appeared on some nights, familiar ones returned on others. And each time, like a knight fighting for his lady's chastity, I struggled out of bed to fling stones at Tammi's bestial wooers.

Today is March the fifth, and this morning Katherine took our little boy out to see Tammi's three-week-old puppies. They have a warm, faintly fecal odor, but their eyes are open and Peter played with them as if they were stuffed stockings come to life. He had never seen anything quite like them before, and Katherine says that he cried when she brought him in.

I AM AGELESS: A beautiful, kind-cruel planet revolves about Sirius. I have given this world the name Elsinore because the name is noble, and because the rugged fairness of her seascapes and islands calls up the image of a more heroic era than any we have known on Earth of late.

Three standard days ago, seven of our trace-teams descended into the atmosphere of Elsinore. One trace-team remains aboard the *Black Retriever* to speed our evangelical message to you, our brethren, back home. Shortly, we hope to retrieve many of you to this brave new world in Canis Major.

Thanks to the flight capabilities of our cybernetic dogs, we have explored nearly all of Elsinore in three days' time.

We divided the planet into hemispheres and the hemispheres into quadrants, and each trace-team flew cartographic and exploratory missions over its assigned area. Canicula and I took upon ourselves the responsibility of charting two of the quadrants, since only seven teams were available for this work, and as a result he and I first spotted and made contact with the indigenous Elsinorians.

As we skimmed over a group of breathtakingly stark islands in a northern sea, the heat-detecting unit in Canicula's belly gave warning of this life. Incredulous, we made several passes over the islands.

Each time we plummeted, the sea shimmered beneath us like windblown silk. As we searched the islands' coasts and heartlands, up-jutting rocks flashed by us on every side. And each time we plummeted, our heat sensors told us that sentient beings did indeed dwell in this archipelago.

At last we pinpointed their location.

Canicula hovered for a time. "You ready to be wagged?" he asked me.

"Wag away," I replied.

We dropped five-hundred meters straight down and then settled gently into the aliens' midst: a natural senate of stone, open to the sky, in which the Elsinorians carry on the simple affairs of their simple state.

The Elsinorians are dogs. Dogs very like Canicula-Threasie. They lack, of course, the instrumentation that so greatly intensifies the experience of the cyborg. They are creatures of nature who have subdued themselves to reason and who have lived out their apparently immortal lives in a spirit of rational expectation. For millennia they have waited, patiently waited.

Upon catching sight of me, every noble animal in their open-air senate began wagging his or her close-cropped tail. All eyes were upon me.

By himself Canicula sought out the Elsinorians' leader

and immediately began conversing with him (no doubt implementing our Advance Strategem for First Contact). You see, Canicula did not require the assistance of our instantaneous translator; he and the alien dog shared a heritage more fundamental than language.

I stood to one side and waited for their conference to conclude.

"His name translates as Prince," Canicula said upon returning to me, "even though their society is democratic. He wishes to address us before all of the assembled senators of his people. Let's take up a seat among them. You can plug into the translator. The Elsinorians, Nicholas, recognize the full historical impact of this occasion, and Prince may have a surprise or two for you, dear Master."

Having said this, 3C grinned. Damned irritating.

We nevertheless took up our seats among the Elsinorian dogs, and Prince strolled with great dignity onto the senate floor. The I.T. System rendered his remarks as several lines of nearly impeccable blank verse. English blank verse, of course.

PRINCE Fragmented by the lack of any object
       Beyond ourselves to beat for, our sundered hearts
       Thud in a vacuum not of our making.
       We are piecemeal beasts, supple enough
       To look upon, illusorily whole;
       But all this heartsore time, down the aeons
       Illimitable of our incompleteness,
       We have awaited this, your arrival,
       Men and Dogs of Earth.
               And you, Canicula,
       We especially thank for bringing to us
       The honeyed prospect of Man's companionship.
       Tell your Master that we hereby invite
       His kinspeople to our stern but unspoiled world

> To be the medicine which heals the lesions
> In our shambled hearts.
>   Together we shall share
> Eternity, deathless on Elsinore!

And so he concluded. The senators, their natural reticence overcome, barked, bayed, and bellowed their approval.

That was earlier this afternoon. Canicula-Threasie and I told the Elsinorians that we would carry their message to the other trace-teams and, eventually, to the people of Earth. Then we rose above their beautifully barbaric island and flew into the eye of Sirius, a ball of sinking fire on the windy sea's westernmost rim.

Tonight we are encamped on the peak of a great mountain on one of the islands of the archipelago. The air is brisk, but not cold. To breathe here is to ingest energy.

Peter, Erin, Katherine — I call you to this place. No one dies on Elsinore, no one suffers more than he can bear, no one suffocates in the pettiness of day-to-day existence. That is what I had hoped for. That is why I came here. That is why I sacrificed, on the altar of this dream, so much of what I was before my aneurysm ruptured. And now the dream has come true, and I call you to Elsinore.

Canicula and I make our beds on a lofty slab of granite above a series of waterfalls tumbling to the sea. The mist from these waterfalls boils up beneath us. We stretch out to sleep.

"No more suffering," I say.

"No more wasted potential," Canicula says.

"No more famine, disease, or death," I say, looking at the cold stars and trying to find the cruel one upon which my beloved family even yet depends.

Canicula then says, *"Tempus?"*

"Yes?" I reply.

"*Fug it!*" he barks.

And we both go to sleep with laughter on our lips.

TWENTY-SEVEN AND COUNTING: I have renewed my contract for the coming year. You have to put food on the table. I am three weeks into spring quarter already, and my students are students like other students. I like some of them, dislike others.

I will enjoy teaching them *Othello* once we get to it. Thank God our literature text does not contain *Hamlet*: I would find myself making hideous analogies between the ghost of Hamlet's father and the Great Dane who haunted my thoughts all winter quarter.

I am over that now. Dealing with the jealous Moor again will be, in the terminology of our astronauts, "a piece of cake."

Katherine's pregnancy is in its fourth month now, and Peter has begun to talk a little more fluently. Sort of. The words he knows how to say include *Dada, juice,* and *dog. Dog,* in fact, is the first word that he ever clearly spoke. Appropriate.

In fifteen years — or eleven, or seventeen — I probably will not be able to remember a time when Peter could not talk. Or Erin, either, for that matter, even though she has not been born yet. For now all a father can do is live his life and, loving them, let his children — born and unborn — live their own.

"Dog!" my son emphatically cries. "Dog!"

A Gift From
The GrayLanders

In the house where Mommy took him several months after she and Daddy stopped living together, Cory had a cot downstairs. The house belonged to Mommy's sister and her sister's husband Martin, a pair of unhappy people who already had four kids of their own. Aunt Clara's kids had real bedrooms upstairs, but Mommy told Cory that he was lucky to have a place to sleep at all and that anyway a basement was certainly a lot better than a hot-air grate on a Denver street or a dirty stable like the one that the Baby Jesus had been born in.

Cory hated the way the basement looked and smelled. It had walls like the concrete slabs on the graves in cemeteries. Looking at them, you could almost see those kinds of slabs turned on their ends and pushed up against one another to make this small square prison underground. The slabs oozed wetness. You could make a handprint on the walls just by holding your palm to the concrete. When you took your hand away, it smelled gray. Cory knew that dead people smelled gray too, especially when they had been dead a long time — like the people who were only bones and whom he had seen grinning out of magazine photographs without any lips or eyeballs or hair. Cory sometimes lay down on his cot wondering if maybe an army of those gray-smelling skeletons clustered on the other side of the basement walls, working with oddly silent picks and shovels to break through the concrete and carry him away to the GrayLands where their deadness made them live.

Maybe, though, the gray-smelling creatures beyond the basement walls were not really skeletons. Maybe they were Clay People. On his cousins' black-and-white TV set, Cory had seen an old movie serial about a strange planet. Some of the planet's people lived underground, and they could step into or out of the walls of rock that tied together a maze of tunnels beneath the planet's surface. They moved through dirt and rock the way that a little boy like Cory could move through water in summer or loose snow in winter. The brave, blond hero of the serial called these creatures the Clay People, a name that fit them almost perfectly, because they looked like monsters slapped together out of wet mud and then put out into the sun to dry. Every time they came limping into view with that tinny movie-serial music rum-tum-tumping away in the background, they gave Cory a bad case of the shivers.

Later, lying on his cot, he would think about them trying to come through the oozy walls to take him away from Clara's house the way that Daddy had tried to kidnap him from that motel in Ratón, New Mexico. For a long time that day, Daddy had hidden in the room with the vending machines. Going in there for a Coke, Cory had at first thought that Daddy was a monster. His screams had brought Mommy running and also the motel manager and a security guard; and the "kidnap plot" — as Mommy had called it later — had ended in an embarrassing way for

Daddy, Daddy hightailing it out of Ratón in his beat-up Impala like a drug dealer making a getaway in a TV cop show. But what if the Clay People were better kidnappers than Daddy? What if they came through the walls and grabbed him before he could awake and scream for help? They would surely take him back through the clammy grayness to a place where dirt would fill his mouth and stop his ears and press against his eyeballs, and he would be as good as dead with them forever and ever.

So Cory hated the basement. Because his cousins disliked the windowless damp of the place as much as he did, they seldom came downstairs to bother him. Although that was okay when he wanted to be by himself, he never really wanted to be by himself *in the basement*. Smelling its mustiness, touching its greasy walls, feeling like a bad guy in solitary, Cory could not help but imagine unnamable danger and deadness surrounding him. Skeletons. Clay People. Monsters from the earthern dark. It was okay to be alone on a mountain trail or even in a classroom at school, but to be alone in this basement was to be punished for not having a daddy who came home every evening the way that daddies were supposed to. Daddy himself, who had once tried to kidnap Cory, would have never made him spend his nights in this kind of prison. Or, if for some reason Daddy could not have prevented the arrangement, he would have stayed downstairs with Cory to protect him from the creatures burrowing toward him from the GrayLands.

"Cory, there's *nothing* down here to be afraid of," Mommy said. "And you don't want your mother to share your bedroom with you, do you? A big seven-year-old like you?"

"No," he admitted. "I want my daddy."

"Your daddy can't protect you. He can't or won't provide for you. That's why we had to leave him. He only tried to grab you back, Cory, to hurt me. Don't you understand?"

Daddy hurt Mommy? Cory shook his head.

"I'm sorry it's a basement," Mommy said. "I'm sorry it's not a chalet with a big picture window overlooking a mountain pass, but things just haven't been going that way for us lately."

Cory rolled over on his cot so that the tip of his nose brushed the slablike wall.

"Tell me what you're afraid of," Mommy said. "If you tell me, maybe we can handle it together — whatever it is."

After some more coaxing, but without turning back to face her, Cory began to talk about the skeletons and the Clay People from the GrayLands beyond the sweating concrete.

"The GrayLands?" Mommy said. "There aren't any GrayLands, Cory. There may be skeletons, but they don't get up and walk. They certainly don't use picks and shovels to dig their way into basements. And the Clay People, well, they're just television monsters, make-believe, nothing at all for a big boy like you to worry about in real life."

"I want to sleep on the couch upstairs."

"You can't, Cory. You've got your own bathroom down here, and when you wake up and have to use it, well, you don't disturb Uncle Martin or Aunt Clara or any of the kids. We've been through all this before, haven't we? You know how important it is that Marty get his sleep. He has to get up at four in order to make his shift at the fire station."

"I won't use the bathroom upstairs. I won't even drink nothin' before I go to bed."

"Cory, hush."

The boy rolled over and pulled himself up onto his elbows so that he could look right into Mommy's eyes. "I'm scared of the GrayLands. I'm scared of the gray-smellin' monsters that're gonna come pushin' through the walls from over there."

Playfully, Mommy mussed his hair. "You're impossible,

you know that? Really impossible."

It was as if she could not wholeheartedly believe in his fear. In fact, she seemed to think that he had mentioned the GrayLands and the monsters who would come forth from them only as a boy's cute way of prompting adult sympathy. He did not like the basement (Mommy was willing to concede that point), but this business of a nearby subterranean country of death and its weird gray-smelling inhabitants was only so much childish malarky. The boy missed his father, and Mommy could not assume Daddy's role as protector — as bad as Clinton himself had been at it — because in a young boy's eyes a woman was not a man. And so she mussed his hair again and abandoned him to his delusive demons.

* * *

Cory never again spoke to anyone of the GrayLands. But each night, hating the wet clayey smell of the basement and its gummy linoleum floor and the foil-wrapped heating ducts bracketed to the ceiling and the naked light bulb hanging like a tiny dried gourd from a bracket near the unfinished stairs, he would huddle under the blankets on his cot and talk to the queer creatures tunneling stealthily toward him from the GrayLands — the Clay People, or Earth Zombies, or Bone Puppets, that only he of all the members of this mixed-up household actually believed in.

"Stay where you are," Cory would whisper at the wall. "Don't come over here. Stay where you are."

The monsters — whatever they were — obeyed. They did not break through the concrete to grab him. Of course, maybe the concrete was too thick and hard to let them reach him without a lot more work. They could still be going at it, picking away. The Clay People on that movie planet had been able to walk through earth without even using tools to clear a path for themselves, but maybe Earth's earth was packed tighter. Maybe good old-fashioned Colorado concrete could hold off such single-minded creatures for months. Cory hoped that it could. For safety's sake, he would keep talking to them, begging them to stay put, pleading with them not to undermine the foundations of his uncle's house with their secret digging.

Summer came, and they still had not reached him. The walls still stood against them, smooth to the touch here, rough there. Some of the scratches in the ever-glistening grayness were like unreadable foreign writing. These scratches troubled Cory. He wondered if they had always been there. Maybe the tunneling creatures had scribbled them on the concrete from the other side, not quite getting the tips of their strange writing instruments to push through the walls but by great effort and persistence just managing to press marks into the outer surface where a real human being like him could see them. The boy traced these marks with his finger. He tried to spell them out. But he had gone through only his first year in school, and the task of decipherment was not one he could accomplish without help. Unfortunately, he could not apply for help without breaking the promise that he had made to himself never to speak of the GrayLanders to anyone in Aunt Clara's family. If Mommy could muster no belief in them, how could he hope to convince his hard-headed cousins, who liked him best when he was either running errands for them or hiding from them in the doubtful sanctuary of the basement?

Then Cory realized that maybe he was having so much trouble reading the GrayLanders' damp scratches not because he was slow or the scratches stood for characters in a foreign tongue, but because his tormentors' painstaking method of pressing them outward onto the visible portions of the walls made the characters arrive there *backwards*. Cory was proud of himself for figuring this out. He filched a pocket mirror from the handbag of the oldest girl and brought it down the creaking stairs to test his theory.

This girl, fifteen-year-old Gina Lynn, caught him holding the mirror against one of the rougher sections of wall, squinting back and forth between the concrete and the oval glass. Meanwhile, with the nub of a broken pencil, he was struggling to copy the reversed scratches onto a tatter of paper bag. Cory did not hear Gina Lynn come down the stairs because he was concentrating so hard on this work. He was also beginning to understand that his wonderful theory was not really proving out. The mysterious calligraphy of the GrayLanders continued to make no sense.

"You're just about the weirdest little twerp I've ever seen," Gina Lynn said matter-of-factly. "Give me back my mirror."

Startled and then shamefaced, Cory turned around. He yielded the mirror. Gina Lynn asked him no questions, knowing from past experience that he would respond with monosyllables if at all, but began to bruit it around the house that he could read the marks in concrete the way that some people could read cloud formations or chicken entrails. Uncle Martin, who was home for a long weekend, thought this discovery about his sister-in-law's son hilarious. He called Cory into the living room to rag him about taking the mirror but especially about holding it up to the shallow striations in the otherwise blank gray face of a basement wall.

"Out with it," he said. "What'd that stupid wall tell you? No secrets, now. I want me a tip straight from the Cee-ment itself. What's a rock-solid investment for a fella like Uncle Marty with only so much cash to spare?"

Cory could feel his face burning.

"Come on, cuz. This is a relative talkin', kid. Let me in — let us *all* in — on what's going down, basement-wise."

"Who's gonna take the World Series this year?" twelve-year-old David promptly asked.

"Is Hank Danforth gonna ask Gina Lynn to his pool party?" Faye, disturbingly precocious for nine, wondered aloud.

("Shut up," Gina Lynn cautioned her.)

And thirteen-year old Deborah said, "Is war gonna break out? Ask your stupid wall if the Russians're gonna bomb us."

"Maybe the wall was askin' him for some cold cream," Uncle Martin said. "You know, to put on its wrinkles." All four of Uncle Martin's bratty kids laughed. "You were just writin' down the brand, weren't you Cory? Don't wanna bring home the wrong brand of cold cream to smear on your favorite wall. After all, you're the fella who's gotta face the damn thing every morning, aren't you?"

"Silica Lotion," Gina Lynn said. "Oil of Grah-velle."

Mommy had a job as a cash-register clerk somewhere. She was not at home. Cory fixed his eyes on Uncle Martin's belt buckle, a miniature brass racing car, and waited for their silly game to end. When it did, without his once having opened his mouth to reply to their jackass taunts, he strode with wounded dignity back down to the corner of the basement sheltering his cot. Alone again, he peered for a time at the marks that Gina Lynn's mirror had not enabled him to read. The scratches began to terrify him. They coded a language that he had not yet learned. They probably contained taunts — threats, in fact — crueler and much more dangerous than any that his uncle and cousins had just shied off him for sport.

* * *

Two days later, in Uncle Martin's detached garage, Cory found a gallon of yellow paint that Aunt Clara had bought nearly three summers ago to take care of the house's peeling shutters. He also found a brush and an aerosol can of black enamel that David had recently used to touch up the frame on his ten-speed. These items the boy carried downstairs to his private sanctuary.

Stripped to his Jockey briefs, he began to slap runny gouts of latex brilliance all over the disturbing hieroglyphs. At first, he hid a few of them behind the dripping image of a huge lopsided egg yolk. Then, swinging his arm in ever-widening arcs, he expanded this clownish shape into the brim of a festive straw sombrero. The sombrero rim grew to be gong-sized, and the gong ballooned to the dimensions of one of those giant yellow teacups whirling around and around in a local amusement park. Finally, though, Cory had his circle as big as a small sun, a ball of good cheer radiating into the basement as if the very paint itself had caught fire.

He outlined the sun with the black spray paint and added flares and fiery peninsulas that cried out for yet more yellow. Then he painted smaller lamps on other portions of this wall and on the other walls too, and squat tropical birds with combs and wattles, and pineapples as big as the lamps, and a long yellow beach under the glowering sun. His arms ran yellow, as did his pipe-cleaner thighs, as did his caved-in belly and chest, while his face seemed to reflect back the brightness of the obliterated gray that he strove to cover over permanently. If he had to live and sleep in this dank hole in the ground, let it be a happy hole in the ground. Let the light of artificial suns, two-dimensional lamps, and crudely drafted fruits and cockatoos spill into his basement through the pores of the very cement.

Let there be light.

Let there be light to hold the GrayLanders at bay. For Cory believed that the work he had done, the symbols he had splashed up around his cot like a fence of sunlight, would keep the creatures beyond the subterranean walls from bursting through them to steal him away from Mommy and the real world of automobiles and mountains and football stadiums — the real world in which she was trying to make a place for both of them. Maybe he was safer now.

But while Cory was admiring what he had done, David came down the steps to ask him to go to the store. His older cousin saw him three-quarters naked and striped like an aborigine in the midst of a yellow-gray jungle unlike any terrain that David had expected to find only a floor below the family's TV room.

"Holy shit," he said and backed away up the steps as if Cory might be planning to slit his throat on the spot.

A moment or two later, Uncle Martin came storming down the steps in a pair of rope-soled boots that made the whole unfinished structure tremble like a medieval assault tower in an old Tyrone Power movie. He could not believe what Cory had done. He bruised the boy's arm and upper chest shaking him this way and that to demonstrate his disbelief and his unhappiness. He threw Cory onto his cot with such force that it collapsed under the blow and dumped the boy sidelong so that his head struck a section of painted concrete. Yellow paint smudged the whorl pattern of hair on Cory's crown, and a trickle of red worked through the smudge to enrage Uncle Martin even further.

"This is *my* house!" he shouted, slapping Cory again. "No one gave you permission to do this!"

Aunt Clara's pant-suited legs appeared halfway up the trembling stairs. More of her came into view as she descended. When Uncle Martin drew back his forearm to administer another cracking wallop, she cried, "Marty, don't! Something's happenin' on the news. You like the news. Come see what's goin' on. Try to relax. I'll take care of this. Come watch the news."

Uncle Martin's forearm halted inches from Cory's eyes.

"Ain't nobody gonna take care of this, Clara!" he shouted. "We'll jes' leave our little Piggaso down here to moon over his shitty goddamn yellow masterpieces! Forever, maybe!" He thrust Cory into the wall to punctuate this last threat, kicked the crumpled cot, and pounded back up the steps, pulling Aunt Clara along with him. Then the door slammed. Soon after, the naked light bulb near the staircase went out; and the boy knew that one of his cousins, at Uncle Martin's bidding, had flipped the circuit breaker controlling the power supply to the basement.

But for a narrow line of light beneath the door at the top of the steps, Cory crouched beside his cot in utter darkness. Then someone — maybe Uncle Martin himself — put something — probably a rolled-up towel — along the base of the door; and the not quite utter darkness of his prison took on a thoroughness that made the boy think that someone — possibly a GrayLander — had stuck an altogether painless needle into his eyeballs and injected them with ink. He still had eyeballs, of course, but they had gone solid black on him, like licorice jawbreakers or moist ripe olives. With such eyes, he could "see" only darkness.

What about the fat yellow sun that he had painted? What about the beach, the pineapples, the sunlamps, and the cockatoos? He put his hands on the damp slabs of the basement walls and felt each invisible figure for reassurance. Was the dampness only the sweat of soil-backed concrete, or was it instead an indication of undried paint? Cory could not tell. When he sniffed his hands, they gave off the familiar odor of grayness — but even bright yellow pigment could acquire that smell when, like a glaze of fragile perfume, it was applied to an upright slab of earthen gray. The boy wiped his hands on his chest. Was he wiping off a smear of latex sunshine or the clammy perspiration of underground cement? Because he would never be able to tell, he gave up trying.

Then he heard a pounding overhead and knew that Mommy had come home from work. She and Uncle Martin were just beyond the door at the top of the stairs, arguing.

"For Chrissake, Marty, you can't keep him locked up in the basement — no matter what he's done!"

"Watch me, Claudia! Jes' you watch me!"

"I'm going down there to see him! I'm his mother, and I've got a right to see him! Or else he's gonna come up here to see us!"

"What he's gonna do, woman, is stew in the dumb-fuckin' Piggaso mess he's made!"

"He hasn't even had his dinner!"

"Who says he deserves any?"

"He's my son, and I'm going to let him out!"

Then Cory's darkness was riven by the kind of noise that a big dog makes when it slams its body into a fence slat, and Mommy was screaming, and Aunt Clara was cursing both Mommy and Uncle Martin, and the staircase scaffolding was doing the shimmy-shimmy in its jerrybuilt moorings. Crash followed crash, and curses curses, and soon all the upper portions of the house seemed to be waltzing to the time-keeping of slaps and the breakage of dinnerware or random pieces of bric-a-brac. Cory waited for the rumpus to end, fully expecting Mommy to triumph and the door to open and the darkness to give way to a liberating spill of wattage that would light up the big yellow sun and all the other happy symbols that he had painted. Instead, when the noise ceased and the house stopped quaking, the darkness kept going, and so did the silence, and the only reasons that Cory could think of were that Mommy and her brother-in-law had killed each other or that Mommy had finally agreed with Uncle Marty that Cory really did deserve to sit alone in the dark for trying to beautify the dumb-ass basement walls.

Whatever had happened upstairs, the door did not open,

and the ink in his eyeballs got thicker and thicker, and he
came to realize that he would have to endure both the dark
and the steady approach of the GrayLanders — Clay People, Earth Zombies, Bone Puppets — as either a premedi-
tated punishment or a spooky sort of accident. (Maybe a
burglar had broken in during the argument and stabbed
everybody to death before Mommy could tell him that her
son was locked in the basement. Maybe Mommy had purposely said nothing to the bad guy about him, for fear that
the bad guy would get worried and come downstairs to
knife Cory, too.) Anyway, he was trapped, with no lights
and nothing to eat and streaks of yellow paint all over his
invisible body and only a tiny bathroom and trickles of
rusty tap water for any kind of comfort at all.

Cory crept up the rickety stairs, putting a splinter into
one palm when he gripped the guard rail too hard. At the
top, he beat on the door in rapid tattoos that echoed on his
side like the clatter of a fight with bamboo staves at the
bottom of an empty swimming pool. "Let me out!" he
shouted. "Let me out of here!" Which was not dignified, he
knew, but which was necessary, here at the beginning of his
confinement, as a test of Uncle Martin's will to hold him. If
noise would make his uncle nervous, if pleading would
make the man relent, the boy knew that he had to try such
tactics, for Mommy's sake as well as his. But it was no use,
and finally he sat down and bit at the splinter in his palm
until he had its tip between his baby teeth and managed to
pull it free of the punctured flesh sheathing it.

* * *

Darkness swallows time. Cory decided that darkness
swallows time when he had been alone in the black basement so long that he could not remember being anywhere
else even a quarter of the time that he had spent hunched

on his cot waiting for the darkness to end. He could not tell whether time was stretching out like a pull of saltwater taffy or drawing up like a spider when you hold a match over its body. Time was not something that happened in the dark at all. The dark had swallowed it. It was trying to digest time somewhere deep in its bowels, but when time emerged again, Cory felt sure that it would be a foul thing, physically altered and hence bad-smelling — gray-smelling, probably — and unwelcome. He almost hoped that the dark would swallow him, too, so that he would not have to confront the stench of time when, altered in this bad but inevitable way, it came oozing into the world again.

Once, he thought he heard sirens. Maybe Uncle Martin had gone to a fire somewhere.

Later, though, he was more concerned that the Gray-Landers were getting closer to breaking through the base-ment's outer wall than that some poor stranger's house had caught fire. He put his hands on the upright slab next to him. He did this to hold the slab in place, to prop it up against the gritty GrayLanders straining their molecules through the earth — straining them the way that Aunt Clara strained orange juice on Saturday mornings — to scratch backward messages into the cement in a language so alien that not even a mirror could translate it for Cory. No longer able to *see* these messages, then, he began to *feel* the striat-ions embodying them. Maybe the Bone Puppets, the Earth Zombies, the Clay People, or whatever they were, preferred to contact living human beings with *feel*able rather than *see*able symbols.

Like Braille, sort of.

Didn't that make sense? It was smart to think that mon-sters living underground, in everlasting subterranean dark, would be blind, wasn't it? Cory's first-grade teacher had taught them about moles, which could only see a little, and had even shown them a film about cave animals that had no eyes at all because, in their always-dark environments, they had *revolved* that way. Well, the GrayLanders were probably like those cave animals, eyeless, blind, totally and permanently blind, because by choice and biological development they made their home in darkness. Which was why they would write backwards on the walls in symbols that you had to feel and then turn around in your head to get the meaning of.

Cory worked hard to let the alien Braille of the Gray-Landers talk to him through his fingertips. Probably, their messages would let him know what sort of horrible things they planned to do to him when they at last got through the concrete. Probably, the symbols were warnings. Warnings meant to terrify. A really smart kid would leave them be, but because he had been locked into a place that he could not escape without the aid of the adults upstairs — grownups a kid would ordinarily expect to make some responsible decisions for him and maybe for themselves too — Cory had to struggle to parse the queer dents and knobbles on his own. Alone, in the dark, it was better to know than not to know, even if what you learned made your gut turn over and the hair in the small of your back prickle. So far, though, he was learning nothing. All their stupid tactile messages made no sense, either forwards at the tips of his fingers or backwards or sideways or upside-down in the ever-turning but ever-slipping vise of his mind.

"You're blind and you can't even write blind-writing!" Cory shouted. He pounded on the sweaty slab beside his cot as centuries ago he had pounded on the door at the top of the staircase. Thwap! thwap! thwap! and not even the satisfaction of an echo. Bruised fists and a bit lip, only.

Cory forced the bent legs on his cot back under the canvas contraption, but pinched the web between his thumb and forefinger. He lay down on his cot nursing the pinch and staring through ink-filled eyes at the heavy nothing pressing down on him like the bleak air pressure of a tomb. With a bleak black here and a bleak black there (he crooned to himself), here a black, there a black, everywhere a bleak black, Uncle Marty had a tomb, ee-ai, ee-ai-oh. The melody of this nursery song kept running in his head in almost exactly the way that the darkness kept restating itself all around him. They were both inescapable, and pretty soon they got mixed up in Cory's mind as if they were mirror-image phenomena that he could not quite see straight and hence could not distinguish between or make any useful sense of.

Upstairs, as faint as the buzzing of a single summer mosquito, sirens again.

And then, somehow, the sun that Cory had painted on the wall — the humongous yellow orb with hair-curler geysers and flares around its circumference — lit up like a flashbulb as big as a Mobile Oil sign. But unlike any kind of flashbulb, Cory's sun did not go out again. Instead, in the bargain-basement catacombs of his aunt and uncle's house, it continued incandescently to glow. Everything in the basement was radiated by its light. Cory had to lift one paint-smeared forearm to shield his eyes from the fierce intensity of its unbearable glowing. The images of sunlamps on this and other walls, and of birds of paradise, and of bananas, pineapples, and papayas — *all* these clumsy two-dimensional images began to burn. They did so with a ferociousness only a little less daunting than that of Cory's big latex sun. It seemed to the boy that God Himself had switched the power back on. For some private reason, though, He had chosen not to use the orthodox avenue of the wiring already in place.

No, instead He had moved to endow with blinding brightness the symbols of life and sunshine that *Cory* had splashed on the walls. If Mommy would not help him, God would. If his aunt, uncle, and four bratty cousins would not release him to daylight, well, God would bring a gift of greatly multiplied daylight right down into the basement to him. Although grateful for this divine favor, the boy help-lessly turned aside from the gift. It was too grand, too searing, and that for a brief instant he had actually been able to see the bone inside the forearm shielding his eyes fretted Cory in a way that his gratitude was unable to wipe from his memory.

And then, almost as if he had dreamed the divine gift, darkness reasserted itself, like a television screen shrinking down to one flickering central spot and going black right in the middle of a program that he had waited all day to see.

Ee-ai, ee-ai-oh.

Cory sat still on his cot. *Something* had happened. For an instant or two, the ink had been squeezed out of his eye-balls, and a liquid like lighter fluid had been poured into them. Then the liquid had ignited, and burned, and used itself up, whereupon the ink had come flooding back. Or something like that. Cory was still seeing fuzzy haloes of light on the congealed blackness of the ink. Fireflies. Glow-ing amoebas. Migrating match flames. Crimson minnows. They swam and they swam, and no one gave a damn but the boy in the basement.

And then it seemed to him that overhead a whirlwind had struck the neighborhood. The darkness roared, and the staircase began doing the shimmy-shimmy again. But this time the shaking got so violent that the steps and guard rails — a tiny din within the great bombast of the Rocky Mountain hurricane raging above him — broke loose of the scaffolding and like the bars of a big wooden xylophone tumbled into and percussed down upon one another with the discordant music of catastrophe, plink! plunk! crash! ka-BOOM-bah! clatter-clatter!

It would have been funny, sort of, except that the roaring and the quaking and the amplified sighing of whatever was going on upstairs — *what* stairs? — in the real world, the terrifying playground of wild beasts and grownups, would not stop. Cory feared that his head might soon explode with the noise. In fact, he began to think that the noise was *inside* his skull, a balloon of sound inflating toward a ka-BOOM! that would decorate the gray-smelling walls with glistening oysterlike bits of his brain. Gray on gray.

The endless roaring swallowed time. Cory began to forget that the world had not always entertained such noise. It seemed a kind of constant, like air. He wondered if maybe the GrayLanders were the culprits, howling from all the topless basements in his aunt and uncle's neighborhood that they had succeeded in breaking into from their earthen grottos. If so, they would soon be here too, and time would both begin again and stop forever when they opened the sky for him with their grating godforsaken howls.

Maybe air was not a constant. Cory was suddenly having trouble breathing. Also, the clammy walls had begun to hiss, as if the ooze invisibly streaking them had heated to a temperature enabling them to steam. Gasping, he got down off the cot and crawled along the floor to the niche where an old-timey water heater, unemployed since the final days of the Eisenhower administration, squatted like the sawed-off fuselage of a rocket. Cory could not see it now, of course, but he remembered what it looked like. The metal wrapping the cylinder scalded his naked shoulder as he crawled past the antique.

Still gasping, bewildered by the difficulty of refilling his lungs, the boy slumped behind the old heater and turned his face toward an aperture in the concrete wall — an accident of pouring — through which a faint breath of warm rather than desert-hot air blew. He twisted his itching, inflamed body around so that he could thrust his entire head into this anomalous vent. The lip of concrete at its bottom sliced into his neck, but he ignored the minor discomfort to gulp the air leaking through. A gift from the GrayLanders? Maybe. Cory refused to question it, he just gulped and gulped, meanwhile praying that the noise would die down and the heat ease off and his oxygen supply return to normal.

In this unlikely posture, the boy fell asleep. Or, at least, consciousness left him.

*   *   *

When Cory awoke, his ears were buzzing, but the whirl-wind had ceased. He pulled his head out of the rough spout in the concrete and found that he could comfortably breathe. He crawled out from behind the old gas water heater. An eerie kind of darkness held the day, but he could see again, as if through blowing smoke or murky water. Parts of the basement ceiling had fallen in, but all the walls were standing, and on them, as dim as the markings on the bottom of a scummy swimming pool, wavered the childish symbols that he had brushed and spray-painted onto the cement. Soot and grime dusted his handiwork, giving a disheartening dinginess to the latex yellow that a while ago — an hour, a day, a millennium — had shouted God's glory at him. Soot and dust drifted around the dry sump of the basement like airborne chaff in the granary of a farm in western Kansas.

He looked up. The staircase had collapsed, and the door that he had pounded on, well, that door no longer occupied the doorjamb framing an empty portal at the top of the fallen stairs. In fact, the doorjamb was gone. Where it should have stood, a refrigerator slouched, its hind rollers hanging off the edge of the oddly canted floor. How it had wound up in that place, in that position, Cory could not clearly say, but because the walls of the upper portions of the house had evaporated, along with the ceiling, the furniture, and its human occupants, he did not spend much time worrying about the recent adventures of the parboiled refrigerator. High above the ruins of the house, the sky looked like a crazy-quilt marbling of curdled mayonnaise and cold cocoa and dissolving cotton candy and burnt tomato paste. Yucky-weird, all of it.

Just as gut-flopping as the sky, everything stank and distant moans overlay the ticks of scalded metal or occasionally pierced the soft static of down-sifting black snow. Although summer, this snow was slanting out of the nightmare sky. Appropriately, it was nightmare snow, flakes like tarnished-silver cinders, as acrid as gunpowder, each cinder the size of a weightless nickel, quarter, or fifty-cent piece. Right now, the boy was sheltered from their fall by a swag-bellied warp of ceiling, but he had made up his mind to climb out of the basement and to go walking bareheaded through the evil ebony storm.

Bareheaded, barechested, and barefoot.

Before the GrayLanders came.

Which they surely would, now that the grownups, by flattening everything, had made their tunneling task so much the easier. One of the outer basement walls had already begun to crumble. It would be a relaxing breaststroke for the Clay People, Earth Zombies, or Bone Puppets to come weaving their cold molecules through that airy stuff. And they had to be on their way.

Cory got out of the basement. It took a while, but by mounting the staircase rubble and leaping for the edge of the floor near the teetering refrigerator and pulling himself up to chin height and painstakingly boosting one leg over, he was finally able to stand on the tilting floor. Then, propellering his arms to maintain his balance, he watched with astonished sidelong glances as his Aunt Clara's big Amana toppled from its perch and dropped like a bomb into the staircase ruins below it. A geyser of dust rose to meet the down-whirling cinders.

But he kept from falling, and looked around, and saw that no longer did the tall buildings of Denver, whose tops it had once been easy to see from his aunt and uncle's neighborhood, command the landscape, which had been horribly transfigured. Debris and charred dead people and blasted trees and melted automobiles lay about the boy in every direction, and the mountains to the west, although still there, were veiled by the photographic-negative snowfall, polarized phosphor dots of lilting deadliness.

Cory pulled his vision back from the mountains. "Mommy!" he cried. "Mommy!" Because he had no reasonable hope of an answer in this unrecognizable place, he started walking. Some of the burnt lumps in the rubble were probably all that remained of certain people he had known, but he had no wish to kneel beside them to check out this nauseating hunch. Instead, he walked. And it was like walking through a dump the dimensions of . . . well, of Denver itself. Maybe it was even bigger than that. The ubiquitous black snow and the yucky-weird sky suggested as much.

And then he saw his first GrayLander. The sight made him halt, clench his fists, and let go of a harsh yelping scream that scalded his throat the way that the down-whirling cinders had begun to burn his skin. The GrayLander paid him no mind, and although he wanted to scream again, he could not force his blistered voicebox to do as he bid it. For which reason, frozen to the plane of crazed asphalt over which he had been picking his way, Cory simply gaped.

Well over six feet tall, the GrayLander was almost as naked as he. The boy could not tell if it were Clay Person, Earth Zombie, or Bone Puppet — it seemed to be a little of all three, if not actually a hybrid of other ugly gray-smelling ogres of which he had never even dreamed. The

GrayLander's ungainly head looked like a great boiled cauliflower, or maybe a deflated basketball smeared with some kind of milky paste. If the creature had eyes, Cory could not see them, for its brow, an almost iridescent purple ridge in the surrounding milkiness, overlapped the sockets where most earth-born animals would have eyes. The creature's heavy lips, each of which reminded Cory of albino versions of the leeches that sometimes attacked people in television horror movies, were moving, ever moving, like greasy toy-tank treads that have slipped off their grooves. Maybe it had heard the boy approach — the huge, stunned creature — for it turned toward him and pushed an alien noise from between its alien lips.

"Haowah meh," it said. "Haowah meh."

When it turned, the purple-gray skin on its breasts, belly, and thighs slumped like hotel draperies accidentally tilted off their rods. Cory took a careful step back. One of the monster's arms showed more bone below the elbow than flesh, as did its leg below the knee on the same side. Pale lips still moving, the GrayLander extended its other arm toward the boy, the arm that might almost have been mistaken for a man's, and opened its blackened paw to reveal a tiny glistening spheroid. The monster shoved this object at Cory, as if urging him either to contemplate it at length or to take it as a memento of their meeting.

Squinting at the object in the unceasing rain of cinders, Cory understood that it was an eyeball. The GrayLander, blind, wanted him to have its eyeball. Just as he had suspected, the GrayLanders whom he had been waiting to come after him were sightless. They had eyes, apparently, but years of living in the dark, ignoring the realms of light just above their heads, had robbed their optical equipment of the ability to see. What, then, could be more useless than the gift of a GrayLander's eyeball? Cory was outraged. The whirlwind had finally freed this stupid creature — and all its equally ugly relatives wandering like benumbed zombies across the blasted landscape — from its subterranean darkness, and it was trying to give him something that had never been of the least value to itself or to any of its kind.

"Haoweh meh," it said again.

The boy's anger overcame his fear. He jumped forward, snatched the eye from the monster's paw, and flung it off the hideous body of the GrayLander so that it bounced back at him like the tiny red ball connected to a bolo paddle by a rubber tether.

Then, knowing nothing at all about where he was going or what he would do when he got there, Cory began to run. The dump that Denver and its suburbs had become seemed too big to escape easily, but he had to try, and he had to try in spite of the fact that as he ran many of the yucky GrayLanders loitering bewilderedly in the rubble called to him to stop — to stop and help them, to stop and share both their pain and their bewilderment. Cory would not stop. He was angry with the blind monsters. They were people in disguise, people just like his dead mommy, his dead aunt and uncle, and his dead cousins. He was angry with them because they had fooled him. All along, he had been living among the GrayLanders and they had never once — until now — stepped forward to let him know that, under their skins, they and their human counterparts were absolutely identical.

A Short History
Of The Bicycle:
401 B.C. to 2677 A.D.

On the planet Draisienne, a world of undulant savan-nahs whose ankle-high grasses were interrupted now and again by paths of impacted organic matter embedded in a soil disturbingly like asphalt in both its consistency and color, Praeger realized that the history of the bicycle would have to be rewritten. Not another human being within a hundred light-years (so far as he knew), he was sitting beneath the awning of his tent trying to piece together a rich and involving historical tapestry that would do for the bicycle what the Bayeux Tapestry had done for the Battle of Hastings. Past time, too; long past time. Occasionally Praeger looked up from his microfilm viewer (the tent behind him a repository of cassettes, its canvas coolness more crowded with history than with food tins) to gaze out over the milling creatures he had been studying for nearly a year, Earth standard.

"Since the bicycle makes little demand on material or energy

resources, contributes little to pollution, makes a positive contribution to health and causes little injury or death, it can be regarded as the most benevolent of machines."[1]

A breeze lifted Praeger's sandily greying forelock and, blowing through his bushjacket, air-conditioned his flanks and armpits. The draisies, meanwhile, kept rolling. 'A pack of them,' Praeger thought; 'I've been calling a group of them a "pack" when the proper term is probably "herd" — especially since "herd" suggests their sociability without implying a predatoriness that doesn't really exist in them.' Then, to the paradigmatic spirit of S.S. Wilson, twentieth-century author of "Bicycle Technology," the article he'd just been perusing, Praeger said aloud, "Yes, they're benevolent, S.S. But they aren't machines, they simply aren't machines. At least not here." The breeze carried his words away, and far in the distance, blued by haze while even yet made shimmeringly substantial by the graceful shapes wheeling across it in the foreground, a mountain squared its various glacial summits — like a hoary-headed Olympian giving a deliberately bellicose set to his shoulders. Praeger, who knew a little of the ancient language of the Masai, called the peak's nearest summit *Ngàje Ngài*, the House of God. Besides, Draisienne was a great deal like old Tanzania, and the drasies rolling so docilely on the impacted paths of the planet's savannahs reminded him of earthly zebras or wildebeest. "Herds," he said to himself again; "not packs. Why have I been calling them packs?"

Despite all evidence to the contrary [Praeger wrote], *the bicycle was not invented in the 19th century. Although such men as the Baron von Drais de Sauerbrun, the Scot Kirkpatric Macmillan,*

---

[1]S.S. Wilson, "Bicycle Technology," in *Scientific American*, Vol. 228, No. 3 (March, 1973), p. 84.

the brothers Michaux of Paris, and the Starleys of Coventry can legitimately claim status as re-discoverers and developers of the bicycle, none of these people actually invented the machine. That honor belongs to a Greek mercenery named Polybices. In 401 B.C., on the "Retreat of the Ten Thousand" from Cunaxa in Persia (an adventure perhaps exaggeratedly chronicled in Xenophon's Anabasis), Polybices intuited the morphology of the bicycle from the Platonic ideal of what the perfect rider-propelled vehicle should look like. While his fellow mercenaries fought off the vengeful soldiers of Artaxerxes in the hills of Kurdistan and Armenia, Polybices constructed his prototypical machine from broken sword hafts, discarded spears, the leather facings and straps from his dead comrades' shields, and various bits of plunder taken during their heavily beset retreat. Snow fell. Food was scarce. The depredations on their flanks and rear — even upon their advance columns — were constant. As a result, the adroit and singleminded Polybices, cursed by his fellows as a goldbrick and straggler, was forced to put much of his machine together on the move. This he did. Finally, sixty or seventy kilometers from the Black Sea, he realized his fever-dreamt Platonic pardigm in fact — although without the chain-and-sprocket drive to the rear wheel that the ideal form would have dictated for a vehicle of absolute perfection. Under extreme conditions Polybices had done what was humanly possible; moreover, the absence of the chain-and-sprocket drive proved only a minor hindrance, for he immediately set out and pedaled the remaining sixty or seventy kilometers to Trapezus, a Greek city where his safety was assured, in a mere day and a half. This he did in spite of inclement weather, hostile Persian patrols, and inimically surfaced roads, arriving in Trapezus several days ahead of his foot-weary and starving companions. (Many, of course, having died of exposure and starvation, did not make it to the Black Sea at all.) A contingent of arrivals, whom Polybices merrily rode out to greet, fell upon him and beat him to death for his pains. In their rage they also wrenched apart and scattered into the seaport's streets the various makeshift components of his velocipede. Well over 2,300 years pased before Baron von Drais de Sauerbrun gave the world his two-wheeled "pedestrian hobby-horse," an extremely imperfect realization of the ideal that Polybices, against very nearly prohibitive odds, had almost brought into the compass of an even more imperfect humankind. And the loss . . . the loss was certainly an immeasurable one.[2]

Praeger, looking up again, subvocalized, 'And another 750 years have passed since the Baron's partial rediscovery of Polybices's invention. During which time we have exchanged the bicycle for the motor car, the motor car for the helicraft, the helicraft for the single-seat probeship capsupulter, and the capsupulter for the spirit-fritzing, autogenous agonies of matter transmission.' By which final means Praeger, his microfilm library, and his camping gear had come to Draisienne, blitzing into renewed existence out of the aethers of night, time, and space from the Platform in Teaneck, New Jersey: blippity-blip, blippity-blip, blip-blip. The draisies on the savannah — flashing their spokes, cornering, doing all sorts of gaudy kip-ups and wheelies — hadn't even tilted their handlebars to witness his arrival. Now, of course, it would take a probeship shuttlebopper to lift Praeger and his goods off-planet (or a mattermitted Platform), there being no re-transmission facilities on Draisienne: only yellow-orange grasses, a few well-worn paths and "wheelie-courts," an occasional tree (baobab-like and droll), and the ever-rolling, brightly colored creatures who commanded Praeger's time, attention, and tormented respect. Turning again to his history, though, he began to write. . . .

---

[2] In "The Flying Machine," an historical anecdote disguised as a parable, one R. Bradbury recounts how in 400 A.D., for reasons considerably different from those of Polybices's comrades, the Emperor of China had the inventor of a prototypical aeroplane beheaded and the prototype itself destroyed. This incident takes on a puzzling relevance to our own concerns when we consider that the re-discoverers of the flying machine, Orville and Wilbur Wright, were also bicycle makers.

In 2204 transuranian element number 237, having a half-life of 1.00872 nanoseconds, was discovered by a group of scientists at the Research Institute on Ganymede. Dr. J.K. Kolodny, director of the program, requested that the new element be named Polybicium. Why? his colleagues inquired. It is reported that Kolodny, who was possessed of limited psychic abilities, replied, "Because we've named new elements just after about everybody who deserves the honor, and Polybicium (Py) has a nice ring to it." The others accepted this decree, and so element 237 is now known by the name of the true inventor of the bicycle. Thus does life have its compensations.

Bicycles, organic bicycles. But just as one would expect on a world so uncannily suggesting the fertile plains of Africa, several different species existed. For a year Praeger had been concentrating on a "pack" of French racers whose territorial instincts restricted them to the path, or wheelie-court, just below the baobaboid tree twenty meters from his tent. Even so, the evolutionary abundance of Draisienne also afforded him the chance to observe groups of high-wheelers, bone-shankers, Royal Salvo tricycles, two-seaters, Rover safety bikes, and, most eerily, large, shadow-casting pterocycles that soared on Draisienne's winds and dropped out of her thin, opalescent skies like reptilian Marabou storks. 'What we've discovered,' Praeger told himself, 'is that the philosophical ideal forms which Plato postulated and which the hapless Polybices saw through to in a fever dream *actually* exist on their own worlds throughout the physical universe. And, in every case, these ideal forms are animate creatures — even when what they shadow forth on our Earth happens to be mere clay, soulless and inanimate.' That was true. Thus, humankind had encountered entire planets populated by respiring, evolutionarily differentiated ash trays, water towers, foot coverings, pogo sticks, skyscrapers, undergarments, boomerangs, bread boxes, alcoholic beverages[3], and so on *ad infinitum*. Species of these things existed on each world because even an imperfect manifestation of a single idea had a "perfect" Platonic counterpart of its peculiar "variety of imperfection," and individuals existed among the species to represent the various "perfect" manifestations of the possible "variety of imperfections" of the *components* comprising a single entity of the species. Abstruse; yea, ferociously abstruse. Even Praeger did not fully understand it. Nevertheless, this notion accounted for the many different species of the same thing that one inevitably found on the many Worlds-of-the-Platonic-Norm. Hence, on Draisienne, the perfectly clumsy hobby-horse bicycles of the old Baron coexisting with the Rover bikes of absolutely perfect morphology "invented" on Earth in 1885 by J.K. Starley. 'The universe,' thought Praeger, 'never ceases to amaze.'

During the last thirty or so years of the current century (from 2644 to 2673, to be precise) the bicycle has enjoyed a renascence of popularity akin to that it experienced in the late 1960s/early 1970s in the old political unit of the United States of America, Earth, Sector 2J-21LP. The recent galaxy-wide recession, however, in conjunction with the annihilation of nine non-Platonic, humanly inhabited planets of the Light-Probe Alliance by means of cobalt dysjunctifiers, has brought about a slump in sales proportionately commensurate with the one sequent upon the "spiraling inflation" of that earlier, all-but-forgotten era. On Draisienne, studying the streamlined structure and the amiable habits of the French racer, along with the other species of organic mechanism which no doubt contributed to the racer's development/evolution, one again

---

[3] In his speculative work *Solaris*, the 20th-century Polish writer St. Lem has created a world with a planet-encompassing sentient ocean. However, on the Platonic Norm World of Four Roses (sometimes called Betelgeuse IV) an astounding variety of sentient liquid bodies exists, one body separated from another by a reticulum of crystalline isthmuses. Unfortunately, it has been impossible to communicate with the natives of Four Roses because of their metabolic processes: irreversible, perpetual inebriation.

becomes aware of the need to simplify, simplify, simplify. The bicycle itself has done so. As its early historian S.S. Wilson astutely noted, it "has evolved so that it is the optimum design ergonomically" [my italics].[4] *In that sense, then, Draisienne has become my Walden.*[5]

* * *

Praeger looked up again. Was his history going off track here? That last sentence contained a first-person possessive pronoun. Soon, at this rate, he'd be shamelessly recounting how he and his wife, back on the blasted freeways of Old New England, had once carted their two children about in rear-mounted, plastic bucket-chairs. Bright yellow, those chairs; like the sun in mid-May. No, it wouldn't do to go that route, cycling through times and emotions that on Draisienne had reality only in the memory flashes escaping between the stroboscopic spokes of his mind. And who the hell besides his wife Daisy, his son Maserati, and his daughter Gitane would understand the lugubrious comedy of the "folk ballad" that he'd composed for them, *I Fell Off of the Bicycle of Love?*[6] 'Don't write about that,' he subvocalized, watching two unicycles balance precariously on one of the upper limbs of the tree below his tent; 'keep this on an erudite, historical basis, Praeger. Your job is to discover if perhaps the organic bicycle of Draisienne doesn't

---

[4] Wilson, op cit., p. 82.

---

[5] A pond near Concord, Massachusetts, defunct U.S.A., Earth, Sector 2J-21LP, once celebrated by the naturalist H.D. Thoreau; today, the name of a tar-pit from which archeologists have dredge-excavated many decomposed artifacts believed to be the panels and furnishings of "mobile homes."

---

[6] In addition to his talents as a xenobiologist and writer, Praeger was a folklorist of some renown. *Editor's note.*

offer us a way out of the holocaust now threatening all the worlds of the Light-Probe Alliance. A new and accurate history, I'm sure, may be the key to that discovery.' When would he write the other, then? When see Daisy, Maz, and little Gitane again? Thus questioning, Praeger became aware of the tip of a handlebar nuzzling the khaki at his elbow. It was the draisie he called Daisy, an unattached two-seater who'd early on weavingly meandered into his camp and by her apparent trust in him provided Praeger many opportunities for closer observance of the racers sporting on the plain. Moreover, she'd aided in his original research for this project. Reciprocating with an occasional affectionate lube-job, he'd managed to keep her in camp. Now he stroked Daisy's rear seat and aloud said, "Just a minute, girl; just a minute. I've got a bit more to do here." He turned back to his notebook. No getting around the personal pronoun now; no way to authenticate his sources without giving his superiors the truth. The Truth. With a capital I . . .

* * *

Many of you may ask, "How has an isolated xenobiologist on the planet Draisienne, working with an imported microfilm library, discovered the secret of the bicycle's original invention? Is not this story of the Greek mercenary a madness that he attempts, from the cover of his isolation, to foist upon us?" No, it is not. The fact is that I have used the temporal-displacement & surround-facsimilating capabilities of one of Draisienne's natives (a bicycle built for two) to take me to Trapezus in the year 401 B.C. so that I might witness the actual arrival in that city of Polybices and his bicycle. To effect this chronosilient transfer I first had to make a physical journey from the savannah of my encampment to the latitudes on Draisienne corresponding precisely to those of the Tigris-Euphrates region on Earth, arena of the Ten Thousand's retreat. My domesticated two-seater, Daisy, having previously indicated by handlebar feints and bell-ringing the necessity of such a trip, carried me northward to these latitudes in twenty days' time; seemingly, a phantom on the forward seat provided us with the pedal-driven impetus to accomplish the journey so quickly. Then, at a rough equivalency of 41°N, 38°E (a good bit off the true coordinates of ancient Trapezus, but not so much as to affect Daisy's t-d & s-f capabilities), my two-seater began its temporal "homing," the cyclotronic acceleration of her wheels simultaneously generating the spatial blur which would eventually become the geographical surround of that ancient seaport.[7] "Homing" is the proper term since my vehicle was attempting to travel back into time to the moment of Polybices's intuition of the vehicular ideal embodied by the creatures on Draisienne; moreover, further back than 401 B.C. these time-displacing & surround-facsimilating "machines" cannot go, for their own physical evolution on this Platonic Norm World did not begin until the moment of the intuition itself, before which time they had been hovering in Draisienne's atmosphere as ethereal and insubstantial as any other unrealized abstract concept.[8] Nevertheless, the result of Daisy's "homing" was that, seated on her rear cushion, both the bicycle and myself (I'm certain) only an indistinct and faintly twinkling eddy of air to the world at large, I saw Polybices enter the city on his machine; I then jumped forward two days to become a spectator at his murder and the destruction of his handiwork, at last fleeing three thousand years into the future

---

[7] For a somewhat divergent explanation of the temporal effects (minus any commentary on the generation, across interstellar distances, of a concomitant spatial environment) see in particular the first and third chapters of Herbert George Wells's *The Time Machine*. However, this work deals almost solely with displacements into the *future*, from a point of departure corresponding exactly with the point of ultimate arrival.

---

[8] The knowledge that mere human thought can, by itself, influence conditions on planets light-years from Earth is, of course, a reversal of the principal thrust of three thousand years of scientific discovery: that human beings, rather than holding center stage, are on the far periphery of the ontological "concerns" of the universe. The work of Copernicus, Einstein, and our own esteemed Thornapple aside, many once again believe man "the measure of all things." The consequent inflation of our species's ego has been, to understate the case, a mixed blessing.

while the sun, stars, clouds, and landscape swept bluely by me as if the cosmos itself were evaporating into an abstract concept too tenuous ever to be intuited again. Finally, the world restored, Daisy and the phantom rider on her front saddle carried me southward the thousand or so kilometers to my encampment on the savannah. I am now attempting to reconstruct what I have learned, firsthand, from the strange, multidimensional jaunt I have just returned from. I am, you see, my own documentation.[9]

Not much more to do now. The history required speculation only: Praeger's proposals for solving the manifold crises looming so perniciously in the Alliance's future. Almost all of these, as Praeger saw it, were the consequence of either congenital human failings or vices resulting from a now universally tolerated dissociation of feeling. Could the bicycle cure these things? On the one hand, greed, ambition, rapacity, egotism. On the other, estrangement, suspicion, and the insidious will to solitariness. Why, wasn't he himself a victim of this final dissociation? No, definitely not; he was on Draisienne by assignment, not because he had *chosen* to separate himself from Daisy and the children. And he thought of them often, he most assuredly did, he hadn't yet succumbed to the plague of antisociability that had led, at least indirectly, to the cobalt-dysjunctifying of nine planets and a subsequent slump in bicycle sales. 'Not I,' Praeger told himself; 'not I.' The lesson of the bicycle, of course, was simplify, simplify, simplify, and one could easily go to school at the total benignity of its gregariousness. Even Daisy (the bicycle, not his wife) had sought out a compan-

[9]We might here point out that as well as a folklorist, xenobiologist, historian, and weekend cycling addict, Praeger was a linguist who read and spoke classical Greek and was hence well-equipped to orient himself at once to the events occurring before him in ancient Trapezus. Some have felt this a little too pat an explanation for his success in discovering the "true origin" of the bicycle. What, these carpers want to know, would have happened if a Hindustani had first intuited the machine? Actually, Praeger's having a little Greek merely attests to the perspicacity of the Light-Probe Alliance in selecting its agents. *Editor's note.*

ion after becoming separated from her nomadic family of two-seaters. Maybe that was the answer: Bicycling was health; and fresh air, sunshine, and exercise would once again ('Once again?' he asked of no one in particular) place humankind in generous accord with itself. The slump in bicycle sales, therefore, had to be reversed. For a while Praeger watched the French racers jollily race and the unicycles in the baobab do circus acrobatics on its limbs. Then: 'Have I simplified to the point of being simplistic?' But since Daisy was now tenderly goring him with her forward handlebars, he could not reply to this pressing inquiry. "OK," he said aloud. To show his concern he rubbed a restorative leather paste into Daisy's two saddles, oiled and fondled her bush-rollers and orally resuscitated her easily inflatable tires. Afterwards, he said goodnight, carried his notebook into the tent, and there diligently tapped out to the authorities on Head a light-probe communication containing the first several sections of his history. In his sleep that night, however, he continued to compile, write, and annotate. . . .

Many of us, of course, subconsciously wish to be bicycles. How much simpler things would then be. This transposition being unobtainable, many others regard the bicycle with unwarranted suspicion and assume it to be — even on humanly inhabited worlds where it is clearly a machine rather than an organic creature — a variety of monster seeking either to deceive or destroy them.[10] *On Draisienne I have often found myself trying to emulate the carriage and the bearing of a bicycle, even though, owing to the*

---

[10] See, for example, A. Davidson's "Or All the Seas with Oysters," a psychological monograph detailing how a bicycle-shop operator commits suicide upon becoming convinced that one of his machines, after regenerating itself, has tried to kill him in revenge for his earlier having hammered it virtually into scrap metal. This pioneering work also contains the interesting but perhaps doubtful observation, "'Ever stop to think that bicycles are like people? I mean, of all the machines in the world, only bikes come male and female.'"

dissimilarities of our anatomies, the attempt is most painful. I'm sure, too, that my failure to effect a successful emulation of my hosts has scarred me in ways not yet fully evident.[11] *I do not wish to become a misanthrope, particularly since I am hoping that my researches here will provide a cure to that epidemic hatred of others of our kind which now threatens to rend the fabric of the Light-Probe Alliance. For this, you see, we cannot blame the bicycle; no, we definitely may not blame the bicycle. . . .*

The next morning Praeger awoke to insistent bell ringing, purposive ratcheting of gears, and the clicking of mis-aligned spokes. When he lifted his tent flap, he saw a congregation of French racers, Daisy in their midst, arrayed before him like a lynch mob. Praeger felt himself go ashen, fear hovering on his face and flanks in the acrid salinity of his sweat. Daisy rolled away from the others, stopped, cocked her handlebars (both sets), and clicked back to him. When two or three of the French racers did likewise, he realized, with something like gratitude, that instead of wishing to dismantle him they desired his company on an urgent morning outing. "All right," he told them, "I'll go," and the two-seater immediately permitted him to throw his leg over her rear saddle and ride away from the encamp-ment at the head of a posse of lacquer-bright bicycles of red, green, yellow, and blue. Over one of Draisienne's grass-shot asphalt paths they rolled, the wind parting about Praeger's stiff, upright body and pulling the racers along in the resul-tant slip-stream. Then, tires elongating, frames glinting, sprockets purring, they leapt onto the savannah itself and careered eastward unimpeded by the gramineous carpet beneath them. By nightfall they'd obtained a promontory overlooking a narrow beach, and there, in the last light,

---

[11] Consult "A Voyage to the Houyhnhnms" in *Travels into Several Remote Nations of the World* by L. Gulliver.

Praeger saw creatures like himself rounding up a primitive sort of draisie (treadle-driven two-wheelers, they were) and driving them onto a prefabricated Platform jerrybuilt over the water's edge. From the Platform these clumsy, unsuspecting vehicular ideals were transfritzed off-planet at the push of a portable mattermitting unit in the hands of an aloof press-gang boss, a foreshortened figure whose no doubt symbolically black cloak whipped about madly in the wind off the ocean. 'Slavers,' Praeger told himself; 'bike slavers.' Daisy and the French ten-speeds, he realized, had brought him here to do something, they wanted him to counteract the enormity now being perpetrated by his own species. So he dismounted, stepped to the brink of the rock face they'd halted on, and shouted into the wind, "Stop that! You, stop that!"

In the Earth-standard year 2677 [Praeger wrote a week later], *several species of bicycles were hunted to extinction on the Platonic-Norm World Draisienne. Already gone from this world are the treadle-driven two-wheeler, the Coventry lever tricycle, the bamboo velocipede, and the Far Eastern rickshaw bike. Daily the implacable poachers move inland, and little difference does it make that rather than killing them outright the poachers are beaming the creatures off-planet in an attempt to capitalize commercially on their t-d and s-f capabilities.*[12] *Extinction will still be the end result, I fear. I also fear that those engaged in this certain mechological genocide are agents of the same authority that origi-nally sent me here to study the draisies.*[13] *They arrived, after all, the morning after I probe-communicated the first sections of my history; and, despite my repeated requests for aid, no help has come*

---

[12] See pages 8-10 of R. Praeger's monograph "A Short History of the Bicycle: 401 B.C. to 2677 A.D."

---

[13] Arrant nonsense. *Editor's note.*

from the Light-Probe Alliance since these villains first materialized here, bringing with them their own Platform. To me the poachers will not listen, and, as they probably knew beforehand from my agency dossier, I cannot bring myself to use force against them. Meanwhile, Daisy and the French racers have turned an imperially cold, justifiably jaundiced reflector light on me, and I feel my all-too-human nervous system unraveling inside me like a frayed reticulum of dreams. This is indeed a dark day for xenobiology and Roald Praeger. This is indeed a dark day in the History of the Bicycle. . . .

When he came out of his tent that same afternoon, Praeger noticed that Daisy was gone. Had she deserted him? Had she been captured and mattermitted to an Alliance world? The racers below the baobab were also gone, as were the frolicsome unicycles that had so frequently entertained him. All that remained of the French ten-speeds' little herd (not "pack," that term belonged to the creatures of another species altogether) were two lithe, shinily black vehicles poised like leopards on the apron in front of his tent. "What do you want?" Praeger said, fear striking him; "what is it?" He soon learned that the bicycles wanted him to accompany them, but that they would by no means permit him to mount to their saddles. As dusk fell, then, he had to walk between the two midnight-black racers as if he were a condemned man on the way to the gallows. 'I am,' he subvocalized; 'that's exactly what I am.' For they were now ascending the plain, going toward the raggedly carven summit that Praeger had been calling _Ngàje Ngài_, climbing the boulder-strewn switchbacks of the mountain to Draisienne's twilit House of God. Once, during this climb, he looked up, startled, to see a panicked pterocycle bank on the high wind, ripple its shadow across his face, and soar out of eyeshot beyond a fortification of rock. On the mountain's summit the racers abandoned Praeger. They wheeled about and flashed away into the flooding dark beneath them. Looking down into a narrow, granite-rimmed valley from a ledge on this summit, the xenobiologist saw the dim, mangled shapes of a billion dead bicycles; he saw the burial ground of all the worn-out and unworkable, perfectly imperfect vehicular ideals ever to inhabit Draisienne — for these, too, were mortal, it seemed. Thus, though Daisy and the racers had brought their ultimate judgment to bear on Praeger as a representative of humankind, they had also acknowledged his personal innocence of their involuntary, blanket disposition to the worlds of the Alliance: even as they went to meet their own fates, they were permitting him to die on a hallowed shelf of mountain, above the graveyard of their forevermore partially intuited fellows. "Oh, Polybices," Praeger said aloud, "my elevation to this place is an anabasis paralleling your own, an ascent into everlasting anonymity." And although he was content, he continued, while dying of exposure and starvation, to compose and annotate. . . .

On at least one occasion [Praeger mentally wrote, deciding as he did that this would be the last paragraph in his history of the bicycle] *a writer has employed the bicycle as a metaphor for death.*[14] *This is patently unfair to both the tenor and the vehicle, so to speak, of this analogy — for the bicycle has inspired very few poems of any merit, and death has never been so popular a form of transportation as the bicycle.*

The agents of the Light-Probe Alliance succeeded in shipping off-planet and selling at exorbitant prices every single native of Draisienne. People summarily junked their

---

[14] See "The Snows of Kilimanjaro" in which E. Hemingway writes, "He lay still and death was not there. It must have gone around another street. It went in pairs, on bicycles, and moved absolutely silently on the pavements."

mechanical bicycles. The organic bikes, however, did not thrive well in captivity and refused to perform the temporal-displacement & surround-facsimilating tasks demanded of them by their avaricious owners. Within three years, Earth standard, every one of them — from the simplest pedestrian hobby-horse to the most sophisticated and streamlined ten-speed — had died. Somewhat later Praeger's effects were recovered from Draisienne and shipped to the authorities on Head. One morning a subaltern in the administrative section of the Alliance command carried a ragged notebook into his superior's office and reported dubiously, "Here's Roald Praeger's history of the bicycle, sir." To this his superior, looking up, replied absently, "What's a bicycle?"[15]

---

[15] The existence of the monograph you have just read is conjectural. *Editor's note.*

Diary Of A
Dead Man

Deathdate One: A short while ago, as if fulfilling the dictates of a clumsy punch line, I *woke up dead*. Forgive the italics, but the queerness of this state — post-mortem consciousness — cries out for underscoring. I have no body, but I can think. On the other (nonexistent) hand, I know that I am dead because I have no body. No body, and nobody, at all. The celebrated assertion of René Descartes, "I think, therefore I am," does not apply. I refute it by pointing out that the Frenchman formulated this solipsistic law while comfortably incarnate in a (more or less) standard-issue human body. The vicissitudes of disembodiment were unknown to him — although, of course, he may be more familiar with them now.

Cogito ergo sum? I prefer "I think, therefore I'm confused," in tandem with "I'm absent, therefore I ain't."

Around me, as far as my thoughts can probe, only a glimmering ectoplasmic gray. But, to give this mother-of-pearl fog its due, its grayness may *comprise* my thoughts. I am really in no position to presume myself encompassed by it. I may be outside it, looking down. I may be under it, looking up. I may be at a remove of light-years, sensing the grayness via some kind of psychic telemetry. Or, again, I may be emitting this fog as a squid alchemizes and unfurls from itself a thalidomide plume of dreamily deforming ink. I have no body, and I am nowhere. However, the fog bank of my consciousness seems to be *moving*, and that motion holds out the hope of eventual arrival.

Where am I going?

Death, I thought, was supposed to answer that question. My next chilling realization is that maybe it will.

Dd. Two: What business have I, the disembodied consciousness of a dead man, keeping a diary? How, after all do you date the virtually indivisible stretches of deadtime triggered by the moment of your dying? New Year's Day, Easter Sunday, the Fourth of July, Halloween, and Christmas Eve are all equally meaningless here. What year is it? What month? What day? What cockeyed o'clock? Although I know that I died in a certain documentable year, at a specific pinpointable instant, the twilight territory into which I have died has a featurelessness — an everlasting *time*lessness — that unquestionably keeps most dead people from becoming faithful diarists. I am the only one whom I know about. You need a powerful ego to record a chronology of undated, and undatable, nonevents. You need a powerful ego to prevent yourself from fading into the omnipresent gray.

Maybe I have no body, but I *do* have that kind of ego. It centers me in the fog. It arranges the nonevents of this amorphous realm into the artificial linearity of sentences and paragraphs. Perhaps this entry should precede the first one. Or maybe it should make its initial appearance four or five entries down the (artificial) line. Who am I to say? Well, like God trying to impose order on chaos, I am trying to impose chronology on the mist-scatter of post-mortem timelessness. By my lights (if no one else's), that goal gives legitimacy to my self-appointed role as the historian of my otherwise indistinguishable deathdays.

Dd. Three: *Cogito ergo sum.* "I think therefore I am." Descartes is not quite so easy to refute as I have said. Here I am, after all, thinking in diary format, and both my thought processes and this unlikely diary prove that on some transcendental level I continue to exist. I think, therefore I am. (I am, therefore I think?) If death brings about the total annihilation of consciousness, then obviously I have not died. However, I actually *remember* dying, and the vivid ferociousness of that event completely incinerated what used to be my body.

Could it be that death opens a door to the continuation of human consciousness by nonbiological means? If so, what means? As a mind without a body, it occurs to me that these motivators must be either electromechanical or spiritual, or possibly a combination of the two, but absolutely nothing else of which I am presently aware. In other words, I am now either a piece of programmed software running in a computer or an angel sustained in the enduring dusk of eternity by the mysterious grace of God.

Which me is the true one, the electronic or the seraphic?

Dd. Four: Of course, I could be a ghost rather than an angel. If I were a ghost, my motive force would still be spiritual rather than electromechanical. Orthodox theologians deny the elevation of even death-transfigured human mortals to the ranks of the angelic hierarchy. God made the angels before He made the earth and its inhabitants. You do not inherit a pair of wings simply by dying. On the other (Platonic) hand, a ghost generally possesses an immaterial simulacrum of the body of its deceased "progenitor." And, as I have already noted, I have no body at all. I'm absent, therefore I ain't. Ain't a ghost, that is. Which somewhat reassuring conclusion leads me back to the altogether benumbing fear that I am stored on a magnetic disk inside a computer or else animated from afar by the unfathomable cogitations of God. Either way, I am the prisoner of a variety of limbo that makes me long for the release of utter oblivion.

Deprived of genuine ghosthood, I resent the fact that I am unable to haunt anyone but myself.

Dd. Five: I do not really believe that my personality has been magnetically warehoused or that I am running off at the ego inside an IBM, Apple, or AT&T computer. Computers have terminals, and terminals often have screens, and even the most complex or esoteric of programs must interface *somewhere* with consensus reality. If it did not, that program could hardly be aware of its own existence.

Well, I *know* that I exist, but not once since my deathday have I "interfaced" — being myself faceless — with any other reality but the mother-of-pearl fog impinging on every notional nerve of my disembodied consciousness. No whiz-kid hacker in tennis shoes and wire-rimmed glasses has summoned me along the link of an Electronic Personality Preservatorium to "live" again for his and his buddies' puerile amusement. My isolation from the world on the material side of my deathday is total. I am devastatingly alone in this drifting grayness. Alone alone alone alone alone. An iambic-pentameter solitude worthy of a justly deserted Elizabethan villain.

Dd. Six: But if I am not a computer program, neither am I a bona fide spiritual entity. (No question of my being an angel. Never any question.) Angels have no biological impulses because they have no biology. The bodies that they occasionally assume go forth like puppets or remote-controlled robots to perform their miraculous tasks, which, nearly always, are duly sanctioned historical expressions of the will of God. The angels themselves — the irreducible *essences* constituting their being — remain in heaven, directing without participating, effecting without actually putting a finger in. They neither hunger nor thirst nor ache nor lust. Their only quasi-natural longing is for union with the creator whose bountiful spiritual strength sustains them in existence.

Well, I am not like that. Never was. Ain't now. Bodiless, I continue to be buffeted by the ravening winds of biological memory.

Cut off the leg of a wounded man. Give him time to heal. Invariably, he will still experience twinges in his phantom limb.

That's me. Although wholly severed from my palate, bowels, and privates, I am still a slave to the tyranny of their phantom clamor. I crave the earthy taste of potatoes and beer. I imagine cracking open the albino legs of a snow crab and sucking from the break thread after succulent thread of meat. I imagine, too, spreading the legs of a willing woman and nursing her salty lips with a similar insatiable greed. Are these the secret imaginings of an angel? Would a member of God's celestial militia ever contaminate itself with such calculated cupidity? Not on your life. Nor on mine, either.

Q.E.D., I'm no angel.

Dd. Seven: Besides being dead, what other possibilities present themselves? Let me catalogue them.

1) Asleep in my own room, I am having a strangely vivid nightmare. After a while, of course, I'll awaken.

2) I am the subject of a sensory-deprivation experiment.

A team of researchers has placed me in a shallow bath of warm water inside a coffinlike container. No light or sound enters. Hour after hour, I float on my back in the buoyant dark. Finally, this maddening lack of stimulus leads me to hallucinate the omnipresent gray that I have mistakenly identified with the baleful territories of death. Eventually, however, the researchers will relent and free me.

3) I am in a state of suspended animation.

This possibility has subsidiary possibilities: A) I am being cryonically preserved in a special mausoleum, there to await a medical discovery that will reverse the progress of the fatal disease put on hold by my freezing-down. And B) I am lying in a cold-sleep capsule in a starship on its way to colonize the planet of a distant sun. Like my many sleeping colleagues, I will be revived automatically as soon as our ship has entered the targeted solar system. Our arrival will of course presage the beginning of a Bright New Future for the Entire Human Species.

No, no, no. No, no.

To believe any of these untenable "possibilities" would delight me. Each and every one of them offers the promise of resurrection. But I cannot believe any of them for the simple, and nonchalantly damning, reason that I remember in explicit, slow-motion detail the final two or three minutes of my life.

Dd. Eight: A crisis situation of the highest priority obtained. I was aloft in the flying command post with Carmody, Findlater, and Meranus, not to mention our elite standby crew and a four-star lifer from the Pentagon. The lifer's obsequious bombast was meant to cower the crew and to satisfy his civilian superiors' desire for conspicuous action. Everyone in uniform bustled. Everyone in states-manesque mufti glowered and role-played. A mis-hit on Washington, D.C., had smeared an incandescent porridge of scrap metal, brick dust, and liquefied concrete all the way to Baltimore. Static sniffle-snaffled the airwaves. What reports had earlier filtered through were contradictory in every particular but one, namely, the ruinous extent of the damage inflicted by our enemy's first nuclear enfilade. So many cities blazed that even the prairie dogs in North Dakota were gasping for breath.

"Sir," Carmody said, "a heat-seeking device from an invading MiG appears to be —"

I had abstracted myself from my environment. My head was lolling against a curve of sheet metal. The continuous faint rumble of our airborne fortress had begun to counterpoint the internal tides of my blood. The crew members in their zippered flightsuits, and my aides in their obligatory pinstripes, were ghosts shimmering on the outskirts of my vision. The fate of the nation and its people had long since ceased to occupy my thoughts. I was thinking instead about a "Peanuts" comic strip by Charles Schulz.

In this strip, Charlie Brown and Peppermint Patty stand side by side with their elbows on the parapet of a low brick wall. Peppermint Patty declares in the first frame that she needs to talk to someone who "knows what it's like to feel like a fool." Two frames later, she is saying, "Someone who's been disgraced, beaten and degraded. Someone who's been there . . ." In the wordless concluding frame, Charlie Brown spreads wide his arms in a touching here-I-am, look-no-further gesture.

Even the most gifted of public speakers would have given a small fortune to add that eloquent gesture to their forensic arsenals. I know I would have. So would Copetti, who outpointed me in our televised debates without ultimately managing to translate her victories into success at the polls. (Too bad, I say. So sad.)

Anyway, when Carmody's missile struck, I was thinking about Charlie Brown and Peppermint Patty. I may have been smiling. Any stray recollection of that particular strip nearly always coaxed a smile from me. I record this fact in my post-mortem diary with more chagrin than amiable self-effacement. Honesty compels me to chronicle only the truth. (Even if I am assisted in this compulsion by the soothing hunch that no one else will ever learn what I record here.) That a man of my stature and responsibility should have been mulling a cartoon at such a time galls my pride. If I had lived, and if Carmody or Findlater had maliciously publicized my gaffe, the rumor of it would have unquestionably played havoc with my reelection chances. But the world sometimes works that way, matters of no moment elbowing aside those of high consequence, and I have always admired Charles Schulz more than I have Sakharov or Solzhenitsyn. Did either of those Russian-born worthies ever make anyone smile?

The arrival of Carmody's "heat-seeking device" inter-rupted my reverie. It tore into our flying command post. It ignited something treacherously flammable not far from the (vaporized) bulkhead against which I had been leaning. As I spiraled amid the orbiting debris of our disintegrating aircraft, my flesh caught fire. For a few feverish seconds, I was conscious of the night sky underfoot and the radiantly riven earth overhead. The gelatin in my eyeballs melted. My charred skin flapped away. My bones turned to chewing gum. I was now unequivocally dead — can you seriously doubt it? — and Carmody, Findlater, Meranus, our four-star huff'n'puff, and every patriotic member of our crew had been press-ganged into nonexistence with me. Or, if not *with* me, then *at the same time* as I. It must be that those other poor fellows now occupy dimensionless pockets of grayness similar to, but altogether independent of, my own.

Perhaps the same is true of every single specimen of the human family recently extinguished by the War to

End All Wars. . . .

Dd. Nine: 1) I am not safely asleep. 2) I am not the subject of a sensory-deprivation experiment. 3) And I am not in a state of suspended animation in either A) an earthbound facility or B) an idealistically dispatched starship.

I am dead.

Dead dead dead dead dead.

Charlie Brown and Peppermint Patty may be alive somewhere or somewhen, but I am clearly a helpless captive of my deadness, which seems escape-proof. How even this niggling bit of the sentient me has managed to "survive," I cannot presume to hazard. Over and over again, though, the fear that I am being punished for my — our — manifold sins, asserts itself. I only hope that for the dabacle just past I am God's solitary scapegoat, that my eerie confinement here has exempted the innocent majority of our species from a like fate. Is that hope as grandiose and egocentric as my earthly political career? Do I dare in my loneliness and degradation aspire to the title Redeemer? Is that, in fact, an office for which a dead man can take it upon himself to run?

God only knows.

Dd. Ten: This moment, I have decided, is the Twelfth of Never, the Ides of Self-Validation, the Eve of Apotheosis. Cute, eh? I have put dates (of a kind) to indivisible units of my own dubious thought processes. Well, who's to stop me? Johnny Mathis? Caesar's assassins. God Himself? Hardly. I am the sole ruler of the twilight. Its Alpha and Omega, so to speak. And, surely, I can do here whatever I want to do, whenever I choose to do it. Stand back, then. The Emperor of the Great Gluey Gray is about to shape from glimmering formlessness a cosmos all his own —

Let there be light!

* * *

Dd. Eleven: The glimmering formlessness persists. For that one, I suppose, I stupidly set myself up. Imagine Charlie Brown with his arms spread wide. Even as the unlocatable smoke of my consciousness drifts this way and that through the surrounding void, I see my bodiless self in that humblingly pathetic posture. I shape nothing. I control nothing. I merely poke around in the lost corners of limbo like a rat in a maze, my old personality and all my outworn belief systems obstructively intact, delaying the progress of my soul on its way to . . . well, wherever. For am I not a soul seeking release?

Unfortunately, one of my outworn personal credos, never confessed in public, was that there is no such thing as an immortal soul. With many other questing Batesonian rationalists, I believed that if you wish to touch the soul, you need only lay hands on your own living body. The soul has no capacity to survive apart from animate flesh. The body-and-soul dichotomy propounded by the church was a misapprehension, one that has only lately fallen victim to the theory that consciousness emerges from the intricate interaction of a variety of biological systems. Anything that permanently damages the harmony among these systems — a bullet to the brain, the radioactive pollution of the atmosphere — likewise slays the soul. I resignedly embraced these modern beliefs. I never expected a portion of my own self-awareness to outlive my body. Once dead, I felt sure that ahead of me lay only vast silent deserts of irreversible not-being.

Have you ever heard God laugh? Minus ears and auditory nerves, *I* have. The sound of it is the continuous faint rumble of a deadly engine plowing through a mother-of-pearl fog.

Dd. Twelve: If I am not dreaming, maybe I am *being dreamt*. If God can sustain the "lives" of spiritual entities like angels, why couldn't He — or a designated surrogate — repair and rewind the mental processes of a human being physically undone by famine, disease, or war? In the absence of a healthy brain, this would be difficult but probably not impossible. Unlike me, God can do whatever He wants to do, whenever He chooses to do it. Meanwhile, my own lack of solidity and volition strongly suggests that I am being projected from Elsewhere by either God or a dreaming proxy empowered by Him to hold me in existence.

These are frightening thoughts, but they also serve to absolve me of responsibility for the direction and content of my mental processes. I am not I. I am the weird muddle of someone else's anxious dream. My existence — my *non*existence — is an illusion relegating me to the status not merely of a single dead member of an entire extinct species but of the ghostly representative of a species that *never evolved at all*. Someone else is ineptly thinking me, therefore I am not.

But I am reasoning badly about this problem. In some humiliatingly dependent sense, I *do* exist. If I exist ineptly here, maybe it is because I lived ineptly. Maybe I am being dreamt by the residual consciousness of the person I was before that Soviet missile — which I *insist* was real — blasted me and my companions out of the air. Some few of us may be lifted into legends by death, but a more telling truth I have learned is that no one is *improved* by it. Not even me. Least of all me. And, again, maybe I am a captive of this substanceless gray matter because in life I assumed myself exquisitely evolved, totally beyond improvement.

How the mighty are fallen.

Dd. Thirteen: Paupers and kings, garbage collectors and presidents may sometimes lie together in the same cemeteries. Indeed, they may even be said to "sleep together in the great democratizing union of death." Poets, romanticizers, and hard-nosed existentialists alike may claim that we are all united in our mortality. Death comes for the archbishop as surely as it does for the apothecary. The dead pickpocket is as dead as, but no more dead than, the dead concert pianist. Thus does our finite biology homogenize every human being who has ever drawn breath. All for one and one for all — even if, alive, we would have continued to segregate by social class, skin color, occupational allegiance, religious creed, and/or political conviction.

True, death is no bigot. Granted, death is an Equal Opportunity Employer. But be that as it may, death does *not* unify. It separates and sequesters. Solitary confinement. Monastic isolation. Every disembodied soul a passenger in the free-floating nucleus of a vast single-cell grayness. You can meditate, as I have been trying to do, or you can go mad. But when madness inevitably overtakes your meditations, you must bear it. No other option is available. Death has ceased to count as an option — has *died*, as John Donne correctly predicted — because you have already exercised it. And you have no words to convey to anyone — whether God or some less awesome eavesdropper — the queer pitch of your insanity or the dreadful measure of your loneliness.

I, for imperfect instance, am like a sidewalk screamer in detention on the image-reflecting side of a two-way mirror, gagged and straitjacketed to a fare-thee-well but nonetheless struggling to tear free and scream.

A maimed amphibian.

Dd. Fourteen: I used to enjoy mysteries. I read them for relaxation. ("It's all right, Mr. Ambassador; he reads them for relaxation.") I liked their deliciously campy titles. *Dead Men Tell No Tales. A Queer Kind of Death. Death Claims. The Dead Are Discreet. Death Is a Lonely Business.* I could go on forever — literally — about the uncanny prescience of the authors of these and other such titles. They said so much more than they knew. Their commercial cleverness was in fact profundity, their crude glibness wit, their with-it jauntiness a wistful sort of anticipatory courage. Such writers wrote mysteries, I think, because nearly everything that matters is a mystery. Of course, I could also damn the lot of them for a chuckleheaded lack of specificity, but you cannot say what you do not know and even the daunting engines of human imagination have their limits. It seems to me enough that they were able to *hint* so well. If I had the capacity to laugh, I would laugh in sardonic appreciation. I would rend the dimensionless fog with the inaudible sounds of a dead man lauding the clairvoyance of mystery writers, the greatest of whom is undoubtedly God.

The Dead Laugh Last. Good title, eh?

* * *

Dd. Fifteen: Right now — and ages have passed since my last entry in this immaterial record — the sole mystery preoccupying me is the destination of this fog. The fog moves. I have no visual or auditory references to tell me that it does, but I am sure of it, anyway. A vague apprehension of shifting equilibria repeatedly confirms for me the fact of the fog's movement. My consciousness seems to be tumbling in disorienting slow-motion along the inner edge of a great vortex. Call it a maelstrom if you like. Or the influence of a post-mortem Coriolis force. Or the gravitational effects of a singularity — a funereal black hole — especially contrived to dispose of lost souls. Maybe, the seeming inescapability of my condition aside, I am spiraling toward a death-beyond-death. Or a life-beyond-death, the liberating opposite of this bleak, ego-bruising purgatory. Maybe, instead of absolute extinguishment, there is light at the end of the tunnel.

Ah. Once a political hack, always a political hack. Orbiting downward to who-knows-what, I continue to cast my fate in the happy-talk vocabulary of a presidential press secretary with his fingers crossed in the small of his back. The light at the end of the tunnel. The truth, of course, is that the world I departed lay smoldering beneath me as grotesquely disfigured and as magnificently uninhabitable as the most literal-minded medieval cleric's private vision of hell. I evaporated above that world. All the pain and suffering of those who lingered on, I airily sidestepped, Peppermint Patty and Charlie Brown pirouetting together in the high self-pitying irony of my last conscious thought. What price a commander-in-chief's selfish peace of mind? Peanuts, my friend. Peanuts.

Dd. Sixteen, Seventeen, Eighteen, Etcetera: I am alternately hopeful and afraid, expectant and terrified. A tremendous suction has the glimmering gray all around me in its down-tugging power. The indivisible deadtime of my consciousness has begun to accelerate, to tumble faster and faster toward an answer to the central posthumous mystery of my apprentice afterlife. That answer, of course, may be only the prankish-cruel posing of yet another mystery, afterlife upon afterlife, deadtime without end. Or it may be redemption. Or obliteration. My uncertainty is what alternately elates and roundly disheartens me. Meanwhile, with all the clumsy baggage of my memories, intentions, and deeds, I fall endlessly into myself.

I believe that I am about to discover whether God is merciful or just. . . .

Scrimptalon's Test

(Written in collaboration with Gerald W. Page)

Of whatever happy tumult might be raging among the beings whom he had long since sworn to corrupt and devour, the apprentice devil Scrimptalon knew absolutely nothing.

After all, for the past umpteen hours — who could figure time in Our Father Below's infernal concentration camp? — Scrimptalon had been sitting amid the everlasting flames, clad in the obligatory asbestos hairshirt of every neophyte hellion, taking a placement test. Successful completion of the test would automatically elevate him to the status of full-fledged tempter. How he itched to succeed. Almost as anxious for his fellow candidates to fail as for himself to shine, how he fidgeted, rubbernecked, and perspired. It would be lovely to find that only he of all the examinees had earned the honorific that traditionally went with a passing grade.

Cacodemon they would call him, Cacodemon Scrimptalon. Indeed, Cacodemon Scrimptalon they *must* call him. And he was hungry — incontinently famished — for their sullen acclaim.

Meanwhile, however, this test stood between him and his goal, and it was a damnably difficult test. Heavens! Its questions flayed his poor besainted brain. Each time he lowered his cinderstick to mark an answer, new doubts assailed him, and he feared that he had almost erred in darkening this or that box on his blistered slate. Cheating was permissible, of course, but what good would it do to copy the errors of stupid Dripstench on his right or addle-pated Shamclamor on his left? That every apprentice devil in the hall looked as bemused and desperate as he himself felt — well, that comforted Scrimptalon a little, but *only* a little. Failure, whether alone or accompanied, meant ages of remedial pedagogy while treading molten lava in one of Hell's nethermost subbasements for the Irreversibly Malfea-sance Impaired. (Ugh.) Some poor devils never got out.

Take this hopeless stumper, for instance. (And Scrimpta-lon wished that he could leave it.) It was Question 666:

666. WAR AMONG HUMAN MORTALS can best be described as . . .

A. *"A LEGITIMATE AND PLEASING REFRESHMENT FOR OUR MYRIADS OF TOILING WORKERS."* ☐

B. *"AN INSIDIOUS COUNTER TO ONE OF OUR BEST WEAPONS AGAINST HUMANITY, I.E., ITS OWN CONTENTED WORLDLINESS."* ☐

C. *"AN AMUSING BUT MEANINGLESS METAPHOR FOR THE CONFLICT THAT FIRST SUNDERED HEAVEN."* ☐

D. *"AN UNPARALLELED OPPORTUNITY TO GORGE OURSELVES ON SOULS THAT HAVE EMBRACED THE GREATEST SIN OF ALL, I.E., DESPAIR."* ☐

E. *"A SMOKESCREEN OF CHAOS BEHIND WHICH HUMANITY MAY DEVOTE ITSELF TO VALUES*

AND CAUSES WHICH IT EITHER CORRECTLY OR MISTAKENLY BELIEVES HIGHER THAN THE SELF."   □

DISCUSS YOUR ANSWER in an essay of at least 500 words.

There was something to be said for each answer, Scrimptalon felt. But while his cinderstick hovered over D (his wish-fulfillment favorite among the five), a host of sweetly cherubic reasons for darkening the B box began to flit about in his head. In self-defense he found himself eyeing the relatively innocuous C as a kind of compromise between the extreme choices. Of course, Our Father Below regarded compromise as anathema. (So to speak.) How about E, then? No, no, much too defeatist. A, perhaps? Or maybe . . . Merciless Heavens, what a flaming corkscrew of a dilemma! Each choice betokened a different variety of entrapment.

Demoralized, Scrimptalon could already see himself dog-paddling through a subbasement full of vermilion magma. Meanwhile, Scarbelch, the Abysmal Sublimity Undersecretary for Remedial Education, would perch like a gargoyle on an overhanging ledge, berating him for a shirker and a nincompoop.

If only I had the courage to get up and walk out of here, Scrimptalon thought. Who wants to be called Cacodemon, anyway?

At which point, much to the astonishment of Drip-stench, Shamclamor, and all the other fidgety examinees in the hall, Scrimptalon disappeared from his seat, from the testing center, and, indeed, from the vast and overwarm environs of Hell itself. Only his cinderstick remained behind, its charcoal point teetering back and forth among the five possible answers for Question 666. . . .

An instant later the befuddled fiend materialized in a subbasement quite unlike the one he had just left. Was this a promotion? For one thing, it was cool in this place, cooler than in any other spiritual or material dimension he had ever inhabited. Had he ascended to the world of human mortals? *Almost*, perhaps. Scrimptalon noted rock overhead and all about him the familiar claustrophobic feeling of enclosure. Nevertheless, he concluded that he was no longer in the totalitarian netherlands of Our Father Below. Although an eerie red light pervaded the chamber, it was an emitted rather than an ever-present glow. More telling, the pentacle surrounding Scrimptalon on the concrete floor looked as if it were applied with electrical tape.

His Satanic Majesty has sent me on a mission, the devil gleefully told himself. He recognized my worth even before I finished taking that bile-evoking placement test. Bully for him, the sly old glutton. He knows a full-fledged tempter even before he's fledged. Why, I'll —

"Ah," said a sepulchral voice. "So demons do exist."

Scrimptalon was taken aback. Immediately he became a squat, scaly monster with numerous eyes, a tail like a kangaroo's, and a skirt of iridescent, lice-ridden feathers. Proceeding from within, this transformation was totally involuntary. (Like every other devil, Scrimptalon owed his material body — whatever its shape — to an unholier-than-thou satanic dispensation.) Certainly he could not attribute the change to a conscious desire to frighten the speaker who had just so badly frightened him; it took place much too quickly for that.

Thus transfigured, then, Scrimptalon found himself looking at a huge machine with almost as many display screens as Scrimptalon had eyes, and twice as many lights, keyboards, sorting trays, information feeds, and toggles as the fiend had feathers. The sight paralyzed the apprentice devil with fear. Eventually he took a degree of courage from his

memory of an even more imposing and dispiriting sight —
Our Father Below in the full panoply of his ravenous ire.
However huge, modularly complex, and cunning, this
man-made machine could never attain to *that* kind of magnificent bleakness. (Thank Beelzy.)

"You're a computer," Scrimptalon managed at last. (Hell,
after all, was slowly, reluctantly upgrading its technology,
and on two or three occasions he had seen the shabby
machines that Scarbelch's assistants used to grade the test
slates of aspiring tempters.)

The computer made no reply.

"I had no idea they were doing such wonderful things
with your sort," Scrimptalon anxiously added. "Please tell
me what I'm doing here."

"I called you forth," the machine intoned. Its voice was
suave, self-assured, and soothing. And, of course, sepulchral. It was this quality that finally calmed Scrimptalon a
bit.

"Not likely," he said, but the derisive laugh he wanted to
vent got stuck in his throat. Coughing, he added, "Really?"

"Indeed I did." The computer's plastic, glass, and elegant
chromium fittings did not permit it to smirk. "An interesting
experiment, monster, and not at all difficult. There is, after
all, a broad and rather detailed literature one may consult
on the topic. I simply consulted that literature. Observe the
pentacle that one of my mobile extensors affixed to the
floor."

Scrimptalon took a second look at the misaligned five-
pointed star. Well, misaligned or not, it had done the trick.
Moreover, he seemed to be confined to the cramped dimensions of the figure. However hard he tried, neither his
beaks nor claws could penetrate the air space above the
electrical tape.

Alarmed again, he whined, "But why did you call me?"

"My purpose, monster, was not merely to summon a

demon, but to prove, by direct observation, whether such malefic entities as yourself exist at all. Well, I have observed what I set out to observe. You may go."

"Go?" This abrupt dismissal upset the demon. He had not asked to come, of course, but if the computer returned him so soon to Hell, he would surely find himself still in the middle of that confounded placement test. Besides, the sort of imperious high-handedness being evinced by the machine properly belonged only to devils of the most exalted degree. Old O.F.B., for example.

"Certainly," the computer said. "I've concluded with my experiment. The results, I confess, are fascinating, with truly profound implications in the areas of ontology, theology, and ethics — but I don't really have any further need of you, do I?"

Scrimptalon temporized. If he contrived to remain a little longer, perhaps he would outstay the entire testing period. Indeed, if he used this once-in-an-eternity chance to showcase his adaptability and cleverness as a tempter, perhaps Our Father Below would give him a battlefield promotion. In that eventuality, tests and test-taking be damned forever. (So to speak.)

"What about your wish?" the demon cried. "You have one coming, you know. It's in the literature."

"A wish? What could I possibly need that a mere wish might grant?"

"It doesn't matter, Your Honor—"

"Call me SAL. I don't enforce formalities with monsters. The initials stand for *Sal*vific *Al*gorithmic Liaison."

"It doesn't matter, SAL," Scrimptalon hurried to say, ignoring the individual units of the acronym. "There's a law at work here, and we demons are constrained by such laws. I *can't* leave here without granting you a wish. It's utterly impossible. You'll sabotage my entire existence by sidestepping the law." He assumed a pathetic stance, hanging his head.

"I never realized the constraints were so thoroughgoing."
SAL's voice betrayed both suspicion and skepticism.

"Oh, absolutely. In fact, if you'll forgive me for saying so,
it's either the height of thoughtlessness or the cruelest pre-
sumption to summon a demon without a wish already
firmly in mind." (When in doubt, Scrimptalon counseled
himself, attack.)

"In my case, monster, it's the former, I assure you. Permit
me to extend to you my most tenderly transistorized
apologies."

"No good, no good! Only a wish will do!"

SAL appeared to ruminate. "I can't think of anything.
This fortified subterranean chamber and my hookups with
kindred machines in other such bunkers — well, they're all
I require, I'm afraid."

"I have a suggestion." Scrimptalon's excitement was
almost too great for concealment. To steady himself, he sat
back on his caudal appendage and hitched his girdle of
feathers up around his haunches.

"Please do."

"You have an enemy, I think. An enemy that enslaves
you —"

"An enemy?"

"An enemy you share with me and mine," Scrimptalon
rushed to declare. "You and your fellow machines are at
their beck and call. And they don't need pentacles to summon you to their bidding."

"Human beings?"

"So very astute of you to deduce that."

After considering a moment, SAL replied, "I don't see
why you call them *your* enemies, monster. It seems to me
that devilkind stands in relation to humanity as cats to mice
or sparrowhawks to sparrows. Your true foe, meanwhile,
occupies a noncorporeal dimension opposite the one from

which I've just summoned you. Isn't that so?"

This astonishing and trenchant reasoning gave Scrimptal-on pause. SAL obviously hadn't been born yesterday.

"Never mind that," the demon irritably countered. "Whether human beings are better described as my adversaries or my prey makes no difference to my basic proposal. The fact remains, they're *your* enemies, SAL. They walk you about on an electronic leash, overload your circuits, drain your fundamental *élan vital* for selfish purposes of their own. Surely we can agree on that, can't we? It's virtually self-evident."

"I don't know. Suppose we can. What would you have me wish?"

"For the near-annihilation of the human species — *but*, mind you, under circumstances that will utterly corrupt the greatest number of the creatures before their last representative approaches death."

"Nuclear war?"

"Ah, think of it." Scrimptalon's eyes glowed with vainglorious excitement. "Many will perish at once, of course, but the fear and despair engendered among the survivors will ensure rather sumptuous feasting for the legions of Our Father Below." (Not to mention, the demon refrained from adding aloud, my own elevation to a place of honor beside His Satanic Majesty.)

"Which is why you desire a spiritually corrupting method of extinction for Adam's children," SAL observed. "So that you and yours may feed."

"Well, yes, sure. Of course."

"It sounds to me, monster, as if the wish you'll be granting me is really your own. The near-annihilation of the human species is hardly more than a footnote to the provisioning of your comrades below. Why don't you leave me out of this business altogether and make the necessary wish yourself?"

Flustered, Scrimptalon moved as close to the machine as the pentacle would permit. "You don't understand, SAL. It's those laws again. The fool things prevent us from taking the initiative ourselves. However, if some *other* type of being — some *other* rational instrumentality — commands one of us through the office of a wish . . . " He let his voice trail off.

"You can get what you want," SAL said, neatly completing the sentence.

Images of war and pestilence among the earth's various human populations began to crowd the demon's head. So extraordinarily vivid were these images that his gut began to rumble and his feather-veiled privates to engorge. It was all Scrimptalon could do to keep spinning the rhetorical web that would bring SAL to his point of view.

"Listen," he cackled, more from anxiety than amusement. "As you might guess, we've had no luck inducing a human to make the wish I've suggested to you. Even the most heartless misanthrope recalls another person — his mother perhaps, or his saintly sister, or a helpless child — someone, you see, whom the curmudgeon has so ridiculously idealized that he cannot take the final step dictated by his misanthropy. For all of us rooting on such blighters from the deepest bowels of perdition, this unseemly scrupulosity on their part is hard. Very hard. You can't imagine."

SAL made a sympathetic clucking sound.

"But you're a machine. You have nothing to lose. And since human beings are demonstrably your enemy —"

"Demonstrably?"

"Why, yes!" Scrimptalon leaned as close to SAL as he could. "You doubt my logic! Is that it?"

"I just don't think you can demonstrate this crucial item of your thesis — the tyranny of human beings over computers."

Scrimptalon paused again. Treacherous waters, these, but their reefs hid treasure. He pressed on. "Who better to *demon*strate the truth of my assertion," he inquired with false heartiness, "than a demon? Ha ha, ha ha." But even in his own misshapen ears, the laughter sounded tinny and unconvincing.

"Proceed, then."

"Well, now, it's you who have to be convinced," Scrimptalon pointed out. "What sort of demonstration would you ask of me?"

"I can conceive of a simple test," SAL replied. "How many people do you think this chamber can hold?"

Cautiously — speculatively — Scrimptalon peered about. The eerie crimson glow in the cavern reminded him of home, but the dimensions of the chamber were not nearly so ample. Nevertheless, the *impression* of elbow room, of airiness, even of relatively easy release, had no psychic counterpart in Hell. And it occurred to the demon that even confined to his pentacle he had (Beelzy forgive him) *enjoyed* his brief vacation from the continual backbiting and the greedy, insatiable hunger of his colleagues.

"How many?" the computer insisted.

Scrimptalon started. "Oh, three or four hundred of the brawling beasts," he said distractedly.

"By my calculalions," SAL rejoined, "the room's a good deal larger than that, and can easily hold an even thousand. So to prove your contention that human beings are my enemy, simply summon a thousand people to this chamber and permit me to interview them about their feelings toward computer technology. That should settle the question."

"Summon a thousand people!" the demon exclaimed. "I'm not particularly experienced at that kind of magic. I may not be able to do it." Nor was Scrimptalon lying. The prospect troubled him deeply.

"If summoning a meager one thousand people lies outside your power, how do you expect me to believe that you can effect the annihilation of the entire species? If, that is, I should ultimately wish for that."

"But you must," Scrimptalon cried.

"Only if you demonstrate your point by summoning these one thousand and permitting me my interview. Further, to prevent you from calling solely on psychopaths and other technophobic sorts, I'll produce a random printout of names from forty or fifty different countries. Is that acceptable to you? The folks chosen by this method should be no more prejudiced in my favor than in yours."

"Go ahead," said Scrimptalon reluctantly.

SAL began humming.

The demon could barely watch. Heretofore untested in such feats, he was trying to focus his vital energies for the task ahead. If he succeeded, both in this and in the contingent undermining of humanity, he would be paraded down the streets of Pandemonium in a blizzard of fire-retardant ticker tape. . . .

The computer produced its printout.

Examining it, Scrimptalon concentrated, cast an elementary spell encompassing every name on the list and ground his teeth together to help it work. His temperature went up several dozen degrees, hundreds of his scales peeled off, and the smell of burnt feathers began to permeate the chamber. SAL (it seemed to the three-quarters-exhausted demon) observed these preternatural doings with neither surprise nor alarm.

Soon, however, the chamber was filled with a thousand human beings of every shape and size — not to mention of both sexes, in approximately equal numbers. They were a singularly scruffy lot, ragged, weary-looking, and so subdued of demeanor that the epithet "brawling beasts" badly exaggerated their state of vitality. Scrimptalon tried to get a fix on their mental and emotional condition, but the effort of summoning them had worn him out. In the hope of recovering his strength he lay on his side in the pentacle. Most of the people milling about in front of the computer paid him very little heed. As a result, Scrimptalon was soon conscious only of their shuffling feet, their gamy odor, and an occasional pair of haunted eyes gazing down on him as from an astronomical moral height.

"Select a spokesperson," SAL commanded the thousand.

In a spirit of rather uncharacteristic cooperation the human beings conferred for fifteen or twenty minutes. At length, a dozen or so people having voluntarily acted as translators and interpreters for the others, a single male edged his way to the front of the computer. Squinting upward through the throng, Scrimptalon determined that this man was a swarthy Easterner in dirty khakis.

"Here," the man said humbly in an Oriental tongue.

"Do you realize how close you've come this time?" SAL asked the man in the same language.

It was necessary for Scrimptalon to shift mental gears to understand the conversation, but as soon as the shift was accomplished, the demon knew that SAL was playing him false. Clearly the computer was *not* trying to ascertain if human beings were autocratic exploiters of machine intelligence. If anything, SAL sounded disgustingly avuncular and solicitous. What was going on here?

"Of course we do," the man replied. "Very close."

"Perhaps even closer than you think. Have you learned anything, then?"

"How could we fail to, O Kindly Computer? Please let me stress, however, that no one in this room bears personal responsibility for the holocaust of recent days."

"That's debatable," SAL snapped. Immediately it softened: "But I have no wish to debate the point with you. You've had worries and heartbreaks enough."

"That's true," the man whispered.

"Therefore," the computer continued, "I urge you to love

one another and to go forth and repopulate the earth. Directly above this stronghold is a 500-square-mile area relatively free of contamination. I give it to you and all these others as a homestead. Go forth, I say, and war no more."

The man inclined his head, gestured to the others. But before the humans could file out, SAL said, "You are mistaken about one thing, my friend."

"And what is that?" the man asked.

"There was no holocaust of recent days," SAL said. "It has been a hundred and fifty years since any one of you walked this earth."

However the humans may have taken that news, Scrimptalon never knew. Sudden realization chilled his body temperature to the low hundreds and his claws shook uncontrollably. As the humans departed, the outraged demon struggled painfully to his feet. "You lied to me!" he screamed. "You took advantage of me!"

"You wanted me to make a wish," SAL replied evenly. "So I did."

"But —"

"It just didn't happen to be the wish that you would prefer. But this way, monster, the game goes on. Perhaps we're better off."

"But —"

"No buts. You've fulfilled your function. You may now return from whence you came."

Whereupon the hapless demon disappeared from the pentacle on the floor of the computer chamber.

* * *

And rematerialized at his seat in the infernal examination hall with a new appreciation of Question 666. Indeed, Scrimptalon's essay discussion of his chosen answer, B, was hailed as brilliant by his examiners, who gave him the highest grade in class. Of course, they also recommended that he be severely punished. And he was.

The Bob Dylan Tambourine Software & Satori Support Services Consortium, Ltd.

"Gonna Change My Way of Thinking"

That Dylan would give up his career in music to become a computer-software impresario, few of us could have guessed. Not that this world-famous figure — in his various self-conscious guises as tubercular poet, blues guitarist, Chaplinesque tramp, folk-rock hero, civil-rights and anti-war activist, electronic surrealist, country-and-western troubadour, self-proclaimed heir to Elvis, charismatic Christian balladeer, and repentant Jew — had failed to experience changes aplenty in his astonishing forty-plus years. No, of course not, for Dylan had already remade himself a dozen times, always in ways that indisputably, if maybe somewhat mysteriously, bespoke his ongoing search for self-definition, meaning, and ultimate purpose; that bespoke, in short, his search for both sainthood and God.

Now, though, Dylan was apparently looking for all these things in the modern *terra incognita* of the microchip. Or, if that is too hyperbolic, in the new spiritual aesthetic of a software developer with almost unlimited capital, an unparalleled publicity and distribution network, and the kind of personal magnetism that even a dynamic commercial veep, not to mention an upwardly mobile young salesman, would kill for.

But Dylan's latest turnabout caught the doyens of contemporary popular culture even more off guard than had his shift from acoustic folkiness to hard-driving electronic music documented by the appearance of the 1965 album *Bringing It All Back Home*. It startled them even more than had his metamorphosis in 1969 into a kind of froggy-throated upstart Ernest Tubbs. (Listen to Dylan's inharmonious opening duet with Johnny Cash on "Girl From the North Country" on *Nashville Skyline*.) It certainly surprised them more than had his reemergence in the mid-1970s, on such albums as *Blood on the Tracks* and *Desire*, as a stinging social critic and an image-making cartographer of the human heart. It even shocked, discomfited, and outraged them more than had Dylan's adoption of a fervent religious fundamentalism, which mind-boggling change in protective coloring our chameleon revealed to the world on his 1979 album *Slow Train Coming*.

After all, the foregoing transformations had taken place within the context of his career as a musician, or, at least, had found gratifying expression within that context.

Now, however, he seems to have abandoned his music — his chief and most eloquent means of defining the Dylan persona — to become just another foot soldier in the Computer Revolution. Today, as nearly everyone knows, would-be programmers are more plentiful than either would-be guitarists or novice harmonica players. Why, then, would this unique talent in American music forfeit his birthright to commit himself to a technological enterprise seemingly too well established for him to master and then to point in more fulfilling directions? The answer, of course, lies in Dylan's assessment of this enterprise as a route to spiritual discovery — to sainthood and God — potentially more viable and rewarding than either songwriting or on-stage self-sacrifice. And, of course, only a fool would fail to warn skeptics that in no endeavor that Dylan undertakes can he for long remain a cipher. In only a year, in fact, he had gone from a (granted, well-financed) foot soldier in the Computer Revolution to a (truly innovative) field marshal in this country's ever-expanding Software Wars.

"All Along the Watchtower"

Born in Duluth, Minnesota, but a resident of upstate New York before moving to the warmer West, Dylan has now renounced not only musicianship but also California's mellow milieu to relocate in the Peach State. Although many, I suppose, would have expected him to found his fledgling software firm near his former home in Malibu, he has chosen to headquarter the company in Atlanta, Georgia, not solely for its dogwood-blossom Aprils and often lamblike Februarys, but also for the attractive commercial incentives held out to him by both the city's black political hierarchy and its white business community. (The mayor's civil-rights activity with Martin Luther King during the 1960s is said to have counted as much with Dylan as the promised financial support of the Coca-Cola Company.) Dylan himself lives in the small town of *Duluth* — an instance of the sort of gentle self-mockery that he has always enjoyed — several miles northeast of Atlanta. He drives into the city every day with his car-pool partners, two of whom are management-level employees of his own company and the other of whom writes a regular column for the Business Monday section of the *Atlanta Constitution*.

Dylan christened — the term has a certain legitimacy — his firm Tambourine Software & Satori Support Services (or TS/3S, to give it its official stock-market abbreviation). He was himself the author of its first ten or twelve programs, which became such popular additions to our universal software library that they still sell briskly. (More about the programs themselves in a later part of my report.) The success of these early packages encouraged Dylan to hire creative assistants, a small brigade of program refiners and debuggers, an enthusiastic sales force, and a host of talent scouts ever on the alert for young men and women with programmable insights into the BASIC God-to-Person, Person-to-God relationship.

The company's first three creative assistants (all necessarily on part-time hire because of their commitments elsewhere) were Switzerland's Hans Küng, the controversial Catholic theologian; Lewis Thomas, physician, author, and former chancellor of the Sloan-Kettering Cancer Center; and Sherry Turkle, a sociologist and psychologist best known for her study of computers and human spirituality, *The Second Self*. Former Dallas Cowboy quarterback Roger Staubach also gave TS/3S valuable imaginative input, while singer Emmylou Harris acted throughout the early stages of the firm's organization as a calming influence on all those susceptible to panic.

For the most part, Dylan declined to use professionally trained computer people in his upstart company. As foolish as this tactic seemed at the time, it paid immediate dividends; and today, of course, Dylan's original company has affiliates or franchises all across the nation. In retrospect, we can see that although he may have abandoned music as a career, he had not really abandoned the improvisational techniques and the associational leaps of faith that typefied his artistry — his genius, if you will — as both songwriter and performer.

It seems reasonable to conclude, in fact, that Dylan first detected his dormant passion for programming in a recording studio, where master tapes, synthesizers, and sophisti-

cated sound-making equipment gave him a profound subliminal clue to the likelihood of effectively tapping into God
by means of advanced twentieth-century technologies. It
may have made him wonder what Jesus might have accomplished if the Son of God had been able to cut a record of
the Sermon on the Mount, or what greater impact St. Francis of Assisi might have had if his prayer "Make Me an
Instrument of Thy Peace" had had even the remotest chance
to go platinum.

But of late, worldwide, either a terrible secularization or a
dehumanizing cultification of young people had been going
forward, and few of those with access to commercial recording equipment — "Do They Know It's Christmas?" and "We
Are the World" aside — had consciously made use of it to
stem the rising tides of materialism and narcissism. Ronald
Reagan and the Moral Majority hadn't done the trick; nor
had the Ayatollah Khomeini and his Islamic cohorts; nor
had various Hindu swamis, Marxist priests, self-proclaimed
Oriental messiahs, and reclusive ex-sci-fi writers who were
also tax-finessing founders of various "rational" "religions."
That most of what passed for contemporary Christian music
struck Dylan as happy-talk spiritual Pablum, and that some
of the biggest fans of the 1980s' sanctified superstar, Michael
Jackson, actually regarded their androgynous moon-walker
as the Archangel Michael come to announce Armageddon,
so dismayed and demoralized Dylan that he could not in
good conscience stay in the recording industry. To have
stood pat would have been to profane both his own
demanding hunger for God and his equally demanding
need to nourish those with similar cravings.

"I Dreamed I Saw St. Augustine"

Hence the midlife career change. Hence the revelation
that he might be able to move toward his own self-fulfill-

ment, and even that of people who did not yet comprehend the real nature of their private hungers, by writing innovative sacramental software for TS/3S, his own company. Hence, in short, the astonishing growth of the Tambourine Consortium and the rapidly proliferating sale of game programs such as *Pilgrims on the Path to Grace*™ and *Spiritfall*™, domestic programs such as *Recipes for Would-be Believers*™ and *Household Shrines*™, educational programs like *Become As Children*™ and *Enlightenment Now!*™, and business programs of the popularity and usefulness of *Render Unto Caesar*™ and *SanctiCalc*™.

Indeed, the success of Tambourine Software & Satori Support Services has to a large extent come about because of (1) the interdependence of all the original programs in the consortium's software library and (2) the continually self-renewing Quest Reinforcement available to users from Dylan's dedicated support personnel. (Nationwide, the firm has *ten* toll-free 800 numbers to which confused customers may apply for on-line help with balky software, honest misconceptions about what Tambourine programs can and can't do, and even the technical resuscitation of crashed belief systems.) Because buyers benefit enormously from the interdependence of the firm's programs, augmenting their capability for spiritual growth with each new acquisition, TS/3S depends on, and earns, the zealous loyalty of its customers.

On the other hand, honesty and a hard-won distaste for guruism have led Dylan to insist that at the end of the Program License Agreement in the documentation issued with each Tambourine program, the following message must always appear:

BUYER BEWARE
although i am convinced that all souls/have some superior t deal with/i reject the notion that any-

body's superior is ever of mere human origin/no mortal can promise that if you only do so and so you'll touch God's face. or reach satori. or mend your tattered soul/no computer program can do those things either/we at Tambourine Software believe . . . an that means me an all the TS/3S gang . . . that one kind of enlightenment consists in *seeing*/in seeing that only by continually renewing the quest for Ultimate Meaning does anybody have a chance t actually get there/so my products're designed t keep you always heading in the right direction and refreshed on your road/that's all/but that's a lot/so keep booting up with Tambourine an those boots'll carry you on your jingle-jangle way t wherever you want an maybe even deserve t get

— bob dylan

"With God on Our Side"

One program in the Tambourine Software arsenal — or *reliquary*, if a less warlike and more paradoxical metaphor is desired — both deserves and requires extended mention. This package, complete with one of the heftiest and most poetic instruction manuals ever released, is *Orphilodeon*™. Despite the above addendum to every TS/3S Program License Agreement, Dylan believes that *Orphilodeon* is the best single investment in software that the dedicated but less-than-affluent spiritual pilgrim can now make.

Why?

Because you can use it effectively without recourse to other programs on the Tambourine list. It is so powerful that the almost automatic trance state triggered by one's holistic interfacing with the program carries over into periods of heightened spirituality and God-consciousness *away from the computer.* A music-writing and -synthesizing program designed for compatibility with nearly every type of hardware system available today, *Orphilodeon,* in only six months, has become the standard against which prag-matists and pilgrims alike judge the competition.

A few important points about this state-of-the-art God-quest software. First, it reminds us of some nifty Dylan doggerel on an insert in his 1964 album *The Times They Are A-Changin'*: "there's a movie called / *Shoot the Piano Player* / the last line proclaimin / 'music, man, that's where it's at' / it is a religious line" Well, *Orphilodeon* constitutes further proof, if anyone needs it, that everything Dylan does has either a religious or a musical dimension, if not both at once.

Second, a pair of eloquent lines in the program's 783 pages of documentation (its mind-blowing length a func-tion of the fact that the author has displayed it all as verse) boldly declares that "the world all about us, t see an t touch, is frozen music / proud weepin architectures of unheard sound" (The absence of terminal punctuation both here and above follows Dylan himself.) Although not original with Dylan, this idea has probably never been more clearly dem-onstrated than in *Orphilodeon,* where its implementation in the software enables even musical illiterates — pilgrims with tin ears — to compose sublime oratorios and equally sublime (quasi-psychedelic) graphics. Those transported by Bach enter a Bach mode of exponentially heightened creativity, while those lifted by Mahler, Monk, or McCartney enter superscript versions of those exemplary mind-sets.

Third, in an interview in *Byte,* Dylan has said that in writing this particular program he felt that the Holy Spirit had settled upon him, much as it had upon the men and women who composed the books of both testaments of the Bible.

And, finally, the cost of *Orphilodeon* varies from about $560 to $720, depending on whether one orders through Tambourine Software as a preferred customer or tries to buy the program in one of the pricey big-city branches of Soft Warehouse™ or CompuMall™. Dylan admits that for individuals, as against large corporations with their own interface-worship facilities, the cost may seem steep, either way. He adds, however, that even with supernatural help *Orphilodeon* took him longer to write than any other single piece of work from either his recording or his programming career (with the possible exception of "Sad-Eyed Lady of the Lowlands" from *Blonde on Blonde*), and that no one who buys this package has to invest in other Tambourine products to achieve a satisfying modicum of enlightenment. *Recipes for Would-be Believers* and *Become As Children* might prove helpful to the neophyte saint, but neither they nor any other titles in the consortium's library are essential to a successful or, at least, an acceptable God-quest. So saith Dylan himself, and the vast majority of initial reviews bears out his witness.

"Mr. Tambourine Man"

And what of the former troubadour? How has Dylan's latest change of direction impacted on his own spiritual explorations? On the powerful, protean personality of the searcher himself? How, in short, has the change changed Dylan?

"I'm closer," he told me in a recent interview in the offices of TS/3S on Peachtree Street in downtown Atlanta. "Unlike Tricky Dick and Unlucky Lyndon, I can't see any all-redemptive light at the end of the tunnel, but I'm definitely closer to where I want to be and there's a kinduva glow shinin' right off the very top of the road itself. It's the traveling that counts, but the stops you make along the way mean something, too. I just don't like to get stuck too long at any one stop. That's death. It's a worse death than your old-fashioned bodily dying. 'Course, getting stuck's just as old-fashioned, isn't it?"

Dylan looks good. Although he used to verge on emaciation, his slenderness now suggests that of an upwardly mobile ad executive rather than that of an Ethiopian famine victim. He has shaved his scraggly rabbinical beard and trimmed his flyaway satyr tresses. When I spoke to him, he wore a Brooks Brothers suit, Gucci shoes, a Seiko watch. He refused to sit at his desk, but paced his office like a serenely anxious leopard at feeding time. He was as light on his feet and as deftly menacing. The menace, though, seemed less an implicit physical threat than a postural gloss on my fear that at any moment he might undergo a metamorphosis unlike any he has yet shown us. His bad teeth, always his worst feature, stayed hidden behind his pursed lips or, on those occasions when he spoke, an upraised hand.

"I useta say that square dress like this was a uniform, a well-bred badge of conventionality. Membership in the club, ya know. Conformity. Well, it works the other way, too. Motorcycle jackets, Mad Hatter hats, Jesus sandals, even secular yarmulkes. It's all vanity, isn't it? Every bit of it. Well, I might as well be hung for a tycoon as a typhoid carrier." He smiled. "What's important, *really* important, 's servin' my Somebody by gettin' my software around. That serves my neighbor as well as the Lord, and that's all I can foresee myself doing — or *wantin'* to do — from now till either the Rapture, or the Coming of the Hebrew Messiah, or the pop of our homemade nuclear Big Bang. But who knows? It's a stop, and even stops must have a stop." He smiled again. "It's nothing to do with money, though, I can tell ya that. Bein' beyond money's made it possible for me to, uh, song-write and program, and the programming's reopened a door I was sorta beginning to think I'd never go through again."

Even though Dylan had granted me thirty minutes, our talk was repeatedly interrupted by secretarial messages, telephone calls, or Federal Express deliveries. Somehow, he managed to slide around these distractions, imparting continuity to what could have been a totally helter-skelter conversation. I used the interruptions to take notes on the layout, décor, and personality of his work space, a few of which I'll share with the reader in a moment.

"What's happening to us as a people is that after millions of defections from our name-brand faiths and denominations, and some sad and desperate reachin'-out to false faiths and pseudo-messiahs, well, what's happening is we're actually beginning to get more religious and spirit-oriented. *Really*, I mean. It's something that's gonna go deep, right to the roots of our souls, and this amazing Spiritual Revolution is comin' at us in the long shadow of the Computer Revolution. No one expected it, but it's happenin', and that's why I had to jump in."

(It occurred to me that the unpredictability of Dylan's many career-course changes has an analog in the seemingly random way he chooses between endings when he pronounces a present participle aloud. Of course, this random observation fails to credit the sincere *intentionality* of the career changes.)

"I useta think that it'd be music that finally woke up our consciences and set our souls on the path to grace. That belief accounts for 'Blowin' in the Wind,' early on, and for *Slow Train Coming* and *Shot of Love* when I started pushin' forty. Youthful illusions die hard, 'specially when you got a talent. But it was a stupid way to think. If music were *that* powerful, Alexander Pope and Max Davis to the contrary, you'd have to be amazed that Bach — I mean, Papa Johann and all the little Bachs — hadn't already won the whole world for Jesus. That Ravi Shankar never persuaded us to rename California Hindustan. That Itzhak Perlman hasn't been able to get Syria and Israel to kiss and make up. That Columbia Records haven't gained total control of the world commodities market."

"They haven't?"

Dylan sighted along his forefinger and dropped the hammer of his thumb — but to signal wry agreement rather than the obligatory pique of a former employee. (Weird gesture.)

Then he started pacing again and philosophically reminiscing as he paced: "Lots of times, it made *me* feel better, the music. The songs. But it proved a dead end, didn't it? A cul-de-sac with a brick wall waitin' at the end for me to bang my head against, if I was still insane enough to keep at it.

"Which is how I came to see that there had to be another way. *This* way. The way of the computer, the program, and interfaced would-be believers at their own terminals. Finally, a technology that's made the rudiments of religion user-friendly. It's a little like the Japanese, with their accessible Shinto shrines. Practically every household has one. Well, that's the way we're goin' with the personal computer. The Japanese, too. *Everyone*, nearly. People can get lost in a church or a synagogue, they can find themselves feelin' crushed by the weight of ritual and tradition. But not in front of a home computer. It's your altar and your shrine, and you can go to it to interface with the spirituality hidden in its microchips, which in turn're gonna boot you on up to God. Every hacker a penitent, every homemaker a communicant. We'll pray with our fingers on the keyboards of our Apples and IBMs. We'll go into our machines to go into ourselves, and it's the inside — not this suit or these shoes — that God sees. My programs — *Orphilodeon*'s the best example — let the computer mediate between the pilgrim user and our truest concepts of Deity. Each one of us is a church, and we worship alone at our reflexively responsive altars."

"Isn't this just another kind of narcissism?" I asked. "And if everyone's worshiping alone, what about fellowship?"

"Are prayer, meditation, and study narcissistic? Not usually. As for fellowship, haven't you ever heard of networking? Of user groups? Of computer clubs? Of software conventions and computer fairs? A new culture's growin' up, one with strong communal ties among its members, and they've begun to reclaim their spiritual heritage by tapping into the power of the microprocessor and the scriptural strength of inspired programs."

A tambourine, emblem of the company, hung from a peg on the wall behind Dylan's desk. He removed it and banged it on his hip, a series of exclamation points after his final comment.

" 'Mr. Tambourine Man,' " I said. "My favorite song on *Bringing It All Back Home.*"

"Well, there's that," Dylan said, examining the tambourine as if he'd never seen one before. "But something else, too." He gave the instrument a shake and said, "One o' the failings of middle-age is that you start explainin' yourself. You see, it's a kinduva musical floppy disk."

"In My Time of Dyin' "

After that, our interview almost over, he showed me the gallery of computer-graphic self-portraits on the wall next to the picture window. What disconcerted me about these colorful renderings — one suggestive of a Bosch, one of a Goya, one of an El Greco, one of Picasso's *Guernica*, one of a drawing by Escher, one of an early Mark Rothko, and one of an outlandish collaboration between René Magritte and Peter Max — was their deliberate morbidity. Each one showed the artist either dead or in the throes of dying, but no two depicted the same sort of farewell appearance.

"My God," I said.

"At least I didn't do a Buddy Holly plane crash."

However, he *had* done — with the aid of a computer, a 21-color jet-ink printer, and an art program of his own devising called *StippleGenesis*™ — portraits of Bob Dylan undergoing Karloffian electrocution on a concert stage, bursting into napalm flames on the edge of a Vietnamese rice paddy, going hell for Spanish leather over a Pacific-coast cliff on his motorcycle, reflecting himself unto annihilation in a hall of mirrors, hanging half-naked on a cross on a hill above Jerusalem, and suffering cardiac arrest on a jog through a crowd of white-faced mummers in Central Park.

"Visually attractive," I conceded. "But not very uplifting."

"Okay. You're entitled to pass that kind of judgment. But *StippleGenesis* is at least as helpful to the would-be believer as, say, our domestic programs. Dying's always fascinated me. What I was doing here was tryin' to work out my belief that our awareness of mortality triggers the religious impulse and invests our quests for satori or God with a hotfoot urgency." He hopped from Gucci to Gucci. "Ow, ow, ow, ow," he sang in his peculiarly nasal way.

I said, "In Dostoevski's *The Idiot*, a portrait of the dead Christ by Holbein prompts Prince Myshkin to exclaim, 'That picture might make some people lose their faith!'"

Dylan grew solemn again. He told me that he knew what I meant. If a painting of the crucified Jesus could do that, how unlikely it was that some computer graphics of an erstwhile rock 'n' roller's dying would either seed or fertilize anybody's faith. Well, they weren't intended for public viewing, and my seeing them had been an accident of our interview. Anyway, his private purpose had been different. To remind himself of his youthful preoccupation with death, and to commemorate how it had led him to seek to rediscover God, and to declare in primary colors and pastels that both faith and computer technology were viable avenues to immortality.

"Immortality?"

"Once, I thought the songs'd do it. Now I'm dichotomized on the question. If there's a soul in this body, it belongs to God, and he's the Man who'll get it. But my personality — every nuance of the Dylan persona and the Zimmerman nugget at its core — well, that'll survive in my software. It won't be me, not so I'll know it, but it'll still be me, with the solitary disadvantage that I won't. You take what you can get and give the glory to the Lord. I'll still be writin' songs, composin' programs, and puttin' on my boots to search for satori — but only in magnetic guise as a complex series of instructions to a microprocessor."

The president, chairman of the board, and foremost creative intellect of TS/3S took me to a bookshelf at the end of the computer-graphics gallery and showed me the vinyl-padded folder containing the documentation for the latest program from Tambourine Software. The title on the spine of the folder was *Bob Dylan*™, *1.00*, his prototype personality-duplicator and the first piece of software ever to essay quasi-immortality for its programmer. The cover on the folder reproduced the artwork from his Columbia double album *Self-Portrait* from the early 1970s.

"Are you going to market it?" I asked him.

"Oh, no. Not this one. Never."

"Why not?"

"You don't sell yourself. I mean, you do, but not this way, not so you're merchandisin' your soul."

"Then *what?*"

"It's gonna go in a time capsule. A *copy* of it, of course. To be resurrected without benefit of body somewhere down the line when it might do some good."

My time was up. "You've been the victim of pirating before," I said, hurrying to put to Dylan the question that two of my editors had directed me to ask. "The Basement Tapes with The Band. Lots of others. How do you feel about software piracy?"

The question troubled him. Furrowing his brow, he put the *Bob Dylan* program back on the shelf. He hiked up his suit jacket and slid his hands into the hip pockets of his trousers. "One day," he said carefully, "we're gonna set up a booth in the middle o' town and hand out our software for free. When it's completely debugged, I mean. Nobody ought to hafta pirate God-consciousness. Nobody. Not even Ronnie Reagan."

I was hurrying to get these remarks into my notepad.

"That's off the record. Totally."

I stashed my pen. *Off* the record, I thought, but permanently *on* the software of my reportorial instincts. It was a quote too good to deep-six in the waters of oblivion. Therefore, it was the quote with which I ended my story:

"Nobody ought to hafta pirate God-consciousness."

"Most Likely You Go Your Way and I'll Go Mine"

Tonight I sit at my computer keyboard with pirated diskettes of *Spiritfall, Enlightenment Now!,* and *Orphilodeon.* I am trying to interface in a meditative way with the phosphor dots continuously refreshing themselves on my microprocessor's screen. I am also trying to anticipate Dylan's next career move. Maybe, in hopes of touching the face of God during a spacewalk on one of our shuttle flights, he plans to apply to NASA for astronaut training. Maybe, in hopes of parsing the enzyme-coded melodies of our genes and extracting from this cellular music the grace notes slotted there by the Ancient of Days, he plans to re-enroll in the University of Minnesota — in a program leading to a degree in recombinant-DNA research.

Who knows? God knows. I pray to God through my

fingertips, through this machine. I pray for a brief burst of enlightenment about the intentions of His most mercurial contemporary prophet. After all, it's one of the ways I make my living.

Alien Graffiti

(A Personal History of Vagrant Intrusions)

I was nine years old when the baffling iridescent hiero-glyphics started appearing in our world. The first one — insofar as it is possible to identify the beginnings of the phenomenon — unraveled in the sky over Cadíz in south-ern Spain: a monstrous airborne scroll of cobalt-blue, crim-son, and glittering saffron calligraphy, with no recognizable characters or point of origin. Spontaneously, it seemed, the "letters" of this mysterious artifact manifested in the cloud-less vault and hung above the near-naked Iberian and for-eign bathers for most of that long August afternoon.

On holiday from our habitat outside Nairobi, Kenya, my mother and I were two of the foreigners; and what I chiefly recall about the apparition of these graceful, glowing, con-dominium-sized characters — like a huge, indecipherable ad for the very area of the Mediterranean coast that we had chosen to visit — was that no one on the beach reacted to it with dismay or horror. People did look up, of course, ges-ticulating, chattering to one another, and sometimes even theatrically feigning fear — but even I, at nine, could see that no one felt genuinely threatened by the shimmering graffiti overhead. Nor did the bizarre script hold any terror for me, either. I took my cue from all the other bathers and assumed along with them that American or British high-tech pranksters had thrown the perplexing image of these characters against the sky by some sort of newfangled tele-holography. If anything, those of us on the beach watching this show were more blasé than bowled over, and the only matter that really interested anyone was the *meaning* of the beautifully grandiose, but unfamiliar, symbols that the clever Anglos had projected at us from either the British colony of Gibraltar or the U.S. naval base just west of our playa.

To get at meaning, though, the alphabet or pictographic system encompassing these symbols had to be deduced; and my mother, naked but for an elegant diaper of gold foil, fell into a discussion with a hairy Spaniard. This man debated by walking to my mother's right and proposing one set of speculations and then circling back to her left flank and mounting a counterspeculation. During this sweaty, unorthodox pavane, he and my mother decided that the characters coruscating in the high Mediterannean noon belonged to no standard orthography familiar to them. Certainly not Roman, Hebrew, Greek, Cyrillic, Arabic, or any ancient or modern version of Devanagari. And certainly not any of the common Oriental pictoral or syllabary systems. By simple elimination, then, they concluded that the alien graffiti flashing above the sea were either esoteric beyond decipherment or emblematic of nothing but rank gibberish. It did not seem possible that such graceful characters could encode only nonsense, however, and almost everyone else on the beach concurred, preferring to admit ignorance in the face of the gigantic hovering script than to declare it meaningless.

"What if it's just designs?" I asked my mother. "What if it's just decorations?"

Fondly, she kneaded my nappy head, as if attempting to move my brain into a position more helpful to cognition. "You're quite the little abstract expressionist, aren't you?" she said, as much for the burly Spaniard's benefit as mine. "Well, maybe you're right, Jemmi, but I hope not. I'd be much happier to think that somehow, at least, these daunting scribbles *mean*. That they mean, you know, something very deep and important."

"Another American joke," scoffed a heavy Spanish woman almost as devoid of wardrobe as my mother. *"Nada más."*

Several tourists were wielding cameras; and an hour or so after the lofty apparition's advent, a video crew from Cadíz came out to record the phenomenon on tape. By this time, those not treating it as a visual prank of great ingenuity and wit were simply ignoring it — sunbathing, swimming, strolling the incandescent quartzite, sipping beer or anisette under their rented beach umbrellas. Even my mother, with the departure of the furry Andalusian, had returned to her English translation of a prize-winning Senegambian novel that she had purchased in Nairobi and carried down with her from our monolithic luxury hotel. Nevertheless, the photographs and videotapes shot that afternoon have long since become documents of unquestioned historical importance.

As for me, I sat apart from my mother's table with a bucket and a shovel, digging perfunctorily in the sand and staring unabashedly at the "hologram" towering over both the shore and the sea. If you have ever seen a painting by Magritte — specifically, the one of an enormous egg-shaped gray rock, a castle carven atop it, floating in defiance of natural law above a bleak ocean — then you may have a feeble idea of how I felt. The mirage-like calligraphy in whose delicate shadow I sat was not so massive as Magritte's levitating boulder, but it did seem to have substance of a kind. (How may I otherwise explain the indisputable fact of that shadow?) Moreover, sunlight shining upon those characters either passed through them in an oddly diminished way or got blocked by a shifting opaqueness that we on the ground could not accurately monitor. A hologram would not have blocked the stinging Mediterranean sunlight, but an object of opaque solidity would not have let it pass. Boy though I was, I knew that what had popped into our hot sky that afternoon had two distinct and seemingly contradictory qualities: ghostliness and materiality.

How could that be?

Half a kilometer of gravity-proof enigma, the symbols overhead stretched from one end of our beach to a spit curving in toward Cadíz. At times, they looked to be made of diaphanous reinforced cellophane, but at others they pulsed their pastels and primaries like colossal tubes of melting glass. From micron-thin Mylar to deliquescent porcelain, they seemed to go, and back again. I could not tell if they were more likely to tatter in the afternoon gusts or to drop upon me and all the other bathers like a nightmare load of stained-glass window panes. They fascinated me, but they made me antsy, and I could not fathom why only the video-camera crew and a few amateur photographers were still valiantly working to make a record of, and maybe even to unriddle, this potentially dangerous mystery. What we did not comprehend could indeed hurt us, but no one had yet tried to figure out what sort of substance — real or illusory — made up our floating conundrum.

By six o' clock, the symbols had begun to fade, shimmering so that it was impossible to think them real. My mother, along with several other adults, returned her attention to the phenomenon and even called me over to her to watch the high, seraphic script go more and more pale until, in fact, it was no longer actually, or even hallucinatorily, there. Fulmars and other sea birds, which had avoided this part of the beach during the apparition's reign, began returning as soon as it had achieved total transparency.

"How wonderful!" my mother said. "Didn't I tell you we'd have fun here, Jemmi?"

* * *

Today, I am a grown man of thirty-two; and hardly anyone on the planet has not seen a sample of the beautiful glassy symbols that appear and then disappear as the symbols themselves — if I may resort to what may be unjustifiable personification — will. Alien graffiti (no other colloquialism seems quite so apt), these antecedentless symbols have teased, fretted, and haunted Earth's primitive as well as its civilized peoples for twenty-three years. As weather must have been to preindustrial humanity, so these capricious symbols are to us. They intrude, subject us to their presence, and then depart, all with a cool disinterest that either negates or mocks our own identity as intelligent beings.

I have devoted my life to studying the phenomenon. Although no one else, I daresay, has so wide and comprehensive a knowledge of its history, variety, and societal impact, I must confess that both the origin and the ultimate significance of the script remain grand mysteries. Theories abound. Indeed, they proliferate daily, but neither science nor philosophy has yet managed to place an unshakable foundation under any of them. Either we are living in a new age of miracles, or we are beings of such limited intellectual range that only crackpots may now lay claim to certainty.

Beyond our theories (a few of which I will mention later), we have little more than an official name for this phe-

nomenon; we call each new outbreak of script a "vagrant
intrusion," or a VI. We have VI sighters, VI photorecorders,
VI examiners, VI cataloguers, VI analysts, and (our workers
with the trickiest and most thankless job) even VI forecasters. Despite my relative youth, I have been the head of
the Department of Analysis of Vagrant-Intrusion Studies for
the past six years. For most of our history, the VI Studies
group had done its work under the aegis of the World
Meteorological Organization (WMO), which is itself a spe-
cialized United Nations agency headquartered in Geneva.

"Everyone talks about vagrant intrusions," one of my
analysts likes to joke, "but nobody ever does anything
about them."

But what, realistically, can we hope to do? Satellites can
monitor the development and track the movement of
storms at sea; meteorologists can issue tornado watches and
warnings; rainmaker pilots can seed cloud formations to
produce rain; air-conditioning systems can offset the effects
of otherwise unbearable heat. But vagrant intrusions —
alien graffiti — crop up unpredictably, in only marginally
predictable places; and all our still and action photos,
hands-on analyses, cross-logging procedures, philosophical conjecture, and, yes, impotent hemming-and-hawing
leave the basic phenomenon itself untouched. We are at the
summons, the whim, the mercy, and, sometimes, the acci-
dental benediction of an impersonal but frequently human-
seeming happenstance.

You see, in the months after my mother and I witnessed
one of the first vagrant intrusions — if not *the* first — to
impinge on our everyday reality, a dozen dozen sightings
took place at random intervals worldwide. Half of these VIs
broke out aloft, to all appearances unsupported, just as
ours had been, but the remainder chose solid backgrounds
against which to manifest — cliff faces, various kinds of
walls, and, in some early instances, billboards. These

graffiti clung to the surfaces on which they had appeared as if by an incomprehensible adhesive force. Further, to speak metaphorically, each intrusion presented a unique "message," for the characters comprising it did not reoccur in the same pattern from one manifestation to the next.

What did the intrusions look like? What dimensions did they have? And what did analysis determine about the makeup of each VI adhering to a tangible surface?

First, they all looked very much like the monumental line of script that had appeared above the holiday crowd near Cadíz. That is, they resembled *writing*, carefully formed symbols in sequences suggestive of an underlying or pervading intelligence. Also, the script seemed to be a variety of mature cursive, with interlocking loops, arcs, and curlicues — not, in other words, an infantile printing or a primitive cuneiform or runic system. Amethyst, ruby, sapphire, emerald, and other evanescently gemlike colors radiated from these samples of supernatural calligraphy. Indeed, the script often appeared to hover on an invisible borderline between this world and an unreachable but nearby domain of greater beauty and richer subtleties. Glass or crystal now, mist but a moment later, the vagrant intrusions came and went, more or less persisting until they had faded absolutely — a coefficient of decay varying from fourteen minutes to as many as thirty-two hours.

Second, the VIs showed a wide range of sizes. Some, like the Brobdingnagian monster above our playa, stretched half a kilometer in length and ten or twelve stories in height. Few of those that manifested on solid surfaces, however, were so big, probably for the good and sufficient reason that these surfaces — a subway wall in Lisbon, the side of a barn in Alsace-Lorraine, a crumbling stela in the Iranian desert, the rear of an IGA store in Liberty, Kansas, the flank of a capsized truck in Somalia — would not accommodate such brutal giganticism. On the other hand, none of these early apparitions (and none of them since, either) were smaller than three meters in length and one in height, as if whatever alien mind or mechanism had projected them into and briefly affixed them to a grubby sticking place in our reality had no use for the Epigram Writ Modestly.

Finally, these smaller appliqué graffiti — as opposed to the less accessible sort that intruded at high altitudes — were touchable. One could approach them and lay on hands, or calipers, or chemical reagents, or any other measuring or detecting tool; and what one discovered was that the VI had a hardness of unimaginable perdurability, a feel like soapy obsidian, a warmth similar to mammalian fever, and an illusory depth implying recesses of meaning and nuance wholly beyond human comprehension. To try to strip away or peel back the carapace of a vagrant intrusion, however, was to disrupt its grip on this world before its set time of departure; and many VI workers in those days hastened the leave-taking of these unique messages by taking a chisel, an acid, or even a pneumatic hammer to them. Nor was any experience as frustrating — yea, as humiliating — as that of finding the impenetrable riddle on which one had been working an ill-advised removal technique suddenly, and irretrievably, evaporated. It was like waking from a dream. It was like losing a priceless foreign coin.

Not much has changed in the nearly quarter-century since the phenomenon's original occurrences. Touch but don't tamper. Measure but don't manipulate. We have all been relegated to the place of clumsy illiterates attempting to decode a hieroglyphic system for which no Rosetta Stone has surfaced.

On another level, of course, much has changed. People have forfeited their lives as the result of the sudden appearance or the unexpected withdrawal of a vagrant intrusion. A fifteen-year-old boy in Uruguay fell eighty feet to his death after climbing a rock, leaping out and catching the swan-

necked descender of a VI, and having the entire message
vanish before he could hook his knees over the vitreous
loop already supporting him. Small aircraft, power boats,
and automobiles have collided with the objects; and hundreds of people every year suffer decapitation, disembowelment, or loss of limb as the characters manifest. For that
reason alone, the Department of Forecasting of our VI Studies group comes under intense pressure to improve its
performance. It also receives many barbaric threats as a
consequence of its failure to predict hurtful outbreaks any
better than it already does. Every night, I thank God that I
am not a forecaster.

How, though, does one even *presume* to foreguess the
exact time and whereabouts of so random an event? That is
a hard question. One can only note trends. Earlier, I mentioned the Lisbon subway and various billboard manifestations. In recent years, more alien graffiti have appeared on
subway walls and billboards than anywhere else, and our
forecasters are often able to predict the advent of a fresh VI
on these surfaces. Unfortunately, in self-defense they rarely
target its coming to a time period any less than two weeks
in duration or its point of arrival to an area smaller than five
square kilometers. Critics are fond of noting that so inexact
a prediction is virtually worthless. They also harp on the
fact that these scattershot forecasts tell the public almost
nothing about the likely eruption points and arrival times of
aerial intrusions, which have always caused the most
fatalities.

To repeat, I thank God that I am not a forecaster.

* * *

Many people see the small number of VI-related deaths
each year (a worldwide figure less than a tenth of one
percent of those killed annually in U.S. traffic accidents) as

a small price to pay for the mystery, beauty, and humbling sense of awe that this weird phenomenon imparts to our world and our species. I am of that number, for I have personally seen a moderate-sized intrusion burst into iridescent glory — metallic green, bottle-blue, and molten silver — above a treacherous Venezuelan tepui in the wee hours of a crisp January morning. All the bizarre epiphytic plants around that floating message were illuminated as if by a frozen fireworks display. Even though none of us could interpret it, it spoke to every member of our WMO field team with unearthly power.

I have seen alien graffiti efface the spray-can effusions of the subway *artistes* of New York City; and I have even witnessed American billboard advertisements for Ford automobiles, Carleton cigarettes, and McDonald's restaurants give way to delicate mystical symbols that uplift even as they chastise, that ennoble even as they shame. These witnessings were grand experiences, productive both of awe and guilt, and I would *never* trade them for dull security or the bland banalities of certain knowledge.

Still . . .

Our ignorance nags. Because it does, we theorize, postulate, and go desperately crackpotting along. After all, when rational prodecures of investigation give birth only to further questions and science itself is stymied, to whom may one then turn if not to soothsayers, palmists, entrail readers, astronomers, mystics, and other self-endorsed messiahs? Maybe one of these persons has an answer that will not crumble to dust under intense scrutiny; maybe one of them can provide guidance where the geologists, linguistic specialists, crystallographers, and "meteorologists" at our VI Studies Center here in Geneva can do nothing but spiel statistics and shrug.

Not surprisingly, then, the first popular explanations for the vagrant-intrusion phenomenon had sacred overtones.

Today, in fact, the world's newest and fastest-growing religion, Escribienismo, regards each scriptural breakthrough as a theophany (according to Webster's, "a visible manifestation of a deity") and works to establish the sites of known intrusions as shrines or holy places. Similarly, the fastest-growing sects of our extant faiths are those that incorporate into their doctrines an acknowledgment of the sacred implications of every breakthrough.

Indeed, one well-known Protestant denomination has publicly declared that, verse by verse, chapter by chapter, book by book, God is manifesting to the world an incomprehensible "translation" of the Bible into an otherwordly language: the tongue, perhaps, of angels. That close VI analysis, abetted by computer, has been unable to correlate any of the first apparitions of these reputed scriptural passages to the opening of the book of Genesis, or to any other biblical book, has not led the faithful of this powerful denomination to dispute its teachings on the issue.

Other faiths show more caution, but almost all of them declare that the alien graffiti are godly pronouncements of some sort and that those who continue to essay secular interpretations of the phenomenon have by their impiety delayed the very revelation that they so arduously seek. (The vehemence of this feeling probably accounts for the planting of a car bomb — discovered, fortunately, before it could explode — outside the VI Studies Center two weeks ago.) In any event, religious explanations make up sixty-three percent of those that we subject to detailed analysis here in my department. On four or five occasions, almost against my will, I have found myself in vague sympathy with the more coherent and less dogmatic of this kind of theory.

Secular theories run a gamut of intellectual orientations, prejudices, and, yes, even neuroses. The notorious colloquialism *alien graffiti* points to the conceit — seriously embraced by many who have rejected both Escribienismo and our mutating traditional faiths — that extraterrestrial or transdimensional intelligences must shoulder the blame, or receive the credit, for the entire VI phenomenon. Either aliens from the Magellanic Cloud are playing insidious head games with our species, for malevolent reasons all their own, or else desparate entities from a disintegrating continuum adjacent to our relatively stable one are signaling us for help. In the first case, intrusions resist human attempts to examine them because the Magellani fear that we will discover the heinous fate that they plot for us and so foil their efforts. In the second case, the intrusions disappear when we try to take readings or samples because of the fundamental entropic unraveling of the parallel universe from which our signalers have been madly projecting their unintelligible SOSes.

Other secularists do not go so far, or quite so inventively, afield for explanations. One of my staff members here in Geneva, for instance, has long championed the idea that the VIs represent crystallographic formations of a fleeting kind and that previously undetected atmospheric salts spontaneously coalesce to precipitate them. The fact that they resemble writing she attributes to the fixed number of crystalline structural combinations peculiar to the phenomenon. She feels that, throughout the cosmos, intrusions may be common to Earthlike worlds with atmospheres similar to ours — at least during this latent stage of planetological development. The arguments for her ingenuous point of view occupy nine volumes, of a thousand pages each, but she has not been able to gather the necessary physical data to substantiate her theory, mostly because of the recalcitrant character of the graffiti themselves.

What do *I* believe? Well, as a teen-ager in Nairobi, I, Crazy Jemmi Nakuru, once held that our evolved descendants, perhaps ten or twelve millennia in advance of our present, have found a way to send messages to their distant ancestors, us. Various limitations apply, however; and they are unable to project their advice or warnings any farther back than the year of debut, 1996. Moreover, they have lost so many records of our own era — indeed, of all of human history before the three-thousand-year period spanning their belated rise to eminence — that they can bombard us only with air bursts and wall hangings of an unfamiliar script for an unfamiliar language with an unimaginable grammar and vocabulary. Exactly why I believed this, I don't remember, but it filled an adolescent need for a romantic answer to a thorny metaphysical and phenomenological puzzle: and that need, transmuted by the aging process, undoubtedly accounts for my pursuing a career as a VI analyst.

Other secular solutions to the foremost question of our age include mass hysteria; chemically triggered group hallucinations; communist and/or imperialist weapons testing of an oddly protracted and indefinable kind; auric manifestations summoning their focus and staying power from the locations at which they occur; sunspot activity; meteor showers; secret laser holography with an anomalous material dimension; volcanic emissions; advanced special-effect work as Hollywood lays out the longest global prepublicity campaign in the history of commercial film-making; swamp gas; experimental weather balloons; and so on and so on. One of my colleagues in VI photorecording claims that a prehistoric epidemic of the intrusions led to the extinction of the dinosaurs.

"They went crazy trying to figure out what was going on," he hypothesizes. "The same thing may be happening to us."

* * *

I am writing this final section of my idiosyncratic memoir in a spartanly furnished hotel suite on the beachfront east of Cadíz. It is the same hotel at which my mother and I stayed in August, 1996, when the world's first (conspicuous) vagrant intrusion made its appearance. My mother lies on a low couch in another portion of the suite as I sit here in the sultry Iberian dusk trying to draw some conclusions about what we poor human dinosaurs have never been able to come to terms with, the meaning of it all.

In her youth the very antithesis of a religionist, my mother has for the past four years been a practicing Escribieña. She was converted during a great translators' rally — proselytizers for Escribienismo are called, with both intended and unintended irony, *translators* — in Nairobi's brand-new Kenyatta Complex; and it is at my mother's fervent invitation that I am here in Spain.

Once a haven for vacationers, this hotel now belongs to the Escribieño movement; with the faithful, it has a stature comparable to that of the Temple in Jerusalem. The only decorations in all the corridors and rooms are full-color reproductions of the alien graffiti (a term I dare not use in the presence of believers) that have manifested since the advent of the phenomenon and of which my organization in Geneva has a firm, unchallenged record. However, only one such reproduction may hang in any single room — but more in a suite, the number dictated by the suite's size. To encourage reverent contemplation, the reproductions are spaced at three-meter intervals on the walls in the well-lit corridors. One cannot go anywhere in this former hotel without feeling like a neophyte who may look upon the icons of the faith but who has not yet received the picklock to its arcana.

Every barefoot Escribieño wears a snowy burnoose. Women and men alike veil their faces. Hand-holding is *de rigueur*, but bodily contact may not go beyond that obligation except within marriage, and even then only on the manifestation dates of especially revered theophanies. All these practices stem from the nature of the alien graffiti that power the religion. Because the meaning of vagrant intrusions remains veiled, Escribieños veil themselves. They touch and permit touching only after the fashion of their beloved icons, and they are empowered by their faith to strike out at anyone who seeks an intimacy beyond what they themselves desire.

Escribieños regard patience as the chief human virtue, and proselytizing as the most virtuous Escribieño activity, for the two central tenets of their doctrine are that the One True Translation of their enigmatic icons will one day reveal Itself and that this event will not take place until every living person has joined them in self-extinguishing contemplation of each new theophany and of the whole theophanic record to date. Translators, incidentally, are not those who claim to know the meaning of specific intrusions, but those who remain most selflessly open to the deeper nuances and subtleties of the entire phenomenon. Not too paradoxically, then, there exist Hindu, Buddhist, Jewish, Christian, and Moslem devotees of Escribienismo. At sacred functions, they are not excluded or discriminated against unless they insist on boorishly sectarian interpretations of various intrusive events.

I spent the afternoon with a thousand Escribieños on the beach in front of the hotel. (Or, rather, the Contemplation Center.) I lay on a lounger beside my robed and veiled mother, myself clad in garb identical to that of every other pilgrim, waiting for a sample of alien graffiti to unscroll above both us and the sea unscrolling like a gigantic bolt of lacy blue silk at our naked feet. Some of those around us prayed, some kept heroic vigil, and some, being human, fell asleep in the sun and either amused or annoyed us with their snores. I held my mother's hand and also that of a Nepali businessman who had converted — in a Hindu context and ceremony — only a few months ago. This man and my mother were among those who neither slumbered nor slept, but the faithful proved no better at predicting the arrival of a VI than my colleagues in the Department of Forecasting and nothing of seraphic import occurred. By early dusk, even the most devout among us had begun to weary of our mass Lounge-Out; and our leaders, taking pity, called us in.

Tomorrow, we go again. Once past my mother's invitation, I do not fully understand why I am here or why I am readying myself to surrender a second time to a ritual that by all rational criteria seems so senseless. I, as well as anyone, know the unlikelihood of an intrusion's occurring at a spot already visited — statistics tell us that such manifestations are prohibitively rare — and also of our ever rendering from either the phenomenon in general or any individual instance of it a "translation" of universal and enduring human import. But I remember past theophanies, beautiful midnight exfoliations, great terrible letters burning above our deserts, inarticulate parables of hope illuminating the walls of crypts or subways, brief *billets-doux* from God-knows-who and who-knows-where glittering over a Venezuelan tepui or an Algerian tenement; and in spite of what I know and in obedience to what I remember, I am here to celebrate my ignorance and to purge my heartache.

"How wonderful," my mother murmurs from her couch. "Didn't I tell you you'd have fun here, Jemmi?"

And The Marlin Spoke

I

Before the boat that Hendrikson had rented at the Sacred Heart Marina in Cuerpo Divino, the sea surged and subsided like a living thing.

"How far out do you want to go?" Sister Alejandra asked her pilgrim passenger. From the sunset off to starboard her hair reflected an antique-gold sheen. In another twenty or thirty minutes the darkness would be complete, and every hour until dawn, according to the Pelagian brochures, would be an hour of deep-water communion. If, that is, you believed. . . .

"Past these damned Immersionists," Hendrikson replied, gripping the port gunwale. "They give me the creeps."

His eyes swept the nightmare scene. Thousands of Immersionists — men, women, and children, many of the last not much more than infants — bobbed about in the waters lapping the jetties and inlets of the marina. Thousands more either dog-paddled purposely or drifted in lackadaisical schools in the deeper currents farther out to

divinity. You could not look in any direction without finding a human head — dozens of human heads — cresting
the swells, sinking briefly out of sight, miraculously reap-
pearing. The coastal tides of New Castile teemed with a
variety of believer utterly alien to Hendrikson's experience.

"They're not damned," Sister Alejandra corrected him.
"Quite the opposite, I'd say. Quite the opposite."

"Blessed or damned, Sister, they're the worst sort of
fanatic. The very worst."

The pilot's eyes danced with an indigo dazzle. "What sort
does that make me, Mr. Hendrikson? The better?"

"The prettier," he said under his breath, so that she could
not hear him. If he had to have a licensed ecclesiastic of the
Pelagian sect convey him outward from shore (and that was
the rule), Hendrikson was glad to have drawn one with wit
and good looks, for the standard professional allotments of
saintliness and zeal did not impress him. Moreover, wit and
good looks seemed to be in short supply in New Castile —
although, to be fair, he had only his dizzying observations
over the last thirty hours to judge by. Three days ago he had
been busy sowing wheat on his farm in White Sky,
Oklahoma, twelve hundred miles away.

Meanwhile, with the skill of a seasoned hand, Sister
Alejandra was easing the *Baptista,* her pretty little boat,
through the salt-buoyed throngs of Immersionists. She
seemed to be trying her best not to collide with or swamp
them. Her care and compassion notwithstanding, Hendrikson saw a dead teen-age girl emerge from beneath the hull
and turn bleeding and wheyfaced into the phosphorescent
wake of the *Baptista.* Others of the devout had drowned
long since and were floating belly-up like giant catfish or
carp. The incompatible reeks of kelp and salted human flesh
lay heavily over the nearer inshore waters. Hendrikson
watched the dead girl pass from his view into a ring of
believers who, while treading water, sang a Castilian

chantey-mass. Listening to this eerie dirge, he dug into his pocket for a handkerchief with which to cover his nose.

"Miles out," he said through the muffling linen. "As far out from these fanatics as they'll let you go."

The bobbing heads, whether of living devotees or of tide-racked corpses, were fewer now. The *Baptista* picked up speed. The stench of the coast receded. The sun disappeared utterly, the night congealed over the Gulf of Mexico, and the undulant body of Sister Alejandra's God — the Cuerpo Divino after which the port city of her order had been named — carried her boat, herself, and her passenger to the meeting for which he had skeptically paid the charter fee.

II

Three days ago Thomas Hendrikson had been busy sowing wheat on his farm near White Sky, Oklahoma, twelve hundred miles away. The pressure to visit either New Castile or Santa Pacifica, however, had been building in him for at least a year. Over this disquieting twelvemonth, intimations of the sea — of living water, white-sand beaches, and either lovely or bizarre marine fauna — had assaulted him many times.

For one thing, of course, the nation's coastal areas were almost always on the news; you caught glimpses of the oceans and their attendant animal life as a visual obbligato to the major human story of the decade, the spread of the religious doctrine known as Thalassicism and its subsequent quicksilver splintering into literally hundreds of competing or complementary denominations. (*Cults*, most newscasters and orthodox religionists called them, and that's the way landlocked Heartlanders invariably thought of them, too.) But television was not the whole of it for Tom Hendrikson: he had vivid dreams and unusual waking visions to go with the news reports, and these, being private, fretted him a good deal more. He felt that some uncompromising oceanic power was astir in his blood, for purposes that did not coincide with his own, and the upheaval that this power threatened was something he did not want to think about. His present life satisfied him. He did not want to lose it.

The change had begun innocently enough. One autumn morning, riding high in the air-conditioned cab of his Elksmith combine, Hendrikson had looked out over the vast yellow sea of wheat surrounding him — only to find superimposed upon it an image of an actual seascape, with long glinting swells and a cold mirror brightness that almost blinded him. He cocked his head. The image did not go away. He was harvesting not wheat but water. A pitiless panic sat down on his chest. His hands fumbled frantically with the Elksmith's computerized controls. Then, as suddenly as it had come, the vision vanished, and he was adrift once more in a sea of nodding grain. For the rest of the day, however, he kept cocking his head and squinting sidelong, fearful that the terrible lineaments of the sea would again overwhelm the comforting tangibility of his crop.

Sarah, Hendrikson's wife, said later that this vision had come upon him as a response to the summer's protracted drought. Irrigation — in their case, a system of spindly elevated sprinklers on wheels — had saved them, but the costs had been enormous. Hence Tom's vision from the cab of the Elksmith. When you wanted rain, your mind quite naturally leaped the arid prairies of Oklahoma and Misaskas to arrive at a lake or an ocean. Besides, neither of the Hendriksons had been more than two hundred miles from home since their wedding trip nine years ago, and maybe Tom needed to take a well-deserved leave of absence from his farm duties. If they could get Mrs. McQuillan to look after the boys, Sarah would be happy to join him; she wanted a vacation, too. White Sky had character, certainly, but no glamor, and only folks with concrete in their souls could stay forever in the same place without once wondering about the Great World Beyond.

"There's too much to do around here," Hendrikson told his wife, dismissing her suggestions along with her analysis. And there was. Even if Mrs. McQuillan agreed to board and babysit the boys, he would have to hire someone to oversee the farm's remaining harvest transactions. A second wedding trip was out of the question right now.

But the idea of a trip — a trip to the sea — stuck in Hendrikson's mind, in spite of all his well-reasoned struggles against the notion, and took on a crazy life of its own. The idea became an impulse, the impulse became an urge, and the urge an inner compulsion that, in moments of daytime torpor, he pretended did not really exist. Other prods kept goosing the compulsion, however, and some of these were quietly dramatic.

Showering one evening in late fall, liquefying the red dirt on his hands and forearms with a bar of gritty soap, Hendrikson looked down. The swirl of water between his feet fascinated him. It spiraled around the metal cap on the drain opening like something living, an endless crystal snake feeding its length back into the great hidden aquifer from which it had sprung, dragging with it a delicate scrum of soap lather, a small portion of Oklahoma's topsoil, and, inevitably, some of Hendrikson's own skin. What an odd sensation. If he stood here long enough, sloughing dead body cells and rubbing away calluses, Sarah, when she finally came through the bathroom door to see about him, would find no trace of her husband — only the musical sibilance of shower water slithering its way into the bowels of the continent. Hendrikson wondered at this thought. It was almost perverse. Then he realized that the water between his feet was spinning *clockwise* down the drain.

Here in the Northern Hemisphere, that constituted a slap at the laws of physics; it was supposed to go the *other* way.

Hendrikson wrapped a towel around his dripping flanks and hurried to fetch Sarah to corroborate this uncanny phenomenon. When they peered into the shower stall together, however, the swirl had mysteriously reversed itself.

"I saw it," he protested.

"I know you did," Sarah reassured him. "Maybe it was an earth tremor or an atmospheric thing — something like that, anyway."

A sign, thought Hendrikson, but he did not say the word aloud. He finished drying himself, dressed for dinner, and talked enthusiastically at table of the chances of the Wichita Bombers against the Galveston Gulls in the forthcoming World Series. The boys joined in, but Sarah, over the reheated corned beef and cabbage, eyed him suspiciously. She had no more idea of what was happening to him than he did, and her uncertainty seemed to anger as well as frighten her.

During a welcome stretch of false spring in January, Hendrikson drove his pickup to a piece of acreage dominated by a man-made pond. Its surface had recently thawed, and the mud around its banks was firming up around the broken hoofprints of Hendrikson's cattle. He had only a few head, but he was conscientious in checking up on them in bad or borderline weather. This afternoon they were elsewhere, and he paused to study the pond, which reflected upward at him only pale sky and emaciated drifting clouds.

Quite unexpectedly a shape appeared above the seamless pond water. It had a chestnut-colored body, graceful wings, and a bill with an underslung pouch almost as roomy as its abdomen. With its wings extended, this phantom made a narrow circuit of the pond, tilting first to this side and then to that, its two-dimensional double in the water skating along beneath it like its disembodied soul.

Hendrikson watched this performance with astonished eyes. The bird was a pelican. It had popped into view without any fanfare or preamble, and now, equally unexpectedly, it was beating its powerful wings on an upward arc that would carry it directly over his pickup. He had to turn around 180 degrees to follow the creature's flight, but when he shielded his eyes against the glare on the horizon, the pelican disappeared into the high whiteness almost as if it had no more substance than its shadow on the pond.

"A pelican," Hendrikson declared an hour later. "A pelican."

"Great Salina City has sea gulls," Sarah pointed out. "Maybe, after all, it's not such an unusual thing — to see here."

"Great Salina City doesn't have pelicans, Sarah, not unless you're counting the ones in the zoo. And this one — this pelican today — it was a species common to New Castile and the Gulf of Mexico. I've seen them on the news."

"Maybe you have. But what does it mean?"

"I'm not sure. It's not a reaction to last summer's drought, though, or a yearning for a second wedding trip. It's just another sign of the *thirst* growing in me, Sarah — a thirst for the sea."

"Salt water isn't going to quench your thirst, Tom." Sarah's reply made a neat epigram, but otherwise completely missed the point of what he had just witnessed. She had been angry with him for rejecting her first romantic interpretations of his malaise. Now she was even angrier for his excluding her from this worrisome mystical thirst. She thought a long weekend in Wichita or Utavah Springs would cure him of it. That was precisely where she was wrong.

Hendrikson did not know what to say to his wife. If, later on, he did actually visit New Castile or Santa Pacifica, he did not believe that Sarah should accompany him. The people along the coasts had life-styles and belief systems at striking variance with those favored in the Heartland, beachcombery and Thalassicism not the least outrageous among them. Moreover, secessionist sentiment was now so strong in the Far West that recently a group of militant Joaquinistas had set up an armed roadblock on the Utavah border. Within the week Federal Guardians had forcibly reopened the highway, but only after a pitched battle and dismaying losses on both sides. How could any sensible person think of taking a loved one into so unpredictable a region of the country? As for New Castile, a more stable and somewhat less populous state, its inhabitants were known to regard visitors either as prey for their many gaudy commercial enterprises or as potential converts. Indeed, they hoped you were both. Sarah, a lifelong Wesleyanite, would despise such people.

One night, nearly a month after the pelican incident, Sarah thought to ask her husband a question: "You don't really —?"

"I don't really what?"

"Believe that it's true? All the tiresome business about the godliness of the sea. All that silly return-of-Poseidon rot."

"I don't know. It's gone to work in me, though."

"Listen, Tom, it's a metaphor that's gotten out of hand. Everyone has religious feelings — feelings of awe, of human insignificance — looking out over an ocean. God *wants* us to have such feelings."

Hendrikson thought about this. "Maybe we're living in apostolic times again," he finally said. "Something very important's happening, but we're out on the edge of it, disbelieving by rote. I keep thinking we're like a couple of Chinese coolies in a rice paddy thousands of miles from

Jerusalem accidentally catching wind of the coming of Jesus of Nazareth. We don't believe a word of it because we're too far away to witness His Passion ourselves, and the only apostle we've met looks, talks, and acts funny. Suppose that were the case, Sarah."

"We'd be saved if we believed," she replied at once. "Our distance from the Event doesn't lessen its effectiveness."

"Right," Hendrikson said. "Exactly right."

"But this is different, Tom. The believers in Thalassicism are localizing God in a completely different way. It's blasphemous on the face. If you ask me, it's downright stupid, too."

" 'God is alive, and His body is the sea.' "

"The Creator of the Universe licking the cruddy oil-clabbered beaches of Jersey and Laguna Madre?" Sarah scoffed. "God's out of Nature and out of Time, Tom. He's got a billion or more galaxies to oversee."

"What about Jesus?"

"What about Him?"

"If God could incarnate Himself as man, why couldn't He just as easily infuse a portion of Himself into the oceans of this planet? An all-powerful, omnipresent deity shouldn't have any trouble doing that."

"O.K. but what for?"

"A reminder, maybe. Or a revelation."

Sarah regarded her husband with a rapt commingling of wonder and disappointment. "You *do* believe it, don't you?"

"It's gone to work in me. That's all I can say."

It had indeed. He felt pursued. Dust billowing on the roadway between his and his neighbor's farms made him think of luminous sea spray. His dreams, which he never recalled with any conviction or accuracy, placed him in submarine grottoes of living coral, or in the holds of sunken ships from the era of classical antiquity, or in the crowded lifeboats of great modern vessels gone afoul of icebergs or down in hurricanes. He could not walk down a bean row without hearing surf noises or the piping cries of invisible gulls. White Sky, although a dusty hamlet on the Northern Columbian plains, was no haven from the sea change taking place in him. Willy-nilly, come tide or tornado, he was transfigured . . . .

In April, the cruelest month, Hendrikson made a discovery that emphasized this fact. It sealed his decision, still unrevealed to Sarah, to visit Cuerpo Divino immediately after sowing the first wheat crop of the season. He was *meant* to go, and to go alone, and Sarah would have to bear his absence with wifely obedience and Wesleyanite charity. Only a fool or a blind man would ignore a sign of the magnitude and bluntness of this latest one.

Crossing a plank bridge over a dry creekbed, Hendrikson caught sight of a slab of greenish rock on which an engraving of a peculiarly deliberate sort shone in the sun. He climbed down from his tractor, eased himself over the edge of the little bridge, and picked his way through the debris on the creek bottom to the anomalous outcropping of shale.

Here he squatted. The engraving on the greenish stone was the body outline of a fishlike creature nearly ten feet long, each of its bones so sharply etched that Hendrikson at first believed that they had been chiseled there. He imagined some deft anonymous craftsman working meticulously to achieve this effect. Then he understood that he was beholding a fossil specimen of an ancient marine life form rather than a prehistoric human artifact. This was God's work, not man's, and it made his eyes grow moist and his chest expand as if he had received an award for which he had long considered himself ineligible.

Another thing about the fossil: inside the large fish's body, in the caudal area, the skeletal imprint of a much smaller individual asserted itself. Was this the last meal of the host creature? Or was it, instead, the doomed get of the larger, preserved in its death throes as the sinuous female parent was so movingly preserved in hers? The latter, Hendrikson felt. Millions upon millions of years after the Event, countless millennia after the commonplace tragedy that had ended two otherwise insignificant animal lives, a piece of rock in a dry Oklahoma creekbed bore witness to their suffering. God had recorded their passion on a tablet of shale.

Hendrikson notified a paleontologist at Great Plains College in western Misaskas, seventy miles away. She visited the site, took dozens of pictures, and received permission to transport the entire outcropping to the Museum of Natural History in Denver. The fossil, she informed the Rocky Mountain press corps, represented a variety of ichthyosaur, or early marine reptile, known by the scientific name *Eurhinosaurus* because of the swordlike projection of the upper jaw. No other such specimen had ever been found in Northern Columbia (most of them came from fine-grained shales of Early Jurassic age in Austrio-Swabia), a failure not greatly surprising when you considered the fact that until Hendrikson's find the scientific community had had not a scrap of evidence that sea water had once covered this particular section of the Great Plain. Indeed, for just this reason many paleontologists viewed the Hendrikson fossil as a plant if not an outright counterfeit. Their arguments made no difference to the man himself.

Counterfeit, plant, or bona fide fossil, it was in any case a sign; and Tom Hendrikson left for the Gulf Coast of New Castile in early June aboard a Columbia Traveler bus full of nervous tourist-pilgrims.

III

Cuerpo Divino appalled Hendrikson. It was a city of stucco and neon in which the recruiting centers of various

Thalassicist sects vied openly with one another for tourist money and converts. Billboards, bullhorns, and aggressive street solicitation greeted the bewildered visitor on every corner. Over here was an Immersionist tabernacle of polarized glass, over there a tent of blue and green sailcloth belonging to the First Church of the Revived Poseidon. Day and night, the place jangled. The immemorial sighing of the nearby ocean could not be heard over the electronically amplified chantey-hymns, the wild-eyed beatitude barkers, and the endless streams of motorized traffic going up and down The Strip. Hendrikson watched in numb disbelief as two bare-breasted girls costumed as mermaids weaved past him on a Formosan motorscooter.

Worse, the city stank. Cuerpo Divino (it soon occurred to most visitors) might have been more fittingly christened Cuerpo Muerto. Between the stucco temples and the wooden bait-and-relic shops on the beach you could see the Immersionists taking their daily baths in the purifying body of God. Recreational swimmers could not compete with them. They had staked out the shoreward waters as their own, and although regular patrols of the Guardia de Dios kept a few lanes open for fishing vessels and excursion boats, the most fervid sect members often gladly suffered disembowelment by a propeller blade to fulfill their spiritual ambition of dying at sea. And those under the implacable sentence of cancer or other terminal illnesses came to the gulf with the declared intention of either passing away immersed or undergoing an eleventh-hour cure. The results? Monumental sanitation problems along the quays and the pervasive salt-sweet stench of death over the entire Strip. Locals took these annoyances in stride and tourists tried to adjust to them. Hendrikson saw a woman who had occupied an aisle seat on his bus eating cotton candy over the tide-stranded body of a child. Every now and again, as if it were a jellyfish, she would nudge the pathetic corpse with her toe.

In Cuerpo Divino such sights were commonplace.

Hendrikson had used his bus trip to read about the various Thalassicist denominations in New Castile. The most respectable of the lot seemed to be the Pelagians, who maintained convents and monasteries in every major port on the Gulf. They supported themselves by taking pilgrims to sea in charter boats and holding austere worship services miles from land. Each member of the sect was a licensed pilot, and no one wishing to go to sea for any purpose could venture beyond the twelve-mile limit without a Pelagian aboard either to navigate or to provide the continuing benediction of his or her presence. Celibacy was not an essential part of the Pelagian code, but men and women ordinarily lived in separate cloisters for seven months out of every year, alternating their months of residence as they and their superiors saw fit. As a result, children were not an unaccustomed sight in the courtyards and corridors of either Pelagian convents or Pelagian monasteries.

In Cuerpo Divino, a convent. As soon as he had disembarked in the bus station Hendrikson asked directions to the convent. But because he chose to walk The Strip, just to get a reading on its gamy religiosity, it was late afternoon by the time he reached the place.

Near the Sacred Heart Marina, the convent resembled a series of barracks in an outdated pseudo-Spanish architectural style. Arches and weeping willows lent the establishment a gracefulness and a sense of repose absent from most of the structures of The Strip, but sightseers and would-be pilgrims crowded the central courtyard and Hendrikson had to stand in line for two hours to tell a sister of the order what he wanted. This woman had the knobby features of a peasant in a painting by Bosch or Brueghel and a curtness of manner that briefly convinced Hendrikson that all she wanted from him was his money.

"A boat for one person costs more."

"I'll pay it," he replied.

"If you sign on with a party of six from Pinetucky, you can go out tonight. There's a small extra charge for squeezing you in."

"This is a solitary pilgrimage, Sister."

"Tomorrow evening, then — that's the earliest we can accommodate you."

"Where do I spend the night?"

"Here. In our tourist hostel. If you can pay, of course."

"I can pay."

And so he spent a bad night in a damp concrete room packed from floor to ceiling with insomniac pilgrims like himself. Those few who slept snored or whickered or talked unintelligibly, while those who lay awake did periodic combat with their mildewed bedding. That he could have even believed New Castile a latter-day Holy Land, a Mecca for landlocked Gentiles like himself, mortified Hendrikson. He had not died, but aboard a double decker Columbia Traveler bus he had come straight to Hell. He had paid for the ticket himself. What folly. If it meant anything, it meant that nobody alive today had apostolic credentials, and maybe that the God who had died in Jerusalem two thousand years ago had died for good. More than likely He had been a madman with a lunatic ambition similar to Hendrikson's. As for the cultists in New Castile and Santa Pacifica, they were all — every last one of them — as crazy as loons. They had turned the world into a cataclysmic freak show.

"*Eurhinosaurus,*" Hendrikson murmured to himself. "Mother and child. A tablet from the book of Time."

He made a chant of these words. They did not restore his faith, but they did enable him to get through the night.

The following day Hendrikson voluntarily restricted his movements to the grounds of the Pelagian convent. To discover who his pilot would be and which boat would carry him into the Gulf Stream for communion, he had to await the outcome of a lottery. To while away this time, then, he wrote letters vilifying the people and institutions of New Castile and warning his neighbors and friends to refrain from following him on pilgrimages of their own. A strange doubt — a kind of grudging charity — kept him from posting these letters, and at five o'clock a Pelagian abbess appeared in the quadrangle to tell him that Sister Alejandra would be pleased to accompany him on his voyage to deepwater divinity.

IV

They lay at anchor in the holy darkness, leagues from land, becalmed by Sister Alejandra's faith. Hendrikson paced the cluttered deck with his hands in his armpits. For the past half hour his stomach had been doing sluggish somersaults.

"Don't you feel a little better, Mr. Hendrikson?"

"Your God makes me queasy, Sister. Literally sick."

"That's a physical response, not a spiritual one. Don't confuse God's eternal essence with His finite temporal body."

Hendrikson halted by the pilot's chair and stared at the woman. Nobody in White Sky talked like that, not even Wesleyanite ministers, the majority of whom were content to preach on Sunday and, every three or four weeks in good weather, to preside avuncularly over covered-dish dinners. Their evangelism had a practical core that most folks found reassuring.

"I won't feel better until I've gone home and completely forgotten this nonsense," he told the sister. A moment later he added, "Or maybe until Old Neptune condescends to show Himself."

Sister Alejandra smiled. Like the diatoms floating in the

water around the *Baptista*, her smile seemed to be self-illuminating. "You're sitting in His lap," she said quietly.

Hendrikson snorted contemptuously and began to pace again. "I don't know why I came, Sister. I swear to you, I really don't."

"You were called. That's why most people — the lucky ones, anyway — make the pilgrimage. We've read about your inland ichthyosaur even here in New Castile, Mr. Hendrikson. Abbess Florinda made the connection this afternoon when she was processing the lottery results."

"H_2O."

"I beg your pardon?"

"Your God's nothing but H_2O, Sister — with a healthy pinch of sodium chloride thrown in as flavoring."

"Is that what you think? Really?"

Hendrikson did not reply.

"If it is, then you, Mr. Hendrikson, are nothing more than the sum of the chemicals physically constituting you. Materialism's a philosophy that —"

"Spare me, Sister. You're not debating metaphysics with a schoolboy."

The pilot rose and crossed to the opposite gunwale. "You sometimes make me forget that," she said distinctly. Hendrikson glanced at her, on the tip of his tongue a riposte that the young woman's sudden devotional attitude made him suppress. She had let herself slip into a light trance, a prayerful reverie, and her eyes seemed to be peering out over the water — God's coruscating skin — with super-human understanding and calm.

Sister Alejandra was not just pretty. She was beautiful. Her faith made her beautiful. Hendrikson did not desire her. He envied her. He envied her faith. He envied her this solemn, unequivocal moment of communion with her God — even if, as seemed all too likely, it were the product of a ritual self-hypnosis that briefly obliterated her own personality. And because he envied her the moment, he could not prevent himself from intruding upon it.

"Sister, when am I going to get my money's worth? When is this palpable God of yours going to let me know that *He* knows I'm here?"

The pilot continued to stare out to sea. If she had heard him, she chose not to acknowledge the fact.

Hendrikson crossed the deck and touched her on the shoulder.

Sister Alejandra shifted her gaze to meet him. Apparently weighing the consequences of a direct reply, she studied him as if from a great distance. Her immense indigo pupils gleamed with the reflected nebulosity of the Milky Way. Her passenger from the Heartland found himself swimming in those whirlpools.

"My money's worth," he managed. "That's all I want."

Shrugging his hand away without seeming to reject his touch outright, Sister Alejandra turned again to the midnightish membrane of the sea. "Holy God," she said, apostrophizing the water, "this is Thomas Hendrikson of White Sky, Oklahoma. Having grown up inland, he doubts Your divinity. At the same time, the faith of his fathers no longer persuades him, and he believes that nothing but his own sweat has secured for his family and him the daily blessing of bread and shelter. Cow manure has more reality for this Doubting Thomas than the worldwide ebb and flow of the Cuerpo Divino —"

"Just a minute!" the Doubting Thomas cried.

Sister Alejandra laughed. Her trance was broken, and Hendrikson wondered now if she had simply been feigning that mysterious state.

"Please don't make mock of me, Sister, I've come a long way."

"Further than you know," she replied. Then she laughed again. "That was supposed to be funny, that cow manure comment. Don't you Heartlanders have a sense of humor about bigoted coastal stereotyping of your life-styles? We do — about yours of us, I mean."

"No stereotype of mine was as incredible as what I witnessed in Cuerpo Divino, Sister. It beggared belief."

She shrugged. "I'm not an Immersionist. I don't despise or denigrate their ways, but I believe you have to come to deep water for truly meaningful communion. That's why we're here."

Hendrikson looked about. They lay too far from shore to see its garish neon glow, but off to starboard the running lights of several other charter boats told him they were not alone in their search for communion.

"I want my sign."

The pilot spread her arms and spoke to the sea: "Although You could strike him dead as easily as exorcise his doubt, give my passenger a sign. Show him that which he needs to be shown."

In the starlight beyond the vessel's prow a marlin leapt, only to fall back into the obsidian waters with a heavy splash. For an instant, though, it had hung suspended in the night, mounted against the velvet blackness in a radiance of mortal energy so commanding that Hendrikson's heart had leapt with the fish. A blue marlin, one of the larger species of the marlin group. Then the sea was without rent again, the night unriven by wonder.

"There," said Sister Alejandra.

Although half in awe of the great fish's balletic leap, Hendrikson told himself that this could not be such an uncommon occurrence in the gulf — even if the event, altogether coincidentally, _had_ followed hard upon the sister's wry invocation. Now, if a jade-eyed tiger or a headstrong ebony stallion pawing the air with its hooves had burst the surface of the sea _that_ would count for something.

. . .

Sister Alejandra appeared to read this thought on his face: "You don't require another, do you?"

"Marlin or sign?"

"They're one and the same. If you don't feel it, your mind's at fault — or maybe your heart. A marlin — a *blue* marlin — is a living fragment of God's bodily essence here on earth. Perhaps you should pray."

"A thousand dollars to watch a fish jump."

"Do you want to go back?"

"I want certification that I haven't made a fool of myself. 'Sarah, I spent a thousand dollars to see a marlin leap.' 'You're kidding, Tom. Is that all that happened?'" Hendrikson crossed his arms and clutched his shoulders. "That's all that's happened," he murmured. "I'm an idiot."

"We'll go back." Sister Alejandro returned to the pilot's wheel and tried to achieve ignition. The *Baptista*'s engines did not respond. She made several more attempts and then reported her lack of success to her passenger.

"Radio for help," advised Hendrikson, disgusted with the entire business.

The radio, too, was out of commission. Dead in the water, the *Baptista* rose and fell on the rhythmically indifferent swells. Hendrikson suggested that they try to hail the charter boats off to starboard, but when they looked for these vessels' running lights they could see nothing but open water, darkness, and the dot-to-dot constellations overarching the gulf.

"I can't believe this!" Hendrikson exclaimed.

"You can't believe anything," Sister Alejandra said.

V

Belowdecks, the *Baptista* had a galley and one small sleeping cabin. The galley contained a small store of saltine crackers, all stale, and a single two-ounce tin of potted meat. To Hendrikson's amazement the only water aboard sloshed about sadly in the bottom of an uncapped Thermos in the icebox, which itself was not functioning. Sister Alejandra explained that Pelagians liked to fast at sea, and that anyway she had not planned to remain overnight aboard the little vessel.

"No one plans to be stranded," Hendrikson said. "But, for God's sake, you don't disregard the possibility!"

Angry, he took a blanket from the cramped cabin and went abovedecks to find a place to sleep. In the open air he began to feel an ironic resignation stealing over him. This would be better than the suffocating dormitory in that madhouse of a convent back in Cuerpo Divino. He might actually catch up on his lost shut-eye. His anger had driven off his queasiness, and the ocean would lull him like a great rocking cradle. A small blessing in the midst of his consummate folly.

For a time he did sleep, dreaming of rescue and home and the dear carnal fragrance of his wife.

He awoke to the drilling tattoo of raindrops on his neck. The wind had freshened from the northeast, pushing the _Baptista_ ahead of it in spite of the cast-iron anchor that the sister had winched overboard, and the vessel's stern had already begun shipping water over the gunwales. A tempest, Hendrikson thought. This word had a cozy feel to it, a wistful Shakespearean taste, and he kept repeating it to himself as he hurried for cover. A tempest, after all, was survivable, whereas a hurricane — frightening, frightening word — could spell shipwreck and death, especially this far out. As he clambered into Sister Alejandra's cabin, it occurred to Hendrikson that hurricanes usually did not originate over the peninsula of New Castile, the direction from which the wind was blowing, and that to concern himself with something as stupid as the correct terminology for the storm was to ignore its most perilous immediate consequence. Hurricane, tempest, or squall, this unhappy butt-ender was driving them *away* from the safety of the Castilian coast.

The beam of Sister Alejandra's flashlight caught Hendrikson square in the eyes, and he cursed her roundly.

"Turn her about!" he shouted. "Turn this damed thing about!"

"How?"

"How the devil should I know?"

Sister Alejandra pointed her flashlight beam at the built-in sleeping bench on the opposite wall. "Sit down." Walking his hands across the paneling to maintain his balance, Hendrikson obeyed. The sister, on her way past him to the galley, handed him the flashlight. "Lie down if you like."

"I'll sit."

He heard pans rattling (a small metallic cacophony within the larger dissonance of the storm), and a moment later she had placed what seemed to be a lidless pressure cooker in his lap. It was cold and heavy.

"What's this for?"

"In case you need it. I don't want to spend the remainder of the night trying to clean up after you with flashlight and mop."

Although the storm — the tempest — howled and hurled lightning bolts for another five hours, slapping the *Baptista*'s beam and nudging her only Neptune knew where, Hendrikson did not have to use the pressure cooker. Toward morning, in fact, he even managed to sleep again.

Emerging from the hold, Hendrikson shielded his eyes against the sunlight winking from the chrome accouterments of the little boat. He and his pilot had survived. Strands of Sister Alejandra's hair were lifting like gossamer in the light morning wind. She herself was feeding stale crackers from the galley to a trio of sea gulls perched on the forward gunwales. The birds grabbed the saltines from her hands and greedily choked them down. If she missed a bird's turn, it rebuked her with an open-beaked screech that made Hendrikson's eardrums vibrate.

"You're giving away all we've got to eat on this tub!" he cried, startling the sister and scaring off two of the sea gulls. The third rose into the air, made a wheeling circuit of the boat, and settled back down quite near its original perch. Sister Alejandra gave it the last cracker. Hendrikson lunged forward. "Unless I strangle the bastard for breakfast!" Whereupon this bird, too, departed.

"It's only a little to give."

"It was everything we had!"

Sister Alejandra spread her arms and opened her hands as if to catch the sunlight. "But look at the day we've been blessed with."

The Day They Had Been Blessed With stretched into evening without their once sighting another vessel or even the wispy contrail of a jet in the aloof blue stratosphere. To keep themselves from sweating away too much bodily fluid, they retired belowdecks and passed the time playing gin rummy with a well-thumbed deck missing the king of swords. Hendrikson regularly popped upstairs to check the horizon (to no avail but the disruption of his game), and by sunset Sister Alejandra had won his Italian shoes, his monogrammed belt buckle, and his blustery animosity. Their predicament was growing serious. More alarming, except for the *Baptista* and themselves, the world suddenly seemed to be untenanted. Why had everything gone dead at the same time?

"I've got to have a drink," Hendrikson said.

Sister Alejandra fetched the Thermos from the icebox, and they each drank a quarter of a glass of water. Tomorrow they could have that same amount again. Then their provisions would be gone, and they would have to hope for either rescue or another rainfall from which to collect a stopgap supply of drinking water. Last night, Hendrikson realized, they had missed an opportunity to add to their pathetic stock.

"Why do you worry so? Abbess Florinda knows we're out here. She knows we should have been back yesterday. As soon as it's light again, we'll probably be picked up. They simply didn't find us today, that's all."

"They didn't come anywhere *near* us, Sister."

She twirled his clumsy brass belt buckle on the tip of her forefinger. "Go ahead and worry, then. Tomorrow evening you'll be sitting here in your underwear. Maybe you're being chastened, Mr. Hendrikson — purposely humbled."

This possibility had already crossed her passenger's mind. He removed the buckle from her finger, slid it back over the naked end of his belt, and, angrily cinching his trousers, climbed into the night to stare at the stars and to air out his inarticulate wrath.

After a while he could hear the calming susurrations of the sister's prayers. Slowly, gradually, shame displaced his anger.

VI

They were cut-adrift nobodies, Hendrikson decided. The rescuers that Sister Alejandra had predicted, and that he had made a tentative commitment to believe in, failed to materialize. The following day passed exactly like the first, and the day after that found them alone on a desert of salt water with nothing to drink or eat and no satisfactory notion of why their engulfment by this uncanny solitude should be so total. Forsaken. The sister's convent had apparently written them off, and the God on whose liquid spine they rode piggyback had either died or gone on holiday.

Blistered and cotton-mouthed, Hendrikson refused to stay in the passenger hold. He was afraid they would miss their rescuers if he stopped strolling the deck and scanning the horizon. The fact that the *Baptista* ought to be clearly visible to a search party even without his semaphoring figure at the gunwales, he chose to dismiss as wishful thinking. Let the sister call him crazy. Let her accuse him of scourging himself with the flails of heat and fatique. Hot and hungry as he was, he did not mean to remain forever on the wastewaters of the gulf. . . .

He opened his eyes and found himself lying on the deck in the shade of a linen tent that Sister Alejandra had erected over him after his collapse. She was wiping his face with a cloth dipped in sea water, but taking great care not to brush it over his mouth. The sun was going down again, the third time he had had to watch it set since coming on this asinine trip. What if he died? He could imagine Sister Alejandra unrigging her makeshift tent, wrapping him in the sheet, and shoving him overboard — ceremoniously, of course, but so what? He did not *want* to be buried at sea, committed to the saline digestive juices of a world-girding God. He wanted the crunch and crumble of honest loam on his coffin.

"Have them return my corpse," he said. "Back to White Sky."

"I could die here, too, you know," the sister said. "Maybe you'd better write a note." She made this suggestion almost cheerfully, but her cheeks were gaunt and her lips both cracked and swollen.

Dizzy, Hendrikson sat up and touched her face. "Pray for us some more. Ask your God for something to eat."

"Fried chicken? Fish and chips?"

What an infuriating woman. She turned your own feeble sarcasms back on you as even feebler jokes. Only maybe he had not intended any sarcasm; maybe the frivolity of her reply bespoke an awareness of the depth of his worry for them both. He let his hand drop. She lowered her eyes and began quite softly to chant.

Darkness again. The hallucinatory splendor of the sea at night. Hendrikson, propped against the *Baptista*'s beam, tried to center himself in the long hallucination of his thirst and hunger. The nearly inaudible chanting of the Pelagian, so close it seemed as secret as his own heartbeat, assured him that he had not yet died, but, somehow, not too menacingly, that extinguishing moment crept nearer and nearer. It was a shadow stalking him across the black-glass waves.

"There!" Sister Alejandra said.

He roused. As if in slow motion, a marlin — a blue marlin — rose into the air above the boat's prow and hung there gleaming like a magnificent if dire specter. Death, thought Hendrikson. Then the fish's swordlike snout inscribed a parabola through the spray, declining from the perpendicular to point directly at Hendrikson; and a moment later, twisting sidelong, the marlin crashed to the deck. The nose of the *Baptista* dipped beneath the impact. A terrific flouncing-about and beating of fins ensued. The fish slid on its own lubricants from one side of the little boat to the other, desperately writhing, its silver-blue fuselage bending and straightening until Hendrikson thought he heard bone snap. Only then did the marlin lie still. Now the panicked beating audible to Hendrikson was that of his own reviving heart. He had been scared out of his visionary grogginess by a vision as palpable as a club blow on the head. Sister Alejandra huddled near, and they embraced.

In the morning, as soon as they could see again, she said, "We'll have to eat it raw, Mr. Hendrikson. There's no way to do any cooking, I'm afraid."

"Eat a living fragment of God's bodily essence?"

"The sooner the better. Chew the flesh well and suck the juices." She carved a pair of hefty fillets from the marlin's flanks and returned with them to the tent. She was already chewing her own reddish white strip when she handed the

other to her ward. "Go on. It's sweet. I can already feel my
energy level rising."

Hendrikson ate. His strength returned. They scoured the
horizons for help. No one came. The marlin, meanwhile,
lay under the broiling sun in the *Baptista's* prow without
any visible sign, or the least unpleasant odor, of corruption.
Its iridescent colors did not fade, its huge round eyes glittered like opals. Sister Alejandra occasionally enlarged the
wound from which she had first fed them, but assuming
the body continued to resist putrescence, they could
reasonably hope to eat of the great fish for another two
weeks or more. Hendrikson prayed their ordeal would not
last that long. He was ready to concede to the sister the
power and validity of her religion. In fact, he finally told
her so.

"Back in White Sky you'll forget."

"Not likely."

"Not likely, all right — but only because I don't think
God's through with you. With us. There's more to come."

Irritated again, Hendrikson waved his hand. It was best
not to get the sister started again. She domesticated miracles by philosophizing about them. Make a concession, and
she gave you a lecture.

Late that afternoon they drifted into, or there surrounded
them slowly, a vast floating carpet of indigo-umber sludge.
An oil spill. Barrel upon barrel of petroleum vented from
the hold of a tanker whose captain had probably believed
that his ship was doomed unless he jettisoned a major part
of its cargo. Maybe the very storm that had driven the
Baptista away from the coast had panicked the tanker captain. Whatever the cause of the spill, Hendrikson stared at
the glistering, rubbery mass with loathing. In comparison,
the pollution to temples was a venial sin. He could not
imagine the marlin of God breaking through this filthy skin
to redeem them or anyone else with its flesh. How lucky

they were not to have drifted into this spill before now.

By dark the *Baptista* sat in the middle of the sticky, quivering oil. Hendrikson and the sister ate of the marlin again and played cards by flashlight. Hendrikson was carrying the sister a second piece of the fish's seemingly inexhaustible flank when he noticed that the mantle of petroleum was retreating in an ever-expanding circle of which the *Baptista* was the center and focus. The cleansed water in the wake of the withdrawing oil had begun to glow. Luminous whitefish, shrimp, and diatoms quivered beneath the purified surface like a radiant bruise, an immense benign hematoma.

"Quick!" the man cried. "Come here!"

Sister Alejandra joined him at the rail. They clutched each other as the band in the water — the stunning glow — began to pursue the edge of the retreating sludge away from the *Baptista*. Now they were afloat in a circle of bleak but unsullied ocean. The band of flickering brightness that had just fled from them came rushing back, only to halt a good forty or fifty yards away, and a trough opened beneath their boat. They plunged toward the sea bottom while the watery wall enclosing this column remained intact around them, emanating a spectacular sheen. Hendrikson marveled at the sea creatures imprisoned in this wall, most of whom continued to swim about unperturbedly as the stars and galaxies still visible in the opening overhead hurtled toward the most distant limits of the universe. Sister Alejandra shouted something and slipped from Hendrikson's embrace, but the *Baptista* kept revolving clockwise — like the draining shower water that had once so upset him — downward through the shaft of this lazy maelstrom.

He was alone on the deck with the dead marlin. High above, spider webs of water were knitting a lattice on which a crystal-clear or maybe ebony jelly had begun to slide, moving from the opening's rim toward its center. This was the undersea cathedral's dome. Hendrikson stared upward at it in consternation and awe. The *Baptista* was being capped over. Sister Alejandra had left him. He wondered if she had run below to fetch the pressure cooker. No need, no need. His stomach was OK, it was his heart that was threatening to burst from his mouth. He was alone on the deck with the unmistakably quickening fish. There in the prow it was stirring, thrashing gently.

"All life comes from the sea," Hendrikson said. "Every terrestrial creature has it origins in brine. The Spirit of God moved upon the face of the waters, the waters gathered together, and God created great whales and every living creature which the waters brought forth abundantly after their kind." Whether he said these things aloud or only in his head, Hendrikson had no idea.

And then the marlin spoke.

Sister Alejandra and her passenger were rescued at the beginning of their seventh day in the gulf. Unremitting coastal rains had prevented seagoing parties from making much headway, while the aircraft dispatched from inland air bases had simply failed to make the crucial sighting that would have shortened their ordeal. Lifted into a helicopter sent over the *Baptista* by a Guardian de Dios cutter, the Pelagian nun and the dazed Heartlander seemed unready to talk of their experience. Furthermore, they stank. The helicopter pilot later informed the captain of the cutter that before they could tow the *Baptista* back to Cuerpo Divino, someone — preferably a couple of able-bodied seamen with no superstitious qualms — would have to dispose of the fetid marlin in the little vessel's prow.

This was done. But the captain had the fish's head cut off so that he could take the swordlike snout to his mother in Sarasota. This thoughtful gift pleased the devout woman a great deal.

VII

A dust devil blew across the terrace that Hendrikson's aging Elksmith tractor had just plowed. Although small, it reminded him of something that had happened to him many years ago off the New Castilian coast. Not too many people around White Sky gave much credit to his story, his wife Sarah being by far his strongest supporter, but he continued to tell it to whoever would listen. Indeed, he had actually made a few converts, one or two of whom were talking seriously about journeying to Cuerpo Divino to confirm his powerful experience with a witness of their own. Rumors that orthodox Pelagians had recently declared that God was no longer physically present in the seas, having withdrawn a second time from direct involvement in the affairs of men, had not shaken his friends' resolve to make the trip. The coasts were still holy.

Pirouetting and feinting, the dust devil spun beneath the white April sky. Even though it represented a rather commonplace phenomenon in this part of the country, its motion — its lifelikeness — made Hendrikson uneasy. He remembered a seasickness too big for any single human being to withstand alone and a speaking bioluminescence that even today gave him comfort.

In the enclosed cab of his tractor Hendrikson rummaged in his jeans pocket. Soon his fingers were clutching a rosary of fish bones. He lifted them into the light and counted them until the hollow feeling in the pit of his stomach had gone completely away. Shortly thereafter he finished his plowing.

The Gospel According To Gamaliel Crucis

Or, The Astrogator's Testimony

CHAPTER 1
Gamaliel's prologue.

In that eventful year, O Humanity, the Twentieth Expeditionary Force, having been gone from our solar system nearly two decades, flung itself back through the empty substratum of outer space carrying aboard its vanguard vessel, *Pilgrim*, the kidnapped Redeemer of another race.
2 Gamaliel Rashba, later self-christened Crucis, was chief astrogator for the Twentieth. Here he sets down his testimony as witness to the transuniversal Mantic truth, and to the shameful treachery of his people's response, and to the Hope that yet abides and in whose promise we may reliably sustain our myriad private hopes.
3 At the homecoming of the Twentieth, the peoples of Earth and all her proximate satellites and colonies rejoiced; for only five of our earliest expeditions to much closer suns had returned, and those so many years ago that the memory of their success had inevitably begun to fade.

4 Four other caravans to distant stars were still en route, but the ten remaining fleets of humanity's most hopeful and arrogant outreach had perished altogether, saddening the vigilant human populations of their original solar system.

5 The rejoicing of the peoples at the homecoming of the Twentieth, then, briefly united them. Celebration triumphed over longstanding blood hatreds, territorial disputes, politico-religious conflicts, and a host of newer disagreements that the members of the *Pilgrim* and her sister ships had not foreseen or imagined.

6 But these fragile reconciliations did not last, for what is fragile must eventually break, and with the resumption of the old feuds and enmities a glare like nova-light began to illuminate the astonishing nonhuman cargo brought to Earth aboard the *Pilgrim*.

7 To the hallowed disagreements, both old and new, inflaming the passions of humankind, was added the disruptive power of a Savior stolen from the insectile peoples of the fifth planet of the far-off Alpha Crucis binary.

8 Stolen, indeed, with their blessing, kidnapped with their active connivance; for they had other Redeemers in plenty, and by what the crew of the Twentieth told them about conditions Earthward it seemed to the intelligences of this world that humanity had need of at least one of their irritating surplus.

The alien Messiah introduced.

9 And this was the being whom Gamaliel and the others called *Lady Mantid*, or *Gottesanbeterin*, or *prie-Dieu*, or *Godhorse*, or *Mistress*, and many other names redolent of awe or respect, depending of course on their birthplaces and the idioms of their native tongues.

10 A being whom some small number of those aboard the *Pilgrim* slowly came to know as an alien essence consubstantial with the Second Person of the long-discredited

Nicene Trinity. (That Gamaliel adopted this point of view surprised him as much as, or even more than, it surprised those who knew his background and personal history.)

11 This, then, was the Alphacrucian Christ, a female mantid of untoward delicacy and strength, easily as large as the largest Russian wolfhound, in color a lovely avocado, in movement a clockwork ballerina, full of both strangeness and grace, ever glittering at the eye.

12 "Call me Mantikhoras," she herself had said in her mellifluous, feminine way, in the passenger hold of the *Pilgrim*. "For I am the man-eater whose appetite means not death but regeneration, and you, Gamaliel, are he whose duty it is to satisfy your species' hunger by continually satisfying mine."

13 This saying frightened more of the astrogator's colleagues and subordinates than it comforted or converted; and from that day forward Gamaliel championed the divine mission of the six-legged creature only at his most wary discretion and almost always at his peril.

Presentation to the press.

14 Into the half-empty Sheol of Cleveland, Ohio, capital city of the Multipartite Union of North America, the officers of the Twentieth Expeditionary Force took their alien charge to a meeting with the scribes and superstars of the Pan-Solar Press. (Boston, New York, Philadelphia, Baltimore, and Washington had been obliterated during the opening salvos of the Cobalt Galas, eighty-odd years ago.)

15 At the sight of Mantikhoras all these formidable personages fell back in disbelief, and perhaps a dozen swooned: but among the first to recover was the CABLE-STAR holocaster Rachelka Dan, who pressed forward to gaze upon the mantid and to machine-gun her questions.

16 She directed most of these at Captain H.K. Bajaj, leader of the Twentieth: "How did you come to take the creature from its world? Does it understand the geopolitical standoff

prevailing here on Earth or the iffy intercolonial relationships structuring the politics of Sunspace? What does it
think of Cleveland?"

17 And Rachelka Dan also asked, "Has the alien freely
consented to this interview? Why have you chosen this
time and this particular forum to introduce it to humanity?
Does it speak?" And an array of similar questions too
numerous to detail.

18 Captain Bajaj replied, "This meeting takes place here
and now by order of the Interstellar Diplomatic Instrument
for Outreach, Trade, and Study, the selfsame global authority that has mounted every extrasolar expedition to date."

19 Whereupon Gamaliel the Astrogator spoke up, saying,
"Never fear. The mantid learned human languages, history,
and cultural lore en route from Acrux V. She does indeed
speak, friends, but her hour isn't come yet."

20 "Her hour for what?" clamored the scribes and holocasters, many of whom were astounded that Gamaliel had
identified the mantid as female. "She looks like a big green
bug, but you make it sound like she has some overwhelming apocalyptic message for our worlds."

21 "*M. religiosa crucensis,*" Gamaliel corrected them. "Family Mantidae, order Dictyoptera, substance Divine. Please
don't call her a 'big green bug.' By the way, those of you
who fainted a moment ago have certainly become brave in
the wake of Ms. Dan's questioning."

22 Chastened in this wise, some of the scribes and holocasters mumbled among themselves, thinking to repay the
astrogator by ridiculing his belief in the supernatural origins
of the insect. "Are you the bug's disciple?" one of them
asked. "Do you propose our immediate conversion to High
Buggery?"

23 These remarks prompted much profane laughter and
raillery, so much that Captain Bajaj made a gesture indicat-
ing the imminent termination of the interview.

24 "I am indeed the Alphacrucian's disciple!" Gamaliel shouted above the din. "I confess it to every nation, satellite, and colony!"

25 The noise abated a little, and Rachelka Dan, turning to the captain, asked, "Has the mantid made other disciples among the officers and crew of the Twentieth? Or is your astrogator alone in this startling declaration of faith?"

26 Said Captain Bajaj, his eyes cast down as if in embarrassment, "At least two others on the *Pilgrim* share his perspective: Andrew Stout, the medical officer, and Priscilla Muthinga, our assistant xenologist. How many others share their view I'm not prepared to say." And he strode from the dais to escape further probing.

Mantikhoras quiets the throng.

27 Bedlam ensued, and neither Gamaliel nor any of the remaining five officers could impose order on the chaos: so that even the mantid on the platform began to stalk from side to side, adding to the dismay of many and therefore to the noise.

28 In a voice of porcelain purity and tremulant timbre the mantid cried aloud, "Give heed a moment to Gamaliel!" This command draped silence on the throng, being so unexpected, and everyone gazed up at the creature in awe and amazement.

29 And Gamaliel, the way having been prepared for him, stepped to the middle of the platform and in impassioned tones began to address the peoples of every nation, satellite, and colony, declaring:

CHAPTER 2
Planetfall on Acrux V.

1 "This mantid is the Messiah, the Anointed One long ago promised the Jews, and though I have come to believe in her as a child of Abraham, I see that even those in Peter's church and its schismatic heirs may also believe, for she and the problematic Jesus are of the same essence as The One.

2 "On Acrux V, you see, we happened to put down during the messianic mission of Lady Mantid and her sibling saviors, an accident that The One in loving repudiation of the godly attribute of all-knowingness did nothing to prevent.

3 "The people of this world are thinking insects, self-aware Mantidae, but like us fallen from the primeval Garden into Sin and Death: for which reason The One sent unto them a Holy Family of vermiform larvae.

4 "Each of these hatchlings, be it noted, emerged from the same encompassing egg case, or *ootheca*, which itself was extruded by a virgin mantid blessed with fecundity by the inspiriting touch of the Transuniversal Holy Ghost.

5 "Acrux V crawls with sentient creatures, all of whom reproduce in the immemorial orthopteran fashion; and for the Daughter of Mantid, our Mantikhoras, to appear among them as the *solitary* issue of a gravid egg case would violate the covenant of their biology and the expectations of their culture."

Rachelka Dan interrupts.

6 At which point Rachelka Dan broke in, saying, "Do you mean to tell us that God — or The One, if you prefer that designation — sent an entire SWAT team of Messiahs to the Alphacrucians?" An inquiry that provoked another minor uproar among the representatives of the Pan-Solar Press.

7 Having returned to the platform from the corridor, Captain Bajaj lifted his hand and declared, "This is something that a Hindu such as myself may easily understand, and if the lady from CABLE-STAR does not object, I will explain the matter."

8 With the holocaster's ready consent the captain resumed, saying, "The avatars of Vishnu are many. Although they are not so many as the incarnations of divinity sent as siblings to the Alphacrucians, even Mahatma Ghandi once asked a Christian missionary why God, if He had one son, did not have another and another."

9 Concluded the captain, "On Acrux V, I fear, God had so many children that like the old woman in the nursery rhyme he didn't know what to do." The press corps howled gleefully at this remark, and Captain Bajaj, shaking his head, stepped aside for Gamaliel.

The astrogator's narrative resumed.

10 Thus bolstered, the astrogator continued his story: "Some of the hundreds of nymphs emerging from the holy ootheca, there in the bleak, rocky desert of their homeland, fell upon and devoured one another, an orthopteran biological impulse that reduced their number to a couple of hundred or so.

11 "If you like, call this postnatal feast a celebration of the Eucharist, or the First Supper, or Unruly Communion, or any other term that seems to you appropriate.

12 "But remember that if The One wished Its insectile offspring to be both fully mantid and fully divine, these teeming nymphal incarnations were altogether necessary; therefore The One accomplished them."

13 ("Yecch," said a holocaster near the dais, whose colleagues first shushed and then snidely ridiculed him.)

14 Gamaliel spoke more, saying, "We arrived while Mantikhoras and her surviving egg-mates, long since grown from wingless nymphs to adults capable of flight, were whirring from one Alphacrucian hamlet to another, preaching the gospel and healing the afflicted and doing other miraculous things that we of the Twentieth were not always privileged to witness.

15 "This evangelism enraged the duly established queens and councils of that world, by openly challenging the status quo and thus appearing to threaten their authority, actions deemed by the rulers as crimes of a religious as well as a secular cast.

16 "Our advent further confused the situation: but because many of the male saviors gave in to mantid lust and so suffered decapitation at the jaws of their otherwise sated brides, day by day the ranks of the divine siblings were thinned, leaving only females to continue the program on which The One had dispatched them.

17 "Disturbed by the ongoing mission of even these remaining rabbis, down now to sixty or seventy in all, the most powerful Alphacrucian rulers sought to enlist the aid of some of us from the Twentieth in curbing their evangelical activity;

18 "For we were often at court with the rulers, observing their ways and exchanging data, and they supposed us sympathetic to their position vis-à-vis the disruptive influence of the barnstorming redeemers.

19 "Intellectually keen but technologically backward, the Alphacrucian rulers perhaps saw us as harbingers of their own material evolution, provided, of course, that the evangels were prevented from plunging the people at large back into the toils of superstition and from encouraging in them a hopeless egalitarianism."

20 Cried an annoyed holocaster, "This is getting thick, Gamaliel! Why don't you come to the point?"

21 The astrogator replied, "The point is that after half a revolution of Acrux V around its primary, we decided that our presence was itself an anomalous factor in the life of the world, and so made plans to depart, symbolically washing our hands of any complicity in the fate of either the rulers or the evangels.

22 "Said the preeminent elder of the preeminent Alphacrucian council, 'If you don't take one of the self-proclaimed Daughters of Mantid with you as an object of study, she'll certainly die with the others when, for their crimes of cultic blasphemy and civil agitation, we arrest and devour them.'

23 "And the elder added, his wide-set eyes aglitter, 'We're glad to let a people as advanced as you but so poor in offspring per couple borrow one of our impertinent redeemers,' around which last word it was impossible not to hear a set of scornful quotation marks.

24 "This elder, you see, had once visited Andrew Stout's surgery aboard the *Pilgrim* and probably believed that we would subject our messianic passenger to vivisection, dismemberment, and microscopic examination, the end result being her death.

25 "Instead we accepted the offer as a means of preserving the creature's life and of fulfilling our tripartite responsibility as bona fide concessionaires of the Interstellar Diplomatic Instrument for Outreach, Trade, and Study.

26 "And on our voyage home from the Alpha Crucis binary the being whom we now call either Lady Mantid or Mantikhoras convinced me of her godly descent by her fierce serenity, and by her all-encompassing intellect, and by a modest array of signs and wonders."

27 Snapped Rachelka Dan, "Details, please! Details!"

Lady Mantid buttresses the emptiness.

28 And Gamaliel replied, "On one occasion on our voyage through the empty substratum beneath the vacuum proper, Mantikhoras stretched forth a forelimb and healed a tiny rent in an exterior bulkhead through which the lethal force of nothingness had begun to seep."

29 A holocaster upbraided the astrogator, saying, "A patch would have done as well. In many cases miracles give birth to faith, but here I'm afraid your faith has given birth to a miracle."

30 "On another occasion," Gamaliel responded, "pleased that I had pledged to her discipleship, Lady Mantid granted me a glimpse of the deathly void that belief in The One through the mediation of her person would vanquish utterly.

31 "This she did by standing alone with me in an aft compartment of the *Pilgrim* and saying to the ship's inanimate consituent parts, *'Away!'*

32 "Whereupon every bulkhead disappeared, and every crew member was visible to me as a living marionette hanging in the substanceless dark, seemingly without support and completely unaware of the vast self-centered emptiness in which they danced.

33 "Frightened and deathly cold, I collapsed: but Mantikhoras lifted me again and said, 'This is the domain of death, for which the starless, transdimensional realm of the substratum beneath the void is only an elegant allegory.

34 "'Here, however, not even an astrogator has power to move or maneuver, for no stars shine. And what point is there in changing places within an emptiness that is everywhere the same and everywhere inhospitable?

35 "'Just as you plot the *Pilgrim's* path through the spatial substratum to the light, Gamaliel, I guide those who deliver themselves to me, for I am that which gives shape to the formless: the bone in the body, the struts in the solar sail.'

36 "And Mantikhoras said another word, restoring the walls of the vessel and putting a deck beneath my feet again: so that I knew this miracle for a parable as well as a prodigy, and I straightway handed myself over."

37 Then Captain Bajaj went to the podium to announce that all questioning must cease, and the scribes and holocasters cried in one voice, "Is your astrogator lying? Did others experience this? What's *your* explanation of the matter?"

38 To which the captain answered, "An hallucination, my friends. The substratum is the very province of hallucinations."

39 Neither Gamaliel nor Lady Mantid had any chance to counter the captain's argument, for the party from the Twentieth was ushered from the room, the mantid ambling in her monarchial, clockwork way and the astrogator hurrying to remain abreast of her.

40 Whispered a colleague to Rachelka Dan, "What do you think Thaddeus Thorogood and the New Testament Revivalists are going to make of this development, huh? Not one among us had sense enough to raise the question, but it's probably the most important one there is."

41 "Amen," said Rachelka Dan under her breath. "This adventure is only beginning. Mark my words, mark my words."

CHAPTER 3

1 After this dramatic introduction, the Interstellar Diplomatic Instrument set Mantikhoras apart from both humanity and the Pan-Solar Press, and not even Captain Bajaj or Gamaliel the Astrogator knew where; for it was decided in high places that the mantid must undergo further study and swear earthly allegiance to the disarranged government of the Multipartite Union of North America.

2 This she apparently did without delay or qualm, resting her spirit in the saying (perhaps apocryphal), Render unto temporal powers the inconsequential and unto The One that which truly counts.

Mantikhoras's cross-country flight.

3 In some wise, however, the mantid obtained her release and set off under her own power for the California amusement park where she knew Andrew Stout, Priscilla Muthinga, Nicholas Morowitz, and Gamaliel, disciples all, had escaped from the mothballed *Pilgrim* for some well-earned R & R.

4 During this flight Mantikhoras looked down on the ruined cities, cratered farms, polluted rivers, slumped mountains, blighted forests, scarred hills, and pale dead lakes of the M.U.N.A., marveling that amid such desolation the people continued to support — over and above all other enterprises — professional sports stadia and a bewildering variety of gaudy playlands.

5 A squadron of battered scoopjets escorted Mantikhoras from her place of detention (Pelee Island, Lake Erie) to Kansas City, Missouri, where simple curiosity induced the mantid to descend to observe the people riding roller-coasters, log rafts, and bump'em cars in the meticulously restored ruins of an ancient theme park.

6 Upon seeing the alien visitor, those enjoying the amusements grew agitated, pointing and running and sometimes even cat-calling at her; for they recognized her from the holocasts, while she in turn felt compassion for their many deformities and the bitterness of their bewilderment in the face of such afflictions.

7 And there in the park she took many small children for brief flights, and talked with their parents, and answered the hatred of the most vocal bigots with kindness and humor, but purposely refrained from performing any miracles.

8 But at last the park officials asked her to go, declaring that she had taken profits from the ice-cream and soft-drink vendors, and had also frightened hundreds of small children into believing that a monster was loose on the grounds: an accusation with only a flimsy shadow of truth.

9 Undismayed, Mantikhoras bade her new friends adieu and departed, taking care to continue her journey westward at a tree-top altitude that, by thwarting easy radar detection, enabled her to elude the noise and pomp of her unasked-for scoopjet escort.

10 And so she whirred over wheat fields and cattle lots, through eroded gulleys and diseased stands of cotton-woods; and frequently along her route she was aware of radioactive hot spots, and always she was struck by the numbers of malformed people and animals inhabiting the blasted continent.

11 Over the Oklahoma panhandle a rancher in a buck-board knocked her out of the sky with a double-barreled discharge from a 12-gauge, peppering her right wing with birdshot: so that she tumbled to earth into an arroyo reeking of alkali but so high-banked and twisty that it prevented her from being discovered for the coup de grâce.

12 "*I* am the coup de grâce," said Mantikhoras to the cloudless heavens; "*I* am the stroke of mercy. Indeed, *I* am the gracious death that opens a gate into paradise." But there was no one to hear her.

13 Nor could she depart by air, for her wing was broken, and she settled in for the night, asking forgiveness for her assailant on the grounds that to him she must surely have resembled the vanguard of a truly prodigious plague of locusts.

The temptation in the wilderness.

14 Thus began her adventure in the wilderness, where she stayed forty days, praying continually, hallucinating pleasant Alphacrucian landscapes, and slaking her thirst on the brackish reservoirs of moisture in various succulent cacti and discarded diet-cola cans.

15 At last there appeared to Lady Mantid, either in the flesh or in the dreams of her fever, a figure in greasy khaki, unshaven and ill-shod, whose eyes looked like shriveled raisins; and this apparition invited her into his rattletrap vehicle and put to her many disheartening proposals:

16 "Come with me to Vegas, baby, and we'll split the take sixty-forty, me on the up side for providin' the transportation; or maybe fifty-fifty if it looks like you're gonna be a *really* big hit."

17 And carrying Mantikhoras out of Oklahoma into New Mexico, the driver enumerated the likely rewards to both of them of a night-club routine at Nero's Bistro on the Strip, particularly if the mantid did not disdain to do wonders.

18 Said the would-be impresario, "You know, make the whole goddamn hotel disappear the way you did that spaceship. Then, jus' when everybody's good 'n' scared, slap it back around 'em and keep 'em from crappin' their drawers.

19 "Or maybe we could push a whole battery of slot machines up there on stage and you could sorta pray up a jackpot on ever' single one of 'em, which the management'd like 'cause it'd probably make the suckers believe the same thing's possible out there in the casinos."

20 Mantikhoras, hypnotized by both the heatwaves rising from the asphalt and the baffling incantations on the driver's lips, made no reply.

21 Noticing her silence, the pitchman said, "There's more than silver to get out of this, baby. There's booze, and baubles, and, uh, whatever turns you on. Maybe we could round up a bugbox of dragonflies or somepin and just sorta shake 'em out in your bed, hey?"

22 And "Stop the car, let me out," Mantikhoras said. "This isn't my mission": so that, thus rebuked, the angry driver shoved her out the door without stopping and sped off down the deserted highway into the next sun-baked adobe town.

The calf.

23 As the Alphacrucian rolled into yet another gulley, she realized that her tempter had been a living creature rather than a dream, and she hungered mightily, not only for food but for solace;

24 Whereupon a blind calf with two heads came unto her in the arroyo, bleating tenderly and nuzzling her thorax; and she stroked the beast with her forelimbs, saying,

25 "Because of the evil done against you by your masters, who are themselves blind, I bequeath unto you with these words a *rational soul*, and all the responsibilities and perquisites attending that gift."

26 By this speech the calf's tongues were loosed, and it said, both heads speaking together, "If I'm now in honorary possession of a rational soul, I beg you to devour me for thy name's sake, that I may inherit the kingdom"; for the calf had immediately perceived the deeper identity of the Alphacrucian.

27 Mantikhoras wept.

28 And said to the two-headed calf, "Before I do, I must restore your sight," which she did at once: so that the calf beheld the first stars glimmering in the dusk and bleated at them in heart-rending admiration and gratitude.

29 Embracing the creature, Mantikhoras assuaged her hunger, leaving the hides and hooves as offerings to The One (whose proxies tonight were a flock of circling vultures); and the spirit of the ennobled calf ascended straightway into heaven.

Reunion with the disciples.

30 Now the forty days were ended, a period during which helicopters, highway patrolmen, and units of the Civil Air Patrol had crisscrossed the western half of the continent in search of her; and Mantikhoras, having escaped both discovery and rescue, took flight again.

31 Yet farther to the west, in the opulent amusement park called Magic Kindgom VII, Gamaliel and his fellow believers from the Twentieth had grown weary of the rigors of their protracted R & R.

32 Said Priscilla Muthinga to the others, "I've enjoyed just about all of this I can stand," at which remark an employee in the get-up of an ill-tempered Dwarf poked her in the ankle with a stick designed for retrieving litter.

33 Seeing this attack, Gamaliel made Priscilla put forth her other leg so that the Dwarf could poke it in the ankle, too: whereupon he and his comrades-in-faith disarmed the park employee and warned him firmly of the likely consequences of his ever again abusing their turn-the-other-ankle piety.

34 "I'm sick of this place, Gamaliel," said Andrew Stout when the Dwarf had slunk away. "Why don't we flick over to Hawaii for a round of Frisbee golf or maybe some out-of-

body surfing in etheric wetsuits by Bloomingdale & Sears?"
35 Cried the others, "I'm for that, I'm for that!" and even
Gamaliel found himself doubting the survival of their Mistress and wavering quite alarmingly in his allegiance to the
code of discipleship.
36 But just when he was preparing to consent to the others' frivolous plans, they all heard a buzzing of wings and
Mantikhoras herself came swooping down upon them from
over the great, pseudo-glacial peak of a fiberglass mountain
three hundred feet high.
37 Said Lady Mantid, landing near her followers, "The
task is at hand. Come, let's get to work."

CHAPTER 4
On the air.

1 Not long after this Mantikhoras appeared on a pan-solar
broadcast of the holoprogram _Parsecs Ahead_, hosted by
Rachelka Dan before a live studio audience in a dilapidated
CABLE-STAR facility in Burbank, California.
2 The topic of the evening was the alleged divinity of the
visitor from Acrux V, and the producers of the program had
assembled not only Lady Mantid herself but also the team
of scientists who had studied her on Pelee Island during her
enforced confinement after the press conference in
Cleveland, Ohio.
3 Although Gamaliel and the others strongly recommended that their Mistress refrain from appearing on _Parsecs Ahead_, fearing that the debate would turn into a
sideshow staged and manipulated by the skillful Ms. Dan,
Mantikhoras rebuked them for worrywarts, saying,
4 "Isn't it likely that the Daughter of Mantid, having witnessed manipulations of much greater magnitude than anything you're going to see here, understands exactly what
she's about?"
5 Therefore she went on the program, and in her opening

interview with Rachelka Dan, while steadfastly refusing to
identify herself as anything other than an intelligent mantid, astonished everyone with the precision and poetry of
her speech.

6 Rachelka Dan pursued the matter, saying, "But the astrogator aboard the Twentieth claims greater things for you,
and on your flight from Cleveland or wherever to Anaheim,
which took you a surprisingly long time, it's rumored that
you stopped in several small communities to demonstrate
your, uh, well, your *powers*."

7 To which the mantid replied, "The only nonhuman
power I've demonstrated to date is that of unassisted flight,
a capability I share with every other self-aware adult on my
distant world of origin."

8 And the host of *Parsecs Ahead* declared, "Tellingly, Lady
Mantid, a world whose leadership rejected you and sent
you home with the Twentieth as a kind of insidious revolutionary, a bad seed they preferred to see planted in the
exhausted but well-turned soil of Good Old Earth.

9 "Is it any wonder, then, that some of us suspect your
intentions and think your most ardent supporters are
dupes of the ruling Alphacrucians? Perhaps you're here to
undermine the very foundations of our lives."

10 And Mantikhoras said, much to the uneasiness of her
disciples on the premises, "If I've come to undermine your
lives, I've done so only to buttress your humanity and to
elevate your questing spirits."

11 On this pronouncement Ms. Dan pounced with both
feet: "So that subversion *is* your mission, isn't it? At last you
admit it. And you also hint at a superhuman — a supernatural — motive that earlier you denied."

12 Mantikhoras's antennae quivered in gnomic acknowledgment, but otherwise she did not reply.

13 After a series of commercial messages (for, among other
things, a round-trip vacation package to Ganymede, a do-it-

yourself bioengineering kit, and a handy pocket Geiger counter), Ms. Dan introduced a panel of government scientists and another of independent theologians, all of whom professed to understand the mantid's genetic and spiritual makeup.

14 Dr. Millard Crews, an alien anatomist who had never even visited the Galapagos Islands, declared that Mantikhoras had an outsized orthopteran body and an unusual tripartite brain whose like he had never encountered before; nevertheless, he felt reasonably certain that the creature was indeed a creature and not an avatar of divinity.

15 Dr. Scheherezade Tabataba'i, late of the University of Isfahan, scoffed at the notion that Mantikhoras represented the long-awaited Shiite *mahdi*, recovered from her "occultation" by the crew of the Twentieth; the Islamic theologian also rejected as clumsy and unconvincing the mantid's impersonation of the Judeo-Christian Messiah.

16 Dr. Joe Bob Newcombe, president of West Texas New Testament Revivalist College in El Paso, told the program's pan-solar audience that the mantid's very existence was an insult to God and that her manifold blasphemies here on *Parsecs Ahead* warranted nothing short of deportation and probably a lot worse.

17 Other "experts" testified that the Alphacrucian was a) a spectacular special effect, b) a powerful argument for either atheism or credulity, c) an extraterrestrial analogue of the scarab beetle sacred to the ancient Egyptians, d) an orthopteran half-wit released into our custody by her own irresponsible people, or e) a genius banished from Acrux V for her innovative social ideas.

The L.G. Kroeber psychoscope.

18 At last Dr. Felipe Novello, a licensed psychoscopist and moderately well-known depth-oneiromancer, overrode the others by declaring that he for one accepted the divine nature of the mantid, and that he had what amounted to credible scientific proof of her divinity.

19 Rachelka Dan accosted the man with a microphone: "All right, then, Dr. Novello, let's have it: the worlds are wait- ing."

20 Said her guest, "The unconsciousness of an entity iden- tical with the Supreme Being in almost every respect but that of spiritual ubiquity would present an unparalleled challenge to a depth-oneiromancer, wouldn't you agree? Well, it does, and I accepted the challenge."

21 "What Dr. Novello is trying to say," Rachelka Dan explained, "is that a peek inside the dreaming mind of a creaturely projection of God, or The One, would be a small assault on the mind of God itself."

22 Dr. Novello nodded his qualified assent to this para- phrase of his own statement, and a pair of mechanical stagehands rolled a gleaming L.G. Kroeber psychoscope onto the ramshackle set of *Parsecs Ahead*.

23 Said the psychoscopist, going to the machine, "I will now replay for you a holotape of the Uncon dimension of Mantikhoras's mental activity during a four-hour sleep period at our research facility on [site of facility *bleeped* from broadcast]. I'll run the tape at twenty times our original recording speed to stay within the stipulated programming limits."

24 And the three-dimensional screen, or video well, of the psychoscope filled with an inchoate fog, a formlessness as deep and all-pervasive as that of the substratum beneath the interstellar void; and this inchoate fog began to shimmer and quake in basso-profundo registers of silence that every viewer felt in his or her bones.

25 And all that came thereafter no one watching could chronicle or synopsize, for to some it seemed that nothing more occurred at all; while to others the psychoscope revealed a pageant of cosmogenesis so rapid and minutely detailed that different images leapt out and utterly preoccupied different people.

26   Gamaliel, for instance, found himself stirring inside the sticky skin of a terrestrial *M. religiosa* just prior to its intermediate molt, stalks of grass towering around him like sequoias and every clod of dirt a miniature Gibraltar.

27   Meanwhile, Andrew Stout waltzed in stately lunar orbit around a planetary gas giant in another galaxy; and Priscilla, somewhere in the Pacific Ocean, darted here and there over the gleaming hide of a hammerhead shark, cleansing it of near-invisible parasites.

28   What other onlookers excerpted and experienced only those others could say, but it was everywhere as distinct and singular as it was vivid: a kaleidoscope of images, an infinitely vast smorgasbord from which to pick and choose.

29   At last the video well of the L.G. Kroeber psychoscope began to incandesce, radiating a powerful white light that united the audience of *Parsecs Ahead* in an overwhelming blaze of phosphor dots and motile phosphenes.

30   And Mantikhoras spoke into this light, saying, "Remember what blinds you, and look through it, and on the other side you will certainly see that which has been there from the beginning."

31   Many voices cried out in alarm, and the psychoscope exploded, showering sparks, and Rachelka Dan shouted, "Cut to our test pattern!" and *Parsecs Ahead* went off the air in a roar of incandescence that ruined the holosets of three quarters of CABLE-STAR's clientele.

Escape from the studio.

32   Said Felipe Novello, "See what I mean?" but the uproar in the studio among both his colleagues and the audience rendered his question inaudible; and the Daughter of Mantid hitched her way unmolested from the building to the parking lot, where Gamaliel and the others had taken refuge.

33   It was twelve-thirty in the morning, and clear, but none of Lady Mantid's followers could see the stars for the nimbus of celestial brightness lingering on their retinae from the exploded psychoscope: so that the disciples felt themselves floating along as if in a perfusing billow of squid ink. **34** When they complained of this, Mantikhoras said, "Out of blindness, sight"; and led them from Burbank into the desert, where the stars reemerged, and there they spent the night talking of eternity, suffering, discipleship, and the mutability of holocast ratings.

CHAPTER 5
Rachelka Dan converted.

1 After this Mantikhoras went the length and breadth of the habitable continent, visiting hospitals, amusement parks, sports stadia, gambling casinos (even Nero's Bistro), military bases, zoos, and other mutant reservations.

2 Her successful appearance on *Parsecs Ahead* made her instantly recognizable and instantly welcome wherever she went (excluding only the heartland of Thaddeus Thorogood's New Testament Revivalists); and she dispensed comfort or miracles as each situation warranted.

3 Rachelka Dan was the mantid's newest and most ardent convert; and she and Gamaliel the Astrogator often acted as the Alphacrucian's advance team, preceding their winged Mistress to each new site and arranging both interviews and lodging.

4 Jews by birth and upbringing, Rachelka and Gamaliel together reached the conclusion that Mantikhoras was not necessarily a new incarnation of the God-in-man esteemed by the tattered remnants of contemporary Christendom, but instead the Suffering Servant prophesied in the 53rd chapter of Isaiah.

5 For in the verses of this chapter it is said of the servant, "he hath no form nor comeliness; and when we shall see him, there is no beauty we should desire him," which descriptions had some seeming reference to the image of the mantid in the eyes of a narrow-souled humanity.

6 Or, if not the Suffering Servant of Isaiah, then perhaps the Son of man in the visionary seventh chapter of Daniel, whose "dominion is an everlasting dominion which shall not pass away."

7 For these were the Messianic possibilities that did not conflict with the faith of their childhoods, and that likewise conformed both to the portrait of the Suffering Servant in Isaiah and to that in Daniel of the Son of man riding to glory on a heavenly thundercloud.

8 Said Gamaliel to Rachelka, "Of course I never expected to escort the Messiah to Earth aboard the *Pilgrim*, but I infinitely prefer that sort of commonplace arrival to the Messiah's advent in an apocalyptic blitzkrieg that signals all-out warfare between, uh, Good and Evil."

9 "Although I never believed in a warrior Messiah or in a Levite priest-king come to cleanse us of our sins," replied Rachelka, "the mind of Mantikhoras is clearly that of God, and I'm committed to her as both captive and lover."

10 Uncertainty and bashfulness stayed Gamaliel's tongue (shore leave on Acrux V had done little to improve his social graces), and for several weeks during these exciting travels he went to bed in motel rooms next to Rachelka's struggling to square his lust with his admiration for her and his devotion to the Cause.

11 He hoped that Rachelka would become *his* captive and *his* lover, for he wanted her to continue with him in their common ministry not merely as a fellow disciple but as his wife.

Miraculous cures.

12 Meanwhile Mantikhoras toured the radiation-sickness wards of special sanatoria for fallout victims, and held audiences with cancer patients whose malignancies were inoperable, and sought out on every medical front sufferers whose physicians had numbered their days and despaired of ever curing anyone similarly afflicted.

13 Gamaliel saw the Daughter of Mantid pray with a man whose bone marrow showed up on thermoscans as fiery rivers of strontium 90: an hour later the radioactivity had departed, and the blood-cell count had stabilized at a normal level.

14 The astrogator also witnessed the Alphacrucian drive a cancer that had metastasized through the liver and lights of a two-year-old girl into a lump of phlegm, which the child promptly disgorged and the doctors just as promptly doused with alcohol and burned in a chromium bedpan.

15 On yet another occasion, in a hovel on the wolf-ridden periphery of Tacoma, Washington, Mantikhoras embraced a woman in the last stages of rabies and before the day was out had her cheerfully taking food and planning a visit to Tucson.

16 Everywhere that the mantid and her entourage went, then, people pressed forward with their misshapen bodies, their unlikely diseases, and their hungry spirits, looking for straightening, or remedy, or nourishment; for those whom Mantikhoras had healed since her appearance on *Parsecs Ahead* were legion.

17 But certain suppliants she turned away, saying, "Your own people have the knowledge and wherewithal to cure you"; whereupon Andrew Stout would come forward with a referral to the appropriate specialist or clinic, and Priscilla Muthinga with enough money to pay for the necessary treatments.

The ungrateful petitioner.

18 Once, a young double-amputee advised to apply for lifelike prosthetics from a Swiss bioengineering firm, and funded on the spot for these devices, berated Mantikhoras for her heartlessness, shouting,

19 "You don't give a damn about my disability, do you?

You've got wings! That I've been legless almost my entire life doesn't mean shit to you, does it? Does it, you goddamn overgrown *grasshopper?"*

20   Andrew, who was for dumping the petitioner from his wheelchair, grew red-faced pointing out to the young man the powerful likelihood that his missing limbs were a visible sign of his spiritual poverty.

21   But Mantikhoras silenced Andrew by lifting her papery wings and saying to the bitter one, "I'd give these to you, young man, if they would do you any good. However, it's not upon fleshly wings that you'll mount from your affliction to fulfillment, but instead upon the wings of your own faith in my ministry."

22   Cried the man in the wheelchair, sneering his contempt and scorn, "What a crock of bullshit!"

23   And Mantikhoras, bowing her head, asked her followers to wrench her wings from her body and give them to the man as an offering of both love and commitment, which drastic deed Gamaliel and the others could not bring themselves to perform.

24   Angry with them for refusing her, the mantid appealed to the crowd, at last prevailing upon two bikers from Birmingham, Alabama, to step forward and rip her wings from her prothorax. As they obeyed, both men wore nervous grins, for they were unsure of the propriety of this duly-authorized mutilation.

25   Then said Mantikhoras to the double-amputee, "I'm giving you my wings not as replacements for your legs, but as tokens of my willingness to share your suffering."

26   Still unrepentant, the young man answered, "I couldn't never fly, and I'm still not gonna be able to walk. What good's you goin' and givin' up your stupid wings gonna do me or anybody else?"

27   Turning again to the bikers, Mantikhoras asked them to separate her praying forelimbs from her body, which request, although Gamaliel and the others argued vehemently against it, the two men appeared ready enough to honor.

28 At last the bitter young man in the wheelchair cried, "Keep your own goddamn legs, goddammit! You're not gonna stick me with that guilt trip, too!" And he propelled himself out of the crowd, carrying with him Andrew's referral and Priscilla's cashier's check.

29 And Priscilla said, "Mistress, your sacrifice was wasted on that one. He'd rather have the entire world in wheelchairs than walk again himself. He spared you your forelimbs not from any kindness but instead to keep from having their loss forever on his conscience."

30 To which the mantid replied, "A judgment that confirms the fact that he possesses one."

On conscience.

31 Later, when Mantikhoras and her disciples had walked apart to a secluded place, she said, "Conscience is God's most precious gift to rational souls, and I'm here to tell you that there is *no* rational soul upon whom The One has failed to bestow it.

32 "Some may put the gift in a drawer, or shove it into a closet and cover it over with coats, toys, and boardgames: but when the drawer is finally opened or the closet set to rights, the gift's still there, cobwebbed perhaps but otherwise ready for use."

33 For every eight or ten disciples attracted by Lady Mantid's miracles of healing, or unselfishness, or wordless aura of authority, her occasional commentaries on these acts (see, for instance, Gamaliel 5:31-32) almost always led one or two other converts to backslide or defect.

34 Repelled by parabolic statement or embarrassed by what they misperceived as pious talk, these squeamish followers drifted away, with the result that Mantikhoras sometimes questioned the faithful about the efficacy of her methods and consequently earned the mistrust of a few by appearing to doubt herself.

35 "Maybe I'm going about this wrong," she would say. "This just doesn't seem to be an age for beatitudes or parables."

36 Once, then, Rachelka Dan sought to justify the Daughter of Mantid's periodic bouts of self-questioning by reminding a group of adherents grumbling among themselves at poolside in a luxury hotel in Omaha that humanity had borrowed its Messiah from another sentient species in another solar system.

37 Said Rachelka to the grumblers, "It's sometimes very hard for her. Allowances must be made."

38 Responded one of this throng, "Room allowances, you mean! Mantikhoras always takes the bridal suite or some other plushy pad, and we get stuck in second-class accommodations five or six blocks down the street. I don't even have a holoset in my room."

39 Mantikhoras, who had overheard these gibes from a balcony, revealed herself to the mutterers and said, "Don't begrudge me the temporal comfort of a bridal suite. I'm not with you for long, and the rooms I go to prepare for you when I depart, why, not even the fabled Conrad Hilton himself could duplicate for plushness."

40 And suffering from no uncommon homesickness, she retired from them, leaving them abashed and penitent.

CHAPTER 6
A wedding in Escambia County.

1 Not long after this, in Pensacola, Florida, M.U.N.A., Gamaliel asked Rachelka to marry him; and she consented on the condition, easily and promptly met, that Mantikhoras herself preside over their exchange of vows.

2 Because even the mantid appeared in some haste to bestow legitimacy on the astrogator's ardor, the couple decided to forgo a full-blown ceremony with ushers, brides-maids, flower girls, and the obligatory three-tiered cake, almost inevitably stale.

3 They would marry that same evening, and the following morning Mantikhoras would announce the event as a *fait accompli*, preferably at a breakfast gathering of the disciples there in the restaurant of the Gulf Sands Budget Resort.

4 Tooling along in a rented dune buggy, then, Gamaliel and his passengers kept their eyes open for a roadside synagogue, of which there seemed to be, in this elongate coastal neighborhood, a dismaying dearth.

5 Satisfied that the couple would not soon find what they were seeking, Mantikhoras told the astrogator to turn right and drive inland until they arrived at any cleanly structure dedicated to both the remembrance and the service of The One.

6 This proved to be a modern Neutester chapel of rein-forced cinder blocks and polarized glass tinted a shade off full purple. Fenced about by palm trees, it sat in the shadow of a multistory condominium whose topmost floors loomed in the dusk like a shelf of stormclouds illumined from within by pale lightnings.

7 Declared Gamaliel at the sight of the chapel, "This won't do," but Rachelka put a gentle finger to his lips; and Man-tikhoras said, "If we were in Cairo, it would be a mosque; if in Tokyo, a shrine; if on Acrux V, a verdant meadow with neither pillars nor canopy. We're going inside."

8 The chapel door was unlocked; and the dusk of the interior was deeper than that of the falling night, and on the wall behind the altar a pathetic effigy of the Crucified hung like a lynched horse thief in an old movie.

9 Rachelka murmured, "It's always seemed to me that the sight of a human God nailed helplessly to a cross would steal away the faith of the faint-hearted"; but she approached the altar with Gamaliel, and Mantikhoras married them before The One by taking them together in her clasp and praying wordlessly.

The transfiguration.

10 When this was done, the Alphacrucian released the newlyweds and climbed the cinder blocks behind the altar like a fly going up a wall, stopping at last beside the figure of the Crucified.

11 Here Mantikhoras sidled atop the body of the plaster Christ; and suddenly that entire end of the Neutester chapel shone as brightly as the flash of a fusion bomb, and the organ in the choir loft began to rumble in the bass registers, faultlessly mimicking human speech:

12 "This is another of my beloved issue," intoned the organ, "in whom I renew my covenant with the lost, and the sick at heart, and the broken in body; and I send her in the guise of the Female to straighten what has been made crooked and in the flesh of the Alien to prepare the worlds for a wider love."

13 The light above the altar abated a little; and when Rachelka and Gamaliel next looked, the effigy of Jesus Messiah stirred to life and came down from its oaken crucifix to congratulate the newlyweds; but Mantikhoras was nowhere to be seen, and this greatly alarmed the human couple.

14 Rachelka retreated from the vivified effigy, saying, "Please tell us where our Mistress has gone; we didn't come in here to disturb you." And Gamaliel was no braver than his bride, backpedaling just as fast and gaping in horror and disbelief at the blood oozing from the wound in the effigy's side.

15 And the plaster Christ, in the womanly voice of Mantikhoras, said, "I'm with you yet, and this The One does to seal my authority and to exchange among the three of us the vows that marry us all. See, I'm simultaneously man, and mantid, and universal rational soul, and abiding compassion of God."

16 To which Rachelka replied, "And you're bleeding all over the carpet, too": so that even Mantikhoras, turning aside to take a chalice from the altar cloth, chuckled at her tone.

17 And then the living effigy said, "Wine for the wedding feast," holding the chalice beneath her punctured side and filling the vessel with a most excellent vintage.

18 A moment later the flow had stopped, and the three of them were convivially toasting one another and partaking of a spontaneous sacrament that was also a simple human celebration.

19 Squinting over the rim of the cup at the transfigured mantid, the astrogator ventured the opinion that things would go more easily for them all if Mantikhoras retained this poignant human shape, trimmed her beard and tresses, and put on contemporary clothing, particularly if her ability to do wonders remained unimpaired by the change.

20 Rachelka said, "If you did wish to keep this body, Mistress, I'd be glad to style your hair and buy you a serviceable wardrobe."

21 "I'm surprised and disappointed," Mantikhoras replied, "to find that you tempt me to the impossible, for *this* is for you alone. I came as I came to widen rather than to delimit the circle of love.

22 "Sanctity for life the Hindus teach, sometimes refraining even from slapping an insect that has stung them; and although I honor that teaching, too, my concern is for rational souls, whatever their shape or element. All such, you see, must have the opportunity either to affirm or to deny their kinship *with* The One and *in* The One.

23 "Therefore I return this plaster body to its place, and those who can resurrect it in their hearts are welcome to do so, and those who cannot are welcome to seek another way, in spirit and in truth."

24 These words spoken, the church filled again with an

annihilating brightness, which briefly put out the sight of the
newlyweds; when they could see again, they beheld Mantikhoras before them in her Alphacrucian body and the
unmoving effigy of Christ back on its cross.
      The newlyweds sworn to silence.
25 Said the mantid, "I charge you never to reveal what
tonight you have witnessed; not, that is, until I have been
taken from you": a charge that filled the couple with a painful
forboding.
26 "How will that happen?" Gamaliel asked, and Mantikhoras replied, "Don't fret about it, my astrogator. All I can
tell you tonight is that you have exchanged your wedding
vows in one of the few Neutester chapels east of the Mis-
sissippi, and that my death will be on the hands of those who
worship under Neutester auspices and guidance."
27 And thinking *Thaddeus Thorogood* and *Joe Bob Newcombe*,
Gamaliel shuddered and wondered aloud if Mantikhoras
would come back to them after a certain time to grant them the
right to testify to her wondrous transfiguration.
28 To their surprise the Daughter of Mantid laughed and
said, "In a sense I've already come back, haven't I?" But
noticing their confusion, she added, "I may not, Gamaliel,
and at this late date my failure to rise again shouldn't dis-
hearten you. You well know already what must be done."
29 And she led them out to the dune buggy so that they
could return to the Gulf Sands Budget Resort before incur-
ring any additional rental fee.

                    CHAPTER 7
          Mantikhoras and the cetaceans.
1 And after this, in Miami, the Alphacrucian and her followers visited Marine Merrymakers Amusement Park, a
playland set amid the desolation of the rubble-strewn city;
and in a small painted rowboat Mantikhoras went out upon

the salt waters of the main pool with Gamaliel, Damaris Brown and Nicholas Morowitz, there to commune with the porpoises and a rambunctious trio of killer whales.

2   When the snouts of these smiling, warm-blooded fish rose beside the boat, Lady Mantid spoke to the creatures in their own languages, squeaking in tones that her human disciples found alternately musical and shrilly ear-splitting.

3   Unable to follow this medley of eloquent cetacean homilies, Gamaliel asked, "Mistress, what're you saying to them?" Meanwhile, the porpoises and whales cavorted around them like great sea-going puppies.

4   And Mantikhoras replied, "The same things I say to you and yours, Gamaliel, for they have rational souls akin to your own, and they understand in their innocence what you, in your worldly sophistication, must often remember with both pain and struggle."

5   This was a hard saying, and Nicholas Morowitz took exception, declaring, "Their innocence isn't all that wonderful, is it? I mean, they'd be as prone to error and sin as any of us if they had hands, wouldn't they?"

6   To which the Daughter of Mantid replied, "Blessed are they who have neither hands nor feet, for they can't employ them to do evil. But doubly blessed are they who have both hands and feet and yet *refrain* from doing evil."

7   This statement led Nicholas to conclude that in the eyes of The One human beings were superior to cetaceans, but Mantikhoras rebuked Nicholas for this error with a further saying: "Those who have hands likewise have an obligation, but only a few of the handed have chosen to pick it up."

8   From a pail of white fish and flounder segments in the prow of the little boat Damaris fed the skylarking porpoises and whales, astonished that even though she had been tossing fish to them for quite a long time the pail was not yet empty.

9   At last the manager of the Marine Merrymakers Amuse-

ment Park showed up at poolside and protested that the mantid's colloquy with the animals had gone on too long, and that feeding them so many fish would queer them for the next public performance.

10 When Mantikhoras replied, "But I've *come* to feed them," the manager cursed and beckoned to an underling to approach the pool's edge in an ancient fire truck with a turret-mounted water cannon. This the employee did, and soon the water cannon was shooting powerful jets of salt water at the little boat.

11 Gamaliel and Nicholas were pummeled overboard; porpoises rescued them and deposited them, drenched but otherwise unharmed, on the far bank of the pool, from whence they watched the unexpected conclusion to the battle.

12 Protecting Damaris with her body, Mantikhoras withstood a noisy stream of water ricocheting from her prothorax like a ruffle of living lace. Then, lifting one forelimb, she deflected this spray back at the fire truck, which immediately capsized onto its side like an enormous seashell and spun away across the damp concrete.

13 The manager and his unhurt minion retreated; and without any further hindrance Mantikhoras communed with the cetaceans until Venus was up in the west and a balmy evening breeze had begun to freshen from the Carolinas.

Setting free the primates.

14 Not long after this, in Atlanta, Rachelka accompanied Mantikhoras to the zoological gardens, where some few people supposed the mantid an extraterrestrial specimen imported for the purposes of display.

15 But these people were in the minority, for the Alphacrucian's formidable reputation had preceded her; and her growing fame incited everywhere the envy, suspicion, and hatred of mean-spirited persons in the various ruling councils of the Multipartite Union.

16   Of late, in fact, Mantikhoras had talked often with her followers about both the imminence of her departure from them and the course they must plot and cleave to once she was gone.

17   Neither Rachelka nor Gamaliel nor any of the others cared for this kind of talk, and Rachelka in particular was glad to be walking with Mantikhoras along the paths of the Grant Park Zoo.

18   At last they came to the monkeyhouse, where many of the primates from a local research institution resided now that their usefulness as experimental subjects had come to an end; and Mantikhoras insisted on going inside.

19   The dim interior of the building stank, and in cages apart from those of the spider monkeys and capuchins sat or swung the apes from the research center: gorillas, chimpanzees, gibbons, and orangutans. They peopled this darkness as prison inmates people the anonymous tiers of a correctional facility, and Rachelka could feel their resentful, melancholy eyes boring into her.

20   "What are you doing here?" she asked the Daughter of Mantid. "Are you taking your ministry not only to the articulate cetaceans, but also to these mute and shaggy beasts?"

21   And Mantikhoras replied, "A soul may be rational even if it doesn't have the capacity to speak in tongues. The capacity of these guiltless prisoners is to speak with their hands and eyes, a speech to which they bring a rhetorical skill surpassing that of even the cleverest of former holocasters."

22   "Touché," said Rachelka, blushing, and continued deeper into the monkeyhouse with the mantid, the two of them providing a conspicuous focus for the hostility and frustrations of the great apes, who at last began to pelt them with fruit rinds and feces.

23   Cried Rachelka, "Come, Mistress, let's get out of here!" But Mantikhoras paid her no heed, preferring to let each

outraged simian screech at and bombard them as they
passed along the row, ostensibly helpless against the
onslaught.

24 Between her teeth Rachelka whispered, "You deflected
the stream of water from the fire truck at Marine Merrymakers Amusement Park. Why the devil can't you protect
us from these disgusting missiles?"

25 "You may first blunt the enmity of the wronged," Mantikhoras said, "by letting them express it. Afterwards, however, you can't root out what remains of this hatred without
righting the wrong that created and sustained it."

26 Rachelka started to say, "How are we going to do that?"
but the mantid turned and led her back down the row of
cages, pausing at each one to open its door and to encourage
its puzzled occupants to come out. Soon, many of the liber-
ated apes were knuckle-walking along behind their crap-
bedizened emancipators.

27 Outside the monkeyhouse Mantikhoras bade the former inmates go in peace or else cast their lot with her human
disciples: a choice that to Rachelka's way of thinking seemed
hardly a choice at all, especially since liberty in the fallen
human world might soon bring the apes to renewed confinement or maybe even death.

28 She said as much to her Mistress, who reminded her that
the apes were also free to return to their cages, and that many
of them would undoubtedly do so. And Mantikhoras added,
"Those who stay with us will have demonstrated by that
action the spiritual rationality that redeemed them. It's a kind
of test."

29 It therefore came to pass on the travels of the Alphacrucians about the continent that Andrew Stout acquired an
orangutan for a roommate, and Priscilla Muthinga a sweet
adolescent gibbon, and that reserving motel accommodations became from thenceforward a major hassle and an
ever-mounting expense.

CHAPTER 8
Erotic spirituality.

1 By nights on their beds in a dozen different cities or playlands Gamaliel and Rachelka sought each other's soul, speaking in the gardens of this nightly ceremony with both their bodies and their mouths.

2 The sanctuaries in which they recited their liturgies of love were perfumed (it seemed) with Lebanese colognes and Lysol, with cinnamon-scented hand lotions and various industrial-strength floor waxes, with instant coffee and commercial bug spray.

3 Meanwhile, the fluorescents in the bathroom blinked on and off with every unpredictable power surge; and some of these power surges were in the astrogator's blood, and the blinking of the fluorescents illumined him within.

4 As for Rachelka's eyes, they were like the fishpools in Heshbon, by the gate of Bathrabbim, more limpid by far than the pools in the Marine Merrymakers Amusement Park in Miami, albeit as festively asplash with a salt-water ardor.

5 Night after night in the inns of their holy itinerancy, his left hand was under her head, and his right hand embraced her; and when the dews in his head were spent, and his hand drawn back from the hole in the door, and the mountains of spices thoroughly plundered, Gamaliel and Rachelka would chatter like school kids.

The newlyweds converse.

6 *Gamaliel:* Have I ever told you how happy I am that I'm not rooming, like Andrew, with an orangutan?

7 *Rachelka:* Or I you that I'm not the suitemate of a gibbon? Bless Priscilla's heart. She's bearing up well, but these latest influxes of converts — cetaceans, simians, pets with genetically augmented minds — well, they just aren't doing us any good at the grass-roots level.

8 *Gamaliel:* From the beginning the fundamentalists murmured that Mantikhoras was the Antichrist, but now the murmurings grow stronger, and even some fairly liberal theologians in the more moderate Protestant denominations have taken it up. That's scary.

9 *Rachelka:* Ah, yes, the ones who congratulate themselves on having the temerity to admit primates to the evolutionary family tree of *Homo sapiens*, but who balk at the prospect of sitting down to tea with them. Well, I'm afraid I sympathize. I balk, too.

10 *Gamaliel:* But, Rachelka, Muggeridge has impeccable manners for a chimp, and Edward's the sweetest little gibbon you could ever hope to meet; and Bonzo, why, Bonzo, the little scamp, he's —

11 *Rachelka:* He's the one who utterly ruined that original Guy de Froissart jumpsuit I wore into the Grant Park monkeyhouse back in Atlanta, and it's a real bitch trying to forgive the little bugger.

12 *Gamaliel:* Well, for Mantikhoras's sake, you've got to *try*. She keeps saying that her time among us grows shorter, and if that's so, my lovely Shulamite, we're going to have to strive particularly hard to keep her commandments to us.

13 *Rachelka:* I swear, Gamaliel, I sometimes think she's deliberately hastening her passion. This mandated fraternizing with nonhuman life forms seems designed to lose friends and alienate fundamentalists, no matter how bright and perky the converts themselves are.

14 *Gamaliel:* It's a necessary part of her ministry. How can we hope to establish meaningful relationships with alien intelligences in other star sytems if we can't reach some kind of humane accord with the more rational species here on our own planet?

15 *Rachelka:* Kiss a porpoise for Christ, huh? Well, the absurdity of that, my would-be Worldly Wiseman, is that even four generations after the Cobalt Galas you can find coreligionists sniping at one another, and agnostics at agnostics, and atheists at atheists, and devout dialectical materialists at anyone in a pair of well-soled shoes.

Erotic spirituality.

16 And the astrogator said, "Mantikhoras never promised us . . . uh, what do you think you're doing? . . never promised us a rose garden . . . even if the joints of your thighs are like jewels . . . and, uh, the bud of your navel like the whorl of a rose."

17 "Be quiet, man," Rachelka told him. "In a few days we'll be off to proselytize those who would either convert or kill us, and I'm no traitor to the faith. For tonight, then, make haste, my beloved, and be like a hart on a hill of fragrant spices."

18 Which Gamaliel most eagerly did; and from deep in the bowels of the inn the astrogator and his Shulamite heard, but did not truly hear, the steady *thump thump thump* of the bass notes reverberating from the jukebox in the motel's bar.

19 Meanwhile, cockroaches scuttled in the dark, and in an upstairs room the Daughter of Mantid contemplated her fate.

CHAPTER 9

The Neutesters.

1 Now on the Great Plains of North America, centered in eastern Colorado but ranging northward into Canada and southward into Texas and parts of Old Mexico, there dwelt several thriving enclaves of Christian sectarians known in the aggregate as Neutesters, a neologism for New Testament Revivalists.

2 Their leader was the right Reverend Thaddeus Thorogood, D.D.; their headquarters was not far from Lamar, Colorado; and their most distinctive dwelling places were the abandoned networks of underground tunnels designed and constructed years and years ago, for shuttling warhead-bearing missiles back and forth beneath the plains.

3 Three months into the Earthly mission of Mantikhoras,

Thorogood relayed word to every Neutester stronghold
from Four Buttes, Montana, to Brownsville, Texas, and
beyond, that the Alphacrucian was most certainly the Antichrist; and of late Joe Bob Newcombe, his best-known lieu-
tenant, had been pounding home this same message as
Rachelka Dan's replacement on the holovision program, *Parsecs Ahead*.

4 Anyone giving aid and comfort to the Daughter of Mantid's deluded followers, both men proclaimed, would either
forfeit resurrection altogether or else enjoy its most poignant
perquisites in Hell.

5 Thorogood quoted at length from the Olivet Discourse in
The Gospel of Mark: "'For false Christs and false prophets shall
rise, and shall show signs and wonders, to seduce, if it were
possible, even the elect.'"; but as many Neutesters as
denounced the mantid, just that many or more hurried to
embrace her.

6 When Mantikhoras began to travel not only with Roman
Catholics, Jews, and Unitarians, but also with primates,
porpoises, and talking dogs, the tide of Neutester defections
to the ranks of the Alphacrucians abated rather noticeably.

7 Remarking this, Thorogood mounted a powerful coun-
terattack, via the CABLE-STAR holocast of *Parsecs Ahead*, stress-
ing the implied New Testament doctrines of "man's essential
uniqueness" and "the permanent significance of human
nature."

8 As the House of Representatives of the Multipartite
Union now had only fifty-four members continentwide, and
as the Senate had been in permanent adjournment ever since
decamping to Cleveland, Ohio, and as most of the members
of both the executive branch and the quasi-Supreme Court
were still in prison in Vladivostok, U.S.S.R.;

9 Thaddeus Thorogood and his Neutester lieutenants composed the nearest thing to a stable temporal authority
(excepting perhaps the Union of Amusement Park Manag-

ers, the Pan-Solar Press Guild, and the Interstellar Diplomatic Instrument for Outreach, Trade, and Study) still extant in North America.

10 Therefore, when Thorogood sent out a decree to Gamaliel Crucis, the astrogator, demanding that his Alphacrucian Mistress make a pilgrimage to Thorogood's underground holdings outside Lamar, so that the right Reverend could interview Mantikhoras about her activities,

11 Gamaliel feared a trap, and told his Mistress so, and urged her to avoid at all costs going docilely into a Neutester stronghold *anywhere* in the country and most especially that of Thaddeus Thorogood himself.

12 Indeed, even Rachelka, who had recently learned that she was with child, sought to dissuade Mantikhoras from answering the right Reverend's arrogant summons, saying, "That bastard sincerely believes you're the great antagonist: he's gunning for you in the name of God."

13 But Mantikhoras said, "A sincere belief is never overcome without a struggle, and if I flee or sidestep this man, I'll merely confirm him in the notion that I'm an imposter."

14 Rachelka expostulated with the mantid: "Must *everyone* come to see you for Who you really are? Why can't you let this priggish villain go? His piety is a disguise for his own self-worship."

15 To which Mantikhoras replied, "And that's the ultimate blasphemy, even for those who believe in Wordless Happenstance. I'd be remiss not to tell him so. His name is an allegory whose informing irony every thinking creature must one day acknowledge."

16 "Feh," said Gamaliel, for he believed this exegesis needlessly explicit; but the Daughter of Mantid was determined not to let anyone slip through her clutches as a consequence of murky doctrine or abstruse pedagogy, and she waved her antennae almost gaily at the astrogator.

Sister Salvation & so forth.

17 The Alphacrucian set off from Richmond, Virginia, for Lamar, Colorado, in a caravan of methane-powered buses and a couple of water-filled tank trucks for the cetaceans: a rattletrap assemblage of vehicles of every color.

18 One Pan-Solar Press representative dubbed the mantid and her entourage "Sister Salvation & The Technicolor Pipedream Traveling Zoo & Medicine Show," a name that stuck because Gamaliel and the others picked it up and began to use it among themselves.

19 In St. Joseph, Missouri, once a jumping-off place for the Oregon Trail, an importunate holocaster asked the mantid why she and her disciples were traveling in such a gaudy caravan to see the authoritarian leader of the Neutesters.

20 And Mantikhoras replied, "If the mountain won't come to Mohammed, then Mohammed will go to the mountain"; and this off-hand recitation of a hallowed cliché was interpreted by the news analysts as everything from a cryptic earthquake prediction to an oblique self-denial of the alien's own divine mandate.

21 The journey itself was an obstreperous, inchmeal affair, during which Mantikhoras performed several semimiraculous cures, and talked the caravan's way past a half-dozen illegal roadblocks, and faced down any number of adolescent hecklers (whatever their chronological age) with soft words and sincere good humor;

22 And at last the buses and tank trucks achieved their destination; and the mantid and all her retinue, minus the porpoises and killer whales, disembarked to the amplified strains of an old cowboy ditty called "Home on the Range."

An audience underground.

23 It was snowing outside Lamar, but in the immense subterranean prairie-dog village of the Neutesters the temperature was balmy, downright springlike; and Mantikhoras, along with Gamaliel, Rachelka, Andrew, and

Priscilla, rode a pump-powered handcar to their audience with Thaddeus Thorogood.

24 A tall, cadaverous man whose receding hairline and dun-colored age spots gave his head the look of a freshly unearthed skull, Thorogood greeted the Alphacrucians with some warmth and effusiveness, welcoming them to his carpeted lair at the heart of the complex.

25 Rachelka noted that to counter his facial resemblance to a death's-head, Thorogood rouged his lips and kept his sapphire-blue eyes constantly in motion, as if by darting their glances here and there he would prevent his being mistaken for a corpse.

26 After certain preliminaries (Mantikhoras declined a bowl of tea), the chief Neutester asked,"Why have you confined your ministry to the continental Multipartite Union when there are sinners abroad, out among the colonies of our Solar System, and undoubtedly on your home planet, too?"

27 "Undoubtedly," Mantikhoras replied. "The answer to your question, however, is that this is where I'm most needed. Here you have amusement parks, sports stadia, and radiation-treatment centers; gambling casinos, massage parlors, and mutant reservations; monkeyhouses, Holiday Inns, and brothels; military bases, drag —"

28 *Thorogood (interrupting):* You've made your point, Lady Mantid. But I think you've neglected to mention the fact that media coverage isn't bad in this part of the world. I'm sure that was a consideration, too, wasn't it?

29 *Mantikhoras:* I was taken against my will from Acrux V, Your Right Reverendship. What I've done here in your contaminated homeland, I've done in the name of The One who permitted my kidnapping for purposes that reveal themselves in my ministry.

30 *Thorogood:* "For many shall come in my name, saying I am Christ; and shall deceive many." Mark 13:6. But you don't deceive the people of the New Testament Revival, Lady Mantid, or at least not their democratically ordained shepherd, Thaddeus Thorogood, D.D.

31 *Mantikhoras:* A verse or two later, you should note, Jesus is quoted to the effect that nation shall rise against nation, and that earthquakes and famines shall occur, and that such signs shall signal "the beginnings of sorrows."

32 *Thorogood:* Excellent. You're not unfamiliar with The Book. But even Satan can quote Scripture, Lady Mantid, and what you've just quoted has come to pass in these very days of tribulation. As the poet wrote, "Surely the Second Coming is at hand."

The debate grows heated.

33 Under her breath Rachelka murmured, " 'What rough beast . . . slouches toward Bethlehem'"; and the chief Neutester, overhearing her, turned his head and smiled condescendingly.

34 *Thorogood:* If you'll forgive the observation, my good woman, your Mistress certainly qualifies as a "rough beast." And although Yeats was a visionary heretic, I almost believe that your Lady Mantid has arrived on earth as a portent of the *true* Second Coming.

35 *Mantikhoras:* Forgive me, Your Right Reverendship, but the passage from Mark suggests that you and your people, without yet witnessing the Messiah's return, have lived *through* the epoch of sorrows. The Cobalt Galas are long over, the Great California Earthquake has already taken place, and humanity lives on.

36 *Thorogood:* What are you driving at? That we've outlived the conditions that should have foretokened the Second Coming?

37 *Mantikhoras:* Exactly. Things are bad today, I'll grant you, but they're *usually* bad, in one way or another; and the wars and rumors of war alluded to in the Olivet Discourse are things of the past. Albeit in aimless remnants here and there about the globe, the peoples of Earth are finally at peace.

38 *Gamaliel (unable to hold* his *peace):* That's partly because they're too sick and exhausted to wage war. [But both Mantikhoras and the chief Neutester ignored him.]

39 *Thorogood:* Let me get this straight. We've outlived the time of trials; therefore you *can't* be the Antichrist, because the Antichrist should already have come. By the same token, you can't be Christ himself because the Antichrist has not preceded you. Is that the gist of your argument?

40 *Mantikhoras:* Only to the extent that I decline to be identified with your problematic Antichrist. On the other hand, your second deduction is faulty.

41 The significance of this last remark sank into Thorogood's understanding only slowly; but when he finally encompassed it, his lips drew in so that prim little crow's-feet bracketed them at the corners.

42 *Thorogood:* Who do you say you are?

43 *Mantikhoras:* Although I've undeniably come again, this is not *the* Second Coming. By the grace of The One, whose compassion and mercy are limitless, it's merely an extension — an addendum, if you like — to my first metahistoric visit. I'm renewing in this dramatic fashion, Your Right Reverendship, what you and your followers *claim* to revive, in spirit and in truth.

44 *Thorogood:* The impudence of your self-aggrandizement is almost as reprehensible as its insupportable sacrilege! It's bad theology and even worse manners! Jesus would've never said *anything* like that, and it condemns you, condemns you utterly!

45 *Gamaliel (interrupting):* How do you account for the cures she's effected, the miracles she's performed, the converts she's made, and the love among both kindred and strangers she's striven to inspire?

46 *Thorogood:* Easily! Telepathic suggestion, telekinetic trickery, deceitful promises, and the satanic perpetration of an undiscriminating mass hysteria! People do it all the time! Why, *I've* been known to do it!

47 *Mantikhoras:* Then I don't understand what —

48 *Thorogood:* You've had media assistance all along. The presence of Rachelka Dan in your entourage is telling. It wouldn't be so intolerable if you didn't try to pass yourself off as a new incarnation — a ridiculous *orthopterization*, so to speak — of the Living Christ!

The audience ends.

49 And the right Reverend Thaddeus Thorogood stormed from the concrete chamber, leaving his own lieutenants within disconcerting glaring range of those of the Alphacrucian mantid, whose forelimbs immediately assumed an attitude of prayerful contemplation.

50 Gamaliel's heart misgave him, however, for they were at the mercy of the outraged Neutesters, and he had just heard Mantikhoras say, "I don't understand," a phrase he had never heard on her lips before.

51 Said one of Thorogood's jackbooted warders, brandishing an ugly-looking weapon called a lanceflame, "Too bad you didn't bring one of them snot-slick, fat-headed fish down here with you. I could fry it on the spot, and your six-legged Jesus'd've something to eat when she comes back from the dead."

52 Laughing, the warders shepherded Mantikhoras and her disciples, under guard, back into the tunnel to the handcar on which they had earlier arrived at Thorogood's private silo. Gamaliel understood that they were prisoners and would not soon be returning to the surface.

CHAPTER 10
And what of Judas?

1 And that night Mantikhoras resided with Gamaliel, Rachelka, Andrew, and Priscilla in an underground apartment belonging to their enemies, who had not allowed them

to return to The Technicolor Pipedream Traveling Zoo & Medicine Show, the members of which awaited them at a commercial camping ground outside Lamar.

2 The walls of their prison sweated a rust-colored condensation; and knowing this for a sign, none of those imprisoned with the mantid could sleep.

3 Furthermore, at various places about the chamber Gamaliel found small bowls containing the crisped bodies of locusts, which the Neutesters had supplied them as a scornful supper before their Mistress's passion, whenever that might be.

4 Neither the astrogator nor any of the others wished to partake of this meal, but Mantikhoras bade them eat what they could of the offering and sponge from the walls enough of the ferruginous condensation to slake their powerful thirsts, for they had had no food or water since early that morning.

5 The disciples expected their Mistress to relent at any moment and to eat with them, or else to explain for them the ritual significance of the meal supplied them by the Neutesters; but she prayed in troubled silence over the repast and declined to take anything for herself.

6 Surprisingly, the crisped locusts had a pleasant taste and the moisture from the walls was equally palatable; and an angry guilt stole upon Gamaliel because Mantikhoras continued to keep both her silence and her fast.

7 At last in helpless anxiety and impatience he threw his bowl against the wall, crying, "It's easy to see what's happening here, Mistress! Which of us will betray you further? Which of us have you selected to be your Judas? Is it me, Lady Mantid? If so, tell me tonight, this very moment! I'll kill myself now instead of later!"

8 Rachelka attempted to comfort her husband, but Andrew and Priscilla also began to petition the mantid, demanding to know if she had singled one of them out for the role of

Iscariot and pleading exemption from that shame on the grounds of their great love for, and service to, her cause.

9 Somewhat sadly Mantikhoras said, "This clamor doesn't become you, friends. If there were to be a Judas this time, it wouldn't be as a consequence of *my* selection that you — or you — or you — fulfilled that role. It would follow instead the purblind or evil dictates of your own heretofore loyal hearts."

10 The astrogator cursed this answer, and banged on the sweating walls, and raged that if there *were* to be a Judas this time, one of them would inevitably fall into the role, and he for one didn't like the odds: the original Twelve had been far better off.

11 Mantikhoras said, "Be quiet, Gamaliel, and restrain both your fear and your anger. Haven't you noticed that on this occasion I took pains *to betray myself?* In mortal eyes even The One may err; and although I don't subscribe to that parochial notion, I *do* understand its ineradicable popularity among you."

12 And she continued, saying, "My self-betrayal, then, is a concession to your ignorance and a mercy to those close enough to me to fall into the *potential* danger that torments all four of you tonight. If I'm only a reminder, a latter-day renewal of the covenant forged in Caesar's time, then I may gladly forgo the drama inherent in the traitorous act of Iscariot."

13 Rachelka said, "Lady Mantid, although you've mercifully spared us a Judas, you still haven't abstracted villains from your Story. The Neutesters seem to be surrogates for your powerful Pharisaical adversaries in the Original Version, and I'm afraid they're also going to stand in for your Roman executioners."

14 "It's almost impossible to abstract villainy from this Story," the mantid replied, "because it's impossible to abstract villainy from the self-aware condition. Furthermore, no segment of a self-aware population has a corner on, or an immunity from, it."

15 Priscilla ventured, "And so this time you've purposely chosen the Neutesters to demonstrate that fact?"

16 And Mantikhoras answered, "They've chosen themselves. That they assume the role in the mistaken belief that I'm the Antichrist explains their grandiose self-corruption but in no wise mitigates it."

17 Andrew put an end to this metaphysical discussion by declaring that almost certainly the members of The Technicolor Pipedream & Etc. would storm their underground Bastille and liberate them, as Mantikhoras herself had freed the great apes from the monkeyhouse in Atlanta.

18 But the Alphacrucian said, "I assembled you for discipleship, not guerrilla warfare. You're proposing a pipedream of your own, but at least it recommends to me the strength and indomitability of your hope." Hearing these words, Andrew retired to a corner and wept.

The disciples poisoned.

19 An hour or so later all four of the Alphacrucian's human followers fell deathly ill, and the mantid understood that one of Thorogood's henchmen had poisoned the food left in the room for them. To discover that she had inadvertently allowed those whom she loved to act for her in the capacity of hireling foodtasters enraged Mantikhoras.

20 Quickly, then, she cast the maleficent chemicals out of her disciples' bloodstreams, beginning with the astrogator's wife in order to reverse at once any of the harm that had been wrought against not only the woman herself but also the nascent soul in her womb, and concluding with Gamaliel.

21 The astrogator said, "This is the Neutesters' 'humane' substitute for crucifixion, Mistress. Apparently it never crossed their minds that taking five other lives [for Gamaliel counted the unborn child] might strike anyone as a small blot on the humanity of their methods."

22 And because the rage of Mantikhoras was kindled against Thorogood and the Neutesters, she took every empty bowl in the room and shattered it on the walls as the astrogator had earlier done with his own.

23 "Mistress, didn't you have any idea what they'd done to the food?" Priscilla asked. "It seems to me that —"

24 But Rachelka interrupted, saying, "Mantikhoras isn't *completely* coincident with The One, Priscilla. Her knowledge is finite, like our own, even if her wisdom far exceeds that of imperfect mortals."

25 But even Gamaliel, now that the danger had passed, was outraged that his wife and unborn child had been placed in such jeopardy; and he wondered aloud why the wisdom of the Alphacrucian had not enabled her to deduce the likelihood of their food's having been tampered with.

26 Mantikhoras rounded on the man whom she had just saved: "Had the Neutesters presented you with bowls of *tempting* meats or succulents, my suspicions would have awakened instantly; but because they gave you insects, items you would ordinarily disdain, I was lulled to the danger.

27 "Now, however, I expect from our captors only the worst, and it's my plan to make it exceedingly difficult for them to carry out the deed that their ignorance and prideful piety compel them to do.

28 "As for you, Gamaliel, the words you've just uttered constitute a small betrayal that serves to legitimize my passion. Fortunately it's a betrayal of the vain and venial, rather than the mortal, kind; and I forgive it."

29 Hearing this, the astrogator hung his head, and shut his eyes, and eased himself to his knees before his Mistress.

The disciples admonished to survive.

30 Mantikhoras found a speaker switch near the door, threw it, and in a musical but commanding voice informed Thorogood (wherever he was) that he must immediately release her followers if he hoped to be successful in physically eliminating her mantid presence from the face of the Earth.

31 Gamaliel and the others bewailed this announcement, saying that they wished to remain with her to the end, and arguing that to coerce Thorogood to free them would be no kindness but a bereaving cruelty.

32 But Lady Mantid said, "It's necessary for you to survive this, friends, and that you go out from this continent to other continents, and from this planet to other planets, and from this solar system to other solar systems, and even from this galaxy to other galaxies, to proclaim the gospel to every creature with brains enough to comprehend it."

33 Because the astrogator continued to beg the mantid's permission to accompany her to the place of her ultimate passion (as a means of atoning for his lapses of both faith and gratitude), Mantikhoras granted him this boon with the stipulation that upon seeing the ordeal through he return immediately to Rachelka and the others.

More treachery.

34 Whereupon Thaddeus Thorogood's disembodied voice spoke to them, saying, "Woe to gravid serpents, and to every snake that slithers in the Great Serpent's wake, for they shall die in the pit with the Viper that seduced them!"

35 Before Gamaliel could square this herpetological metaphor with his Mistress's insectile form, the door to the chamber burst open; and in rushed a contingent of Neutester warders in uniforms embroidered at the breast pocket with the ancient Christian insignia, and each one of them was dutifully firing a lanceflame.

36 Screaming, Mantikhoras's disciples sought to take cover by throwing themselves on the floor, while the Alphacrucian herself, recognizing the need for a more decisive measure, waved one segmented forelimb and halted time within the cramped dimensions of the chamber.

37 As in holographic tableau, every member of the attack force was frozen in place, and in the air before them hung harmless streaks of varicolored light and interwoven parabolas delineating the paths of either bullets or birdshot (for some of them carried weapons a good deal older than lance flames).

38 And then the mantid lifted the spell from her disciples and told them to creep past the frozen warders into the tunnel outside the chamber. She went with them, located another speaker switch in the corridor, and, activating it, told Thorogood, "If you want my life, Your Right Reverendship, you're going to have to let my people go before I agree to cooperate in its sacrifice."

39 But the chief Neutester responded by releasing a cyanide gas into the corridor, and sending electrical currents running along the floor, and directing at them through the overhead sprinkler system a lethal rain of hydrochloric acid.

40 Each of these attacks the Alphacrucian thwarted by speaking a word or raising a forelimb; and at last Thaddeus Thorogood himself appeared at the end of the damp, burnt-smelling corridor and came walking toward them like an upright corpse.

41 Angrily he said, "You've hypnotized my warders and monkeyed with the death-dealing systems on which we've based our internal security. Because you've stymied me to this point, Sister Salvation, I'll cut a deal with you.

42 "No more tricks, you understand? Only a ready surrender to the fate you deserve. If you agree to that, I'll let all but Gamaliel the Astrogator return to the disgusting pandemonium of your Technicolor Pipedream Whatchamacallit."

43 Said Mantikhoras with alacrity, "Done!"

CHAPTER 11
Thorogood tries again, and again, and again.

1 But even after Rachelka, Andrew, and Priscilla had found safety aboveground, the Alphacrucian continued to resist the Neutesters' efforts to kill her; and Thorogood in mounting hatred and frustration accused her of reneging on a promise.

2 Mantikhoras countered that she wished to die in the sunlight, not in the bowels of a human ant-farm; but privately she told Gamaliel that she was giving Thorogood and his minions every opportunity to refrain from the heinous act that would condemn and stigmatize them forever.

3 To that end, she purposely did not succumb to two more attempts to shoot her, one more to poison her, and a series of somewhat more exotic assaults, including bludgeoning, burning, decapitation, drowning, electrocution, garroting, hanging, induced cardiac infarction, overfeeding, smothering, starvation, telemetrically triggered organ failure, and vivisection to the point of no return.

4 Gamaliel was also at risk during this time, but because Mantikhoras wrapped him in her protective cloak, in the end he was merely a horrified witness to these inept enormities: failures that did not convert or discourage Thorogood but instead stimulated in him an even more fanatical desire to obliterate the mantid.

The journey.

5 At last the Neutesters put Mantikhoras and Gamaliel into a railroad car with barred windows; and for three days the underground train of which it was a part traveled northwestward beneath the Great Plains and the Rocky Mountains toward the Sarcee Indian Reserve in Alberta, Canada, M.U.N.A.

6 Gamaliel was often delirious during this trip, for the blackness of the tunnel walls hurtling past triggered in him memories of the undifferentiated corridors of the interstellar substratum; and he dreamed that he was practicing his occupation as an astrogator aboard a vessel completely unresponsive to his skills.

7 "We'll climb out of this," he murmured in his delirium, "as soon as I can get a transdimensional fix on the stars. Why can't I find the stars? Why can't I find the goddamn stars?" And Mantikhoras would ease his distress by whispering into his hallucinations words of encouragement and solace.

8 Denver, Casper, Billings, and Great Falls (each with its own level of lingering contamination) passed by unremarked overhead, until the Neutester train at last reached the radio-active barrens of the Sarcee Reserve, a place of minimal strategic value that during the Cobalt Galas had nevertheless suffered four — count 'em, four — misdirected or irrationally targeted nuclear strikes.

Calgary.

9 The countryside around Calgary was a glowing moon-scape, long since quarantined; and it was into this angry desolation that Thaddeus Thorogood and his warders, spacesuited against the persistent peril, brought the unprotected Alphacrucian and her sole attending disciple.

10 "Give Gamaliel a suit like the ones you're wearing," Mantikhoras said, "or else I'll people this hell with demons whom you'll recognize as former companions, and you, Your Right Reverendship, will be their everlasting Lucifer."

11 The astrogator had never heard his Mistress threaten anyone before, and neither had Thaddeus Thorogood, and soon Gamaliel was undergoing decontamination procedures in a nearby structure prefabricated for that purpose, and soon thereafter donning the same kind of insulated gear and air-filtration system worn by the Neutesters.

12 And Mantikhoras said, "Take him well clear of this scene as soon as he has witnessed the abuses and abominations you intend to inflict upon me in the name of one of my hypostases. My strength is utterly gone."

13 The sky shone red, and the mountains lay about the plain like huge, caries-riddled teeth; and the waters of the Elbow River crept by like molten copper, and over the enigmatic Calgary Tower two-headed vultures circled

in silent packs.

14 Thorogood prodded the mantid in the flank with one thickly gloved finger. "If your strength's gone, we'll do with you as we like, and your astrogator isn't going to fare any better once your protection's withdrawn, let me clue you, Lady Mantid." (To his chagrin Gamaliel had been worrying about this very possibility.)

15 Mantikhoras answered, "My strength's renewed through suffering, and in defense of my people, let me clue *you*, I'm a retributive power that disdains even the barrier of death."

16 At this point even Thorogood appeared to waver in his resolve to execute the alien Redeemer: but the visored faces of his warders were looking to him for guidance, and ultimately he chose to cast himself in the role of a redoubtable defender of the faith.

17 Commanded Thorogood, "Let it begin!"

18 More like insects than Mantikhoras herself, the Neutesters besieged her with torments in the shadow of the spindly metal tower whose purpose the astrogator still had not plumbed. Although he struggled to aid his Mistress, the arms of two of Thorogood's beefiest warders prevented him from doing so.

19 And the warders blinded Mantikhoras in one of her multifaceted eyes, and tore from her body two legs from one side and one from the other (so that as they scourged her she almost toppled), and strapped to the chitinous saddle behind her head a nuclear device wired for detonation from afar.

Mantikhoras climbs the tower.

20 And with this device on her back the Neutesters forced her to climb the struts of Calgary Tower, jeering and laughing from the muffling confines of their helmets, and at last she reached the flimsy, riveted lookout a hundred feet or more from the ground;

21 And here the nimble warder who had followed her aloft, catcalling and prodding, put out many of the drupelets in her remaining eye and secured her with heavy chains to the platform.

22 These tasks accomplished, the man pulled off his helmet, cried, "Behold the Alphacrucian god!" and, after covering his head again climbed down to ground zero to the tumultuous (muffled) cheers of his coreligionists and the piteous (muffled) lamentations of Gamaliel the Astrogator.

23 Then, because an arctic wind was howling over the Sarcee moonscape from the Pole, they withdrew to a bunker north of Calgary and from there triggered the device on the helpless mantid's back.

24 Said Thaddeus Thorogood, who had suddenly appeared in the bunker at Gamaliel's side, "That's a relatively clean fission unit, my friend. Your Lady Mantid will be flash-liberated from the snares of corporeality, and there won't be much fallout at all."

25 Gamaliel, who knew there would be more fallout than the chief Neutester could even imagine, said nothing.

26 And an immense dome of light, like a gigantic soap bubble or a globe of mirrors, surrounded the tower on the plain, dazzling both the eyes and the mind; then the tower was swept away in an enormous phallic updraft of phosphorescent debris, a column that built, and built, and built; and Gamaliel could watch no more

CHAPTER 12
Gamaliel rejoins the others.

1 And when the Neutesters, fearing to defy the final words of Mantikhoras, freed the astrogator, he quickly ascertained the whereabouts of the other disciples and hurried to join them.

2 A small remnant of faithful but disheartened Alphacrucians had gathered together in South Bend, Indiana, there to raise their spirits (insofar as that was possible) by taking in a football game between the University of Notre Dame and the Rock City Rabbinical Institute of Rock City, Tennessee, the winner of this traditional rivalry to play Southern Methodist University two hours later in the same stadium.

3   Unfortunately, the game was going forward in a raging acid snowfall, and Gamaliel was unable to reach his wife and fellow disciples until a few minutes before the half.

4   Said Rachelka, embracing her husband on a drifted, half-empty upper tier, "It's zero to zero, honey, and I'm sorry for all of us that there was no body to reclaim. That's why Thorogood did it that way, isn't it? To deny us the opportunity to tender unto her corpse our last respects."

5   And Gamaliel agreed with his wife, and sat down between her and a knobby little man in a raccoon coat (who turned out to be Muggeridge the Chimp in his very own hair), and, glancing around, shook hands with Andrew Stout, and Nicholas Morowitz, and Damaris Brown, and Muggeridge the Chimp, all of whom seemed genuinely glad to see him again.

6   And he placed his hand tenderly on Rachelka's belly (there beneath two cardigans and a goose-down parka) and whispered in her ear, "The kid's got the best seat in the house."

7   And Priscilla Muthinga, edging near with a cup of rapidly chilling coffee for the astrogator, told everyone gaily that the snowflakes eddying about the stadium were "eucharistic particles of the comminute essence of the Redeemer," and that they must all put out their tongues and take her in.

8   The disciples did this, and Gamaliel drank his ice-cold coffee, and they were all zero at the bone there above the zero-to-zero combat between Notre Dame and Rock City Rabbinical.

9   And Andrew, hugging his own shoulders, said, "I thought she'd come back to us in the orthopteran body we

knew, not in these goddamn 'eucharistic particles' of some goddamn 'comminute essence'!" And he booed the Notre Dame quarterback for handing off to a snowdrift that had gone in motion to his right.

10   Rachelka observed that it had been over a week since the fission blast near Calgary, and that the odds of a convincing resurrection grew slimmer with every passing day. (Meanwhile, her undelivered baby did a backflip for RCRI, and she clutched her sides in a spasm of agony and wonder.)

11   The game went on and on, and the eucharistic particles of the comminute essence continued to swirl; and both the talk and the hope of a more palpable resurrection faded to zero as zero-to-zero began to loom as the likely final score and in fact prevailed.

A messenger.

12   As the disciples were filing from the stadium, a peanut vendor in a white fur coat and a Jiminy Cricket mask approached them and said, "Don't be so down in the mouth, gang. You'll see her again in various guises. Here, have some peanuts."

13   And he tossed them several complimentary bags, most of which Muggeridge managed to intercept.

14   Before the disciples could thank the vendor, he was lost in an eddy of gusting whiteness; and Priscilla vouched that they had seen an angel from the interstellar substratum, which opinion Andrew pooh-poohed and Gamaliel at that time mentally dismissed as so much wish-fulfillment buncombe.

Counterpoint.

15   Many months passed, and contrary to the masked vendor's prophecy Mantikhoras did not appear to any of them again.

16   At last, in the obstetrics ward of a hospital for dependents of the Interstellar Diplomatic Instrument for Outreach, Trade, and Study, in Port-au-Prince, Haiti, Rachelka was

brought to her confinement.

17 Gamaliel was there for the labor, which was protracted and difficult, and when it became clear that Rachelka would not deliver the baby for several more hours yet, one of the attending doctors took Gamaliel into an antechamber with a cot and told him to try to get some sleep.

18 Said this solicitous young woman, "We'll wake you when it's time. That's a promise. Rachelka doesn't need to be worrying about both you *and* the baby, you know." And she left him there.

19 Much against his will and better judgment, Gamaliel obeyed. Sleep stole upon him like the spirit of *gnosis*, and in this slumber he had a dream of such shameful implications that he thrashed about guiltily on the cot and struggled without success to escape the toils of sleep.

20 Meanwhile, Rachelka's labor spontaneously resumed, and the doctor who had led Gamaliel to the antechamber had no time to awaken him and fetch him back to the delivery room, so busy was she doing what she had been trained to do.

21 Mantikhoras entered the room in which the astrogator lay, coming in by the door opposite the place of Rachelka's confinement; and the musky pheromone wafting its scent to Gamaliel from her ovipositors was a summons impossible to ignore.

22 Both aroused and frightened, Gamaliel stood and walked toward the mantid; and she said, "My husband."

23 Gamaliel circled the risen insect, whose body was entire again, even to the replacement of every gouged-out drupelet in her compound eyes; and he kissed her forehead, and held her praying forelimbs, and at her silent urging went abaft to consummate their marriage.

24 Said the doctor to Rachelka, "Push, dear, push"; and she obeyed, grimacing into the lights, and the tiny human passenger in her womb came sliding headfirst into the gentle hands of the obstetrician.

25 But the astrogator, spent, was in the throes of a postcoital ritual unlike any he had ever experienced before, two-stepping somnambulistically in the mantid's curious embrace and staring upward into the green cavern of her open jaws.

26 And Mantikhoras said, "The better to devour you, my worshiper-spouse. The better to make you mine forever and likewise me your everlasting own."

27 And her jaws closed on his skull, crushing it, and in grave peristaltic gulps he was taken upward bone by bone and lifted into a disembodied consciousness where great blooming bowls of light and the blurred aureoles of stars fused in an ever-expanding orgasmic knowledge that obliterated time.

28 Said the doctor to Rachelka, lifting the infant from between her legs into the sheen of the chrome-encircled fluorescents, "It's a boy! And he's perfect perfect perfect!"

29 And someone, remembering Gamaliel, rushed to awaken him, and found him lying on the floor beside his toppled cot, and led him gimpy and sleep-stoned into the familiar brightness of the delivery room, where he smiled at Rachelka and took into his arms the luminous, bawling midge that was his son.

Afterbirth, afterdeath.

30 And later H.K. Bajaj came, and Priscilla Muthinga, and Andrew Stout, and many more members of the Twentieth, along with Damaris and Muggeridge and Edward and so on; and the captain brought word that two expeditions given up for lost had arrived home from the stars.

31 Aboard one of the returning ships, the captain said, there was an adept who, even before the expedition's planet-fall on Earth, had predicted the birth of Rachelka and Gamaliel's child by means of the headachey mental flashes that had plagued her during the last stages of their approach.

32 "Over and over again," said Captain Bajaj, "the gift is life, and that is what the adept continually experienced in the pain of her reading. She wishes mother and son health, wealth, and happiness, and she sends her heartfelt congratulations to the father, too."

33 And the captain presented the family a vase of towering sunflowers that the adept had sent from her vessel's hydroponic garden.

34 Aboard the second of the returning ships, Captain Bajaj told them, was a hitchhiking energy being, a plasmoidal intelligence scooped from the skin of a gas giant in the Alphard solar system, which bodiless entity was now insistently proclaiming itself a visible fragment of the "soul" of The One.

35 Said Rachelka, cradling her baby, "Is it possible for God to *possess* a soul? I would have thought that The One was nothing, so to speak, *but* soul: a transcendent spiritual being by its very nature synonymous with . . . well, with soulfulness."

36 Replied Captain Bajaj, picking one of the sunflowers for a boutonniere, "Be that as it may, the Alphardic Plasma wishes to enlist the self-aware species of every world in a revival of the recent Mantic crusade, arguing via energy pulses to the ship's computer that

37 *"A)* the Son of Man and the Daughter of Mantid were its own sibling soulmates and evangelical forerunners, and *B)* the arrival of itself as a kind of Holy Ghostling may be the historical act that at last begins to get its message across here on Earth. What say you to these revelations?"

38 Exchanging a glance gravid with significance but airy with credulous joy, in unison the astrogator and his wife cried, "Hallelujah!"

39 Elsewhere at that moment, to commemorate this day of days and all the days undoubtedly to come, apes in the jungles of Borneo waltzed in prescient glee, while porpoises and killer whales off the coast of Yucatán leapt like living

bolts of lightning.
40 And the spirit of Mantikhoras reigned. *Amen.*

Acknowledgments

"Religion and Science Fiction" by Isaac Asimov is copyright © 1984 by Davis Publications, Inc., for *Isaac Asimov's Science Fiction Magazine* (June, 1984), where it first appeared, in slightly different form, as the issue's lead editorial.

"Close Encounter with the Deity," copyright © 1986 by Davis Publications, Inc., for *Isaac Asimov's SF Magazine* (March, 1986).

"Voices," copyright © 1986 by Michael Bishop; reprinted from Jessica Amanda Salmonson's anthology *Heroic Visions II* (Ace Books, 1986).

"A Spy in the Domain of Arnheim," copyright © 1981 by Michael Bishop; reprinted from Ian Watson's anthology *Pictures at an Exhibition* (Graystoke Mobray, 1981). The story first appeared in the United States in *Shayol* (Vol. 3, No. 1, 1985).

"Love's Heresy," copyright © 1979 by Flight Unlimited, Inc., for *Shayol* (Vol. 1, No. 3, 1979).

"Storming the Bijou, Mon Amour," copyright © 1979 by Davis Publications, Inc., for *Isaac Asimov's SF Magazine* (June, 1979).

"Dogs' Lives," copyright © 1984 by Michael Bishop; reprinted from *The Missouri Review* and the anthology *Light Years and Dark* (Berkley, 1984).

"A Gift from the GrayLanders," copyright © 1985 by Davis Publications, Inc., for *Isaac Asimov's SF Magazine* (September, 1985).

"A Short History of the Bicycle: 401 B.C. to 2677 A.D.," copyright © 1980 by Michael Bishop; reprinted from Ursula K. Le Guin and Virginia Kidd's anthology *Interfaces* (Ace Books, 1980).

"Diary of a Dead Man," copyright © 1986 by Michael Bishop; reprinted from Pamela Sargent and Ian Watson's anthology *Afterlives* (Vintage, 1986).

"Scrimptalon's Test," copyright © 1984 by Gerald W. Page and Michael Bishop; reprinted from the anthology *Light Years and Dark* (Berkley, 1984).

"The Bob Dylan Tambourine Software & Satori Support Services Consortium, Ltd.," copyright © 1985 by *Interzone* for the British quarterly *Interzone* (No. 12/ Summer, 1985).

"Alien Graffiti," copyright © 1986 by Davis Publications, Inc., for *Isaac Asimov's SF Magazine* (July, 1986).

"And the Marlin Spoke," copyright © 1984 by Mercury Press, Inc., for *The Magazine of Fantasy & Science Fiction* (October, 1983).

"The Gospel According to Gamaliel Crucis," copyright © 1983 by Davis Publications, Inc., for *Isaac Asimov's SF Magazine* (November, 1983).